ALSO BY DAN CHAON

Sleepwalk
Ill Will
Stay Awake
Await Your Reply
You Remind Me of Me
Among the Missing
Fitting Ends

ONE OF US

ONE OF US

A Novel

DAN CHAON

Henry Holt and Company
New York

Henry Holt and Company
Publishers since 1866
120 Broadway
New York, New York 10271
www.henryholt.com

Henry Holt® and Ⓗ® are registered trademarks of Macmillan Publishing Group, LLC.
EU Representative: Macmillan Publishers Ireland Ltd., 1st Floor, The Liffey Trust Centre, 117–126 Sheriff Street Upper, Dublin 1, DO1 YC43

Distributed in Canada by Raincoast Book Distribution Limited

Library of Congress Cataloging-in-Publication Data

Names: Chaon, Dan, author.
Title: One of us : a novel / Dan Chaon.
Other titles: 1 of us
Description: First edition. | New York : Henry Holt and Company, 2025.
Identifiers: LCCN 2025003347 | ISBN 9781250175236 (hardcover) | ISBN 9781250175243 (ebook)
Subjects: LCGFT: Novels
Classification: LCC PS3553.H277 O54 2025 | DDC 813/.54—dc23/eng/20250321
LC record available at https://lccn.loc.gov/2025003347

First Edition 2025

Designed by Gabriel Guma

Printed in the United States of America

10 9 8 7 6 5 4 3 2 1

With love and thanks, to mentors:

Ray Bradbury

William Christy

Reginald Gibbons

Peter Straub

Sheila Schwartz

Sylvia Watanabe

And of course, for Sheri, dearest sister

Exordium

•••••••••

They was born out the same womb, two minutes apart, Rosalie says, and her head lolls back. Her eyes stare at the ceiling.

They was born 1901, November of the eighth. A girl came forth and—

Pullt out her brother with the cord wrapped round his foot—

Drug him into the daylight—

Rosalie seems to smile sleepily, not blinking even as a mosquito alights on the glossy surface of her cornea.

Murderers, she says.

Rosalie twitches, her hands gnarling against her chest. A spasm runs across her face as a cool damp cloth is pressed to her forehead. A viscid breath rattles in her throat.

Eleanor is the girl's name, she whispers. *The boy's name is Bolt.*

There is a growth at the back of Rosalie's skull about the size of a gourd, and it seems to have a face, though of course many things resemble faces when they are not. Two soft bulges on the deformity are damp and shiny as peeled hard-boiled eggs, and could be said to look like eyes; an indentation in the center appears to be a pair of nostrils; and below it, a slit—an open wound? a pair of lips?—seems to move when Rosalie speaks.

They are coming, Rosalie says. *They will be—most useful.*

Their Childhood

Their mother was a butcher's daughter with a lovely timid voice, a tinklebell sigh of soft misery. That is what Eleanor remembers most about her. Bolt remembers the sad, pretty lullabies she liked to sing and the pies she made.

She was the sort of woman who made only the lightest of impressions, even when you lived with her every day, a woman of airy, elusive distances. She would not have named them "Bolt" and "Eleanor," she told them once, "I never chose those names," she said, but when they asked what they might have been called instead, she only shook her head. "It doesn't matter," she murmured. "You are your father's children."

They only had blurry memories of their father—their "Papá," as their mother referred to him. She kept a small photograph of him in an oval frame on her nightstand: a mustached, freckled man in a bowler hat and bow tie, with a gap in his teeth, and they were never sure if they remembered his actual face or only remembered the photo.

He had traveled out west for to make his fortune, and their mother assumed that he'd perished there. "I warned him not to go," she said. "He had auspicious possibilities if he'd remained, as I asked, I had a premonition of—" And she grew quiet, drifting off into thoughts she did not share with the children. Then she smiled tightly. "But—here we are."

So now their mother was forced to run a boardinghouse in Oberlin, Ohio—earning barely enough to keep them from being put out on the street. They had no kin that they knew of, no one their mother could lean on for help, only a rotating population of tenants who took the place of aunts and uncles and cousins—old Mr. Humberstone with his bushy sideburn whiskers, who recited limericks at the dinner table; Berthe and her one-toothed infant boy, constantly nursing on her; Miss Belieu ever in her lacey nightgown who liked to wind the gilt clock on the mantelpiece. A tall, nervous young man whose name was Bouldery? Bowdler? Bodley? The twins never could come to an agreement.

Beyond the residents, the only people their mother really spoke to were her fellow congregants at the Progressive Psychic Spiritualist Church. They were a group of women who met on Sundays in a room above Gibson's Bakery, to perform séances and materializations of forms, seeking wisdom and guidance from beyond the veil. Miss Sylvia Ferryman of London, England, was their leader, a powerful medium, who told their mother that twins were often gifted with Second Sight, and Phenomenal Powers of Mind-Reading, and they were encouraged to practice those skills from an early age.

Which—well. Whatever special abilities they might have been endowed with didn't appear to help them that much in this world.

Giving birth to them had taken some essential vitality from her, their mother said. She would talk about this with the congregants of the Progressive Psychic Spiritual Church—four or six ladies sitting around a dining table with Miss Sylvia Ferryman at the head—telling each other their sorrows while Eleanor and Bolt sat in the parlor on a couch that smelled of mildew and mice.

"I feel as if I lost some part of my own spirit in the process," she said, in her stricken but melodic voice. "As if I only have half a soul left."

"Perhaps," said Miss Sylvia Ferryman. "But that piece may not be lost to you! It may only be adrift in the astral realm, and still seeking to reunite!"

"I was so ill afterward," their mother continued, dreamily. "I was not expected to survive. And the two of them were so ravenous. Of course, my husband and I could not afford a wet nurse—"

And Eleanor could imagine her mother slowly shriveling up like a mummy as the infants latched to each breast and nursed greedily. It was true that in the wedding photograph she had a womanly shape, but now she was extraordinarily thin.

"I think a séance is in order," said Miss Sylvia Ferryman. "Let us join hands and call out to that fragment of our Sister's soul which may have been separated from her!"

Their mother died in late September 1914, a little more than a month before Bolt and Eleanor's thirteenth birthday. She was the sort of person whose death from a vague illness was not unexpected; she'd been telling people for as long as the twins could remember that she did not expect to live a long life. "Each time a new season arrives I'm astonished," she said, and sometimes, when the children went to school, she'd touch their hair, musingly. "Oh, I do hope I'll still be here when you get home," she'd say.

So they were not surprised when they found her that morning, propped up on a pillow in her bed, her skin gray and cold to the touch, her mouth open unnaturally, her lips drawn back to bare her teeth. Not surprised, but still Bolt fell to his knees at the foot of the bed and sobbed. Eleanor frowned and pulled a blanket up over their mother's head.

There was no money for a funeral. The children built a kind of coffin out of two-by-fours and wood slats and buried her in the backyard under the apple tree. At first, Eleanor thought that they could continue on running the boardinghouse just as always, but it seemed that their mother's debts were more extensive than they'd known. Bolt thought they might ask their mother's church for help, but Eleanor said she'd rather drink lye and choke blood than beg from those biddies. "I don't want them anywhere near us anymore," she said. "You bring them in, and they'll just try to get their hooks into our property!"

"Okay," Bolt said, and minded her like he mostly did—it was well established that she was smarter and harder than him.

When the bank took the house from them, Old Lady Synott from next door had allowed them to live with her for a time. *As a kindness to your dear mother, nm-nm,* she said. She made a soft nm-nm after nearly every sentence she spoke, as if she was tasting each utterance and finding it satisfactory. Maybe in the beginning she hoped to make them into servants who would care for her in old age, but she grew sour on them quickly, and when the man who called himself their uncle Charlie appeared she seemed relieved to be parted from them.

He came riding up on a horse, it was night and the moon gave the dry, powdery wisps of January snow a blueish cast. They watched from the window as he dismounted heavily, cowboy hat and black beard, long leather coat flapping in the wind, worn heavy boots with rusty spurs that tinkled as he walked up the cobblestone path that led to Old Lady Synott's door. He gave them a wide smile and two of his top teeth were missing and another was black along the edge with rot.

"Childern!" he said and opened his arms as if they would come running to hug him, crying out joyfully.

But they just stood there silently as he tread through the doorway and swept his hat off and introduced himself as their father's brother.

I never heard of no Uncle Charlie, Eleanor thought, and glanced at Bolt, and he agreed. But Old Lady Synott simpered and welcomed him in and offered him coffee and a slice of her awful sour-cream-and-raisin pie and told him how glad she was that he had come, that these youths were too much for her.

"You can't imagine how much they eat, nm-nm!" she said. "I'm struggling to keep up with them!"

"Ha ha!" said the man who called himself their uncle. "I was the same way when I was their age! A bottomless pit, was I!"

Charlie Lambkin—Charles Lamb—Chuck Lumpkin—C.M. Lambert—Dear old Uncle C. with his long black beard. When he was in a cheerful mood he would sometimes weave bones or bells or ribbons into his whiskers. He'd wear black lipstick, sometimes. Eyeliner.

Smoking his marihuana cigarillos while reclining in his underdrawers on a bed of coyote fur.

Cleaning his gun while they sat on their bunk, watching him listlessly, dosed with laudanum so they couldn't run off.

"Don't you look at me that way, you mannequins," said Uncle Charlie. He unhasked the bullet chamber of his revolver and gave it a spin. The sound of a roulette wheel.

"I'm doing you little shits a favor," Uncle Charlie declaimed, and expelled a stream of skunky smoke. He pointed his finger at them. "I am doing you a FAVOR! I rescued you wretches."

He didn't know that they were killers.

The first time it happened, their mother had been crying off and on for days. She wept so much that she could not even leave her room, and the children sat at the foot of her bed as she held her face in her hands.

"There is not enough money this month," she whispered bitterly. "I don't know what to do." Bolt petted his mother's bare foot. It was unbearable to watch her suffering so. Her smile, the rarest of birds—

"If I were a wicked person . . ." she murmured. "I would put poison in that old man's food."

She wiped her eyes with the back of her hand. "But I could never do anything like that."

Dirty old lech.

Bolt did not know what a lech was but he thought it was probably a type of monster.

Eleanor caught his eye sidelong. She sat on the bed gently brushing their mother's hair with her fingers.

"You're such a comfort," their mother murmured distantly, and nuzzled her nose against Eleanor's stroking hand.

"Both of you," she said. "I couldn't go on if it weren't for my babies."

She looked dreamily at the clock. "Stir two teaspoonfuls of arsenic into the tea along with three cubes of sugar. It should be enough."

She reached out and cupped Eleanor's face. She kissed Eleanor's forehead. "You're so good to Mama," she whispered. And then she pressed her lips close to Eleanor's ear. Bolt couldn't hear what she said.

It was Eleanor who mixed the poison but it was Bolt who brought the tea to the old man's room. They exchanged glances, and their minds were linked together, and Eleanor was sitting in Bolt's head as he walked down the hall, the two of them were both looking out of his eyes.

Bolt felt Eleanor moving like ink in water inside his brain, he felt her looking out through him and her tingle running along his forearms and through his hands, which held the cup.

Old Humberstone was sitting in a chair in his room, studying an old Sears catalog as if it were the Bible. He had one milky eye that nevertheless moved as if it could read as well.

"I brung your tea," said Bolt, and Eleanor shifted inside him with encouragement. He held out the cup. "Um."

"I pity you that live only amongst women," Old Humberstone said, and Bolt noticed that the catalog was open to a page called *One-Piece Frocks for the Jaunty Summer Girl.* He held out the cup, but Humberstone didn't take it.

Patient! Be patient! Eleanor thought.

"It ain't healthy for a boy your age not to have a fatherly figger," Old Humberstone said, and then he coughed and fell into a revery. The mug of tea seemed to give off an unearthly glow, and at last Humberstone hooked his bony fingers to the handle and brought the lip of the mug to his trembling mouth.

They maybe could've killed Uncle Charlie the same way, but they lost their nerve. Eleanor thought that Uncle Charlie drank so much liquor the arsenic might not work on him, or else he might realize he'd been poisoned and shoot them before he gasped out his last.

Instead, they settled into a routine. Uncle Charlie threatened and cajoled them until he'd made them into his servants. His accomplices. He insisted that they call him "Father."

They couldn't guess what he wanted them for. For a while they thought maybe they had an inheritance he planned to steal from them—something their father had bequeathed? It seemed improbable that he'd come for them out of charity, but there was no sign of a hidden fortune. He claimed that he had sworn to their father that he would take care of his niece and nephew, and he WAS A MAN OF HIS WORD! He lifted a bottle to toast himself.

In fact, he was not a man of his word. He was a card sharp and con man, who told tales about the West—the gold claim he'd staked with his brother, his time in Deadwood, where, he said, he had seen with his own eyes when Wild Bill Hickok was shot down. "And he was holding black aces and eights, the Dead Man's Hand!" Uncle Charlie—"Father"—said.

They'd heard that story two dozen times or more, they reckoned. They traveled from Oberlin southwest to Dayton, and thence to Indianapolis, riding along in a burlap covered wagon stuffed with his misbegotten belongings as well as what Uncle Charlie'd salvaged of their mother's, and he regaled them with yarns about haunted privies and train robbers, about a riffraff man with a loose tongue who was buried alive in a graveyard. He told them of the crooked gulch at Wounded Knee, full of the bodies of defiant Lakota. He had been hired along with other civilian men, after a three-day blizzard, to pull the frozen corpses from the snow and haul them to a mass grave on the hill. "Stiff as wood they were," he said. "And women and childern dead amongst the warrior men." He fixed his eye hard on Eleanor. "Yes, childern, too. *Childern, too*," and nodded at her, considering. Then he turned and clucked and shook the reins, and the glum black bay mare named Stardust quickened her pace. It was January of 1915.

He found them a shotgun shack on the outskirts of Indianapolis and set up a still to make corn whiskey. Railroad men and dirty hobos and rowdies came to the place to drink and play cards. He needed to earn some money before they headed farther West, he explained.

But Eleanor did not plan to go farther west with Charlie Lambkin. They would find a way to run out on him before they left Indianapolis, she thought. She was at the stove, making taters and bacon in a skillet when she decided that they'd have to murder him. In the other room, she could hear him entertaining some men that he planned to cheat, beguiling them with the anecdote of the Dead Man's Hand, but she didn't really listen. She stirred the taters with a wooden spoon.

"Nellie!" Father called. "Bring us all some more beer!"

He was in a joyous mood. She guessed that to the card playing men, he seemed drunk, but she knew he was not, especially. He was just pretending.

She gathered up some bottles on a tray and popped the tops with a church key. Then she carried them out and set them down, one in front of each man, like she was a tavern wench. The men eyed her, but she didn't look at them.

"Thank you, doll," Father said. She kept her hair up in a tight bun, like an elderly lady or an old maid, and she wore a smock that Uncle Charlie had given her from a box of women's clothes that he had—for some reason. The smock was too big, the hem dragged along the floor.

"She's getting to be that age," he said, and laughed, though the other men didn't. They didn't know what to make of her.

She kept her face stern and neutral, the kind of face you made when you chopped the head off of a chicken. The men fell silent as she distributed the beers around.

"Got some food cooking," she told them. "If anybody wants to eat."

Uncle Charlie nodded. "You are an angel," he said. "Could you bring me a l'il slice of toast with some black jam on it?" And he winked twice so she knew she was to bring a queen of diamonds and a deuce of spades and slip it into his pocket.

So she went, trailing the dirty train of her dress behind her, her bare feet shuffling.

Back in the kitchen, Bolt was sitting at the table. She guessed that he'd come in through the back door, and he was hunched over, loading bullets, half-moon clips, into the Smith & Wesson revolver.

"Hey," he said, and he gave her the smile where he squinted one eye.

"Hey," she said. She lifted her skirt a little. The hem was wet and stiff with filth from dragging along the floor, and the cloth had a yellowish stain that reached up in fingerlings toward her knees. "Are you hungry?" she said.

"Nah," he said, and he didn't look up. "Not really." He spun the cylinder of his pistol, and she listened to the bone rattle of it.

If Uncle Charlie was caught cheating, it was Bolt's job to come in with the revolver.

Bolt didn't mind working with Uncle Charlie, and he might would've stayed with him and learned more about the con man game, he could've been a good bandit, he thought—

But Eleanor kept discovering stuff that made her suspicious. There was, for example, that crate full of women's undergarments. There was a little music box that when you opened it played Bach's Minuet in G and was full of what appeared to be human teeth. There was a blood-spattered diary or journal, which for some reason Eleanor thought was connected to their father, though it was mostly written in some kind of code.

Worse still, there were times when Uncle Charlie seemed to know more about them than he should. Once, after a card game, he was sitting on his bed, trimming his toenails with the stiletto he had confiscated from Eleanor—which she had herself stolen from a drawer in Old Humberstone's room after he was dead. Charlie hummed to himself while the children cleared the table of bottles and emptied the ashtrays. "I wonder," he said, musing. "Do you childern ever get a niggling that you can hear another's thoughts?"

Eleanor stopped mopping a spill and gave Bolt a quick pinch with her eyes. "No," she said, and Bolt gave Uncle Charlie a look of slack incomprehension. "No," Bolt said.

Uncle Charlie fingered a bit of ribbon that he'd braided into his beard, considering. "You know," he said, "your dear pappy had that talent," he said. "He could always tell if a feller was lying. 'Twas most useful."

Bolt could hear the sharp tang of Eleanor's voice in his head. *Don't never tell him, don't even give him no reason to suspect—*

"Ahh," said Charlie, and smelled the tip of the stiletto blade, then wiped it on the edge of his blanket and snapped it shut. "You should try it sometime."

And then finally there was the night that Uncle Charlie killed one of his customers with a skillet. It was a well-dressed but unshaven man who had gambled but couldn't pay, and long after all the other card players had left they drank and negotiated and quarreled and then abruptly Uncle Charlie had stormed into the kitchen where Bolt and Eleanor were playing Chinese checkers with marbles on a wooden board. He snatched the iron pan off the stove and bludgeoned the man until his skull caved in.

Bolt and Eleanor did not look. They stayed still, they stared at the marbles arranged on the game board on the table and without speaking they both agreed that they would have to get away from him as soon as possible.

They left in the night while Uncle Charlie was in his cups. They'd mixed all the possible poisons they could find in the house into his beer and then snuck out the back door and run down the dirt road as fast as their legs could carry them. It was mid-April but still a chill and blustering wind blew in their faces. Eleanor had a rucksack with some carrots and apple butter sandwiches and the photograph of their father and the diary of course and she led them splashing through the icy creek and up the bank to the railroad tracks. They were both gasping as they hopped on the boxcar.

It was Eleanor's idea that they should go to an orphanage as if they'd been sent there, that they should act surprised that they weren't expected. She made up the name of a lawyer named Daggett who had supposedly written a letter telling of their arrival.

The train stopped for a few minutes at Fingerton Depot just west of Indianapolis and they had only time enough to hop off. There was a small station, where you could buy a ticket if the station master was there, but it was five in the morning and the ticket booth was closed. Eleanor saw through the window that there were cookies and apples that might be purchased, if the passenger waiting area was open. She saw a sign that said HAIRCUT, and underneath it was a single barber chair. She touched her hand to the cool metal knob and tried to turn it: locked. Bolt nosed up behind her curiously and he couldn't help himself, he also had to try the knob. It was still locked.

For the first time, he was taller than she. Up until now, ever since they were born, he had been a bit smaller and shorter, he had been her baby, her responsibility—a wide-eyed, dreamy, placid boy—and she loved his openheartedness, his clumsy uncalculated enthusiasm, but he needed to be protected from it as well. He was not stupid, as sometimes people thought, but his intellect was uncurious, and he was a poor judge of character.

"You think everyone is your friend," she often told him. "They're not."

"Are *you* my friend?" said Bolt, sassily. "Maybe you're not!"

"I'm your sister," she said.

Beyond the station, there was the tower of a grain elevator, and beyond that a smatter of simple houses and main street storefronts and at the edge of the town was the orphanage. They knew it was the orphanage because it looked like an orphanage. It was a fort-like brick structure with long, narrow windows and a flat roof, surrounded by a high cast-iron fence. Even from a distance, they could see that the fence had spiked tips, like spears. Beyond, there were some long fields of snow melting into brown mud and gray stubble, the sun rising in a haze of clouds.

Eleanor stood there holding their sack in her left hand while Bolt held her right, and he squinted around for a while suspiciously, as if someone might be sneaking up on them. He wanted her to know that he was guarding her, he wanted her to know that if she said "Bite!" then he'd bite.

Meanwhile, far in the distance, Uncle Charlie woke up spitting and coughing. He knew immediately that his little angels had poisoned him and fled, and now he rose on his fingers and toes, arching like a cat, vomiting and shitting at once and he bellowed like a man falling into a canyon.

It was almost a day before he was well enough to walk. He made some marihuana tea and after another while he was able to get on his horse and in a sickly fury ride off in search of them.

Though really, what did he expect to find? Bread crusts? Footprints?

He galloped along the road, imagining them crouched in the reeds down by the crick, and he checked the nag Stardust and stopped. Stared as hard as he could.

He dismounted, sweating, panting, still green at his gills from being poisoned. Still bitter about being poisoned. The fog curled thickly through the witchy trees.

"I know you're down there," he called, mellifluously. He imagined them as silhouettes, paper-cut illustrations frozen among the tangles. He was almost certain he could see them peeping up at him, their little lungs puffing like rabbits.

"I am your UNCLE," he called down into the foggy gully. "I am your blood kin, and I will love you always no matter what your transgresses! I know that you think you have to go. But you will always have a home with Uncle Charlie."

He peered down expectantly and then became slowly aware that the silhouettes of the children were only tree stumps.

"Dang," he murmured.

Orphan Train

The train arrives at last in the town of Shenandoah, Iowa. Late May, and a mild spring rain is falling as the children disembark. There are twelve of them left now—the other, better children have already been chosen on stops along the way, in Farmer City and Table Grove, Illinois, in Mount Pleasant and Ottumwa, Iowa, and even though they have been given fresh new clothes to wear, by this point they feel a little shoddy and secondhand. The boys wear dark knickers that button below the knee and white dress shirts with neckties; the girls wear a dark low-waisted frock with a white pinafore over it and have large bows in their hair. Each has a badge with a number and their name safety-pinned over their heart, and they are marched two by two from the platform down to the muddy road, oldest to youngest, the littlest ones holding hands, and the keepers herd them along, Mrs. Sweet in front and Captain Nix at the rear, holding two infants in his arms. Outside the train station diner, a man in overalls watches them pass, smoking on his pipe thoughtfully. From the limbs of a tree, a boy tosses stones down, and there is the harsh musky smell of pig farms near town. A gray, wire-haired dog comes barking and harrying them, but Captain Nix hollers at it in his deep voice until it runs off, but now he has startled the babies awake and they've both begun to bawl.

When they were on the train, Captain Nix told them the story of Johnny Appleseed and he said that they were the seedlings who would be spread across this barren prairie to make it fertile as the Lord God intended. He would patrol the aisle of their train car preaching and telling them stories even while most of them were trying to sleep. Eleanor listened and dozed, staring down at the hole torn in the seat cushion between her and Bolt, a dark opening with straw and springs peeking out.

All across town there are posters on walls and in the windows of stores, in the butcher shop and grocer, the hardware store and the pharmacist, on the bulletin boards at the courthouse and the churches.

OPEN YOUR DOORS TO HOMELESS CHILDREN

An Appeal to You!

Have you not a vacant chair, a hungry spot in your heart that you can fill with one of these children waiting for someone to give them a True Home? All children received under the care of this association are of SPECIAL PROMISE in intelligence and health, and are in age from one to fifteen years and are FREE to those receiving them, on ninety days' trial, UNLESS a special contract is otherwise made.

Now the people of Page County and beyond have gathered at the First Presbyterian Church to view and possibly adopt this passel of orphans: yes, there were right-thinking sentimental middle-class folks who had hungry spots in their hearts, and there were cynical farmers who saw a chance for free labor, and there were heartbroken childless couples who had experienced multiple stillbirths and miscarriages, a carpenter who wanted to find a stolid athletic boy to raise as his apprentice, a widower who would go on to make his twelve-year-old ward his bride when she turned seventeen. It was true that children were a burden, but they also had many uses.

"It is a curious fact," wrote Miss Peattie of the *Shenandoah Sentinel-Post*, "but everybody who goes to pick out a child imagines that he or she is an advanced student of human nature."

They walk down the middle of the main street as if they are a parade. Even this far-flung town has begun the transition from horse to automobile, and Model Ts and REO pickups are parked diagonally in front of the storefronts, a rusty Packard truck putters phlegmily, idling at an intersection as the children march by. Bolt blushes as he sees the staring people beginning to gather on either side. He has the kind of cheeks that grow bright red whenever he feels embarrassed or shamed or angry or when he gets to laughing, but his twin sister does not. The skin of her face is cool as a marble headstone, and when Bolt reaches for her hand she flicks him away surreptitiously with her fingers. He hears her voice in his head:

We're too old for that. People'll get the wrong idea.

Bolt nods and licks his teeth, his head low. He doesn't know exactly what Eleanor means, but he trusts her instincts. He trusts her to protect their shared interests.

Folks sometimes assume that Bolt is a simpleton, especially next to Eleanor, who is bright-eyed and tart-tongued, who looks grown-ups in the eye and answers their questions without stumbling, a confident stream of fibs issuing from her mouth as Bolt stands slightly behind. He is not actually stupid, but for years now it has proven to be an effective disguise.

The church doors open and the people turn to look as the children come in, two by two. Hundreds of people have gathered from all over the county, and they murmur and gesture: there is a boy of seven and already he has a good strong back, and the bland, trusting face of a hard worker; there is a girl whose hair doesn't comb very prettily, it won't lay flat and one of her ribbons has come loose and even though she is only ten there is an air of slovenliness, the hint of a dirty, precocious teenager; the boy who crosses his hands behind his back like a little professor seems intelligent; the girl who crosses her hands in front appears to be devout; the big-smiling little man with a polio limp breaks their heart with his shining courageous hopefulness.

Once the orphans are seated in chairs on the chancel stage, Captain Nix comes forward. "Good morning, ladies and gentlemen," he says in a voice that has had training in oratory. Some in the crowd chuckle appreciatively at this tall, stern, gaunt fellow, with his cheek scarred from a battle in the Spanish-American War and his heavy old-fashioned mustache, holding two plump babies under his arm as he speaks: a dark-eyed boy of no more than thirteen months and a sleeping little blond girl, perhaps two, and it is charming to see how calm the wee ones are while the Captain speaks.

The orphans are of good stock, he says, *good stock visited by tragedy*, though this is not entirely true. There are not just orphans on the stage, Eleanor knows, but children who have been cast off by their parents, street children who worked as newsies or shoe shiners or pickpockets or whores, children whose mamas gave them away for a few dollars. Eleanor keeps her face expressionless. She can sense the rustle of Mrs. Sweet's skirts as she walks behind them, poking the backs of the children who slouch with a hard index finger. Captain Nix speaks of Johnny Appleseed.

Then the people come streaming up to look them over. They flock around Captain Nix and his armful of babies, and the ladies make cooing noises that give Eleanor the fantods. She watches a dour old farmer feeling of a boy's muscle, and then he puts his fingers in the boy's mouth and spreads the boy's lips, to examine his teeth. She watches a girl stand and lift her skirt, to show that her legs are straight. Three couples bicker over a cherubic seven-year-old lad whose face is blank as a rabbit's.

Bolt's hands are folded in his lap and his eyes are lowered as people walk by them, his face burning, but Eleanor tries to hold her head up and look the people in the eye as they walk past, she tries to make her expression pleasing and demure, but people glance at her and then away. A couple stops in front of her, but their attention is on the little boy in the chair to her left.

"Oh!" The woman bends down with her hands clasped.

"How old are you?" she asks, and the boy holds up five fingers. His eyes are big and dark and terrified. Eleanor watches the man put his hand on the woman's waist. They are picking out a puppy, Eleanor thinks.

"Yes," the man says. "Yes, I do believe I like him!"

The woman reaches out and strokes the dark-eyed boy's cheek. "Would you like to be my little boy?"

And when the lady opens her arms, he goes right to her.

"Say!" Eleanor says. "He likes you!"

The couple look at her, startled. Not friendly.

But Eleanor tries to smile agreeably. "He's a nice 'un," she tells them. "Good pick!"

And they turn away from her wordlessly, carrying their new son—who stares over the woman's shoulder at Eleanor as they go.

Eleanor knows that she and Bolt are ugly. They learned that early on, their first year in school. "Goblins," the bullies called them, until she gave them reasons to be afraid of her. She has studied her own face in the mirror: it is rounder than is normal, she thinks, and her cheeks are too plump and her nose is too upturned and her skin is too freckled and her carrot-colored hair will not be brought to heel by a comb.

In looks, Eleanor thinks, she got the worst of it, since she resembles Bolt more than he resembles her. She seems like an ugly boy pretending to be a girl, she thinks, and she sits there as more people walk past and avert their eyes when she tilts her head their way.

More than anything, she hates the clownishly large bow in her hair.

In the end, there are only four of them left: a thin and sickly-looking five-year-old girl and the lame, hopeful-eyed eight-year-old boy and Bolt and Eleanor.

Already, the crowd has begun to thin, and Captain Nix, unburdened of the babies he was carrying, steps up to call to the remaining people. "We still have a few more, ladies and gentlemen!" he announces.

He sweeps his hand toward Eleanor and Bolt. "Two twins!" he cries.

"Boy child and girl child, thirteen years of age! Very healthy, no vices! Good hard workers!"

The audience seems to draw in breath, and there is a silence—a moment—maybe just a second—but Eleanor remembers a time when she was just a little girl. They were at the market and a woman was sitting outside with a baby in a carriage, and Eleanor had wanted to peek at the baby, she was curious. But as she approached, the young mother stiffened and held out a hand. "Don't touch," the woman said, her face pinched with disgust. "Your hands are dirty, little girl," she said. But Eleanor knew she meant more than that—it wasn't just a bath she needed.

That's how the people in the church look at her now, she thinks. *Don't touch your hands are dirty—*

And then she sees a man striding toward the stage. He is very tall and has a theatrical voice like a preacher or a master of ceremonies. "Yes," he says, "yes, yes, yes," he says, and he speaks as if everyone should be looking at him, as if he is an actor in a play making his entrance. His coat is a bright dandy red with golden epaulettes, like the conductor of a marching band.

"My, my!" he says and folds his arms appraisingly as he stands in front of them. "What remarkable specimens!"

He bends down toward Eleanor and his face is beaming, his bright blue eyes meeting hers as if he wants to drink her up. He puts his mouth to her ear so that she can feel his breath.

"I see you for what you are," he whispers. "Don't be afraid, we're going to be good friends."

He is a young man, thinks Miss Peattie of the *Shenandoah Sentinel-Post*, and she writes in her notebook: "No more than 30?" as she watches from a pew near the front of the church—yet he has the air and authority of someone much older. Tall and well-built, with pale blue eyes and white-blond hair swept back as if by a wind on a lighthouse island, he wears an old-fashioned tailcoat and high black boots. "Like a circus impresario," writes Miss Peattie. He might have cut a ridiculous figure, but he sweeps his gaze across the audience with a smile of utter confidence.

"I can provide a home for these unfortunates," he announces, and Miss Peattie waits for someone in authority to step forward and object, but no one does.

Years later, when Miss Peattie was the film critic for the *Des Moines Register* during the 1940s, she was struck by the film *Citizen Kane*, the voice of Orson Welles reminded her so much of that man—deep and self-regarding and ageless—and she had a shudder of memory, she could picture him placing his big hand on the boy's cheek. She could still picture the child's stricken look.

The boy, as she recalled him, was resolutely unhandsome—a mean-looking Irish with a lumpy nose and squinty eyes—like Lampwick in Disney's *Pinocchio*, the youth who had been lured to Pleasure Island and turned into a donkey. He'd been cursed with the face of an unlovable child, and Miss Peattie recalls how her heart ached, she had the urge to stand up herself, to say, "No! I'll take them!"

But, in fact, she remains as silent as everyone else. She merely makes a disapproving face, watching as the man ushers the boy and his equally homely sister off the stage. Surely there must be some requirement, Miss Peattie thinks, some application that must be fulfilled. Surely the minister will object, or the orphans' chaperones.

Already the next orphan has taken the stage, a tragically delicate, hollow-eyed girl named Elphilia, aged five, and hearts melt at the sight of her, and indeed she will make a nicer story for the *Sentinel-Post*.

There will be no court proceedings or adoption ceremonies, as the children expected. Instead, Mr. Jengling simply signs a paper that Mrs. Sweet holds out to him, and Bolt and Eleanor are now apparently his property. He leads them out of the church and into the sunlight.

"Are we to call you Father?" Eleanor asks Mr. Jengling.

They are riding in his cherry-red Chevrolet Baby Grand touring car with the top down, the twins in the rumble seat, Mr. Jengling at the wheel, and he turns to look over his shoulder, bemused, as if this hasn't occurred to him.

"Why, yes!" he says, and gives them a smile that shows his teeth, both top and bottom. "Yes, absolutely, if you wish."

Bolt looks at Eleanor and she stares back. Once they could have whole conversations with just their eyes. Sometimes she called him "sister"; sometimes he called her "brother." But it isn't like it used to be. Month by month, it seems like his ability to hear her voice in his head is growing dimmer, and as for Eleanor, he doesn't think she could read really his mind at all anymore.

He reaches across the seat and this time she lets him take her hand. Now she is regretting what she's gotten them into.

"Would you like to see my latest treasure?" says Mr. Jengling from the front seat. He turns and passes back a sharp pointed stone that looks like the head of a large blind bird. It is bigger than his palm.

"I bought this from a local farmer for two dollars," he says. "I believe it to be a claw of a *Megalonyx jeffersonii*, which was a giant prehistoric ground sloth."

Bolt takes the claw from Mr. Jengling. It's smooth and cool, and he offers it to Eleanor, who holds it in her lap without looking at it.

"Did you know that Lassen Peak in California has erupted?" says Mr. Jengling. "That would be a thing to behold, wouldn't it? To see a volcano spewing out lava and ash?" He laughs. "In any case, I take it as a sign that our meeting is fortuitous!"

The circus train is eighteen cars long, each one brightly lettered with JENGLING EMPORIUM OF WONDERS, and Eleanor feels her teeth tighten as she catches a glimpse of the "wonders" who stand on the platform outside. Her first thought is that they are monsters.

They see the three-legged woman with a withered appendage that dangles limply just below her stomach, dressed in a stocking and a black Mary Jane shoe.

They see the Strong Baby, a man with the hairless, toothless head of an infant, but whose body is as big as a grizzly bear on its hind legs, and he holds in his arms a miniature woman, who is giving instructions to a bald man who appears to have nails pounded into his skull.

They see the half-girl, who walks upon the palms of her hands, and the dog-faced boy. There is a giant Chinese man, more than seven feet tall, with a curved horn growing from the crown of his head. There is a muscle lady in a red, white, and blue leotard, and a man whose head seems too small for his body, grimacing like a skeleton.

There is a tall, somber-faced clown in strawberry-blond pigtails, his eyes dark and foreboding, who comes forward as Mr. Jengling's car pulls up to the station.

His face is painted white and two triangles are marked on his forehead for eyebrows, and his lips are bright red. He has a red ball for a nose.

"Did you have any trouble?" the clown asks Mr. Jengling, and Mr. Jengling makes his special smile.

"No—no trouble at all," says he, and he puts his gloved hands on the small of the children's backs. "This is Tickley-Feather," he tells them. "He'll show you two to your bunks."

O Where, O Where?

Charlie hurtles along the midnight roads outside of Indianapolis, his eyes hot, his cheeks burning, worked up and belathered, yes, enraged and blamblustercated. *Oh, how innocently he'd put his faith in the pure-heartedness of the young, how guilelessly he placed his TRUST in them AND WAS BETRAYED!* The wound of it goads him mercilessly, and in turn he spurs poor Stardust harder and harder, pushing her until she's frothing, and still he slaps her flank and hunches forward though there's no trail to follow. *Thankless wretches! Never had he beaten them nor did they want for shelter! Did they think he should feed them on cake and sugar candy and let them lay abed all day long? Had they no notion of how cruelly he might have treated them, if he'd chosen to?*

By God and all the angels, he hates being fooled! The treachery of his beloved moppets eats away at his heart as he rides west, down muddy wheel ruts, past stubbled cornfields and railroad shacks.

Where did they go? Where? WHERE?

If they hope to seek protection of the law, he knows well how to sweet-talk a deputy or railroad Pinkerton, he'll explain how they were lazy, wanton incorrigibles who he was only trying to tame, and the police will gladly deliver them into his firm but loving embrace.

If they try to seek shelter with a kindly widowed granny, he'll come up the path to her house a-singing hymns and shedding tears of joy to be reunited at last with his lost little kittens, whose low moral fiber is no fault of their own, since they was raised by drunkards and blasphemers, and he'll promise to set them again on the right path. *I surely hope they never stole from you, ma'am,* he'll tell the white-headed old bat, *but they don't yet know how to repay a kindness!*

Perhaps they think they'll take to the rails, but they'll be spotted by every tramp and bum along the tracks. It won't take long for Charlie to catch himself a hobo lad and milk every drop of gossip out of him by means of coin or torture—

At last, becalmed somewhat, he and Stardust come to a little forest glade in the midst of the corn-growing country near the Illinois border, and he lets the tired horse slow to a walk as they approach the nicely isolated farmhouse.

Well. He stands there looking at the unlit windows of the house as Stardust slurps thirstily from a trough by the jakes. It doesn't look like they have any neighbors for miles and no dog to guard the house, neither. Judging by the moon it must be after one in the morning.

He's been very good and hasn't done something like this in a while, but he feels as if he deserves some kind of treat, after all the drizzible flusteration he's suffered.

And so
he slips off his boots and enters the home
through the unlocked back door

gliding on little cat feet
up the staircase without a creak,

the axe from their woodpile cradled
gently in his arms like a bride.

He's killed a lot of people in his day, and most of the time it's just a business transaction, he rarely gets to really enjoy it the way he'd like to, to find that sweetness he felt when he'd murdered his stepmother and stepsister after his pap had died. He was only fourteen, but he knew what he had to do. Ah, he recalls nuzzling against his stepmother's neck and lifting her limp hand to make it stroke his cheek. He recalls tucking the little stepsister into her bed and brushing her pretty blond hair and pulling out a few of her nice teeth with pliers and polishing them in his pocket as he lit out toward the territories, toward a new life of rascalry and adventure.

Now that warm and comforted feeling floods him again. Standing in the doorway he bespies a young couple asleep in their marriage bed, the husband no more than nineteen, the wife even younger, their tender, peaceable, dreamless faces turned to each other. They're so fine and beautiful that it puts him in a pleasant trance—

And then when he's finished he covers them over with the sheet and sits on the edge of the bed holding their baby in his lap and feeding it some applesauce he'd found in their cupboard. The infant takes a spoonful into its mouth with grave seriousness, considers it, swallows, considers again, and then opens up its mouth for more. Afterward, it bubbles with laughter as he dandles it on his knee. "Oh where, oh where has my little dog gone," he sings, and the wee one half-laughs, winningly. Charlie tastes the gore spattered in his beard, licks the fur above his lip, wiped the blood drip from his eye.

"With his ears cut short!—and his tail cut long!—Oh where—oh where—can he—be?" He croons softly, just a whisper, and the babe widens its eyes and gazes up at him the way a cat might stare at the moon.

June 1915

Bolt and Eleanor sleep in a berth together in the circus train car, traveling through the night by the light of the moon. Above them is a plate-size circular window and when Bolt opens his eyes, he can see the ragged clouds pulling themselves over the stars.

He is changing into a new person, he can feel it.

Eleanor shudders and mumbles next to him, and he can sense the outlines of the nightmare she's having: Uncle Charlie on his black bay mare galloping on a road through a tunnel of tangled trees. Coming for them. Bolt has told her that he's sure they're safe, Uncle Charlie will never find them, but Eleanor doesn't share his confidence. "We won't be safe until we're in Canada," she says. "Or Mexico. Or Alaska."

They lie together close in the narrow bunk and Eleanor's breath flutters against his bare neck. On the other side of the train car, the man who calls himself Tickley-Feather seems to be asleep. He is a big man—six feet five, maybe, long-jawed, with lank black hair and a scar that runs down from his left eye and across his nostril and upper lip. His big feet stick out from under the covers and twitch like the paws of a dog when it dreams of chasing a rabbit. Bolt would like to think that Tickley-Feather might best Uncle Charlie in a fight.

In the morning, Tickley-Feather sits at his mirror and wipes thick white clown greasepaint onto his face and traces a lipstick outline around his mouth and marks black triangle eyebrows onto his forehead.

Once, early on, Eleanor said to him, "Tickley-Feather can't be your real Christian name. It don't seem fair that you know us as Eleanor and Bolt Lambkin, but all we know of you is made-up! What did your mama call you?"

And he didn't answer, he just gave her a long stare and tucked his hair under the stiff, braided blond wig.

"I wouldn't want to be called 'Tickley-Feather' if I was a feller," Eleanor said. She shrugged and looked demurely at her shoes. "It's kind of girlish, ain't it? Are you supposed to be a pansy?"

"That's none of your concern," said Tickley-Feather in his gruff, deep voice, and he dotted orange freckles onto his white cake-frosting cheeks. "You two do what you're told to, and I'll do what I'm told to, and we won't have no trouble."

Bolt wishes that she wouldn't needle him, though he knows she can't help herself. He wants Tickley-Feather to like them—or at least to be willing to defend them if necessary. But Eleanor doesn't think it matters.

Even though it seems as if Tickley-Feather has been tasked with minding them from day to day, he is not their boss, Eleanor says, nor their protector. In fact, Tickley-Feather was himself adopted as a boy by Mr. Jengling, and so even though he is a grown-up, maybe almost thirty years old with a low bass voice and hard eyes and veiny hands, he could be legally considered to be only their brother, no better than they themselves are.

A brother!? Bolt thinks. It sends a zing through his heart.

This is June, the year of 1915. In the faraway world, German zeppelins drift over the British Isles, floating gently as whales, dropping bombs over Great Yarmouth and King's Lynn, Ipswich and South End, and in the land of Gallipoli, the English and Frenchmen battle the Ottomans, and a few miles from the lighthouse on the Old Head of Kinsale, a U-boat submarine sunk the ocean liner called RMS *Lusitania*, and the heroic heir Alfred Vanderbilt gave up his life vest to a mother and her babies as the vessel sank.

Oh, the world is changing fast. In the brief time since Bolt and Eleanor were born, electricity has become common, and it's not unusual for a farmhouse to have a telephone. Paved highways are being laid down across the country, and automobiles and trucks are steadily replacing horses. The age of the Wild West has only died recently. The outlaw Jesse James's brother Frank had just passed away in February, after years on the lecture circuit, regaling audiences with tales of his days as a Confederate bushwhacker and then as a train robber—but the days of Buffalo Bill are now just another nostalgic circus show.

This is the year of Typhoid Mary. Harry Houdini is touring the vaudeville houses, performing the Water Torture Cell escape. It is the year of Charlie Chaplin playing "The Tramp," and the starlet Theda Bara mouths the words "Kiss me, my fool," and everyone repeats it, delighted, it passes through the culture like a virus: *Kiss me, my fool . . . kiss me, you fool . . .* An ancient meme.

The film *The Birth of a Nation* plays in movie houses in reserved seat engagements, charging premium prices to full houses, and meanwhile the Great Migration of Blacks to the North has begun, and the English American boxer Jess Willard—"The Great White Hope," as he is called—defeats the African American Jack Johnson in Havana and is held up as proof of his race's superiority. T. S. Eliot's poem "The Love Song of J. Alfred Prufrock" appears in *Poetry: A Magazine of Verse* and the German magazine *Die Weißen Blätter* is preparing to publish Franz Kafka's story "The Metamorphosis"—though Eleanor will not read these until much, much later.

In Palestine there is a great infestation of locusts. In Mexico, Pancho Villa is routed by Álvaro Obregón, though Obregón loses his right arm in a grenade attack. The Armenian genocide has begun, and is ongoing.

But most of this is not known to the people of Beatrice, Nebraska—or else it is so remote as to be negligible. They circle in the smallness of their daily lives like June bugs around a porch light, and when the posters for THE JENGLING TRAVELING EMPORIUM OF WONDERS appear pasted all over town it creates an excited stir that no foreign battles or far-off tragedies ever would.

Meanwhile, the sun is rising over the long, sleepy cornfields and the carnival is erecting itself on the outskirts of town—the tents and booths for penny games and the Ferris wheel and carousel, the caged exotic animals and the human and half-human oddities—and Eleanor and Bolt are cleaning out the gorilla's pen when their new father comes along. It's been three weeks since he took possession of them, but he hasn't spent much time with them yet.

Still, he always seems pleased to see them, and today he gives them a playfully theatrical bow. He is wearing a black top hat and a red tuxedo jacket with a long tail and tight black trousers. He has high black leather boots. "Salutations, my dear ones," he says. "Beautiful morning, isn't it?" says he.

"It sure is!" says Bolt, bowing back clownishly and doffing his fiddler's cap.

Eleanor says nothing, just leans on her push broom and nurses her misgivings. What does this man want them for? How can they escape? Where can they go?

The morning smells of alfalfa, and meadowlarks warble in the prairie grass and a worker man hunches past lugging a brightly painted carved wooden seahorse with a pole stuck through its back. In the distance Tickley-Feather lifts a hammer, his thick arms flexing as he smites a stake that secures the big tent. His wig-braids flop up and down, and some of the other men begin to chant a pounding song.

Their new father smiles at Eleanor. "Around here, we like a woman with a strong back," he says, and Eleanor's eyes observe as he touches her, and then she flicks a glance toward Bolt, and then stares at the ground. Her hand loosely holds her broom.

"We are passionately in favor of women's suffrage," Mr. Jengling declares. "We believe girls are the equals of boys."

And he does not look at Bolt at all. He leaves them and goes off to sit with the gorilla, Miss Alcott, who is waiting aloofly in her trailer as her pen is cleaned.

Mr. Jengling often says that Miss Alcott is one of his closest friends.

Eleanor feels so discombobulated, so unmoored.

Is this her life now? It doesn't feel like her life. Nothing has turned out the way she thought it should. She'd really believed that they would continue running the boardinghouse in Oberlin, she'd even told herself that it would be easier, now that their mother was gone—but instead, everything had fallen apart so quickly, each time she tried to grip the reins they slipped from her hands and she and Bolt tumbled lower and lower: first indentured to grasping Old Lady Synott, and then to the foul Uncle Charlie, and now amongst dirty Gipsies and Freaks and Flim Flam men. Next thing they know they'll be living in a cave with only a campfire for warmth.

The townsfolk—the customers, *the gillies*, as they are called by the carnival folk—arrive and they float past her as if she's invisible. As if they're ghosts, or she is. That's a nice feeling, at least. She once read a book that told the story of the Ring of Gyges, which allowed the wearer to become invisible at will. She remembers this: "No man would keep his hands off what was not his own when he could safely take what he liked out of the market or go into houses and lie with any one at his pleasure, or kill or release from prison whom he would, and in all respects be like a god among men." And this, also: "For all men believe in their hearts that injustice is far more profitable to the individual than justice." She thinks that is probably true.

She and Bolt are dressed identically in overalls and boots, wearing fiddler's caps, their shovels slung over their shoulders, and they are not what the visitors are looking for. The people are drawn to the electric lights and neon, the Ferris wheel and carousel and calliope music, the games of chance and the fortune-telling tent and the contortionist's stage. They want to see Viola, the girl with no legs, do a ballet dance on the palms of her hands, and Herculea, the Muscle Lady, lift the shyly giggling three-hundred-pound Strong Baby into her arms while he drinks milk from a bottle. They are drawn to the world's oldest woman, who is weaving spiderwebs of pink cotton candy onto a stick and calling to them in her high, sweet, grandmotherly voice. "Fairy floss!" she calls. "Sweet spun clouds!"

Eleanor and Bolt are not really invisible, of course. But there is something about them that makes people avert their gaze. The two of them trudge along the edges of booths and tents, and it is only when they cross onto the midway that someone calls out to them.

"Hey! Hey, Red," a boy's voice says.

The dog-faced boy runs the milk bottle toss. His hair is the color of an Irish setter and covers his entire face and neck and arms and hands. There is a coal-black smudge on the tip of his nose and on his lips, and also his fingernails are pointed and painted black. He has green eyes and bright white teeth.

"Howdy, miss!" Dog-Face calls to Eleanor as they walk by. "Care to try your skill at baseball? Knock down these here bottles for me and I'll give you a real nice prize!"

Eleanor turns to stare at him and makes it clear that she doesn't like his smile or his appearance. On the walls behind him are displayed pinwheels and some raggedy dolls with crockery heads, misshapen teddy bears with faces that look more like cats, a ukulele and a beaver fur cap and a set of decorative plates that display the Seven Wonders of the Ancient World. She doesn't think much of this junk, either.

Bolt thinks that the dog-faced boy is maybe sixteen, seventeen. He opens his bare, hairless pink palm toward Eleanor.

What would it be like to kiss such a one? A brief fantasy passes across Bolt's mind: his lips pressing against those black lips, running his hands along the flanks, which must be hairy as a goat's. They are only touching through their clothing, their hands only pet cotton and wool, but their tongues touch, their boots kick each other's toes as they press against one another. Bolt imagines the dog-faced boy pushing him hard against a wall, his hairy hands gripped over Bolt's wrists.

"You look to me like you could be the Lady Babe Ruth," the dog-faced boy says to Eleanor, grinning. "C'mon! Show your beau what you can do with that arm."

"He is not my beau," Eleanor says. "We are brother and sister, adopted of Mr. Jengling. We work here, same as you."

"Ha ha," says the dog-faced boy. "I knew that! I was just teasing you all! My name's Elmer, how'dy do? I guess I'm kinda like your brother."

He gives a glint of the eye toward Bolt, makes a sly cluck of his tongue against his teeth.

"This one's a handful, ain't she?" he says.

Is she a handful? Maybe she is.

She doesn't know what Bolt really thinks anymore. His mind is closed to her: though they confide and cuddle she cannot feel his thoughts the way she once did. Once, it was like pressing a palm against a wet window, and her hand passed through the glass, and she could feel the warm pulse of his consciousness. Once, they could share one brain if they wanted to.

Or maybe it was all just fantasy. That's what she tells Bolt now, she tells him it's babyish to think they can *actually* hear each other's thoughts. "Don't be foolish," she tells him. "That was just make-believe. I made it up and laughed that you believed it!"

When they were little they used to pretend to be one another. Age five, six, seven, they would wake up on a Saturday and Bolt would put on Eleanor's clothes, and she would put on his, and if they put on hats to cover their hair they could almost fool people.

But that wasn't the point. What mattered was the game—putting on the costume of Bolt, living inside Bolt, and then seeing him living inside Eleanor, lounging on her bed, reading her book while she played with his tin soldiers—there was something *delicious* about it.

Now, alas, their bodies are changing too much to make the old game possible.

In the mess tent, the man with the nails pounded in his head is ladling up stew from a pot, and he smiles with squinted eyes as they hold their bowls out to him. "Take some extra meat, you kids!" he says. "Come back if you want more!"

When they first arrived, they had played a trick on him, which they now regret.

"Names?" he'd said, in a heavy accent, maybe Polish. Tiny letters in an alphabet they didn't recognize ran across his face.

"Bolt," said Eleanor. She flicked a quick glance at her brother—a reminder of the old game they used to play, a gesture of solidarity.

He hesitated, just for a moment.

"Eleanor," Bolt said.

At least he was willing to play along.

The man tilted his head and laughed softly. "Eleanor! Isn't it one of the Knights of the Round Table?" He dipped his spoon deep into the pot and filled Bolt's bowl.

"I am Viljams Lacis," he said in his gentle courtly voice. "You do not look healthy to me, Bolt and Eleanor. You have not been well-fed in long time I think, and this is very bad for children your age. You need food to grow, you must eat." He gazed mournfully into the steaming stew. The shafts of the nails in his head were not cylindrical but squared, primitive, and he scratched at one near his ear, thoughtfully. The wound where the nail entered was scarred over, puckered like the skin at the base of a deer's antlers. "I have seen the starving," he said. "And you—you are malnourished, I think? Maybe you got poison, eh?"

Eleanor took the bowl he offered her. "Thank you kindly for the vittles," she said, coolly.

But now weeks have passed and he still thinks Bolt's name is Eleanor, and Eleanor's name is Bolt, and the joke has worn thin. Why does she do such things? Bolt wonders. Maybe to make it so they always have private secrets—so he can't ever get close to anybody else.

Two people sit at one of the long folding tables in the canteen area: the lady with the third leg growing out beneath her belly—Minnie, she is called—and Viola, the girl with no legs, and the small woman named Mme. Clothilde. They watch as Eleanor heads toward a table in the corner, far away from them, and Bolt follows.

Mme. Clothilde is two feet tall and at first glance she appears to be a child. Her voice is the high, sweet voice of a toddler and she wears a powder-blue knee-high jumper dress with a pink sash and a large pink bow in her long, ringleted brown hair. It takes a moment to recognize that her face is that of an adult's. But her eyes are a woman's eyes, and she holds Eleanor for a long moment with her gaze.

"There is room at our table," she says. She beckons to them. "Come! Come sit with us!" Eleanor hesitates. But what can she do?

Mme. Clothilde sips green liquid from a shot glass as Eleanor and Bolt take a bench at the sawbuck table. "Do tell us about yourselves," she says, in her French accent. "We are all so curious about you. It was such a surprise when Père Jengling brought you home with him."

Eleanor nods and takes a taste of her stew. She observes that this small person has full breasts, and that the fingernails of her blunt little hands are long and painted red. Mme. Clothilde watches her intently.

"We were born in Ohio," Eleanor says. "Our mama died and we had no one else to turn to, so we were sent to an orphanage and then put on the train. We were so grateful to be chosen."

"Ah," Mme. Clothilde says. "Heartbreaking."

For a second, Eleanor feels a soft touch in the back of her mind—the same sensation she'd felt when she and Bolt used to read each other's thoughts—and she stiffens. She gives her head a shake.

"I'd like to read your palms and tell your fortune," Mme. Clothilde is saying to Bolt. "You should come to my tent. I could lay out the tarot for you, if you like."

"Oh," says Bolt, spooning a stringy dollop of beef into his mouth. "Uh-huh. That sounds like it'd be different."

"No, thank you," says Eleanor.

The ticketed events start after sunset. The people pay to see Mme. Clothilde conduct a séance. They crowd in to watch Alberic, the contortionist who is a Negro man with chalk-white albino skin, whose knees and elbows bend both ways, who can wrap his legs and arms into a pretzel around his neck and then turn his head to face backward, and they are pleased to see Viola the Half-Woman dance on her hands like a ballerina, pirouetting on the tips of her index fingers. They want to gape at the horror of the Piltdown Man, the missing link, as he gibbers and gobbles up chicken guts—"Step up, ladies and gentlemen," calls queenly Gladness, the Half-Ton Princess of Zanzibar. "Spectators can watch this unique exhibition in perfect safety!" They want to gasp at Minnie, with her three legs, who tiptoes across a tightrope holding two goblets of red wine above a white carpet. They want to see Tickley-Feather shot from a cannon, and Dr. Chui, the giant Chinese mesmerist with the horn growing out of his head, who can hypnotize a member of the audience into barking like a dog.

And then Jengling comes out to thank them for their attention and good taste—and one last thing before they go home—

Spotlight:

Jengling in a tweed coat and bow tie with a straw boater hat, holding a bouquet of daisies.

He knocks at a door and the gorilla, Miss Alcott, answers, wearing a pretty frock and a feathered cap.

The crowd roars with laughter.

And yet she takes the daisies with such melancholy dignity that they grow quiet.

Jengling offers his hand, and Miss Alcott takes it. A player piano begins a waltz.

The audience is silent as they dance and it is so sad to see a wild animal trained to portray human motion, as Miss Alcott does; it is so sad to see the person Miss Alcott might've been, trapped in the body of an ape. Their waltzing shadows stretch and contract as the player piano tinkles gently, her leathery black gorilla paws pressed so delicately against his hairless hands, her feet brushing the floor so gracefully, *onetwothree, onetwothree*, and Bolt feels as if he might start to cry. He feels that it is beautiful in a way that he couldn't explain to Eleanor, and they sit side by side, not looking at one another.

Tickley-Feather's trailer smells of the musk of Tickley-Feather, his hairy male body and his big feet, but there is also a tang of oil and kerosene and wet leather, along with the peculiar, braided bundles of incense that he sometimes burns. *Smudge*, he calls it.

Besides the two berths covered with patchwork quilts, there is a locked trunk and a chest of drawers, a cuckoo clock that works only intermittently, a wind chime that tinkles like ice in a glass when the caravan is traveling.

"You know we got to get moving soon," Eleanor whispers. They lie together, limbs tangled, snuggled as they always have been since before they were born.

"I hate it here," Eleanor says.

And Bolt says, "I know."

"We're not like them," Eleanor says. "We're normal."

She knows that's not true, but Bolt says nothing.

"I just," she says, "I want to get back to the way things used to be, before Mama died. Just us—"

"Mm," Bolt says. He keeps his eyes closed, nuzzled against her. "You want to go back to Oberlin?"

"That house was ours!" she says. "We should have gone to the sheriff and asked for justice!"

Bolt's head is resting against her armpit, and when he opens his eye he can see that he is too close to the woman's breast that has been steadily arising there. He lifts up abruptly, abashed, but she catches him by the back of the head before he can pull away.

"You still trust me, don't you?" she says.

In the morning, Bolt and Eleanor again shovel and mop the cages of exotic animals. They shovel the shit of an elephant, and the shit of the lion and the tiger, and the shit of the Piltdown Man, the Missing Link, who eats worms and bugs and chicken guts, who growls and snatches at them through the bars of his cage, his beard bejeweled and trembling with spittle. He takes down his ragged britches and pisses on the floor right in front of them.

Bolt and Eleanor exchange glances as the Missing Link rages. They remember how the lion and tiger sat peaceably side by side in the pose of sphinxes, watching politely as their cage was swept, as the filth was mopped up and the hay replaced.

Meanwhile, the Missing Link will not settle down. In some ways he looks not unlike an ugly Oberlin drunk they used to know, bald with a crown of lank, long hair encircling his head, teeth gray and crumbly. But the Piltdown could also be a caveman, with his heavy brow and square head and squashed nose, his empty piggy eyes. Eleanor fixes him with a stern gaze and claps sharply.

"Here, now! I ain't no paying customer," she says. "And if a wild gorilla can behave like a decent person, so can you. Now, you sit down and mind your manners or it'll be all the worst for you!"

And she flicks her mop toward him, and as always her aim is uncanny, droplets of water hit him square in the eyes and the mouth, and he cringes and grows silent. She thinks he is a human—a lowlife drunk, a man at the very bottom of a lifetime fall. But Bolt is not so sure.

So credulous is Bolt. That is a problem, Eleanor thinks. That is the issue that divides them as they grow older, that is why they can't really touch each other's thoughts anymore. Bolt, she thinks, wants to be a pet. He follows her now, but he could've followed Uncle Charlie just as well, and he could follow Jengling, too. Already he moons over Tickley-Feather, he even moons over that dog-faced boy.

It's sad. So sad.

They haul slop buckets out of the performers' trailers and they collect dirty dishes and straighten the bedding.

They clean the trailers that are full of Mr. Jengling's collections—

Eleanor holds the kerosene lantern up and they can see the rows of jars on the shelf. It's like a fruit cellar but instead of canned jellies there are babies—monstrous babies floating in brine of some sort—babies with long tails but no arms nor legs, babies with eyes like frogs', swollen out of the sockets, babies with arms where their legs should be, two babies twisted and melted together, fused by the backs of their skulls, one looking forward, one looking back.

Eleanor holds the light closer to that one and glances at Bolt, she points with her lips—*you see it?*—and he nods. It's a dream they used to share when they were little, that they were sewed together back-to-back, heads merged so that they had only one set of ears but two faces, two mouths, one throat, two sets of lungs, two bellies but one pelvis, with boy parts on one side and girl stuff on the other, and one set of legs that ended in four feet, toes pointed in opposite directions.

They would dream it and both wake up screaming, holding on to each other, crying for dear life.

Of Tickley-Feather

•••••••••

It's said that Tickley-Feather is Jengling's first adopted child, and that they have the same age and the same birth date.

Tickley-Feather does not comment on this. He does not comment on anything, doesn't socialize with the other performers and workers, the other brothers and sisters—though he is often seen talking privately, in a low voice, to Ringmaster Jengling, or holding Mme. Clothilde in the crook of his arm while she whispers in his ear with a cupped hand. He might be spotted briefly conferring with Dr. Chui as they walk along the circumference of the carnival. Otherwise, he has little to say.

Does he have a real forename, or a family name? What is his nationality?

In those times, with the great influx of immigrants to the United States, ethnicity carried with it, like a zodiac sign, a key to an individual's personality and attitude toward the world.

Caricatures were a common trope for comedians, subjects for vaudeville novelty songs sung in exaggerated accents—not just blackface minstrelsy, but flame-haired, monkey-faced, whiskey-loving Stage Irish—"O'Brien Is Tryin' to Learn Hawaiian," went one schtick—

Just to say "I love you true."
With his "Ar-rah Ya-ka Hu-la
Be-gor-ra Hick-I-Du-lah"
And his Irish "Ji-ji-boo."

—and then the same performer might return to the stage as a slick-haired, brush-mustachioed lovelorn Italian singing, "My Mariuccia take a steamboat—she-a gone-a back-a to the old-a country—" or as a blond and simple Boxhead Swede, belting out "Come Yosephine in My Flying Machine," in a thick, nasally Nordic intonation—or, wearing a Chinese-style queue pigtail, might serenade an audience with a tune called "Chinese Blues": "Chinaman, Chinaman, wash 'em laundry all day / Chinaman, Chinaman, smoke 'em pipe, they say—"

And though these parodies were exaggerated, it was nevertheless widely believed that they contained a grain of truth—that one inherited certain inescapably persisting characteristics from one's ancestors, not just noses and hair color, lips and skin tone and eye shapes but some deeper, intrinsic aspect of nature and soul.

Yet Tickley-Feather remains frustratingly unidentifiable. Many of the carnival folk believe him to have the blood of some native tribe—Sioux, most likely, or Ponca or Fox—mixed together with European of some sort, while others think he is clearly Sicilian; Mr. Lacis insists that he is a Romani, or perhaps a Persian Jew, and Dr. Chui believes he might be Javanese, of the Indo people from the Dutch East Indies. Herculea the Muscle Lady says she always assumed him to be of Mexican extraction, and Elmer the dog-faced boy laughs.

"He's too tall!" Elmer says. He's had a couple of beers, though he's only sixteen, and his table that is occupied by the other teenagers lets out boisterous catcalls. Tickley-Feather regularly bosses and harries them, and he is not popular among their set.

"He's not a human, haven't you heard?" calls out Shyla, the Hindu Dancing Girl. "He is a rakshasa!"

They don't know what a rakshasa is, but they don't disagree. Most of them bear the outward signs of anomaly and divergence—even within their assigned ethnic group, they are outsiders. Freaks.

But what makes Tickley-Feather part of their family? No one can say.

By the Light of the Silv'ry Moon

•••••••••

Uncle Charlie in moonlight, cursing at the road that stretches out before him like a silver ribbon. The horse Stardust trots along morosely because she knows there is no home at the end and she hates him so deeply for constantly rubbing the heels of his boots against her flank.

He has at last traced the missing children to Fingerton, Indiana, to an agency that runs an orphan racket and he stomps in and demands to speak with the MAN IN CHARGE and the women in the office scuttle around in a flurry of insult and alarm.

"I am the UNCLE of these precious children and you had NO RIGHTS to sell them without permission!" he tells them. "YOU ARE NAUGHT BUT SLAVERS," he declaims, "who have hauled my only kin off on a train LIKE LIVESTOCK! Sold them like the Jews of Egypt to some dirty German or Finn! I will have reparations."

Tears of outrage roll down his cheeks and the shocked women creep toward him cautiously as he's bent, weeping, they murmur uncertainly as he covers his eyes and shudders—this mellerdrammer is, of course, the oldest of ancient tricks, and as they approach, making comforting gestures, he thinks of how simple it would be to kill them all with just his fingers and teeth.

They assure him that the children are well cared for, in safe hands. They will only be adopted by the finest of families. They say that the children are on a train headed west. Illinois. Iowa. Nebraska. South

Dakota. They make a list of towns where the orphans will be put up to auction. "Adoption," they call it.

Of course, he is not their real uncle, but the children's father was his true and most useful friend, and when Jasper Lambkin had passed away Charlie had taken his surname as a way to memorialize him. To honor their bond.

Because Uncle Charlie had loved him like a brother, hadn't he? He had lost his mind with grief when Jasper died and he'd gone on a murder spree that to this day continued from time to time.

Jasper was the only true mentalist Charlie had ever known, and he was a mentalist of great power. They'd met in a poker game in Rapid City, in a big barroom where drunken men with holstered guns wavered along searching for a fight, and whores strolled amongst them, working the floor in melon-colored stockings and faded peignoirs, and Jasper sat there as if he were at a garden party. He was a neat little gap-toothed man, freckled and snub-nosed and gentle faced, with a tended mustache and black hair shaved on the sides, parted down the middle on the top. You wouldn't have taken him for a champion poker player, but Charlie watched as he won round after round. He knew when to hold, when to fold, he knew when to quietly pocket his money and leave the table.

"Good night, gentlemen," Jasper said, pushing away from the table, and Charlie had watched as he strolled along unnoticed, past the lewd wontons and stumbling cowboys and the crowd that was singing as a fiddler played a drinking tune. By God! Jasper had the uncanny ability of being the least noticeable person in the room.

Charlie got up and follered after him. He touched Jasper on the back of his neck as he was walking up the stairs to his room, and Charlie gave him a full-toothed beam when he turned.

"My name's Charlie Prine!" he said. "I'd like to be friends with you!"

And soon enough they were drinking out the same bottle! They were a funny pair, people said. Jasper Lambkin was a small fellow, no more than five foot two, a hundred pounds at best, and Charlie Prine was six feet and three, badger-bodied and wild-bearded, but despite that they were well matched.

In the beginning, Charlie only wanted to learn more about Jasper's cons and flumdoodles and stratagems, but it wasn't long before he fully believed that he had happened upon a true Master, a virtuoso beyond compare. Could Jasper truly read minds? Yes, it seemed unquestionable. Could Jasper perform hypnosis? Yes, Charlie had seen it with his own eyes in a saloon in Spearfish, how Jasper had calmed a violent man by holding up a gold watch and swinging it pendulously, speaking softly in a foreign tongue. He could perform what he called "telekinesis" as well, he could make a shot glass slide along the full length of a bar just by looking at it. What a treasure he was as a partner!

Jasper did not touch alcohol, and he eschewed the smoking of tobacco and marihuana, but he had a valise bag full of medications—laudanum and Bayer's Heroin tablets, Sulfonal, along with elixirs that Charlie had never seen before. Jasper only drank water from a Revigator crock lined with radium.

In any case, Jasper was mildly peloothered most of the time, and when they were at a saloon he could be an engaging raconteur. Once he told a tale about a mesmerist performing at a county fair in Indiana who had hypnotized an audience member and laid him out on the stage, flat on his back, and commanded him to levitate. And the man had risen a few feet into the air when the mesmerist abruptly had suffered a stroke and collapsed! The poor be-mesmered rube—still enthralled—had continued to float up and up until at last he was just a speck among the stars, and then vanished completely, never to be seen again. "He's past the moon by now," Jasper told them, dreamily. "And Mars, and on his way to Jupiter."

He told a story about the Piraña Butterflies of the jungles of South America, soft pink in color, no bigger than a rose petal, they would float along in swarms and if a cloud of them surrounded an ox it might be skeletonized in a matter of minutes. The natives there rubbed an ointment on their skin to protect them from these carnivorous butterflies, and scientists had recently discovered that the unguent contained the radioactive element Uranium! The scientists were astonished to find that this Uranium Salve was effective on all manner of skin ailments, from acne to psoriasis, and also soothed joint and back pain. He had some samples in his bag, he said, that he would be willing to part with for a fair price.

When they were alone together, Jasper was quiet and thoughtful, a good listener, and from time to time he would interject with a comment that would startle Charlie with its wise insight.

Like, for example, one night they were tent-camping, sitting around a fire and roasting greasy prairie dogs on a spit, and Charlie held forth on a newspaper article he had read on how the last passenger pigeon had died in the Cincinnati Zoo, and now they were believed to be gone from the earth. "And once upon a time, they would blacken the skies by the millions!" Charlie exclaimed. "They'd shoot them out of the air with cannons! And now we've killt them all!"

"Yes. Well," said Jasper, and peeled off a bit of meat from the thigh of his prairie dog. "Creatures go extinct for a reason," he said. "If they were meant to be on earth, they would be."

"Huh!" said Charlie, and he stared into the campfire, considering. *If they were meant to be on this earth, they would be*, he thought, and nodded slowly, and distractedly braided a prairie dog leg bone into his beard.

"All right," he mused. "I like that." He watched attentively as Jasper took off his boots and socks and warmed his bare feet at the fire. He had cute little feet, Charlie noted, round-toed and flat-footed as a toddle-child, and when they were in the tent Charlie had the urge to snuggle up and wrap Jasper in a hug and Jasper grunted but didn't protest or try to struggle away like some others had in the past. He just stayed still and rigid as Charlie cuddled, and then as Jasper drifted off he relaxed and softened and his breathing slowed, and truly there was no deeper feeling of love than having a warm living person go limp in your arms.

I am meant to be on this earth! Charlie thought. *Otherwise, I wouldn't be here!*

Everything would have been perfect but Jasper suffered terrible from the woofits, and sometimes he needed to be abed for days, lost in his gloom. Charlie tried to sit with him and tell him dirty jokes to cheer him up, but nothing could rouse him. He'd beg Charlie to leave him be, *just go, just go*, he'd say, *I want to be alone.*

But Charlie stayed. He watched over Jasper as he went through some kind of trance, and when Jasper began to scratch gashes in his chest with his fingernails, Charlie held his hands.

He muttered about the wife and twin babies he'd left back in Ohio. *That woman. She was too much for me*, he said. *She loved me but she would have also killed me, and those babies, I don't know . . .*

"Ah," Charlie said. "You think maybe they weren't your . . . ?"

"No, no," murmured Jasper, and he squeezed his eyes shut as if in pain. "I knew they were my kin, but I didn't want them to be . . . like me. They . . . I should never have had children."

"Now, now," said Charlie, and he stroked hair back from Jasper's brow. "Don't you worry. We will reunite you with your loved ones," he said. "You will see them again!"

"No, I will not," said Jasper. "I will never go back there. Gods! I just want to sleep for a while. Don't touch me, please, Charlie, I don't want to be pawed at. Can you please go?"

"All right," Charlie said. "I'm going to go downstairs and see if they have some applesauce! I'll bet that would do you some good!"

After a few days, Jasper would recover and they went back to their travels. They were making very good money. Men would hire Jasper as a diviner—an Auspex, he called himself—and he could often lead them to the spots where metals and minerals could be found under the earth—not just water for wells, but also gold, gypsum, lime, silver, feldspar, gemstones—he had an instinct for dowsing these things, and more, and he had a full act of eye-rolling and trembling and sweating, he would throw his head back and foam at the mouth, and it was very compelling. By God, watching him prophesy was something to behold, and the performance gave Charlie a tingle in his lower regions! Whether the dowsing was real or not, suckers forked over money for it, and Charlie made sure that Jasper was safe whilst in his stupor.

It was possible that Jasper was not right in the head, but who among us is, truly, sane? *Few!* thought Charlie.

Still, he felt sorry that Jasper's kind of madness did not seem to have much room for frivolity. For Charlie, his happiest times had often been when he was most unhinged, but for Jasper it was the opposite. He leant toward the darkness, toward ancient conspiracies and curses and a lingering sense of being persecuted by demons and angels both.

He once told Charlie that he knew how the world would end, and he knew what came after. "But if I told you, you would start screaming," Jasper said. "You'd scream and scream and wouldn't stop." They were sitting at a campfire and coyotes were yipping in the distance, and there was a stew made of rabbit and navy beans in the iron pot over the fire.

"I would not start screaming," said Charlie. "I don't give two shitties about this world. I'd be happy to see it burn."

"Mm," said Jasper, and spooned up some stew and kept the secret of the end of the world to himself.

Jasper wrote feverishly in his journal using an unknown alphabet, and Charlie laid in the tent next to him and dozed as he scribbled. As the cold wind blew outside and they huddled together, Charlie kept Jasper safe from those as might do him harm.

The Dakotas were not as rough as back in the days of the gold rush, but lands were still full of lawless, desperate people, their hearts full of malice. Since they'd enlarged the Homestead Act and you could now grab up 360 acres instead just 160, the immigrant foreigners kept coming in, too—Swedes, Norwegians, Russians, Germans, Irish. The government started opening what they called "surplus" land on Rosebud Reservation, and thousands showed up in Yankton and even worse places for the land lottery drawings. Suckers they were, thought Uncle Charlie. He'd seen their dwellings—at best a tar paper–covered shack with a slanted sheet metal roof, no more than the size of two shithouses, at worst they built their houses out of rocks and roofed it with sod or dug out a hole in the side of a hill and lived in the dirt like moles.

Charlie would've sooner swallowed poison, he told Jasper, and Jasper agreed.

Later, Charlie regretted mentioning poison. He shouldn't have joked about suicide. "I'd sooner pull the Dutch act than lay claim to a patch of barren prairie and try to grow something on it! Put a noose upon my neck and tie my feet to a fast horse!"

Maybe this had given poor Jasper ideas, because it wasn't long after that he did himself in. The woofits had come over him again stronger than ever before, even though it seemed to Charlie that they'd been having a lot of luck, making good money, and the land was full to brimming with ignorant settlers to fleece. But Jasper's dark mood only deepened and deepened, and he took to bed at a little hotel in the railroad town of Murdo and couldn't be coaxed out of his room. Charlie went out and prowled around the railyard roundhouse and found an empty boxcar where some rubes were drinking corn whiskey and playing cards and he joined in and then got chased off when he won too many rounds of poker. Back in '10, a fire had swept out a whole block of Murdo, and he considered that it might be fun to start another.

It was around this time, Charlie guessed, that Jasper had made the choice to hang himself with his belt, but the purple-faced corpse wasn't discovered until late afternoon of the next day, after repeated unanswered knockings had led Charlie to fetch the girl from downstairs and have her open the door.

Jasper Lambkin was laid to rest in the cemetery outside of Murdo and Uncle Charlie paid a preacher to say a few words, and hired the pretty young Norwegian girl from the hotel to come to the graveside service and told her he'd give her extra if she'd cry real tears. But the three of them were the only ones in attendance, apart from the undertaker, who'd charged an arm and a leg to do an embalming. It was a lonely, empty place to leave his one true friend, *the only friend he'd ever had*, he told the girl, and asked if she'd take an extra fifty-cent piece to let him weep on her shoulder and put her arms around him, and she pursed her lips and nodded, but she was not prepared for the intensity of his grief.

"He taught me . . . the true meaning of friendship," Charlie whispered, and the Norwegianess pulled away with a small cry of revulsion when he rested his wet mouth against her bare neck. Dang it, he could feel a murder splurge in the back of his head, and he reckoned it would overtake him before too long.

But now, standing before his beloved friend's final resting place, he swore he would take the Lambkin name as his own so they would always be brothers. He swore that he would seek out Jasper's lost children and fold them in his arms. Charlie had meant this as a matter of honor but also it was true that he hoped these wee orphans might have the same gifts as their father, which could be farmed and harvested—

Oh, who would guess that these adored infants would flee from their uncle's safeguarding and refuge? Who would guess that Uncle Charlie's one and only altruistic feeling ever in his life would lead to this bitter and angry pursuit?

Blair, Nebraska

•••••••••

They're all packed up and on the train and pulling out of Beatrice before noon, and Bolt stands on the back deck of the caboose with Elmer the dog-faced boy, and Shyla the fourteen-fingered Hindu Dancing Girl, and Gladness, the Half-Ton Princess of Zanzibar. Mme. Clothilde sits on Dr. Chui's shoulder and they all wave and throw handfuls of penny hard candy as the children of the town run along behind them, calling out.

Goodbye!

Safe journey!

Come back soon!

Just dumb farm kids, boys in overalls and big rough boots, girls barefoot in smocks, but Bolt can't help but feel flattered by the attention. He waves and laughs and feels a glow puff up his chest.

"Bye-bye! We'll be back," he calls, hurling fistfuls of candy, laughing alongside Elmer and Shyla and Gladness, and even though he himself is not special in the way they are they don't seem to mind that he's mingling amongst them. Elmer makes his *ch-ch* sound, like he's telling a horse to giddyup.

"That wasn't bad," Elmer says. "That was a town full to the brimming with gillies!" He drapes his arm over the shoulders of Shyla and Gladness. "I made some extree money, my girls!" he says. "Can I buy you some Champagne?"

He looks at Bolt sidelong, sly, one eye squinted. "You can come on with us down to the canteen, if you want. I can't afford to buy for you and the girls both, but I'll give you a taste of mine."

Champagne! Bolt has heard of it, and he guesses it would taste like oranges and flowers, and would tickle your throat like soda pop. He considers.

He likes the idea of getting acquainted with them. How easy and natural they are with each other—though Gladness is a proud noblewoman of deepest Africa, five foot high and five hundred pounds, in a crown and royal robes, her hair in elaborate twining braids; though Shyla is a dancing girl from the land of Hyderabad, stick-thin and long-limbed, with her extra fingers and toes and her paisley silks, eyelids painted gold; and the dog-faced boy Elmer Googins is a rough Scotch-Irish street boy from Chicago, sold to a vaudeville manager at age of five—still, they seem like they are true friends of each other.

Yet also they are older kids, sixteen, seventeen—sophisticated. He does not feel quite prepared enough to be in their company.

He shrugs, bashfully. "Naw," he says. "I got to go check on my sis."

Eleanor is on the berth in the train car they share with Tickley-Feather, staring at their papá's diary. She doesn't look up when Bolt comes in. She's leaned into a corner of a wall, tucked in the way she likes, with a blanket over her knees. He used to like to watch her read—the way her eyes flickered, the way little, subtle expressions played on her face and even sometimes her lips would move, as if she and the book were having a conversation. He doesn't know that he had ever fallen into a line of letters the way she does, and so he just stands there quietly watching her be absorbed which is beautiful.

"Where've you been?" she says, at last, not lifting her head. She closes the book, holding her place with a finger.

"Nowhere," Bolt says. "Just back at the caboose throwing out candy for the town kids. I reckon that's what they do as they leave a place. To spread goodwill."

She nods, then turns back to the diary—opens it, stares down at the indecipherable scrawls.

"Are you having any luck with that?" Bolt says.

He makes a gingerly attempt to touch minds with her, but he only brushes across the edge and then slides away. Still, he knows that the diary has not revealed itself to her. He can feel the moist, unpleasantly warm pulse of her frustration. It is nothing but scribbles, an invented alphabet.

"I saved you some pieces of candy," Bolt says at last, and digs in his pocket. "We got peppermint, butterscotch, cinnamon, lemon—"

He holds out a palmful of glossy lozenges wrapped in cellophane—so pretty and fancy—and she smiles in that distant, thinky way, and takes the butterscotch because she knows that's the one he doesn't like.

"Thanks," she says. She scoots over and he gets under the blanket shawl with her and pets her hair.

She calls the book their *Papa's Diary*—though actually, Bolt thinks, actually it's hard to tell what it really is. On the inside front cover it says:

Noli credere
fratri. Hoc scies
legere.

The inscription is in Latin, Eleanor says, and she tells him that it translates as "Don't believe my brother, you will know how to read this." But Bolt wonders. All she knows of Latin is a book she'd stolen from their school called *Latin for Beginners*, so maybe she can read those words and maybe she just believes she can. And anyways, most of the rest of the diary is written in sloppy-looking code, the letters are not real letters but "runes," Eleanor says, "hieroglyphs," she says, like she thinks it's a big word that Bolt has never heard before. He knows what a hieroglyph is.

"Uh-huh," he says. Even if the pages *do* make any sense, they are often blurred by water stains that have made the ink run, or by brownish-red speckles that look like blood. Why is she so convinced that this argle-bargle is important?

Of course, she thinks she can figger it out all by herself, and he knows she would never ask for help, even though Mme. Clothilde knows how to read the tarot and talk to spirits, and Dr. Chui is a wise professor from the Imperial College of Peking, and obviously there is their new father Mr. Jengling who has been all across the world searching for mysteries and lost treasures and unknown species.

She must catch this thought because she suddenly looks up sharply.

"Bolt!" she says. "Don't you never tell nobody about this diary! Promise!"

Bolt shrugs and looks off out the window but she hears him think *I promise.*

They haven't completely lost the ability to read each other's minds.

There was that at least.

Out the window they are passing a field with a farmhand in it, a man in overalls riding on a red tractor, and he lifts his floppy hat and waves as the circus train goes by. Even from a distance you can see that he's beaming, he's a little boy again seeing the carnival train pulling past. "Hullooo!" he calls, or so Bolt imagines.

Bolt lifts his hand and waves back, though of course the man can't see him. But Bolt can feel—what?

He can feel the man's wonderment.

Wonder, Bolt thinks, is that kind of fluttery joy and sorrow of looking at a thing that will only be seen once in a lifetime. A giraffe's long-necked head above the frame of an open boxcar, an elephant peering from behind bars and extending its trunk as if reaching out to touch. Maybe some of the glamour girls sitting on the roof of their boxcar wave their handkerchiefs at him as they pass by, and Bolt is aware that when the young field hand dies some sixty years hence—in 1975 or 1976?—he will recall again the painted gaudy carnival train that passed by one bright June day in 1915, and how it made him want something that he never knew the name of.

That's what Bolt wants, too: to have a life full of moments of wonder that you carry with you, a life of bewitchments and astonishments, and as he watches the fields and farmhouses and dirt roads and barbwire fences rolling past, he considers what he would do if he owned the carnival. He might offer rides on a hot-air balloon, or even an aero-plane!

There might be a Wall o' Death with motorcycles running along the side of a wooden silo, held in place by friction and centrifugal force. He had read about the motordrome at Coney Island in New York and thought it would be a sight to see. What about a magician like Houdini who could perform daring escapes? Maybe he'd add some cowboys doing sharpshooting exhibitions, and an alligator wrestler, wearing only a pair of ragged pants. And why didn't they have a nickelodeon to show moving pictures? Also, more monkeys! Tame ones you could pet.

He touches a finger to the window and watches a ghost of condensation form around his fingertip. *If he is adopted of Mr. Jengling, does that mean he could inherit this place someday?*

Outside of the town of Blair, Nebraska. Monday morning, June the twenty-first.

They wake when they feel the train stop, and then they smell the incense Tickley-Feather burns, a mingling of sage and cedar and sweetgrass, and they feel him tap the frame of their bunk with the toe of his boot. "We're here," he says. "Wash up and come get breakfast."

Bolt doesn't open his eyes, but he dreams of taking a hot bath back at the boardinghouse in Oberlin. He liked to submerge his head and stare up through the skin of the water and watch the ceiling rippling, he liked to watch a bubble of breath wobble upward and vanish, and all the sound was gone except for the strange, beautiful, echoey knell of his feet rubbing against the porcelain. The boarders would get angry with him because they knocked and knocked and it was the only bathroom, though there was also still a jakes out back.

And then a bang comes and he startles awake, both of them sit up in bed as Tickley-Feather hits the train car door with his peg hammer.

"*GIT UP!*" he bellows.

Tickley-Feather has long legs and walks fast and they hurry along behind him. They'd barely had enough time to pull on their shirts and overalls and socks and boots, let alone wash. By the look of the sun's light it must be six thirty, seven in the morning and Bolt feels ashamed to have overslept, he wants to make a good impression, but he feels a little better when he sees that none of the roustabouts are in shipshape, either, after a night of carousing when they'd docked in Omaha the night before.

Still, the train is already mostly unloaded and they are packing the trucks and the wagons and a few have already driven off to the fairgrounds. Bolt sees Elmer hurry by with a box full of composition dolls made to look like Kewpies, and Herculea the Muscle Lady and Strong Baby are part of a crew hauling the spokes of the Ferris wheel onto a flatbed truck and the elephant is lifting metal poles with its trunk and carefully stacking them.

They arrive at the open field outside of town in the back of a horse-drawn wagon, sitting on stacks of bright red-and-black-striped tent canvas, and the carnival is already in the process of being assembled. Many of the game booths are set up and some of the sideshow tents, and the carnival workers are hammering and shoveling and carrying lumber and boxes, and a gasoline-powered generator is puttering loudly. Some town children are watching from a distance, pointing excitedly at the various unusual people they see, gasping and applauding when the Strong Baby comes along riding the elephant, the curlicue of hair at the top of his round head tied with a blue ribbon. Bolt sees, with regret, that breakfast is no longer being served at the mess tent. Mr. Lacis is cleaning up the dishes and pots.

Tickley-Feather brings the wagon to a halt in front of the half-built carousel and hops down from the driver's seat, and Bolt and Eleanor clamber out as well. The tattoo man is sitting on the center base of the still-horseless carousel with his mynah bird on his shoulder. The tattoo man opens his mouth and the bird feeds him, poking a peanut or a raisin between his parted lips with its bill like it's feeding one of its own babies.

"Hey, Bigelow," Tickley-Feather says, and the tattoo man tilts his head up, squinting one eye as the bird feeds him another raisin.

Tickley-Feather points his thumb at Eleanor. "I need you to teach this 'un how to run the carousel, eh?"

Bigelow leans back on his elbows and swallows his raisin. The bird hops on top of his head.

"Alrighty," the bird says, in a high, croaky voice like a gossipy woman, and Bigelow leans back on his elbows, laconically. "Sure, we can show her the ropes!" the bird says, and Bolt guesses that Bigelow must be doing some sort of ventriloquism so that it seems the bird is talking to them. But the bird actually opens and closes its beak as if pronouncing the words. It's pretty convincing.

Meanwhile, Bigelow blinks his big eyes slowly, like he's stoned on opium. He's naked except for a pair of boxing trunks and a necklace made of fangs. All across his bronze-colored skin are vines and flowers and caves of intertwining trees. He shows his teeth, which have been sharpened into points like a shark's.

"I ain't working with this man unless he puts some clothes on," Eleanor says. She glances at Bolt, who cannot take his eyes off the tattoos, which seem to shift and rustle, he thinks he sees faces of snakes and leopards peering out of the branches, a creature like a monkey with goat horns scuttling in between the tree trunks.

"Ain't that right, Bolt?" Eleanor says. "We ain't gonna work with a half-naked man, are we?"

"No, we ain't!" Bolt says, supportively.

Bigelow laughs, and the bird on his head spreads its wings and makes a laughing sound as well. Bigelow curls his bare feet and Bolt sees that the soles of his feet are covered in tattoos as well—glyphs, not unlike the ones in the diary. He nudges Eleanor, but she's not looking at feet.

"What would you like him to wear, sweetheart?" the mynah bird asks. "A gentleman's tuxedo?"

"Pants'll do," Eleanor says to the bird, and then she gives Bolt a cutting look.

As if he has disappointed her? As if he has confused and hurt her? As if she expected . . . ?

What?

Bolt looks to Tickley-Feather. "Don't you think . . . uh . . . ?"

"What're you asking?" Tickley-Feather says. "He ain't nekkid. He's not gonna cover up them tattoos what makes him money! He's not trying to *do* anything to her, is he? If she doesn't like it, she doesn't have to look."

"Uh," Bolt says, not sure how to counter. He gazes at the winding vines and hanging branches that seem to shudder along Bigelow's muscled torso, the slither of a python as Bigelow itches his belly.

"Well," Bolt says, at last. "*I* could learn the carousel, couldn't I? Why don't you just switch us?"

"Cuz I got other jobs for you, that's why," Tickley-Feather growls in his deep monotone. "You ain't tied to her by a invisible cord, are you?"

Bolt and Eleanor look at one another. Her expression is blank, but her eyes ask for something he can't hear.

"No," Bolt says, and he shrugs and a tingle passes unpleasantly across his skin.

One time Uncle Charlie told him about the Premonition. This was back at the run-down shotgun house on the edge of Indianapolis, and Bolt was sitting at the fireplace in the living room, folding up the blankets and sheets that Eleanor had pulled off the clothesline when it looked like a storm was coming. It had been pouring rain for a while when Uncle Charlie came in the front door, sopping and intoxicated and bright-eyed. He gave his wet hair a shake like a horse tossing its mane and wrapped himself in one of the quilts that Bolt had just folded.

"I just had me a premonition!" Uncle Charlie announced, and sat heavily down next to Bolt, holding his legs out straight, his dripping boots almost in the fire.

"Aye," Uncle Charlie said. "You know what that is, don't you? A premonition, as they call it? It's like a PROPHECY DREAM that you know is going to happen in real life, ain't it? Even if it don't always make sense, you reckernize that it's not just deleriums." He reached over and draped his wet arm across Bolt's shoulder. He gave the clavicle muscle a squeeze, pinching a little, fatherly and dangerous. Bolt looked at the cuckoo clock above the fire, won by Uncle Charlie in a card game, he guessed. It was a little German house and the cuckoo only came out to chirp intermittently, not every hour, but it seemed to be after eleven at night, and he guessed Eleanor was asleep.

"You ever had one, Bolty?" Uncle Charlie said. "I'll bet you get the premonitions, dontcha? It's said that they run in our family."

"Nuh," Bolt said, and gave Uncle Charlie one of his most dull-witted looks. "I never heard of that before," he said. "But it don't sound like it's real."

"Lie!" Uncle Charlie cried, cheerfully. "I can smell the dirty fibs on your breath. I know you've had them. I've heard you muttering in your sleep, haven't I?"

He leaned companionably closer to Bolt's ear, and the smell of Uncle Charlie's breath suggested that he'd had sardines and beer for dinner at a pub, then smoked cigars and drank whiskey for a while, then vomited in a ditch while he was stumbling home in the rain.

"Let's make a bargain, Bolty," Uncle Charlie said. "You tell me your premonitions and I'll tell you mine."

He gave Bolt a soft cuff on the chin with his thick, fighter-man's knuckles, then stood. "But I will say," he confided, "that *my* premonition? It concerned you and your sissy."

The Premonition! He feels it with terrible force as Tickley-Feather brings him to the tent at the far edge of the carnival.

Behind the flap is a windowless space that seems larger than it did from outside, a heavy smell of mildewed carpet, and in the center a girl sits in a chair at a table with a crystal ball on it and a candle is the only light.

But Bolt can see the face—a tiny head, no bigger than a baseball—that is pushing out through the back of her skull, draped by her long brown hair.

"Craniopagus parasiticus, is what Father calls it," Tickley-Feather says. "It means she has two heads. She's like one o' them Siamese twins, I reckon, but there's less of him."

Bolt raises his hand and waves at the girl, but she just sits there, blank as a noodle. He feels the spark in his brain harder than ever, it almost hurts, and he says, "Um . . ."

"All you got to do is feed her once a day and then just keep a pertective watch upon them," says Tickley-Feather, and he puts his big veiny hand on the small of Bolt's back, nudging him forward. "But don't look at her eyes. Nor look at the otherin neither."

Bolt nods. The girl, Rosalie, has a normal, sleepy-looking sort of face, almost pretty, but the boy pushing out from the back of her head has large, swollen eyes and a lump of a nose and ruddy, pocked cheeks, and you might think it was made of softened wax but its lips move and twitch. It turns its gaze toward him as if it can see.

Rosalie is never put on display, Tickley-Feather is telling him. "She is only available for special private consultations, eh?" he says. "And you ain't to speak to her neither. If she starts to babbling at you, don't listen."

"Okay," Bolt says, and he does like the warmth of Tickley-Feather's hand on his back, he does like that he is being assigned a special job and Eleanor don't know nothing about it, he can tell her or not, it's his decision.

Though in some ways it don't make sense. Why shouldn't *he* be learning to run the carousel with Billy Bigelow and his mynah bird, and why isn't Eleanor watching over this deformed unfortunate? Isn't running a machine more of a boy's job, and being nursemaid more of a girl's?

After he thinks on it awhile, he's a bit offended.

He sits in a chair before the girl Rosalie with a bowl of gruel and he guesses that she must be about his age. Thirteen, fourteen. He looks into her eyes, which are milky, probably blind, and then flicks down quickly to the gazing pool of the bowl and dips the spoon into the thin milky grits and drudges up a serving and he sees that her mouth has opened wetly, and when he puts the spoon to her lips, she takes the nourishment and makes a gentle slurping sound. The Otherin's mouth begins to move, too, working silently as if nursing. Bolt blushes, as if he's seen something dirty.

He holds out another spoonful of lukewarm grits and she speaks in a language that he doesn't recognize, it's not even vowels nor consonants he's ever heard before. She takes the spoon like a lizard snapping up an insect, she masticates, drools, the spoon judders in his hand as she bites it and sucks on it and then pulls back.

"The junction in the limbs is," she says, "wrath of the clouds, I believe. Or not."

Bolt cringes back as Rosalie turns her slack face toward him, and the Otherin moves its lips as if it is letting out a little prayer, and Rosalie catches Bolt with her bald, empty eyes, which are not as blind as he thought.

"Say," she says, sweetly. "Don't I know you?"

The Premonition!

That night when Uncle Charlie stumbled off to bed, drunken and dripping with rain.

My premonition? It concerned you and your sissy, he'd mumbled cattishly, and afterward Bolt nestled his legs underneath himself and stared at the fire, considering.

The cuckoo came out of the clock and made half of a sound. "Coo—" it hooted softly, and then bowed its head limply, and did not spring back into its house.

Bolt's premonition—just a flash, a lingering image—had been of this tent he is sitting in right now. He had seen Rosalie, and the infant's head pressing out through the back of her hair, and in his mind's eye, in his dream, he had sat in his chair just as he is sitting now, with his arms crossed, and as he tries to make out the edges of the tent beyond the edge of the light of the candle, he is aware that he once dreamt this exact view. Sometimes he's certain he can see the burlap wall; sometimes he's afraid that all he can see is an endless black plain.

Bolt's not sure what to make of it. If he is, in fact, a clairvoyant who can see the future, then why was his vision of this hot, dark tent? It doesn't seem like it foretells anything very interesting. He doesn't really see the point of it, and he hopes that if he gets another presentiment, they'll do a better job.

Rosalie is still at her little table with the crystal ball and the fringed velvet tablecloth, her head nodded, her breath softly ragged. The thing on the back of her head remains awake, its eyes open and blinking up at the black ceiling. What time is it? Afternoon?

Bolt is so bored. He cleans his fingernails with the smallest blade of his pocketknife. He wishes he had a magazine to peruse. Uncle Charlie always had copies of *The All-Story Magazine* and *Argosy* and *Railroad*

Man's Magazine. Bolt had read all of *The Warlord of Mars* while sitting in a kitchen listening to Uncle Charlie cheating men at cards in the other room.

He is half-dozing himself, thinking of John Carter's wife, Deyah Thoris, in her slowly rotating prison along with the Barsoomian princess Thuvia of Ptarth.

He hardly notices when the voice nudges him. It's so soft it's barely the tickle of a single feathery hair, but Bolt opens one eye.

O God help me!
Help me, I'm trapped.

Bolt jerks awake and he can see that the doll-like extrusion on the back of Rosalie's head is softly moving its lips.

Trapt.
Trappttt.

And then the tent flap opens and light streams in. Bolt can see a big man in silhouette with the sunlight backing him, and then the figure takes off its top hat, and his eyes and smile come into view of the candlelight. Bright, pale eyes, teeth whiter than any Bolt has ever seen.

"How are our special twins doing?" says Mr. Jengling, and he stands peering at Rosalie dozing in her chair. Her lips move, and the thing on her head moves its lips in echo.

"Seems like they're doing real good," Bolt offers. He's worried his voice sounds squeaky, he wants to make a good impression, and he stands up and gestures. "Yep! They been real quiet. Behaving themselves!"

Mr. Jengling tilts his head and turns his attention to Bolt with such intense interest that it makes his skin jump.

"Ha ha, I was asking after *you*, my young friend," Bolt's new father says, and Bolt feels himself blush and lower his head. "You—and your sister," says Jengling. "My special twins. Are you settling in?"

"Uh-huh," Bolt says. "We're real grateful to get chosen! We like it here."

"I'm so glad," Mr. Jengling says. He puts his black velvet top hat down on the table next to the crystal ball, and Rosalie glances up briefly, smiling or maybe just stretching her mouth in her sleep. "I've been worried about your sister. She seems unhappy."

"Oh," Bolt says. "No, sir! She's just like that. She's shy."

"Is she, now?" says Mr. Jengling, and he settles into the cushioned wingback chair across from Rosalie, scratching his earlobe thoughtfully. "I suspect that she has yet to fall in love for the first time," he says. "It shapes the girls in ways much different than it does us boys." He gives Bolt a confiding wink. "You know," he says.

"Uh-huh," says Bolt. "I . . ."

Mr. Jengling leans back and flexes his arms in a chicken-wing gesture. He is like Uncle Charlie in the way he acts like he's always known you, like he's been around since you were a small child and your soul is a road he has trod on for years and years—but unlike Charlie Lambkin, Jengling doesn't seem like he's considering your murder. He picks up the tarot deck and begins to shuffle it thoughtfully, and Rosalie watches with interest.

"I had a presentiment that you'd be able to handle her," Mr. Jengling says. "You're not quite the same species, but close enough."

"Uh-huh," says Bolt. Mr. Jengling's pale blue eyes are almost golden in the lamplight, and Bolt guesses that he has some skill as a mesmerist. Miss Sylvia Ferryman had told them that if you feared falling under the spell of a mesmerist you should blink three times and then turn your gaze away for a few seconds, and when you turned back you should look only at their mouth.

"Did she speak to you?" asks Mr. Jengling's lips, and Bolt twists his hands in his lap, rubbing his fingers with his fingers. Is he a chump to hope that Mr. Jengling could be a real father? Mr. Jengling's voice is nice. Kind.

Bolt shrugs bashfully. "I dunno," he says. "I think she said something like 'the junction of the limbs and the rack of the clouds,' but I don't know for sure because it didn't make much sense to me. And then she said to me, 'Don't I know you?' and she looked me in the eye for a minute . . . and it was kind of like she was awake, and that she thought she reckernized me, but . . ."

Mr. Jengling nods encouragingly, and it feels very nice under the light of his attention. Bolt feels his ears grow warm, and he stares at Mr. Jengling's big hands, the thick blond almost see-through hairs on his fingers, his carefully manicured nails. "But . . ." Bolt says, and he thinks to say that it felt as if Rosalie was trying to transfer a vision to him. There had been an electric current that crawled slowly across his scalp, a flash of movement that was too blurred to read.

But he doesn't know how to explain it. Nor does he want to speak of the Otherin, that soft sibilant whisper: ***help me I trapt***

"Isn't it funny," Mr. Jengling says. "Western Union can send printed text by electromagnetic telegraph, can it not? Did you know, Bolt, that Alexander Graham Bell has made a telephone call from New York City to San Francisco? Can you imagine? A voice three thousand miles away speaking to you? That's real. Do you know that there is an invention called Televista which can transfer moving images over wireless?" He gives Bolt an impish smile. "So why, then—why would it seem so outlandish that some humans would have the ability to communicate from brain to brain in the same fashion? Text, voice, image, moving picture . . ."

Bolt watches as Mr. J finishes shuffling the tarot deck with a waterfall flourish and pulls out a card. He holds it so Bolt can't see and points it toward Rosalie, just a few inches from her nose. Rosalie stares at it uncuriously, her head tilted, her mouth a bit slack.

"Tell me what card this is," Mr. Jengling says, and Bolt shifts awkwardly. It seems nasty to touch the mind of someone so insensate, like touching someone's privates while they are sleeping, and he winces shyly as he slides his eyes into hers. He feels a dizzy tumble through dark empty space, and then the image comes into view.

A man in a dark cloak bending over a collection of spilled goblets.

He sees the name.

"Five a cups," Bolt whispers.

"Exactly," Mr. Jengling whispers back.

He bends down and, briefly, dryly, brushes his lips against Bolt's knuckles. "Perfect," Mr. Jengling says. "Son."

Of Elmer the Dog-Faced Boy

•••••••••

He was five when his mother sold him to a vaudeville impresario who was supposed to be his second cousin—some relation. Before that they had tried to hide his condition. He was the youngest of ten, and when he saw his older brothers coming for him with a cup of shaving cream and a straight razor he would run out of the house screaming "Murder! Murder!" and he would struggle and bite when they caught him.

Once he was in the hands of R. M. Googins, his cousin and manager, it was somewhat better. At least he wasn't being held down and shorn every week, and as his hair grew in and lengthened he felt like he always had clothes on even if he was naked. It was his own idea to put a black cork smudge on his nose and lips, and to paint his nails black, so he looked more like a dog than ever.

He crouched in a zoo cage on all fours in a pair of raggedy breeches, and he barked and howled and showed his teeth in a snarl at the customers who peered in at him. R. M. Googins told them that his mother was a human woman who had been ravished by a male wolf, and he panted and lolled his tongue. He could reach his foot up and scritch his own ear with his toe, which took a lot of practice. But he was good at his job, and when his shift was over his cousin would let him have a few beers.

He was almost twelve when Mr. Jengling came to see him. He was taken into a changing room and told to strip down naked and then this tall blond-hair man in a fancy suit came in and stood looking at him.

Arms crossed. Considering. Elmer had his hands over his privates and he kept his eyes on the floor as the man walked a circle around him and then the man put his hand on his back and ran a finger down his spine.

"The hair is vellus," the man, Jengling, murmured, as if he were talking to a scribe who was recording his thoughts. "Smooth and downy, not coarse, not like a *pelt.* Appears to continue to grow in length, like the hair upon a scalp. Possibly exhibiting a hereditary molecule of an unknown hominini."

And then he abruptly turned his bright attention from the imaginary scribe to Elmer.

"I will adopt you," he said. He appeared to be a very young man—in his twenties?—but he had a dark, husky, commanding voice. "We will need to get you some decent clothes. And are you literate? Can you read and do figures?"

Elmer stared back at the man. He wasn't supposed to be able to talk, only to bark and howl, and he wasn't sure whether he was allowed to break character.

"You can drop the dog act," the man said, sternly. "I recognize you as an intelligent *sapiens*, so you don't have to degrade yourself any longer. I'm freeing you from your old master and taking you somewhere where you can be safe and protected."

"Uh-huh," Elmer said, very softly.

"Can you read?" the man said.

"Um," Elmer said. "A little."

"Can you do arithmetic?"

"I can count to a hunderd," Elmer said.

"Good enough," the man said. "Put on your breeches and come with me."

And so he became a ward and his name was Elmer Jengling now, and he was taught to read by Miss Minnie Wilks, who had a leg growing out of her stomach, and he was put in charge of a baseball toss game and learnt how to hold money and how to run a scam, no mention made of his hirsute condition.

Though of course the rubes, the townspeople still came to gawk at him, that was their nature. And he still insisted on blackening his nose and lips with cork, still painted his nails and filed them sharp.

Sometimes, when he was alone, he would go out and howl at the moon.

That was *his* nature, he supposed.

Charlie's Travels

Typically, a massacre will keep him soothed for a good long while. But it's only been a month or so since that sweet little family outside of Indianapolis, and he's already feeling itchy and agitated.

He's in a very beflusterating situation. He has a list of stops that this so-called Orphan Train was to make, but there's no way to know in which town or village his sweet and beloved Lamby-Lambkins have been unloaded and sold into bondage.

And so he is forced to laboriously visit each of the auction sites, find the official or cleric who was in charge of distribution, and confirm that HIS PRECIOUS TWINS were not among the passel of children who were parceled out.

It doesn't help that Illinois and Ioway are amongst his least favorite states—Ioway, especially, with those little prissy towns and their gazebos and marching bands and barbershop quartets. It makes him feel like he can't breathe.

When Charlie was born there were but thirty-seven states in the Union, and now there are forty-eight. As far as he's concerned, most of them don't deserve the title. Arizona and New Mexico are all right, he reckons, he's had some good times in those places, and he feels a little patriotic about North and South Dakota, since he was living in Rapid City when they achieved statehood—the only twin-born states, ratified on the same day, in the same minute, by the hand of Benjamin Harrison!

As for the rest of it, he didn't approve. Why would you give a handful of ranchers in Wyoming a seat at the table of the Senate? Or Utah? What sane person would let a cockeyed Mormon with seven wives legislate for the rest of the country? If Charlie Lambkin were president of the United States, there would be some changes.

But save that for the future. At present here is a county official behind a desk who is assuring him that no children named Bolt or Eleanor Lambkin were on the list of children who were adopted from the Orphan Train.

"Maybe they were going under different monerkers," says Charlie. "They may have been trying to pass under false identities."

"No, sir," says the clerk. "There's no one matching that description recorded."

"All right," says Charlie, "Thank you for your help." And he reaches his hand out and rests his palm across the young man's skinny forearm, with its pale, downy hairs. "I'd love to kill you sometime," he murmurs, hopefully too softly to be heard.

Sunday, June 27

•••••••••

It takes almost half a day to put together a carousel, with Eleanor and Billy Bigelow and two rousties working steadily. They start from the base where the motor is and erect the center pole, and then the overhanging metal spokes like the ribs of an umbrella—"sweeps," Billy calls them. They build the circular platform out of wedges of plywood that interlock around the base, and Billy shows her how the carousel revolves, how the motor drives a pulley and the pulley turns a drive bolt and the shaft is a pension gear, which—

"You understand, yes?" Billy says with his own gravelly voice. His English is softly accented, maybe Spanish or Portuguese, Eleanor thinks—very different from the exaggeratedly American voice of his mynah bird.

"Yes," she says.

"You know how to work a clutch?" he asks.

"I know how a motor works," she says, and he seems to accept this, he shows her his sharpened teeth in a shy grin. "Hokay," he says politely, and his bird settles on his shoulder with a flutter, tilting its blue eye in her direction. "If you have any questions, just ask."

He's not as bad as she thought he might be. He had frightened her when she first saw him, with his naked torso and tattoos and his ventriloquism tricks, but now, even though she had been rude to him, he treats her courteously and with respect, and she softens her opinion.

She helps him lift a carved, brightly painted unicorn onto the platform and fit it into place on the cranking rods that will make it go up and down as if its trotting, and meanwhile the rousties go around with wrenches and screws, fastening the poles in place.

"Make sure you tighten them nuts hard!" Billy calls to them sternly. "One of those comes loose and you'll be answering to the boss, not me!"

He looks at her sidelong, conspiratorially, and his bird lands on a spoke above her head. "You have to keep an eye on those two," the bird tells her softly. "They don't take pride in their work like we do."

The animals on the carousel are a menagerie of different creatures, each one seemingly hand-carved and painted and richly detailed. There is a chimaera with a horse's front, wild-maned and rearing, but its back half is a blue-scaled fish with a serpent-like tail. There is a wolf with the green and scarlet head of a parrot, covered in scalloped feathers instead of fur, and a trotting pig with human hands and feet instead of hooves.

As they work, Billy makes each one sing in turn—"By the Light of the Silv'ry Moon," they intone and quaver, each animal with a different voice and accent. The swan with the head of a bearded man at the end of its slender neck sings in a low drawl like a cowboy; the horned goat with the body of a monkey croons in a high Irish tenor, while the boyish centaur belts out with the brassy voice of a musical hall burlesque, and Eleanor laughs in spite of herself.

Eleanor loves to sing but first she has to be sure that she's alone and no one can hear her, not even Bolt. She knows she can't carry a tune, and people would laugh at her ugly voice, or be repulsed.

Once she was walking to the store for her mama and singing happily when two big boys jeered at her. They were sitting on a fence barefoot with their pants rolled up, smoking corn silk from a pipe and she heard one of them call out, "What's that noise? Sounds like a cat got run over!" and the other one guffawed and she bent down and picked up a rock from the path and chucked it at the laughing boy's face. "Yow!" he cried and fell off the fence and she stomped down the road as the boy bawled behind her. One thing about Eleanor, her aim was always perfect.

Later, the laugher's mother had come to the boardinghouse to complain that Eleanor had broken her son's nose, and Eleanor's mother put her hand delicately to her throat. "Oh! But . . ." she said. "My little girl is only eight years old!" She gazed, gimlet-eyed, at the accusing woman. "Is your boy small and sickly?" she asked in her prettiest, sweetly doleful voice. "Is he *impaired* in some way?"

Yet ultimately Eleanor was the more permanently injured party, for she swore she would never again let herself be heard singing for as long as she lived, and something that she loved was taken away. Once she would sing and it would lift her out of herself until she was astral traveling on the vibrations of her own voice in her throat, but now it was a source of shame, and even in private she sang only very softly and listened for the footsteps of someone who might approach and hear her.

It was especially sad because no one noticed or cared. Bolt tried to sympathize, but he didn't understand her sense of loss—he had no affinity for music, though he would cheerfully bellow out silly songs like "Alexander's Ragtime Band" and "In My Merry Oldsmobile."

Their mother had sung to them when they were very small, but by the time they started school, she had stopped. She was content to only listen. She would sit in a rocking chair with her head tilted toward the petunia-shaped mouth of the gramophone, silent, her eyes nearly closed. She liked "Moonlight Bay," the high, echoey monotone of the American Quartet—a barbershop group—or Harry MacDonough and Olive Kline singing "They Didn't Believe Me," her mother almost imperceptibly mouthing the words.

And when I told them
How beautiful you are—
They didn't believe me . . .
They didn't believe me!

—words that made the back of Eleanor's neck prickle with a terrible, bottomless feeling, and her mother would play it over and over, the music emanating a softly malevolent glow.

After they've thrown a red-and-blue-striped burlap tent over the peaked sweep rods, and assembled the carved rounding boards and electric blinking lights along the crest of the carousel, above the mythical creature mounts, she and Billy sit on the base as it revolves like a phonograph album at the lowest speed.

"Don't think we're not working," he tells her. "We're listening for rattles and boomphs, and we're feeling for vibrations that don't seem right. Are the horses going up and down smoothly? Is anything dragging? This is the most important part of the job, to make sure that it ain't going to fall apart with little children on it." He takes out his makins and sprinkles a little tobacco along the middle of a rolling paper. "Because I tell you, those Irish rousties are shirkers, you got to know from the beginning that they aren't going to tighten those screws the way they should."

Eleanor nods, and then she says, "I'm Irish."

"You smoke?" Billy Bigelow says, and hands her a thin cigaret, which she takes wordlessly. She puts it between her lips and draws a match out of her pocket to light it. She and Bolt have both smoked from time to time since they were ten or so. She likes it more than he does, and occasionally will pick up a half-smoked butt from the street and save it in her pocket.

Bigelow lights his own cigaret, watching her sidelong. They both breathe out smoke, and it dissipates under the blinking golden electric lightbulbs, as behind them a miniature golden whale bobs up and down beside a trident-holding merman.

"How old are you?" Billy asks, in his own deep, dreamy voice. The mynah bird is a distance away, pecking some spilled popcorn kernels from the ground.

"Thirteen and a half," Eleanor says. "How old are you?"

"Twenny-seven." He sighs, and leans back on his elbows. "Twice as old as you! My pai was fourteen when I was born, and my mãe was twenny! That's the kind of man he was! Ha!"

She breathes a little smoke ring, not looking at him and his tattoos, the tangle vines along his arms and torso and legs, the branches through which you can see jungle animals lurking. Not looking at his odd greenish-blue eyes.

"Where are they now?" she says. "Your father and mother?"

"Dead, Garota," he says. "Dead, dead."

"Mine, too," she says, and shrugs. As they circle slowly around and around, the carnival is a flurry of busy movement. She sees Elmer the dog-faced boy hurry along carrying a bouquet of helium balloons, maybe fifty or more in every color, so many that they seem to almost pull him off his feet, and Strong Baby is walking the tiger on a leash, and the world's oldest woman is riding an elephant, and Viola the Half-Woman paces slowly by on the palms of her gloved hands, lost in some moody thought, and in the distance Tickley-Feather is striding along with a sledgehammer slung over his shoulder. Beyond the fairgrounds to the east, she can see the railroad bridge that brought them across the Missouri River, across the Nebraska state line and back into Iowa again—to the town of Sergeant Bluff, just south of Sioux City. To the west, she can see in the distance where the trees begin to peter out, drifting off into an endless range of sod prairie.

"So—" says Billy Bigelow at last. "What kind of crooked are you?"

"What?" she says, and Billy cocks his head gamely, as if he thinks she's teasing him. His bird abruptly flutters down.

"*What kind of crooked are you?*" Billy repeats, and the bird tilts its head and examines her with its bright blue eye. "Everybody here is crooked in one way or another. Otherwise, Senhor Jengling wouldn't take you."

Yes. Well.

She supposes that she is *crooked.*

She had thrown a rock at that boy and broken his nose and never felt regret for it, only a lingering, resentful wish that she had killed him. They had poisoned old Humberstone so that their mother could steal what meager money he had. They had cheated men at cards for Uncle Charlie, and helped him to bury the body of the man he'd beaten to death—

But that's not what Billy Bigelow means. By "crooked" he means some special ability or aberration, he means that there must be something not normal about her, and she's not sure what that is—what did Jengling *see*, she wondered, when he came forward to choose them?

Bolt still believes in the mind-reading nonsense that their mother built up to get attention from the Progressive Psychic Spiritual Church, but Eleanor doesn't anymore. Not really. That they, as twins, could guess each other's thoughts and moods did not seem particularly supernatural.

She used to half-believe that she had special powers, and she'd convinced Bolt of it—he thought she could give him warts on his hand if he didn't mind her, he thought she could bring down hail and cause branches to fall out of trees when she was in a bad mood, and for a time she'd encouraged this idea but now she thinks it was just coincidence. It's true that she gets blisters on the back of her hands when she's really angry, but that is probably just a nervous condition.

"I'm not . . . crooked," she says. "We're just orphans. I don't think we belong here."

"Pff," Billy says. "If he chose you, then you're one of us, even if you don't know it. Senhor Jengling has a keen eye. He's a connoisseur, as they call it."

"What's a *connoisseur*?" Eleanor asks. She prides herself on having a good vocabulary, but she doesn't know much about French or Portuguese words.

"It is a kind of scholar who collects and studies," Billy says, lowering his voice and glancing around as if there might be a spy listening. "Senhor Jengling has a great collection of oddities here, wouldn't you agree? And do you know when we die he still keeps us? Sometimes our bones. Sometimes our brain or our heart in a jar of formaldehyde."

"That's a load of bosh," Eleanor says, frowning. "You're just trying to scare me, and it's not appreciated."

"Ah," he says, and he gets to his feet and brushes off his bare knees, and the bird flutters its wings as he rises. "Well! I am not the type of man who likes to frighten young ladies." He steadies himself on the pole of the crimson-saddled golden whale and the bird gives his earlobe a soft bite as he goes to the center of the carousel to shut down the motor.

"I talk too much," he says. "I apologize, Miss Eleanor. I am sure you're right that you do not belong here."

He turns away from her and she feels embarrassed, she lowers her head and thinks about how ugly she is, she thinks of the man and woman in Iowa and how they doted over that little boy and ignored her, how she has always been a repulsive person. She lets the toe of her shoe drag along in the gravel beneath the slowly turning base of the carousel.

And then the mynah bird lands on her. "Ack!" she says, and the bird pokes at her mouth and feeds her a raisin, and she spits it out. The bird lifts off from her shoulder and then lands again on her head, then lifts off in a noisy beat of wings and comes to rest on her knee.

"You've been angry your whole life," the bird says to her, gently. "Haven't you?" And she shoos it away.

"Probably," Eleanor says.

"Me, too," says Billy Bigelow, and he gives her a melancholy, conspiratorial smile.

Billy has the Wurlitzer calliope playing "In My Merry Oldsmobile" on repeat, and the carousel is slowly revolving, calling out to the rubes of Dakota City, Nebraska, even before the carnival opens for business. It must be close to dinnertime, Eleanor thinks, when Tickley-Feather shows up to fetch her.

"Mme. Clothilde wants to see you," Tickley-Feather says, without expression, and behind him the clown known as Thistle-Britches smiles at her warmly. Thistle-Britches has no nose—apparently he was born without one—and the space where his nose should be is just smooth, slightly indented skin. But his face isn't disturbing so much as endearing, with his wide-set eyes and broad mouth he has the look of a sweet rag doll whose button nose has fallen off. Though he cannot speak—or chooses not to—his expression is gentle, and he beckons to her encouragingly. *Come. Come. It will be okay. Nothing bad will happen to you.*

Tickley-Feather's stare, on the other hand, says just the opposite.

"Is she pullin her weight?" Tickley-Feather asks Billy Bigelow, and Bigelow shrugs.

"She'll do," Billy says, and he gives an almost imperceptible wink in her direction. "She's a quick learner, and she don't believe in nonsense."

Eleanor is accompanied to the tent of Mme. Clothilde with a clown on either side of her like sentinel escorts, and when they pull back the flap Mme. Clothilde is sitting in the center at a child-size table in a child-size chair, sipping from her shot glass of ghostly green liquor. The space is illuminated by tiny, tear-shaped electrical bulbs, transparent so that the glowing thread of each golden filament is visible.

"Ah," Mme. Clothilde says, and beckons. She is in a lacy white dress with a pink pinafore over it and has an enormous pink satin bow in her hair. Her cheeks are brightly rouged. "Eleanor! So pleased to see you!" She makes a fluttering gesture with her fingers and the clowns back out.

"Sit, my darling," she says in the piping voice of a three-year-old child, but with the authority of a matron.

And Eleanor obeys. These chairs are not meant for Eleanor's awkwardly growing teenaged body, so she has to squat down with her knees almost to her chest, as if she's sitting on a milking stool. Clothilde gives her a small, mischievous smile, as if to say that she half-regrets the accommodation, and she's half-delighted by it.

"Now then," Mme. Clothilde says. She pauses to roll a cigaret and lick it closed, running her tongue delicately along the seam. Eleanor watches as she lights it and a trickle of smoke comes out of Mme. Clothilde's nose. "How are things coming along, my dear?" she says. "Have you met any nice friends?"

"No," Eleanor says.

"Well," says Mme. Clothilde, and raises an eyebrow mildly. "You will." She takes a sip from her glass, and Eleanor looks down at the miniature teacup and saucer at her place setting, which would hold perhaps three thimblefuls of tea.

"You will find your place here, *bien-aimée*," she murmurs, in her light French accent. "Your father and I have endeavored to provide a home for our family that is safe and welcoming, and yet provides challenges and stimulation of the intellect and innate abilities, and room for the growth. You should not be afraid."

"I'm not," says Eleanor. She picks up the little teacup and fingers it, puts her thumb in its bowl, feels the cool smooth porcelain indentation.

"Good!" Mme. Clothilde says. "Then I will do my best to help you." She takes a slow drag from her cigaret and pops her lips to let out a smoke ring. "After all, in some ways I am your mother, since Mr. Jengling is my husband. What should we call it? A stepmother? A new mother for you after your tragic loss? I would not presume—"

Mme. Clothilde pronounces Jengling with a soft *J*, as in Jacques, much prettier than the way Eleanor has been saying it—"Jingling," with nasal midwestern *I*, and for some reason she feels embarrassed of her accent, even as she tries to absorb what Mme. Clothilde is telling her.

"It is surprising, I know," Mme. Clothilde continues, since Eleanor says nothing. "Your father and I met in Montpelier, where I was quite well known as medium and reader of tarot. I was known as Clothilde Moreau then, but"—she taps her ash into a saucer and then delicately stubs the cigaret out—"an arrangement was made between us. We have been wed for seven years, and we are still *as one* in our opinions."

She knits her fingers together, and Eleanor thinks of the hand game she and Bolt used to play as children: *"Here's the church and here's the steeple, open the door and see all the people—"* And that's all she can think. Otherwise, there's only mute uncertainty and a softly pulsing trepidation. Vague resentment, too: no doubt Bolt will be eager and pleased to have *a new mother*. He will probably make her a Mother's Day card with a pressed flower in it, like he did for one of their insipid teachers at school.

"In any case," Mme. Clothilde says, after Eleanor has churned silently for a few seconds, "we thought that I should speak with you of womanly matters."

"Oh," Eleanor says, and her trepidation begins to edge into alarm. "Thank you, but—"

Mme. Clothilde takes another sip of her drink. "Have you experienced your menses?" she says, and Eleanor's alarm begins to slip upward into soft panic. In the distance, she can hear the carousel calliope still playing the same song, and she can smell the exotic allspice and black pepper scent of Madame's cubeb cigaret.

"No," Eleanor says at last, speaking quickly. "I have not. But I know all about it. My mother explained it very clearly, and also I have seen a cat giving birth to kittens, so I understand how it . . . happens."

She stares down at her lap. She actually has very little information about the transformations that are enacting themselves. The ugly dark hairs that are beginning to unfurl down there, the way the aureole of her breast is darkening, the sudden clenching cramps at the base of her torso, the clear discharge that comes out which has a kind of smell like mouse's nest.

Bolt knows none of this. Maybe there was a point when she could have told him about it but it has passed, whatever they might have shared about the bodily changes is now beyond what can be explained.

Well.

He knows about her chest, of course. They used to snug comfortably around each other as they slept, but now he gingerly avoids touching her breast, he's even careful when he hugs her, and his hesitation makes her lonely.

At the same time, Eleanor is not going to take advice from a stranger who is half her height—this midget pretending to be her mother?

"You're very kind," Eleanor tells her. "But I feel most uneasy speaking of such things, and I wish not to."

"Of course," says Mme. Clothilde. She makes a courtly gesture. "I only want to offer my hand to you—and my help, if it is needed."

"That's much appreciated," says Eleanor. "Thank you."

"There are also girls who are closer to your age, you could speak to them?" says Mme. Clothilde. "Shyla . . . ?"

"Thank you," says Eleanor, and the small woman laughs gently.

Gentil.

"I cannot tell what you are, my dear," she says. "You are mysterious to me. But—my husband, he goes to these child auctions frequently, I find them repellent, but he is more practical than I. Still, you are the only ones he has ever brought back, so I think you are not just a common urchin. Would you like me to read your cards? Here," she says, and she picks up her miniature, Clothilde-size deck of tarot cards and fans them out in a swift, practiced gesture.

Oh, Eleanor knows what they will be: Ten of Swords. The Devil. The Lovers. Five of Pentacles. The Tower, perhaps. All the bad cards, and she chooses not to see them though she knows they are hanging invisibly over her.

"No, thank you," Eleanor says, and Mme. Clothilde nods slowly, sympathetically.

"I'll remember you in my prayers tonight," she says.

Of Herculea the Muscle Lady

Herculea sees the new girl leaving Mme. Clothilde's tent, and she thinks to say hello. She considers it and even starts to lift her hand and open her mouth. "H—" Herculea says, but the girl marches off with her head down, and Herculea watches her go. The kid must be—what? Thirteen?—a kind of homely tomboy sort of girl, not unlike Herculea herself had been at that age. *Poor thing*, she thinks. Mme. Clothilde does not particularly like tomboys, and this new girl seems—if not of the same immediate family as Herculea, then at least a cousin of it.

Oh, well. *She probably wouldn't want to associate with you anyway*, Herculea thinks.

Once upon a time Herculea had been a skinny little girl named Mona Finkel who worked every day at the Piper Textile Mill in Philadelphia, changing the bobbins on the spinning frames, and later as a drawing-in girl, who sat on her high stool and with her little hook patiently caught the thousands of threads one by one, feeding them into the loudly clapping and clanking machine to be wound together into cloth. She was at the mill for eight or twelve hours a day and then would go home to her father, who was gently but definitively mad, and did not work—could not work, except to write mathematical philosophy onto sheets of newsprint that he stacked in a special crate. She remembers her Totty eating soup at the table, the way he would jerk his spoon as if it were a puppet and he would listen intently as the spoon seemed to give a speech. And then he would go back to eating with it, and there were trickles of soup that dried in his beard.

And so she was shy and didn't make friends with the other children at the mill—cruel and cliquish, they were, and it was even worse once she started growing. At twelve, she was barrel-chested and heavy-shouldered, and her jaw broadened and thickened, and she knew that she was by far the ugliest girl in the mill, maybe the ugliest girl in Pennsylvania. Then she grew ten inches in a year—from five feet four at age fifteen to six feet two at age sixteen—and she was so strong, *so incredibly strong*, without even trying.

Dakota City, Nebraska, is just to the southwest of the town of Sioux City, Iowa, and it's surprisingly crowded for a Sunday night. She finishes up her stage performances for the first night—lifting barbells over her head, and then doing the schtick with Strong Baby, holding the bald, diapered three-hundred-pound man in the crook of her arm and feeding him milk from a nipple bottle, and then calling out to passersby to challenge them to wrestle or box with her this upcoming Friday. "Any man that can defeat me gets a ten-dollar purse!" she calls. "Any woman—gets TWENTY!"

The people laugh, and she bends her arm and makes her biceps bulge and dance. She's wearing a sleeveless leotard in the colors of the American flag, bare-armed, bare-legged, barefoot, and she rises on her toes like a ballerina. Her entire body quivers with tensed muscles. She grits her teeth in a hard smile.

After-hours, she wanders back to the commissary to see if Mr. Lacis is still awake. She often lingers around the kitchen after the carnival has closed down, helping to wash the pots and haul the slop out to the ditch, and afterward she and Mr. L will sit together sipping brandy from small, cut-glass tumblers, smoking cigars. Sometimes the mute, noseless clown named Thistle-Britches will join them. That's when she feels most at her ease, in the company of gloomy, philosophical middle-aged men.

Mr. Lacis seems to recognize her as a kindred spirit. He never makes her feel like a woman.

And she's a good listener, as good as mute Thistle-Britches is, sitting attentively sipping her brandy while Mr. Lacis recounts his adventures during the Revolution in Latvia in 1905, and how the peasants had tried to rise up against the German nobles, the land barons, how he had joined the Latvian Social Democratic Workers' Party and how they had burned many castles and manors, but at last they were put down and many were executed, and he himself was exiled. To Herculea, it sounds like a fairy tale—nobles and peasants and manors—and she enjoys picturing the ragged serfs holding torches aloft and setting fire to the mansions of the oppressors. It made her think of her days in the Piper Textile Mill, how nice it would have been to set it ablaze.

The three of them sit quietly at the corner table, smoking their cigars, and Thistle-Britches blows out a perfect smoke ring that rises, wavering, up toward the canvas ceiling of the commissary tent.

"And then I came to this country," Mr. Lacis says, and exhales, running his palm across his smooth, bald scalp. His entire head is hairless, no beard or stubble, no eyebrows, only rows and rows of tiny tattooed symbols—Latgalian runes, he says they are—and an iron nail that sticks out near his left ear. "I was working as a blockhead and sword swallower on Coney Island when Mr. Jengling found me and adopted me, and now—" He lifts his glass and toasts Herculea and Thistle-Britches. "Now! Look! I am family with you lovely people!"

FAMILY OF FIVE MURDERED IN SHENANDOAH, IOWA

JUNE 11, 1915

Axe Used in Killing Found,
but No Trace of Slayer.

Militia on Guard.

FOOT PRINTS ARE SEEN

Sister of Dead Man Not in House as Was Thought. She Is Divorced.

SHENANDOAH, IOWA, June 11.

Twenty-four hours after the murder of the entire Loving Mitchell family, five in all, which occurred Thursday night, the authorities have been unable to get a single trace of the murderer and have little or no clue to his identity. The crimes were committed at night while all the victims lay asleep in their beds, and all came to death by means of blows from an axe.

A revised list of the victims follows:

LOVING B. MITCHELL
MRS. LOVING B. MITCHELL, née Sara Horsfield
HERMAN MITCHELL, aged 15
CATHERINE MITCHELL, aged 13

BOYD MITCHELL, aged 10

Bloodhounds brought in from Beatrice, Nebraska, arrived in the late evening and were immediately taken to the Mitchell home. Within ten minutes, they found a scent which took them over a circuitous route to the edge of the town and thence to the banks of the river. They were followed closely by their keeper, Hansel Noffsinger.

Entering a deep woods along the river, the hounds led their followers over several miles of rough timber land in the bottoms.

After an hour the hounds returned to the river where those following the dogs found fresh foot prints in the soft muddy bank and leading to the river. Those following the trail took the hounds across the river, but were unable to find any trace of the fugitive on the other side. At midnight the posse returned to town and will start afresh in the morning.

The bodies of the five murdered persons were viewed late tonight by a coroner's jury and turned over to an undertaker. They were removed to the city hall to be prepared for burial. A detail of militia guarded both the Mitchell home and city hall all night.

The first intimation of the crime was given when an "odd stillness" in the Mitchell house was noticed by next-door neighbor Mary Peckham. Finding the house locked, the window shades all down, and no one about, she notified the neighbors and, with assistance of a hired hand, Huitzy Banuelos, forced entrance to the house through the back door.

The dead, with one exception, were found in their beds in natural attires of sleeping and until the crushed condition of their heads and the soaked pillows were discovered, it was impossible for the searchers to believe that anything was wrong.

An axe showing without doubt it was the weapon used, was found in an upstairs room where it was left by the assassin after he had completed his deadly work.

BEDS NOT DISTURBED

Mr. and Mrs. Mitchell were in one bed, the clothing of which was not the least disturbed. In another bed were the two boys, Herman and Boyd. The sister, Catherine, occupied a third bed. In neither instance was the bedding of the children disarranged. The face of each victim was covered with articles of clothing and the bedclothes were drawn up over their heads.

The tragedy is one of the most mysterious the officials of Iowa have ever had to deal with. There is absolutely no evidence upon which to warrant an arrest and the utter absence of a possible motive has left the authorities in a maze of perplexity and doubt.

Early identification of the young girl who was slain, owing to the terrible condition of her face, led to a report that she was Mrs. Van Gilder. Mrs. Van Gilder is a sister of Mr. Mitchell.

Blood stains, which will require the work of experts to handle in relation with the crime, including finger prints of the murderer, are absolutely the only clew the officers have to work upon. Blood stains were found on the front door near the knob and finger prints were found in the house.

LIGHTED LAMP FOUND

A feature of the tragedy which indicates that possibly the murderer left the house quickly was the finding of a lighted lamp upon the floor of the Mitchell bed room. All the blinds of the house were closely drawn, the doors were all locked and all the windows.

As a posse was hunting in the railroad yards this evening, a tramp, becoming alarmed, gave himself up to the leaders for protection, fearing he might be a victim of the wrath of the people before they had

had time to examine into his identity. He later was identified by the railroad men and released, badly scared, and quickly left town.

Feeling is high and few persons slept in Shenandoah tonight. News of the crime traveled fast and there are hundreds of country people who soon came to the village.

Some are concerned about the recent arrival of the Orphan Train in Shenandoah, and particularly about the older adopted boys who may be from unsavory backgrounds in the Eastern Cities from whence they came.

Others have expressed suspicion of the carnival which passed through Shenandoah several weeks ago, and which was a haven for Gipsies and freak show exhibits and which might easily have sheltered a maniac.

—Helen Peattie for *The Sentinel-Post*

Loving Cup

Bolt emerges from an afternoon in the tent babysitting Rosalie, just for a little break, thinking maybe he'll get himself a bag of candy-coated peanuts and a Moxie soda pop before the gillies start arriving, but he's shocked to see how crowded the midway is already. The carnival is docked outside of a little town in South Dakota called Elk Point, nestled in between the Missouri and Big Sioux Rivers, population 1,200 or so—but it seems as if every single soul of the village has showed up and more besides, people traveling by horse-drawn wagon and automobile across the Nebraska border and the Iowa border and even from as far as Minnesota. Sunday, July the Fourth! Independence Day! They want to see the winking electrical lights and the promised fireworks display at night's end, they want to ride the Ferris wheel and carousel and see the sideshows and wonders and spend their dimes on rigged games of chance.

They want to be changed, they want to be different people for one night at least, Bolt can hear that in their heads as he walks past, *just a dime, it's only a dime*, thinks a glum-faced farmer in overalls, and a girl with a pronounced feather in her hat thinks, *You must seem a little afraid even if you're not afraid*, and a boy of about her age watches her go past and thinks, *Titties, titties, titties.*

The farmhands and cowpokes are lining up to get a chance to box with Herculea the Muscle Lady—men pay fifty cents for a chance to win a ten-dollar purse if you can defeat her in the ring! Women can challenge Herculea for free and win a twenty-dollar purse!

I'd pay money to see two ladies boxin, thinks a little man with a waxed mustache and a bowler hat and Bolt recoils at a nasty image the man conjures in his head.

Meanwhile, Tickley-Feather is selling sparklers to families, a penny apiece, and Mr. Lacis is showing a group of onlookers how he can put an ice pick up his nose, and the world's oldest woman, with her hair hanging down like a shawl almost to her ankles, is hawking candy apples and fairy floss, and a lemon-faced elderly matron limping along with a cane glowers at her and thinks, *That hair ain't real.*

Bolt's mind reading has gotten a lot sharper since he was adopted of Mr. Jengling, but most of the stuff he overhears isn't very interesting, and when Elmer waves to him from his baseball toss booth, he doesn't hear anything at all, he doesn't even know if Elmer likes him.

"Hey, Bub!" Elmer calls. "Can you bring me some more of them composite dolls? I'm runnin out!"

"Sure thing!" Bolt calls back, and gives Elmer a jolly wave, but Elmer is talking now to a female customer, and Bolt watches as he laughs at something the mark says and pushes up his sleeve to display his extraordinarily hairy forearm and cocks his head and says something that makes the young woman put her hand to her mouth and laugh.

"Okay, then," Bolt says.

Bub. Is that a friendly expression, or does it mean that Elmer doesn't remember his name?

Eleanor is running the carousel, but she doesn't look up as he walks past. She is in the center of the carved wooden animals, bent over a book, and he cannot hear her thoughts either, only a sound like putting a seashell to your ear, and she must know he is nearby but she doesn't even acknowledge him, and the tattooed man, Billy Bigelow, wearing naught but a loincloth, ushers children and lovers onto his mounts as the calliope pipes out "In My Merry Oldsmobile."

It has never been worse between him and Eleanor in their whole life, and Bolt doesn't know what to do about it. He is so mad at her that she won't make friends with people, he hates her for being so lonely, he's sick and tired of how she thinks constantly about leaving, about running away.

Even now she is thinking of it, he can feel her mood in his head, in his body, it is like a drink of bad wine that makes his cheeks warm and his head swim and his stomach goes sour as she revolves around and around with her back turned to him. For a moment, the carousel mounts and riders are a colorless blur.

She cannot leave unless he agrees to it. Or at least, she *will not* leave. Not yet.

It had been cold between them since the ceremony.

A week before, Mr. Jengling had gathered all of the carnival people together one night after they'd finished with Dakota City, after they were packed up and ready to leave the next morning, and he'd said that it was high time they welcomed their new brother and sister, and Mme. Clothilde stood beside him on top of a step ladder so that their heads were the same height.

There must've been forty or fifty of them—Mr. Jengling's wards—sitting at folding tables under a tarp. It was a muggy night in late June, and the hanging kerosene lanterns were aswarm with flying insects in silhouette, making shadow puppet shapes on the tent walls. Mme. Clothilde held up a three-handled goblet as big as her head.

"A Loving Cup!" Mme. Clothilde announced in her high, elegant voice, and raised the glass to all of them, then lowered it and drank, and everyone applauded. Bolt did, too. She offered the Cup to Mr. Jengling, who took it in both his hands and drank gravely.

"A Loving Cup!" he boomed, striking an oratorical pose. "Also known as a Tyg! The Knights of the Round Table passed such a goblet from individual to individual to affirm their eternal bond, and tonight we emulate this sacred ritual in order to welcome our brother and sister, Bolt and Eleanor, into our family!"

And all the faces turned smiling to look at Bolt and Eleanor, who sat at the very back, side by side.

"We accept them! They are one of us!" pronounced Mr. Jengling, and all the people applauded and Bolt felt a warm flush, as if he'd been given a prize, even as Eleanor stiffened and grew clammy. Bolt clapped along with them for a moment and then he hesitated because it might be unseemly to clap for yourself, and then he copied Eleanor, who had her fingers clasped in a prayerful position and her eyes lowered.

Ringmaster Jengling passed the goblet to Dr. Chui, who took a businesslike drink and handed off to Tickley-Feather, who sipped from it and passed it to Thistle-Britches, who gave the Cup to the world's oldest woman, and Eleanor murmured almost imperceptibly under her breath to Bolt, "I ain't putting my lips on nothin that old hag slobbered on," and Bolt said nothing.

There should be a word for that cosmic deflation you feel when your whole heart is singing with joy and anticipation, when you are most full of childlike hope and delight, and then the person you love most in the world says something scornful.

His smile faded as the Loving Cup was being passed down from table to table toward them: Gladness sipped regally and passed it to Elmer, who made a show of swirling the Champagne around in his mouth, and then handed it to Shyla, who took it in her slender seven-fingered hand and gave Bolt and Eleanor a nod and a demure, mysterious smile before she transferred the goblet to the thin man with the unusually small head who also worked the Ferris wheel, and Alberic the contortionist took the Cup and helped Strong Baby to take a drink before refilling the goblet with Champagne again and taking a big swallow and passing on along down the row.

"One of us!" they were all chanting. Some beat time with their palms on the tables, or used their spoons as drumsticks. "One of us!" they sang. "We accept them, we accept them!"

And when the Loving Cup reached Bolt he stood up and toasted all of them, and he tilted his head back and took a big swallow. There was just a little bit left in the glass when he handed it to Eleanor, and she rose slowly, uncomfortably, barely acknowledging the applauding Jenglings with an awkward nod. She grasped the goblet in both hands and let some liquid trickle into her mouth and everyone cheered.

Afterward, they were in the bunk together in the train car and her mind was a wasp nest, buzzing but off-limits, and he turned and faced the wall.

All you would have to do is just try a little, people here would like you, he thought, and for the first time in a long while, she heard him. She gave him a stab with her eyes.

People, she thought. *Is that what they are?*

He frowned and closed his eyes, pushed his forehead against the cool train car siding.

What would she want their life to be like? he thought. *Just the two of them, alone? Where would they go? How would they eat?*

I can take care of you better than any Jengling, she thought.

I know that, he thought.

But the idea that he needed to be taken care of grated on him. He was not her baby, nor did he want to be. Soon enough, he was going to be a man, and if he decided to be a carnival man what was wrong with that?

"I could be happy here, Nell," he said into the dark and she turned silently onto her side, facing away from him.

"You could be happy anywhere," she said, under her breath—

—as if that were a flaw in his character.

It's true, though, that he wants to fit in. He wears now a bright red Hussar jacket with gold piping and a Marlow top hat made of brown leather, and jodhpur breeches and high black boots—Shyla and Gladness helped him pick it out from a costume trunk—and it makes him feel more like he's a part of things, that he won't be mistaken as just another rube on the midway. Still, he secretly wishes that there was something special about him—he has heard tell of the Elasto-Man who worked for Jengling once, who could stretch out his skin ten to twelve inches on any part of his body. Bolt wouldn't mind if he could do that! Maybe he could learn to swallow fire, or juggle knives, or he could train monkeys to do tricks. He still didn't know why they didn't have more monkeys in the carnival.

"They'll pr'y turn you into a clown," Eleanor said. This was her only comment on his new outfit, and she gave him a look of kindly pity that made his cheeks heat up.

"Yeah?" Bolt said. "So? What's wrong with that?"

Does she really imagine him in some more respectable life? If he had the nerve he would ask her: *What do **you** think I should become, El? What do you want me to be?*

But he is afraid of what she would say—because she could be cruel if she wanted, she could say something that would wound him, that would linger in his mind forever.

Still, he has to ask himself: Does she have any plan at all for their future, beyond her disgruntlement with her current situation? Would *anything* make her happy?

That's what he'd like to ask her.

Back when they were in school, he could've made friends with other kids but she always talked him out of it, anyone he was drawn to she would make comments about them until he felt embarrassed for liking them, and most of the time it was fine if it was only him and her in the world. When they were little they would have pretend games that would last for days—weeks. They would play as Hansel and Gretel in a forest, or they'd imagine that they'd found a wishing stone, and Eleanor was good at thinking up the trick the devil would use to turn any wish rotten. They imagined that they were Blue-Eyes and Turkey, living with their mother while their father was away at sea, and that they had been so naughty that their true mama had left them in the care of a new mother, with glass eyes and a wooden tail.

They didn't go to school that often, anyway. Their mother felt that because they were in the Spiritualist Church they were the victims of religious persecution. She didn't want them mingling with Baptists or Lutherans, nor with rough immigrant children from Bohemia and Prussia and God knew where else.

And besides, they were needed at home. They had to take care of things at the boardinghouse—for often their mother was unable to move or speak, sitting in her rocker in her black embroidered shawl and her gray housedress, the record on her Victrola circling in its final scratching loop, her lips softly mouthing unintelligible words.

They needed to cook dinner for the boarders and sweep up and do the dishes and later they had to speak to the Pinkerton detective who was inquiring about old Mr. Humberstone—who'd been buried in the backyard garden for over a year. The Pinkerton had been hired by some distant relative to inquire, he said, and he gave them his calling card and said he would come back the next day when, he hoped, their mother would be feeling better, and as he walked away from the boardinghouse a large dead branch fell out of a sycamore tree and struck him in the head, and he was apparently in the hospital with a concussion for a week, and in the end he never came back again.

Later, when they were twelve, in those clouded October days after their mother died, a hail of dirt clods rained down on their house for ten or fifteen minutes.

Bolt stood beside Eleanor at the window and watched as chunks of wet soil the size of plums fell out of the clear sky and when they burst apart on the back garden they were full of earthworms.

He saw her face, her jaw clenched, her cheeks trembling, eyes leaking tears, and he knew that this was something she was somehow doing, he knew that she was bringing forth hail and brimstone—not exactly, but close enough— and he knew it would never be spoken of again.

He always thought that she could see his mind more clearly than he could see hers.

So he walks through the corridor of rubes and their thoughts flicker alongside him as he passes, like the slick underwater plants that brushed his feet when he swam in the old pond: here is a farm boy who thinks he knows where his daddy's gold is hidden, here is the pharmacist's daughter who has laudanum in her pocket to give to the lad she loves, a wife who is going to tie stones to her feet and throw herself down a well, *Will it hurt will it last long*, she wonders, and a churchman is imagining all the positions he could force Alberic to contort into if Alberic were his prisoner—and ugh, Bolt wonders why he only hears the ugliest thoughts, the meanest ones. Why not happy? Why not thoughts of kindness and joy?

Perhaps he is only tuned to a certain frequency.

He comes to the commissary tent and Mr. Lacis gives him a box full of cloth dolls and he strides back through the tunnel of clover-kickers and their awful minds, past the queue for the Ferris wheel and the unusually small-headed man who is cranking a hurdy-gurdy barrel organ while his big fawn-colored pit bull dog dances on her hind legs wearing a red tutu and a red pointed cap, keeping the people entertained and intrigued as they wait to be carried into the air.

It's not much of a Ferris wheel, really—it only takes you maybe 130 feet up—twelve stories or so—but most of these rubes have never seen anything taller than a grain elevator, they've never walked up more than three flights of stairs, and they are astonished by the feeling of the ground disappearing beneath their feet, the sensation of floating up and reaching the top under the vast ceiling of stars and seeing how small everything is down below. *Why the people look like ants!* they think, over and over. He pauses, holding his box of cloth and sawdust dolls, and lets himself feel it with them. From up there you can see for miles in every direction, you can see that the sky was like a bowl closed over you, and you're above everything, overseeing the world like an angel—or as insignificant as the speck of an insect. Or both at once.

Meanwhile the hurdy-gurdy plays "Hello! Ma Baby!" and everyone gazes up at the turning spokes of the wheel and the carts and their laughing, enthralled passengers. The organ grinder has the body of a normal-heighted man, dressed in a single-breasted sack suit and a polka-dot tie, but his head is the size of a child's. The man's hair is shaved down to stubble, and his little face is long and gaunt and grayish in color, thin lips pulled back from protruding teeth. His deep-set eyes have a milky film over them, but he seems to stare back happily at the clodhoppers who are lining up and gawping at him, he gives them a jolly skeleton's grin and cranks his organ with vigor as his dog tiptoes like a ballerina.

From all outward signs it seems the man is blind and mute and perhaps deaf, perhaps he doesn't have much for brains either, but then when Bolt gives a kind of curious prod in the man's direction—like turning over a rock with his toe—the organ grinder twitches and snaps his pale, amphibious eyes in Bolt's direction.

Say! thinks the organ grinder. Bolt startles to hear a reedy, nasal voice in his ear—or in his mind, he's not sure.

Say, kid, the hurdy-gurdy man says. *Mind your own beeswax. Don't look in my drawers and I won't look in yours.*

Their eyes meet through the crowd and the organ grinder lifts his chin in Bolt's direction, a solemn, unsmiling nod.

This is something that's never happened before—not only to be discovered peeping, or snooping, or whatever you would call it, but also to have the offended party speak directly into his inside ear and scold him! He turns to look back at the small-head man and he can feel the prickle of his face heating up and going red—that traitorous blush—and he stumbles a little because he's not watching where he's going.

Clumsy little oaf, thinks a cruel schoolmistress as she strolls slowly past him holding a cheap parasol, but he catches the box of dolls without spilling any. He straightens up and glances back at the Ferris wheel, but the small-head man seems to have lost interest in him. He's grinding his hurdy-gurdy and grinning at the customers, not paying never mind to Bolt.

And that's a relief.

Bolt catches his breath and the blush subsides and he starts walking again and the sound of the barrel organ mingles with the calliope of the carousel, but when he looks in that direction he only sees the tattoo man, standing with his mynah bird perched on his index finger, flirting with some laughing young sunburned farm girls in the line. He can't see Eleanor, but he knows that she's somewhere near the spindle of the machine, he can sense her reading her book, he can hear the words forming in her head—

> "*Why, Pollyanna,*" Eleanor is reading, "*it's only since you came that I've been even half glad to live! But if I had you for my own little girl, I'd be glad for—anything; and I'd try to make you glad, too, my dear. You shouldn't have a wish ungratified. All my money, to the last cent, should go to make you happy.*"

And Eleanor is too engaged in her book to notice that he's listening. The story has her so worked up and tenderhearted that the real world is gone, she's sunk into the dreamland of her book, and there's no point in trying to break her concentration.

Maybe when they are back in the bunk he will tell her about his encounter with the organ grinder, but he doesn't even know if she will believe him. She will probably tell him that it is just his imagination. She will probably say that there is no such thing as mind reading—it's just a wishful idea that their mother put in their head, it's as fake as the séances and Ouija boards and ectoplasm, it's just a grift—*But he* can *hear the voices! He **can**!*

There are a buzz of them up ahead, and though he's not yet sure what they're thinking he can see that a crowd has gathered in front of Elmer's ball toss booth, he can feel their bright curiosity as they form a circle.

Elmer is standing on a raised platform next to the gorilla, Miss Alcott, and as Bolt arrives Elmer sweeps off his straw boater hat so that people can get a better look at the fine wavy auburn hair that covers his face, the long wavy hair that spills down his back.

"Ladies and gentlemen!" Elmer says, and gives them his bright-toothed, black-lipped grin. "May I present to you my dear cousin, Miss Lois Alcott!"

Elmer makes a barker's gesture, and Miss Alcott rises up from her knuckles to stand on two legs. She curtsies with stern dignity.

Bolt is afraid that someone will make a smart remark and get the crowd laughing, but they are silent. Even their minds are only softly pulsing whispers, anxious, anticipating—not only is this jungle animal uncaged, unchained, but she considers them with such a queenly stare, her amber eyes daring them to annoy or insult her—and a woman in front of Bolt takes an unsteady step back and whispers hoarsely, *O mine Jesus*, and Miss Alcott flares her large flat nostrils to make a delicate, imperious sniff.

"The gorilla is a most powerful creature," Elmer declaims. "With the strength of three to five of our largest human men! And yet Miss Alcott is no beast, but instead a refined Lady of gentlish spirit and impeckerble manners!" The gorilla stands there regarding them with her heavy-browed, melancholy eyes and none of them move.

She is about five feet, five inches tall, a little over three hundred pounds. Her high-domed head is larger than a human's, and her long arms hang down almost to her knees, luxurious with black fur, though her chest and belly are bare, and the skin is shiny as black leather. She has nipples and a belly button just like a person.

"The nice thing about being friends with Miss Alcott," Elmer says. "She can always give me advice about how to groom my hair!"

Bolt watches as Elmer takes off his red-and-white-striped vest and undoes his bow tie.

"Are there any fellers named Harry in the audience?" says Elmer, and Bolt watches as a couple of men sheepishly raise their hand.

"What a coincidence!" says Elmer, and he unbuttons his shirt from the top neck button all the way down and he opens it and pulls his arms out the sleeves and the lady in front of Elmer draws in a breath because Elmer's torso is much more hirsute than Miss Alcott—it's almost like a pelt—and the hair on his bare biceps hangs down thick as a mane.

"That's funny, because I'm hairy, too!" Elmer says jovially, and the crowd chuckles uncertainly, and Bolt hears a schoolboy think, *This ain't right*, but mostly Bolt doesn't hear anything, he's like the rest of them, mesmerized as Miss Alcott settles into a sitting position as Elmer lowers himself, shirtless, into her lap.

"I know all you fellers know what it's like to try to scratch your own back!" Elmer says. "But imagine what it'd be like to try to put a comb to it!"

They are all silent when Elmer hands Miss Alcott a bristled ivory hairbrush, and she takes it in her big paw, and he bows his head and she gently rests one hand on the top of his skull, her fingers thick and wrinkled for walking on her knuckles, and with the other she begins to softly, courteously run the brush through the long hair on his back—

There's no laughter, no whispering, no catcalls, as there sometimes is with this kind of act, it's as if the noise of the carnival, the calliope and barker calls and screams of laughter all muffle and fade far away and dissolve.

Bolt: almost touching the mind of Miss Alcott
—not thoughts, she doesn't have thoughts—
only a kind of focused tender feeling
the brush in her hand   the bristles sliding through Elmer's
thick hair through   glooms and winding mossy ways
Bolt can feel his own back tingle as if the brush
is gliding along *his* spine,

just above the skin so he can only feel a feathery stroke
his own hand holding the brush,
the way the hair has thickness and gravity
as he smooths the tangled strands into a line of sleekness
his own hair the tingle of scalp
for a second almost inside both of them at once,
the comber and the combed
—a burst of butterflies in his chest

And then a heavy hand is resting on his shoulder, and he comes aware of himself again.

The noises of the midway return in a jumble, and actually it's not as reverently silent as he'd imagined it was. People are whispering and snickering and a wiseacre in the back is singing out lyrics from "Aba Daba Honeymoon."

Aba daba daba daba daba, said the monkey to the chimp—

Bolt turns and Tickley-Feather is leaning over him. Flat-eyed, grim, despite his clown makeup and braided yellow wig and bulbous red rubber nose.

"You're needed back to Miss Rosalie's tent," Tickley-Feather says. "Come with me, they're waiting on you."

The canvas flap is pulled open with the whap of a blanket being shook out and Bolt, backlit, squints into the dimness, into a hazy darkness swimming with dust motes, and he doesn't move until Tickley-Feather gives him a poke in the small of his back and then he can see the round, scarf-draped table with the crystal ball, candle-lit, a spotlight in a plain made of black velvet. The outside grows dead silent as Tickley-Feather pulls the tent flap closed behind them.

There are three women sitting at the table and they all turn to look at him: first Mme. Clothilde, frowning, and a woman he guesses must be the mark, all dressed in widow black, with a black lace shawl and a veil of transparent organza, so you could only see the hint of a face—the convex of eyes, nose, mouth, but more like stains than features.

And then Rosalie, of course, whose expression is slack but also vaguely amused, as if rolling her eyes at these old fogies: *Just you and me, chum.*

"No!" exclaims Mme. Clothilde abruptly. She stands up on her chair, dressed in her childish sailor suit and her big scarlet bow. "No, no, no," she says, and claps her palms together with each word for emphasis. "These clothings are *ridicules*, *inappropriés*—my dear boy, you must remove this vulgar outfit. Who dressed you in this way?"

"Um," Bolt says.

He looks back at Tickley-Feather, who gives him a small, stony shrug. "C'mere," Tickley-Feather says, and Bolt follows, his face hot, his head lowered, along the curved darkened wall of the tent to where there is a steamer trunk that, in all these weeks, Bolt never noticed before.

Tickley-Feather opens the trunk and pulls out a long piece of black silky cloth. It looks to be a choir robe of some sort, and Tickley-Feather softly grumbles, "Raise up your arms."

And pulls the robe down over Bolt like a sack.

Now he is made to stand behind Rosalie, and he is given a fancy repoussé silver brush and told that he should comb her hair.

He hesitates but does as he's told—carefully sliding the bristles along Rosalie's chestnut-colored hair, and Mme. Clothilde and the widow woman face him and maybe they don't even notice or care that his cheeks are red with mortification.

Oh! To be clapped at and scolded by a bossy miniature woman! To be told that his clothes were vulgar! He will never again wear the scarlet Hussar jacket with gold piping that he'd liked so much, nor the jodhpur breeches. Did Gladness and Shyla trick him when they said he looked swell, had he gone off dressed like an ass and they'd snickered into their hands as he walked away? *They'll pr'y turn you into a clown.* He fingers the neck of his silky robe, frowning gloomily.

Did they mean it, when they all raised the Loving Cup and said he was one of them? Did anybody like him? Or was it just to be him and Eleanor, alone forevermore?

Meanwhile, red and pink and blue candles have been lit, and Mme. Clothilde takes Rosalie's left hand, and the widow takes Rosalie's right hand, and Mme. Clothilde speaks words that might be French or Latin but it's a foreign language, and her voice grows lower until it is like a deep purr: "If a man die, shall he live again?" she says. "Is not the soul immortal? The mysteries of Isis and Osiris, as practiced in Egypt, and those of Eleusis, in Greece, taught the doctrine of the immortality of individual being, as did the great minds of antiquity, Socrates, Pythagoras, Plato, Aristotle. The Divine Master of Arcane Knowledge, Christ, proclaimed the same!"

She tilts her head back, eyes closed. "Spirits!" she says. *"Fantômes!* We seek colloquy with thee—"

She opens her mouth wide in an oval, as if she's a caroler singing a long note, and expels a long sigh and a stream of—what? Smoke? Fog? Frost breath?

The crystal ball on the table vibrates and shudders.

Bolt has been to séances many times before, but the mediums he has seen appear as naught but ordinary fakers compared to Mme. Clothilde. Her exhalation seems to hang in the air, almost like spider silks or fairy floss, twining into suggestive shapes.

The Otherin is staring up at him from the back of Rosalie's skull, he has to brush Rosalie's hair away from the Otherin's lip-like protrusions—

"Spirits," Mme. Clothilde says, and the Otherin's bulbous eyes roll in their incomprehensible sockets and Bolt shudders as they fix

as they

Lock gazes
Lock gazes

Oh! Bolt thinks.

Ow!

Like a fishhook to the eyelid.

He can feel his spine stiffening and arcing, he goes up on his tiptoes, his fingers grasping into claws and making signs, a mucus pours thickly out of his nose—

He jerks, twitches, thrashes, then rises a few inches above the ground, it feels like. He feels words vibrating in his voice box, but he can't hear them.

Of Dr. Chui

•••••••••

What is real and what is not? Dr. Chui is noncommittal. He suspects that Mme. Clothilde is a charlatan, but if so, she's quite a gifted one, for she seems to have convinced even herself. He stands outside Rosalie's tent and listens as the child Bolt emits a string of gibbering monkey-like noises, choking out occasional nonsense words, an American boy's idea of what a primitive language might sound like. Dr. Chui wonders if the lad is under some form of hypnosis, or if he has been drugged, or both. Mme. Clothilde has considerable skill in both mesmerism and experimental pharmacy.

Dr. Chui doesn't necessarily disbelieve in ghosts. It is only that, as a magician, he recognizes the trappings of deception in these Ouija boards and table knockings and spirit photographs, in the trances and automatic writing, the moving furniture and glowing mysterious lights and retching of ectoplasm. He knows how such tricks could be fairly easily achieved—and besides, he doesn't understand why the dead would have such earnest interest in the living. Unless they wanted revenge.

As for Rosalie—there is, he thinks, the possibility that the deformity on her head is also some kind of sleight of hand: perhaps putty and puppetry are involved. Thinking of her, he can't help but touch the horn that pokes up from the fontanelle region of his skull. The horn is smooth, dark amber in color, shaped like the nose of a rhinoceros, but there is nothing demonic or supernatural about it. It's essentially an ingrown hair, an accident of nature. *Hyperkeratosis* is one word for it. *Cutaneous anomaly*. It started as a wart.

As for the growth on Rosalie's head, he has never examined it, nor looked in its supposed eyes, but he wonders if it might, in fact, be something similar—simply an unusual aberration that by coincidence resembles a face.

Still, Dr. Chui, like most of the others, studiously avoids Rosalie and what they call the Otherin. It is said that if you ask them, they can tell you when and how you will die, and that they can tell you the last words that you will say. He doubts this—the poor creature probably has no more cognizance than an infant—but in any case, he has no interest in the circumstance of his future demise.

And thankfully Rosalie and her parasite are not his concern, nor is the boy, Bolt, nor is Mme. Clothilde. For now, his only business is to walk along the perimeter of the carnival with an eye out for trouble, and so he glides along quietly in his long golden silk robe with the aquamarine dragons embroidered on it—a costume, not particularly well made, patterned after Qing Dynasty Imperial fashion—but it lends the "Oriental" touch that the spectators seem to crave. It doesn't matter. He is nearly seven feet tall and if he keeps his chin up, he rarely needs to look anyone in their face. When he casts a gaze over the guests walking along the midway they are merely a series of bobbing hats and bonnets. Are they all not spirits? Nothing but a river of ghosts, briefly encased in flesh.

He hears a group of rough young men calling at him, mocking him with an American version of Chinese, a singsong cluster made up of surnames: *ching chong fu ying dong*—but Dr. Chui continues on serenely. It is not *he* whom they are jeering at, but only a Chinaman they have imagined in their limited dreams—and when he turns to look at them they shut their silly mouths and their smirks vanish.

He is an imposing figure—not just his height, not just his horn, but his large, lithe, long-fingered hands and his big still eyes, a gaze that can catch a person from across a room, a stare that people can feel on the backs of their neck before they turn around.

Later, when these young men are in the audience of Dr. Chui's performance, they will discover that he speaks with the accent of an Oxford-educated Englishman, and he will be able to pick out one of their number to bring up on the stage to be hypnotized. He is an expert at finding the most suggestible, the most easily manipulated; from a distance he can spot a certain credulous gullibility. He knows how to fix a country boy with a soft glare and push him gently down into a trance, like holding a child's face under water until it stops struggling—and once the mark has softened and relaxed, once his eyes have been fastened to the whirling pinwheel and his pupils begin to dilate and he is in what might be called a mesmerized state, Dr. Chui can softly persuade him to cluck like a chicken; he might make him into a plank, stiff as a board and balanced between two chairs; he might draw a long string of pink scarves and scarlet ribbons from the rube's mouth, unfurling and unfurling.

In these times, it is not easy to be Chinese in the United States, and to be seven feet tall with a horn growing out of your head is an added impediment.

The laws from the 1880s that excluded immigration from Asian countries had been amended, and now even people of Chinese extraction who'd been born in America were required to carry papers, "Certificates of Residence," they were called, to prove their legal status. In order to get the certificate, you needed two white witnesses to attest for you.

Two white witnesses to prove that Shing Kai Chui is allowed to remain! Without these papers, he could be arrested and sentenced to hard labor. He could be deported, sent "back" to a land he's never even seen.

He was born in this country. His baba was a traveling merchant, and his mama was a doctor and apothecary, and the two of them had followed along with the railroad camps of Chinese as they built the Union Pacific Railroad line through Nevada and Wyoming. Eventually his parents had settled near a village of miners in Rock Springs, in Wyoming Territory, where his mother gave birth to him, and where he spent his early years.

Is it strange that he remembers his childhood as happy? There were over three hundred Chinese in Rock Springs during that time, most of them miners working for Union Pacific, nearly all of them men. He was the only Chinese child, and their faces lit up when they saw him. He reminded them of their own children, back in Guangdong, their nephews, their little brothers, and everywhere he went they gave him small gifts and treats, they taught him tricks. Dr. Chui knew what it felt like to be beloved.

He can remember how the men came to his mother for haircuts, to have their heads shaved in the traditional queue style, their scalp smooth except for a single tonsil braid, and they would sometimes shed tears of homesickness, to be touched by a woman; he can remember the white people lining up along the muddy streets of downtown to watch the Chinese New Year parade, eager to see the magnificent dragon made of silk and shimmering mirrored scales, measuring close to one hundred feet and requiring a hundred men to carry it. The big shiny eyes worked on a swivel, and almost appeared to flash fire when the dragon was taunted, it writhed with anger, seemingly, and all who were watching gasped and applauded.

His parents, hoping to give him an advantage, sent him to learn English from a British woman named Mrs. More, who had somehow found herself widowed and destitute, stranded at the Pilot Butte Hotel, and he sat with her in her little room while she kissed dewdrops of laudanum from an eyedropper and read Wordsworth and Tennyson and Dickens aloud to him. Her room had a perfumy, musky, dead smell, old fruit and woman sweat and rot, but he endured it because she was kind and patient, and he learned by repeating after her. She made him say tongue twisters over and over until his accent, his stumbling over *r*'s and *l*'s, was gone.

Rory the warrior and Roger the worrier were reared wrongly in a rural brewery.

Brisk brave brigadiers brandished broad bright blades, blunderbusses, and bludgeons—balancing them badly.

To this day, he carries with him a copy of *Great Expectations*.

In 1885, the year of the massacre, he was thirteen years old, and he had somehow lost control of his body. He'd begun to grow higher and higher—already a foot above his father, taller than any of the men in the Chinese camp, and an itchy wart at the top of his head had begun to solidify into something hard and pointed. People did not smile fondly at him anymore.

He was not unaware of the hostility of the white miners but he'd thought that it was directed toward him alone—because he was becoming a monster. His proportions were grotesque, he thought, his arms abnormally long and thin and gangling, his legs like stilts upon which a squat torso rested. He looked, he thought, like the spindly spiders called harvestmen that you'd find along shady walls and in caves and root cellars. "Daddy longlegs," some of the white immigrant children would call him, and pull at their eyes with their index fingers in what he knew were rude gestures but he didn't know at the time what exactly it meant. He kept his face low and couldn't help but cover the top of his head, the extrusion that was now sharp and hard as a fingernail, the terror that they would see it. They threw dirt clods as he hurried along toward the Pilot Butte Hotel, toward his lessons with Mrs. More, his books clutched close to his chest, and Finns outside the saloon joined in jeering at him, and a drunken wild-bearded Swede named Dahlvig, who had once seemed kind and friendly, hooted along.

Dr. Chui didn't know until later that there had been a law passed that banned the immigration of Chinese laborers. He was unaware that many believed there was an ongoing *Chinese Invasion*, "numberless heathen hordes that will, if no check is applied, one day overthrow the present Republic of the United States!" The anti-Chinese sentiment was particularly strong within the burgeoning workers' movements—the Knights of Labor organization had recently established a chapter in Rock Springs, and its members said that the Chinese kept wages low, the Chinese were strikebreakers, they were the enemy of the white workingman.

From a distance of thirty years, Dr. Chui can look back dispassionately and see how these social and political forces had arranged themselves, like a chessboard puzzle, tending toward a particular outcome.

But back then, when he was thirteen, back on the day of the massacre, he still thought that humans were people—that if you saw someone drowning you would try to help them, that civility was preferred over fighting, that all of us were bound by an instinctive revulsion at cruelty.

Alas.

That morning of the massacre he'd wandered lonely as cloud along some shale cliffs and he'd found fossils of ancient ferns and trilobites impressed like cameos into wafers of rock, and he'd been collecting them when he heard the bell ring from the Knights of Labor hall, it was ten o'clock in the morning on a Wednesday, and he saw the men come down the hill toward the Chinese camp, and he saw that they were all carrying rifles and he could hear the angry barking sounds they were making, and he thought, well, they are just bullies making noise.

"A bully is a vulgar coward," Mrs. More had told him. "Taunting, calling names out of ignorance. They are beneath our interest." And he had believed that was true until he saw them shoot a man, until he saw them lighting the shacks of the Chinese on fire, until he saw a person beheaded and the killer carrying away the head as a trophy.

He heard the most awful screams. He knew his parents were down there in the burning houses, but he ran away and hid in the grassy hills beyond the town and he did not go down to try to rescue them, he did not look back to see them being murdered, though later he would read newspaper accounts of the atrocities—

as their hut was burning they had tried to dig a hole to hide themselves, but the fire overtook them when about halfway in the hole, burning their lower extremities to a crisp and leaving their upper bodies intact

shot down in their flight and lay in the creek with face upturned and distorted, charred by flames and mutilated by hogs

He let his mind linger upon each scene of horror as if looking at a photograph, and he would imagine that each description was of his mother and father.

Oh, call upon my baba and mama, Mme. Clothilde, he would sometimes think, *call upon the spirits of the mother and father whose son fled and left them to die—raise them up and let us see what ectoplasm flows from you then!*

And then he thinks: *Forgive me. Forgive my self-pity.*

He survived, and he knows this is what his parents would have wanted. He fled blindly into the inhospitable wilds outside of Rock Springs and then he managed to hop a train that brought him to Cheyenne, and there he met a drunken Welsh magician named Blaidd Jenkins, who took him on as an assistant.

He endured that as well. He portrayed a subservient coolie onstage, a confused and frightened magician's apprentice—though once the show was over, Jenkins could barely find his way back to their hotel room, so intoxicated was he. Blaidd the Bewildering had invented a few good tricks in his younger days, and he still could manage some amusing sleights of hand, but most of his time was now spent in the final stages of poisoning himself to death with alcohol, administering each dose with a tender thoughtfulness. He was not cruel, and he even seemed sometimes grateful when Shing Kai Chui tended to him.

And after Blaidd died there was another magician he assisted, and then another, and then after one night in Denver with the loutish Zolton the Great, Dr. Chui had been met backstage by Harland Jengling.

"I'd like to make you an offer," Jengling said. He couldn't have been more than twenty-one or twenty-two, this Jengling, and Dr. Chui was well into his thirties by then, but this young man had a casual and intoxicating charisma.

"I can see how special you are," Jengling said. "That is my only gift, such as it is, to truly recognize the gifts of others. I can find a place for you in my show, and I promise that you can earn a much better wage with me."

Dr. Chui regarded him silently. "What wage?" he murmured at last. "Give me a number."

"Percentage of profits," Jengling said. "Partnership. A community of equals."

He held out his big, pink-palmed hand, his eyes holding Dr. Chui's steadily. "I have a sort of Ark," he said. "Do you know the story of Noah's Ark?"

"I do," Dr. Chui said, though he didn't say that he found the fable ridiculous, full of logical inconsistencies.

"So I am a new Noah!" said this Jengling. "And we are a gathering of all the diverse tribes of humankind. Of which there are many! You are not alone, sir! You are welcomed, and will be beloved!"

Shing Kai Chui did the calculations and he saw that indeed there was profit to be made, and also a kind of freedom, and now he was—what? A partner? A lieutenant? A cherished specimen for the Ark's menagerie?

He feels relatively safe here, though he is aware as he walks the circumference of the carnival that he is also pacing along the wall of a zoo's enclosure. Protected and yet trapped. Included and collected.

IN RE: *POLLYANNA*

So, what's your dream?" Billy Bigelow says.

They have finished setting up the carousel early and now they sit on the riding board, eating bread-and-butter sandwiches and dunking them in their cups of milk, watching as the other members of Jengling's Emporium hurry about. July Fourth. She sees Bolt, nearly running to keep up with Tickley-Feather's long-legged stride, on his way to babysit for Rosalie; she sees Dr. Chui walking along in his silk robe with his hands tucked in front of him like a lady wearing a muff, and he gives her a long pensive stare—or maybe he's looking through her toward some memory or imagining.

"My *dream*?" Eleanor says suspiciously. "What's that supposed to mean?"

Billy chuckles slyly. He's tickled that she's so untrusting, and he exchanges glances with the mynah bird.

"What do you want to be when you grow up, dolly?" He laughs. "Do you want to be a crafty pickpocket like my sweet bird here? Do you want to get married to a millionaire and have fancy babies? Do you want to be a pirate queen and rule over a crew of savages with sharp choppers?"

He smiles widely, showing his own filed teeth, and scratches his bare thigh, where a jungle cat seems to lurk in a snarl of vines.

"I don't know what I want," Eleanor says. "I'm still deciding."

"Well, you better get to it," Billy says. "Figure it out before somebody else figures it out for you."

He's not all bad. She knows better than to trust him, but so far he hasn't tried to take anything from her. He doesn't stare at her in that way that some men do.

So she relaxes a little. He's not stupid, but he's illiterate, so she reads to him from time to time like she used to do with Bolt, she reads from *Pollyanna*—about how one Christmas Pollyanna had hoped for a doll.

"*You see, I'd wanted a doll, but when the missionary barrel came the lady wrote that there hadn't any dolls come in, but the little crutches had. So she sent 'em along, as they might come in handy for some child sometime. And that's when we began it . . . The game was to just find something about everything to be glad about—no matter what 'twas," rejoined Pollyanna, earnestly.*

And Billy bursts out laughing. "Haw-haw! *Adoro!* This girl is so crazy! She thinks the crutches are a doll?"

"No," Eleanor says. "Her father says that she should be glad because she doesn't *need* the crutches. The idea is that you're always supposed to look on the bright side."

"Fwa-haw-haw-haw!" he cries, and he curls his rune-marked foot soles like a baby. "Ah, poor little chump, to think 'It could be worse,' instead of 'It could be better'! Imagine the kind of brute she will marry! She'll play her Glad Game very hard and often then!"

And Eleanor is miffed for a moment, but Billy's merriment is contagious, and soon they both are bent over and gasping with laughter, they laugh until their stomachs hurt.

Poor little chump.

There is enough time before the gates open to the gillies that she can sit somewhere private and read for a while, and she finds a corner by the gorilla cage out of sight. Miss Alcott is sleeping, and her soft snores are pleasant to hear—a gentle, tremulous coo, like a lullaby. Miss Alcott would've made a good mother, Eleanor thinks.

She opens up her book again. *Pollyanna* wasn't necessarily what she wanted—she'd just chosen it randomly off a stack of books that were on a cart in the commissary—"Take, if you want," Mr. Lacis had told her, gesturing dismissively. "Master Jengling wants us all to read, read, read, become enlightening!" And she'd casually grabbed the first book at the top of the pile, not wanting to seem like she cared.

But as it turns out, she's interested in this novel. Pollyanna isn't foolish, like Billy thinks, she's just strange—and empty—which Eleanor is curious about. Pollyanna is working so hard to solve the problem of emptiness, and Eleanor wants to see what she comes up with.

And she has just gotten to a good part when that dog-faced boy comes along. She hears the clump of his boots and glances up and he's headed toward her with that hungry smirk he has. He has a kind of boyish confidence that makes her teeth hurt, like she's biting down on tin foil.

"Hey there, Red," he says, and gives her a sheepish head-tilt like a friendly mutt. "What's cookin?"

She holds up the book to show him she's engaged.

"Reading, eh?" he says, nodding as if thoughtful. "What's it about?"

"A girl whose name is Pollyanna," she says. She keeps her eyes on the page, even though she can feel him looking at her expectantly.

"Sounds inneresting!" he says, and her face tightens with irritation as he sits down next to her, companionably leaning back against the side of Miss Alcott's cage. He examines his polished black fingernails, and then buffs them against the lapel of his jacket.

"So . . ." he says, at last. He gives her that warm-eyed gaze, like he's confiding. "Listen. Shyla and Gladness are gettin kind of hurt feelings cuz you never want to sit with us at supper."

She keeps reading, or pretending to, and he shifts uncertainly. Why do people always expect that you'll look at them when they talk to you? It's so rude, she thinks.

He hesitates. "Um," he says. "Anyways. They think you don't like them. But your brother says you're just shy. Is that right? You're shy?"

"No," Eleanor says. "I'm not shy."

"Well," Elmer says. He plucks a dandelion and peels its rubbery stalk, considers the milky white juice that drips out. "Is it cuz we look different? The girls think maybe you're embarrassed to be seen in company with the likes of us."

"I just like to be alone, that's all," Eleanor says.

And she realizes: that's it! That's *her dream.*

To be alone with a library full of books, with nobody to bother her, nobody she has to make conversation with, nobody she has to take care of. Oh, that would be heaven.

But also, what a foolish thought! She is not a person of independent means, nor will she ever be one. When people ask "What is your dream?" what they mean is "How do you plan to get money?"

And she can think of no good answer to that. If she leaves Jengling, then what? Could she run a boardinghouse, like her mother? Would she sit there, gloomily reading like her mother sat by the Victrola, listening over and over to her awful songs?

"It's all nothing and nothingness," her mother told her. "And the afterlife, too, I think. I don't really think they are any less lonely in the astral plane."

She would often muse like this when Eleanor was a child, and Eleanor would kneel and rub salve onto her mother's sore feet, listening solemnly.

"Our lives are much too brief, and the universe is much too vast for anything we do to have any consequence," Mother said. "If we had a little more in the bank, that would ease the burden—but we do not, alas."

She sighed and reached down to pet Eleanor's head, as Eleanor massaged her bright red, swollen foot. "This is only between you and Mama, darling," she said softly. "Don't say these things to Bolt. He's much too sweet and simple to understand. It would only confuse him."

"But I understand!" said Eleanor. She was only eight or nine or so, yet such a bright, grown-up girl! Such a hard worker! Mama would be lost without her! Oh, Mama—her anchor, her ankle-chain!

"Yes, my darling. *You* understand the world very well. You will not be taken in and used and discarded like most of our wretched kind."

That's what Mama called women: *our wretched kind.*

"To be in a constant state of unquestioning self-humiliation," her mother said. "Or utter submission. Those are the only choices. The broken heart. You think you will die, but just keep living, day after terrible day!"

And what would Pollyanna do with *that*? Eleanor wonders.

Unlike Pollyanna, Eleanor cannot seem to glad her way out of her unhappiness, because she does not even know its opposite. Oh, sometimes she longs to be less lonely, and it only makes her act more distant, colder, more withdrawn. Whenever she imagines being hopeful and gay, a withering veil of self-scorn settles over her. It's doubtful that she could even manage a heartfelt smile.

She only knows that she doesn't want to be *here*—she hates the crowds of babbling gillies that are already beginning to arrive and mill about, staring and pointing and yawping out horrible, stupid laughter. She hates the constant social niceties she has to perform for her fellow members of Jengling's Emporium and oh! she hates most of all the idea of *belonging* to someone—*my* sister, *my* daughter, *my* adopted ward. What if she doesn't want to be "my" anything, what if she doesn't want to belong to anyone—?

But where would she go? She has nothing, and no relations to help her. She supposes she could become a tramp and hop a train, but she knows how that would play out.

Somewhere far to the south, Ernest Shackleton's Trans-Antarctic Expedition is underway, and maybe that would be the trip she'd most like to take. Standing at the bow of a ship in the hazy blue-white sea, listening to the creaking of enormous icebergs towering in the distance. She would like to see what the stars look like at the bottom of the world, she would like to feel an aloneness so vast that you could melt into it and disappear.

Instead, she's at the center of a carousel wheel, in the middle of a carnival, and there are hundreds and hundreds of people converging, all of them talking loudly and merrily, chattering and swarming and Billy

Bigelow stands with his arms folded over his puffed-out chest, grinning his shark-toothed grin.

He has a name for every type of person he sees—acorn-crackers and barnyard savages, biscuit-nibblers, bog rats, bootchkeys, candle-biters, coppertops, dodunks, guntzels, jaspers, labricks, mincefeet, Scandahoovians—he practically needs his own dictionary to understand him.

"You see that cake-eater?" he says, and points with his lips toward the milling midway. She follows his gaze and sees his mynah bird coasting above the heads of the incoming gillies and she watches with him as the bird dips down and snatches something from the pocket of a prim young man in a checked jacket and docker hat.

"So," Billy says, and looks at her sidelong. "How will you hone a special talent? We all need one." He holds up his hand and the bird lands on his fingers and delivers a folded dollar bill, poking it into his closed palm.

"I don't have any talents," she says, and he makes a cheerful sneering sound.

"Oh, what modest modesty," he teases. "How very becoming of a young lady." And he hands her the bill, which she takes surreptitiously and quickly hides in her pocket. But the young man does not notice that he's been robbed, and he continues off into the crowd, pleased as a prince, holding a candy apple like a scepter.

"Do you like it here?" she says, staring solemnly at the milling crowd of customers walking along the midway. They are curious to see the freaks that are manning the booths, and then are drawn into a game of chance that will fleece them. It's probably more profitable than the sideshow system.

"Do I like it here?" Billy Bigelow laughs. "Of course, of course! Why wouldn't I?" The bird lands on his crooked finger again and delivers another bill, and he puckers his lips and pushes out a raisin that he must have been holding in his mouth, and the bird takes the treat as if giving him a kiss.

"What else would I do, as I look? Go back to work on a ship? No. No. I am through with that life, I don't like sailors. Here, I make enough money. Sometimes I see interesting things. They say they will give me a pension when I get old. Doesn't that seem satisfactory to you?"

He turns, smiling, to take the ticket of a woman in a large, polka-dotted garden hat who blushes, scandalized and titillated by his near-naked, tattooed body. "Choose any mount you'd like, my sunshine," Billy Bigelow says, and then turns to the next customer, and Eleanor goes to the center of the carousel again, ready to pull the lever and set the machine in motion once the seats have been filled.

Food and shelter, security and a few pennies to spend for pleasure, interesting things to see, a pension. What more should a person expect from this life? And yet the idea only makes her feel more trapped. Everywhere, there are only cages within cages.

She sees a boy sit down on a lion-headed seahorse creature and he bends down and grips its mane hard, as if he'll soon go galloping over a cliff on it, and she starts the machine up and the chains and gears groan and the carousel begins to make its slow revolution, and the calliope tootles its tune.

It's all nothing and nothingness, her mother said, but then what? Then what do you do?

"**L**ook," says Billy Bigelow, and he pokes her out of her reverie. "Here comes your brother. Do you want my bird to play a trick on him?"

She looks up and she sees Bolt wandering down the midway in his silly outfit, red Hussar jacket and long hip boots that are too big for him, striding with a big wide-eyed expression, and he looks so stupid that she's furious with him all over again. "No," she says.

And sits irritably, purses her lips and turns her full attention to her book, squeaking her teeth against one another, reading with athletic concentration.

"Yes. I had not meant to tell you, but perhaps it's better, after all, that I do—now." John Pendleton's face had grown very white. He was speaking with evident difficulty. Pollyanna, her eyes wide and frightened, and her lips parted, was gazing at him fixedly. "I loved your mother; but she—didn't love me. And after a time she went away with—your father. I did not know until then how much I did—care."

And she can feel Bolt reaching out, fumbling at the edge of her thoughts, he's listening to her as she's reading, he thinks he can just barge in and start snooping around but she closes the drapes before he can get in closer. She's shutting him out until he gets scared and begs her and even then he's going to have to grovel awful hard before she softens.

He always minded her before. Even when he doubted or argued, he would always capitulate in the end because he had a healthy fear of her, he knew she could hurt him. She had always been the larger and stronger of the two, up until lately.

Oh, now what is to be done about him?

Bolt loves her, she knows that's true, but as she gets older the more she realizes that Bolt would love *anybody*. It won't be long before he's calling himself Bolt Jengling and pretending that he's part of a new "family"—and then where will she be?

Alone, that's where.

But isn't that what you wanted?

She looks up and sees that Bolt is down by the dog-faced boy's booth, at the edge of a crowd, and she thinks, *Maybe I should . . . ?*

But then Tickley-Feather comes up behind him and taps him on the shoulder, and Bolt turns around and Tickley-Feather puts his arms akimbo.

"Oh, he's in trouble now," says Billy Bigelow. Billy folds his arms over his chest and chuckles. "Oh, he's in big trouble, your brother. You ain't supposed to go off and leave that Rosalie, you know."

"Why not?" Eleanor says, and she watches as Bolt follows after Tickley-Feather, casting a gloomy backward glance toward whatever the crowd is watching.

"I dunno," says Billy. "I don't make it my business. But I'm glad I'm not one watching the Rosalie. That's a job *nobody* wants."

She looks at him sharply, not sure if he's teasing. "Why?" she says, and he shrugs.

"Ha ha! You know that fella they call Piltdown Man?" he says. "The one that eats the chicken guts and lives in a cage like a monkey?"

"Yeah," she says, and scowls to remember. "We cleaned his cage once."

"Well, then," Billy Bigelow says, confidentially, "they say he used to be Rosalie's minder, and that's how he lost his wits. Spent too much time in the company of that girl and the Otherin. That's what they say, I won't tell you I believe it . . . but I've seen stranger things."

She wishes that there was someone who could give her good advice, and some nights she'll lie in bed staring at the hieroglyphs in their father's diary and believes that they are full of wisdom—an indecipherable bible, if only she could read it.

If only she could talk to their father, just once. She thinks; she bargains. *Just once!* He could explain it all to her, tell her how to go forward, advise her on how to get Bolt out of this place.

Or maybe he'd tell her that she should stay—maybe this carnival is the best place she could hope for, after all.

By lamplight, with Bolt snoring softly beside her, she'll stay up trying to decipher. If the code is a simple letter replacement, then it's possible she's made some progress. The repeated single-letter rune—a sort of upside-down *U* with a dot in the center—must be either *I* or *A*, and so she looks for instances on page after page.

Sometimes when she is looking at the hieroglyphs in her father's diary she hesitates over a four-letter word and imagines, like a stupid cow, that it might be *LOVE*.

What would his love be like? she wonders. It wouldn't be warm and moist-breathed and dewy soft, like Bolt's. It would be chilly and stern, and without any need of its own. His love would hold her in a thoughtful gaze and have high expectations.

He would say, *Go, Nellie, and find your destiny!*

Or he might say: *Stay, Nellie, and collect your pension.*

She is thinking of this, and keeping an eye on the tent where Bolt babysits for Rosalie, when Dr. Chui comes by. She glances up from her book and sees him coming toward her directly across the circling board, avoiding the carousel animals without even looking as he crosses, smiling politely.

"Pardon me," he says, and stands erect as a toy soldier at the edge of the spinning wheel with his hands folded in front of him. She can hear his voice clearly, even though the calliope is hooting loudly, his voice seems to pass through her like a shudder. "Miss Eleanor?" he says. "Please come with me. Master Jengling would like to speak with you."

What can she do? She goes along quietly, and Dr. Chui places his hand very lightly beneath her shoulder blades, guiding her through the crowd of fairgoers, he must be three feet taller than she is but seems weightless, more like a gust of wind than a person, gliding along in his silk robe as if on rollers, and she finds that she doesn't resent his touch as much as she might another's.

I, too, am an orphan, he says, and she startles, because it's almost like he's whispering in her ear, it's almost like his breath is brushing her earlobe—

But it's not. His face is forward, and she can't even tell if his lips are moving.

"I lost everything I had," he says softly. "When we are children, we think that everything we have is all there is, don't we?"

They come to the far end of the midway, where Ringmaster Jengling's trailer sits facing the big empty prairie sky, full of stars.

"Whatever it was you were once, you will never get it back," Dr. Chui says gently, and she can feel the tips of his long, spidery fingers brushing near the middle of her spine, guiding her along. "Perhaps you will be offered a new sort of life, and you might be wise to consider it."

Eleanor enters Mr. Jengling's private train car—all gold and scarlet paisley felt wallpaper, all glass cases with jars full of horrors and archaeological treasures and objects she can't name. Under a bell jar is a withered mummy's hand holding a snaky-curved dagger; in a terrarium sits a large frog with transparent skin through which you can see all its bodily organs.

Meanwhile, Master Jengling doesn't seem to notice her. He's reading a leather-bound old book in his armchair, wearing his sleeves rolled without his red jacket, and his jodhpur pants without the long boots, only his black stockings, and she stands there for a moment uncertainly, waiting, as he runs his finger across a page, reading avidly.

At last, she taps her knuckles on the doorframe, and he looks up, and she watches his face turn into a mask.

"Ah," he says, and arranges that wide, toothy, artificial smile on his face. "Miss Eleanor!" he says. "Delight!"

She does not know what to make of him. Never once has he ever dropped his jolly, booming-voiced facade, the false warmth that actually, she thinks, makes you feel colder. It's almost as if he drinks up a little bit of your spirit when he fixes you with his eagerly staring eyes, and so instead she looks at an amphibious creature in a jar, a kind of pink eel, which has the plump legs and feet of a human infant.

"I've been meaning to see how you're doing," Jengling says. "Are you enjoying working at the carousel? It's not making you dizzy?"

"It's fine," she says. "I have a steady head."

"So it would seem," Mr. Jengling says, and does he mean to imply something when he tilts his chin down and raises his eyebrows? She can't tell.

"And Billy Bigelow is treating you respectfully, and with kindness?"

"Yes, sir," she says.

"You and he have a lot in common," he says and before she can check herself she mutters under her breath.

"Because we both have so many tattoos—?"

And Jengling looks at her sharply, then tilts his head back and laughs approvingly.

"That could be arranged, you know," he says. "Would you like to be a tattooed lady?"

"No, sir," she says, and when she looks down at her shoes she sees a distorted reflection of her frowning face on the shiny, varnished floor. Why can't she keep her mouth shut? Why must she be a smart aleck even against her own best interests?

"Sorry," she mumbles. "I never meant to be sassy." She tilts her eyes upward and he still has those pale eyes fastened onto her, drinking her, his book closed with his thumb as a bookmark. "I—I need to work on remembering my manners."

"Manners? Ha!" he says. "Mere pantomime and puppetry! I prefer a forthright woman!" That toothy smile again. "But you must allow me to be forthright as well: all of us are concerned about you."

"Concerned?" she says, and if she were Bolt she would go red in the face, but at least she knows how not to blush. Still, her heart quickens. "Have I—done something wrong, sir?"

"Not at all, my dear Eleanor," he says. "It's only—we have all noticed how unhappy you seem."

She glances back, shrugging, swallowing, and she sees a framed display case on the wall with an enormous moth in it, twice the size of her hand. Its wings are blue and shimmering like a still lake reflecting a clear sky, and in the center of the upper wings are two round yellow markings that look exactly like eyes.

And then Jengling reaches out and places his large, cool fingertips against her knuckles, against the back of her hand, and she stiffens, flinches, pulls her hand away and she can't help but let out a soft sound of revulsion.

"Oh!" Eleanor says. What can she do? She tries to conjure Pollyanna, affecting the sweetest voice she can muster. "My—my apologies . . . Father," she says, demurely. "It's just that I'm . . . not naturally sociable."

He regards her, and in recompense for her rudeness she tries to meet his eyes for a moment, and when their gazes meet she counts, three, five, ten seconds, then away. "I . . ." she says, "I just need to smile more. And try to find something to be glad about in any situation."

"Oh, don't be silly," Jengling says. "Ha ha! No one wants you to be a *clown*—and in any case, you haven't the constitution for it. What we want—" And he holds his hands out as if she'll clasp them happily—but she focuses her gaze just above his head, at some kind of giant fang mounted on the wall behind him.

"What we want—all of us—is for you to be your truest self, whatever that might be. We saw you and we knew that there was great potential. Great potential! You're *sapiens* of a sort, but I—"

He seems to consider reaching out and touching her again, but then, to her relief, withdraws. "I think you are not necessarily ordinary *Homo sapiens*—I think there are many more branches of the *hominid* family than anyone realizes!"

He hesitates. After a pause, the tent revivalist in him seems to deflate, and the hungering gleam in his eyes seems to grow dimmer. He clears his throat, and for a moment he seems like almost a person. "In any case," he says, "I think I have a job that might suit you."

He starts to beam out his toothy impresario smile again, but then thinks better of it, lets it fade and instead gives her something more wan, gentle. *Guileful*, she thinks. He's sensed her revulsion and now he's adjusting his face in a way that he hopes is more pleasing to her.

But maybe it is not an act. They are both, in their own ways, guarded people, and maybe he is genuinely making a gesture.

He nods toward a stack of books on a table. *Vestiges of the Natural History of Creation. The Old and the New Magic. Man's Place in the Universe. The Code of Hammurabi.*

"It occurred to me," he says, in a voice now almost shy and ingratiating, "what would you think about being our librarian? We are in need of someone to make a record of the—acquisitions—to catalog them, and you seem like the ideal sort of person. You're bright, you're bookish, you don't mind spending long hours alone—"

She can't help but dart her eyes around, surreptitiously. There are so many books and rings and necklaces and bejeweled pistols in cases, and mechanisms, and stone tablets covered in runes—so many things that she can't help but covet, out of curiosity.

There is a lot here to steal, she hears Billy Bigelow say, and her papá murmurs, *Codes . . . and runes . . . and pistols . . .*

"It might not be a bad use of your talents," says Jengling. "Until you discover one that's more productive."

"All right." She hears herself breathe. "Yes, Father."

It's late and there's a thunderstorm off in the prairie distance when Bolt comes in and gets into bed with her.

He's trembling and when she glances up from *Pollyanna* she sees how strange and pale his face is—an expression she's never seen, it's like he's wearing a mask made from a casting, like the death mask of a corpse.

"What's wrong?" she whispers, and touches his clammy skin, and his lips twitch.

"Nuh—" he croaks, and shakes his head in an odd, sideways jerk.

"Bolt?" She keeps her voice low because Tickley-Feather is asleep in his bunk, she doesn't want to wake him but she feels a spark of genuine alarm.

He looks like he's about to pitch an epileptic fit. She can remember how once at the Spiritualist Church old Widow Hand had a seizure, and how Miss Sylvia Ferryman had put a spoon in her mouth to keep her from swallowing her tongue, and how Missus Hand's eyes had a harrowed blankness, as if she'd just been blinded by a vision. That's what Bolt's eyes look like.

"It's nuh—nothing," Bolt says as she stares hard at him. "I got to help Madame Clothilde with a séance and I guess I blacked out for a minute. But I'm fine. I just feel real tired is all."

She puts her palm on his forehead, and it's shockingly cold to the touch. Is there something that's the opposite of a fever?

"What do you mean you helped her with a séance? Did she send you to the land of the dead and back?"

"Ha!" Bolt says, and smiles wanly. "Maybe. Sure feels like it." He closes his eyes, and relaxes back, his lips parting, almost half-asleep. "I brushed Rosalie's hair . . . and then she spoke . . . and Madame Clothilde said . . . I was the best man for her . . . I did real good . . ."

She puts their blanket over him as he mumbles, even though it's a hot, muggy summer night he's shivering, and she cradles him. The muscles in his arms spasm, and a honey-colored mucus runs out from one nostril.

"She says . . ." he whispers. "She says I'm special." And he hums to himself as he drifts off. "Special," he breathes. "Special. Special."

A Man of Constant Sorrow

•••••••••

Charlie Lambkin, Chuck Lumpkin, Charles Lampwick—poor Chappy so bedeviled by the woofits that the only cure is to give himself a good beating. He makes a fist and clouts himself in the face, blackens an eye, then punishes the knuckles what smote him by biting savagely until they bleed. He pulls out some hair from his beard with a matchstick tied in it, and uses the match to give his big toe a roasting, then squeezes the pus out of the blister and pours corn whiskey on it. He weeps and slaps himself hard on the buttocks. "I'm sorry, Daddy!" he cries, and then, still silently blubbering, hunkers down and dolefully whittles at the bone.

He is bivouacked on the edge of the Missoura river, River of Misery, he thinks, and not even the vilest punishments he can devise seem to lift his spirits this day. He is so terrible lost and lonely, and none to give him comfort nor succor. The nag Stardust, tied to sapling beyond the campfire, eyes him with not an ounce of fellow feeling.

You'd think he'd be happy. He has been a week or two behind his quarry for months now, but at last he has caught up. About a mile or so down the way, the carnival that has stold his childern is setting up at the fairgrounds. He crouches behind some cottonwood scrub and observes the distant scene through a pair of field glasses—but sees neither hide nor hair of his precious angels.

Where are they keeping them? Are the little poppets held in pens like monkeys, crying for Uncle Charlie to save them? He worries that this outfit may be experimenting upon them, using some kind of magic or surgery to transform them into freaks that can be put on display, maybe stitching their skins together like they did with those poor Simease.

Or what if the babes have already escaped? What if they've galivanted off, caught a boxcar back to Ohio? What a laugh they'd have, the little scamps, to have circumvented him! He can't imagine what kind of anger that would arouse.

In any case, he figgers he'll have to go in and take a closer look, but so far he hasn't had the nerve to get close. Not only is there the danger of being spotted by the twins, the fear that they'd warn their keepers of his presence, but also he is afraid of monsters.

This carnival lets their freaks run loose and roam about, that's what agitates and beflusters him the most. He has seen the enormous baby-headed creature, a hulking man three hundred pounds or more, with a bare scalp and no eyebrows nor teeth, and he imagines its hands would be moist and milky-smelling and dreadfully powerful. He has seen it carrying a teensy woman in its arms and he hates the sight of midgets, and their high, imp-like voices give him the collywobbles. In general, the deformed and abnormal make him squeamish, and his palms grow icy cold when he is forced to get close to one.

He spies a red-haired be-pigtailed clown, walking along with a big wooden mallet slung over its shoulder. He holds no enmity toward the Clownish, they seem like a simple, mostly harmless people, but he senses that this tall, lanky fellow might pose a problem.

He's not sure what to do. If he shaved off his beard he could go in disguised as an old woman, but he's loath to lose his whiskers. Ugh. He removes the binoculars from his eyes and returns to the campfire, squats down on a stump and takes a can of beans from his knapsack, considering. He is strongly in favor of canned beans—it's worth the extra money for the convenience. He opens the can with his pocket-knife and uses the edge of the blade to spoon the beans into his mouth.

The nag Stardust watches him reproachfully from where she is hitched, some distance from the fire. He suspects that she's disapproving of him over the extravagance of a second axe murder, so soon after the first, but who is she to judge?

"Don't you look at me that way," Charlie growls at her and brandishes a piece of kindling when she flares her nostrils. "I'll beat you within a inch of your life!" Charlie declares, and then he softens, lowers his stick and gazes into the fire—shadows of merry, frolicking childern in the embers.

"Anyways," he grumbles. "I'm done with killing. I've renounced it."

He says it loud enough that he hopes the spirit of Jasper Lambkin can hear him—whether flitting above in heaven, or curling like smoke in the ether of the astral plane, he doesn't know.

Jasper had believed in ghosts and séances and so forth, and Charlie didn't have an opinion one way or t'other. But he was skeptical. He had seen the flimflam women and the mincing genteel confidence artists plying the medium trade, and he reckoned there was good money in it. Whether there was any truth was another question.

But who knew? He has seen some strange things over the years. He saw a mountain of bison skulls three stories high and he had smelled what the death of ten thousand lives smelled like.

Down in Canyon Diablo, Arizona, he had seen a gang of rowdies pull a newly hanged bank robber out of his grave to give him one last drink of whiskey, and when they held up the corpse out of its coffin it was smiling in such a terrible, knowing way that some of the men covered their faces and began to weep in fear. He had seen a chicken on display, headless but still alive. A farmer had taken a rooster to the chopping block to eat it for dinner but the damned thing had survived its own beheading and earned itself good copper on the traveling curiosity circuit!

At Wounded Knee, after the massacre and the blizzard, he was hired to throw corpses into a pit and he had pulled up a dead child that was frozen in its mother's arms, and it was stiff as a log.

Stiff as a log, it was.

But when you looked at its face you could've sworn it was staring up at you with its black eyes.

You might even think you could feel it breathing.

He wakes and it's long past nightfall and he's feeling better. The dewdrops of hopelessness seem to be draining out of him, and the stars are out, and the Buck moon, and down at the carnival they're setting off fireworks. In the flashes of red and blue and orange he can see the silhouette of a girl in Arabian dress dancing atop the back of an elephant.

That's a vision that will linger in the memory.

And now the fairgoers are drifting away, heading home, and the magic lights electric and neon are winking off, and Charlie stands smiling at the roadside as people go past in their wagons and chugging Model Ts.

He sees a merry young farmer daddy with four daughters in tow—a tall, square-headed Swede is he, freckled of face and broad of chest, clumping along in his big dirty boots with a wee toddle girl riding piggyback, and another, maybe five, holding his thick thumb, and two others in braids, ages perhaps seven and nine, skipping alongside—all of them happy and chattering, all strawberry blondes. He reckons the papa with his ragged pants and suspenders is a widower, and they all live together in a one-room sod hut, and the good Papa took a few coins he couldn't afford from his cookie jar so he could treat his little girls to a night at the fair.

Ah! Charlie can picture himself in silhouette, standing in their doorway with an axe, beholding them all sweetly in their sleep—

Ah! To hug until the beloved in your arms stops breathing. To tenderly cuddle and then cut the throat, to hear the sweet burble of blood in the slit larynx—

But he has renounced such pleasures for the time being, he has other concerns to occupy him, and so he watches them go, watches as they giggle and prance with love for their big smiling bingaloo of a daddy. No doubt poverty and privation will wipe the jolly off Papa's face soon enough.

Then along comes a lad, no older than ten years Charlie reckons, strolling under the light of the full moon and carrying a cloth doll with red yarn for hair and buttons for eyes.

"Howdy there, young feller," Uncle Charlie calls. "What'dya got? Did you win yerself a dolly at the carnival?"

The boy has a pale and girlish face—a son of a dressmaker or a schoolmistress, Charlie figgers—and he seems startled by the appearance of a big, bearded stranger in a long, black fur cape, but he nevertheless stops and nods politely.

"For my sister," the child pipes, and Charlie booms out a hearty laugh.

"Fer yer sissy, eh?" he says in a delighted voice. "Why, what a good brother you are! I'll wager she'll shower you with kisses when you get home, won't she?"

The tyke can't seem to muster an answer to this question.

"So do you live nearby?" Charlie tries again, and the boy nods.

"A few miles down the road," reveals the child innocently, and Charlie makes a note.

"Well, don't that beat the devil!" Uncle Charlie says. "Why, that there carnival is purt'near in your back pasture, ain't it?"

"Yes, sir," the child agrees.

"Did you see that elephant they got?"

"Yes!" the boy says. "And a gorilla that combed a fuzzy man's hair!"

"Bejabbers!" Charlie says. "That must've been a sight! What else?"

"A girl with three legs walked across a tightrope!"

"Three legs!" Charlie says, and his palms grow clammy at the hideous image. "That'd likely make me yurp to behold it!"

"I thought she was purty!" the boy says. "They dressed her up real dandy in sparkly stockings, and wings like a butterfly!"

"Hum," Charlie grunts darkly. "Well, stockings or no, I'd stay away from that kind. They can give you diseases."

The lad takes this in, wrinkling his little forehead with confusion. Then he seems to reach a decision.

"I have to go home now," the child declares, and without another word abruptly turns and trots off down the road, the yarn-haired dolly held by one arm and flopping like a corpse.

Hum.

Hum.

The tyke trots along smaller into the distance.

And now down yonder the lights are out, and he crouches down and tipsie-toes through the brush along the riverbank toward the fairgrounds. The closer he gets, the harder he has to screw his courage to its sticking place. *Three-legged woman*, he thinks, and he imagines her creeping barefooted toward him in the dark, softly padding on her three feet, her toes long and cragged and sharp-nailed, and he almost loses his nerve, picturing that thing out there in the shadows, hidden in the cattails and weeds and scrub branches.

But he comes up from the riverbank alive and finds himself at the rear of a tent, and he huddles at a corner where the canvas is roped to a wooden stake, then scuttles into the pool of shadows behind a stack of crates.

Slowly he sticks his head up and peers around, and Holy Joseph there's that elephant! It's caged, thank God, but nevertheless fearsome. He'd once seen a moving picture about a elephant who had taken a man in its trunk and slapped him like a rag onto the ground until every bone in his body was broke and he was naught but jelly! And they had electrocuted that elephant for its crimes, Charlie had watched the execution happen, projected upon a screen! But still, he would not want to face a elephant in combat.

And now he spies a dandy maestro in jodhpurs and a top hat—it's the Ringmaster, no doubt—walking along with a lad who looks like he was dipped in glue and then rolled through a mound of pubic hair.

"Just be sure you're including him and making him feel welcome and well loved," the Ringmaster says.

They stroll off, and then comes along a man-shaped creature with a head much too small for its body, and it hurries along with a swift and hunching gait, muttering irritably to itself, not speaking in words but more like the soft gnashing sound of a grasshopper, and Charlie huddles down behind the barrel and covers his head with his hands. Oh, God! He puts his hand over his mouth and prays not to breathe.

Then, finally, slowly, he lifts up again.

And lo! He spots the girl Nellie, his darling niece.

She's guarded by a bronze-skinned, be-tattooed devil, nekkid but for a pair of boxer's panties, pr'y a reform cannibal from one of those Pacific Isles. The gollywog could behaps be taken from behind, his throat slit with a razor, and then grab the girl and run!

Problem being, she likely won't come of her own free will. Look at her! Chatting with the savage as if they're old pals, as if she hadn't run off and left her poor Uncle Charlie heartbroke and pining for affection.

If he tries to grab her, he knows that she'll squeal and kick and bite his palm as he covers her mouth. He can handle that well enough. Question is, how does he spirit her off without getting a stirred-up pack of monstrosities to come after him, shaking their torches and pitchforks and scythes as they chase him through the night, lynching on their minds? If they overtook him, who knows what mutilations he would suffer!

Still, he thinks, if he could get the girl, her brother would surely follow. He's not sure if vice versa is true. If he took Bolt first, he thinks, she might just leave him to Uncle's mercy, cold fish that she is.

He figures once he's got her, he'll need to decapastate her—laudanum seems like a good bet, but maybe he'll need to go so far as to cripple her so she can only hobble.

But that won't matter. It won't make no difference if she's lame and can't walk right because Uncle Charlie will take good care of her, if necessary he will tie her to a chair and spoon-feed her applesauce until she learns to trust again, and over time she'll be grateful to him for rescuing her, and that gratitude will blossom into love, and she'll think of him as a father, though they will never forget Jasper's honored memory!

"Ahem," says someone behind him. "May I help you? Are you lost?"

The voice is that of a high-classed British gentleman, but when Charlie whirls, startled, he sees the silhouette of a giant, eight feet tall or more, with a crooked horn poking up out of its skell, leaning over, peering down upon him, and Charlie cannot help but let out a shriek of terror.

Oh God! He runs!

What else can he do but flee as fast as his legs will pump, running blindly through the creek gully, slapped in the face by cattails, stumbling through mud, his madly scrambling hands obscuring his vision and finally falling face-down on a pebbly shoal, breathing hard, until at last he feels safe and lifts his head.

Well!

They may have won this round, but Chuck Lumpkin will not be so easily defeated! He will lie here for a while longer, but in not long brave Charlie Lambkin will rise from the dirt and set about planning how to save his babies!

THE DRUG TERROR

WITH PRACTICALLY UNRESTRICTED TRAFFIC

Cocaine Vice Has Grown So Swiftly That

We Are Most Drugged Nation in World!

4.45 Per Cent of Population Addicted to Habit

Campaign Undertaken by Mrs. William K. Vanderbilt, Sr.

For Extermination of Practice.

One of the Greatest Moral Struggles in History—

Cocaine and Heroin Deadliest of Habit-Forming Drugs.

Bolt has read newspaper articles about the dope fiends. He has heard that if you only accidentally sniff one puff of opium you might become addicted! He once heard a story about a Mexican bandito who became so spifflicated by marihuana that he boiled and ate his own infant son, believing, in his delirium, that the babe was a stewing chicken.

And yet here he is—he and Elmer and Alberic, with Gladness and Shyla in their train car, on their way to Vermillion, South Dakota, and he watches as they smoke marihuana from a corncob pipe, and he is terrified and enthralled in equal measure. He takes the pipe when Shyla passes it to him and puts it to his lips but doesn't inhale. Then he passes it on to Elmer, who is reclining back on the bed beside Bolt, shirtless and shoeless, black-lipsticked, grinning.

"Thanks, Bucko!" Elmer says, and draws long and heavy on the pipe like he plans to huff and puff and blow the house down.

What would Eleanor think if she knew he was in this drug den? He likes to think that she would be scandalized. He imagines her disdainful disapproval, and he tells himself he would not bend before her scolding. *I am my own man now and I'll do as I please!* He would tell this right to her face.

But is she even thinking of him? Is she wondering where he is? He lifts his head and feels around for her, but whatever lighthouse beam she sends out is weak, distant. He guesses that she's probably in the train car where Mr. Jengling keeps all his treasures—*cataloging* them, whatever that means.

It's been a week now since they moved her out of the bunk in Tickley-Feather's cabin. The morning after that séance with Rosalie, Mme. Clothilde sat him down and gave him a long, reproachful look—though only the night before, she'd said he was special.

"You and your sister, you are not little children to share a bed," Mme. Clothilde told Bolt. They sat at her little table in her tent, and she slowly turned over cards from her miniature tarot deck. "We allowed it in the beginning because we thought you needed the comfort of the closeness, since you were in new and frightening surroundings."

She showed him a card: **The Devil**—a goat-horned demon on a throne, with a naked man and a naked woman chained to either side of him. "You see?" said Mme. Clothilde, and she beamed her large eyes upon him, swirling with ineffable thoughts. "Harland and I agree that this is not appropriate at your age, a young lady needs her privacy."

Bolt felt the hated blush heating his face, prickling his cheeks, and when he got back to the bunk that night she had already moved, along with all the possessions he'd thought belonged to both of them—that diary, of course, but also the photo of Father and the locket with the little centipede-size braid of mother's hair in it—but he guessed that Eleanor believed these things to be hers alone.

They hadn't really spoken since.

The train car smells like girl and some kind of flowery incense, and there is a clothesline with ladies' stockings and underwear that blocks his view of the South Dakota badland plains chugging past outside the window, and in the corner is a black sewing machine with SINGER in gold letters, and over it are draped bejeweled garters and sequined belts and brassieres.

Gladness and Shyla sit on the bed across from Bolt and Elmer, with Alberic between them, and Gladness is playing with her snake—a white and pink albino python, five feet long—which winds up around her arm like a twisting vine and rears up, weaving his head as she weaves hers, his eyes following her eyes, his thin, clever tongue flicking toward her lips as she puckers up and makes soft kissing sounds at him; and Shyla is practicing her shadow puppet hands, crooking and twining her fingers into conflabberating shapes; and Alberic is teasing her, bending his fingers so he touches the back of his own wrist, imitating her moody, dignified expression of concentration until she notices and gives him a playful slap alongside his head.

Bolt reaches out gingerly to touch their minds. Ever since he was caught snooping by the hurdy-gurdy man at the Ferris wheel, he has been cautious, he doesn't try to probe too deep. He's aware of the pleasant, circling high Shyla and Gladness are feeling from the marihuana, but when he glances over at Alberic he looks up sharply and catches Bolt staring.

"How're you doing, Banjo-Eyes?" Alberic says, and snaps his fingers like he's breaking Bolt out of a trance. He has one iris that is ice blue, the other is red like a white rabbit's. "Are you feeling comfortable?"

"Uhh?" Bolt says, and nods and sits up straighter, trying to look like he's at ease, even as Elmer breathes out a plume of skunky smoke that almost makes him gag. "Yeah! I was just watching what you all was doing with your hands! That was inneresting!"

"I think the poor boy is afraid of my snake," says Gladness. "Bolt, dear, do you want me to put him away?"

"No, no," says Bolt. "Not at all! I think he's ziggety!" But a blush is burning his ears and cheeks, even as he tries to smile. He hopes that she doesn't bring the serpent any nearer.

"Here, Gladness," Elmer says, and reaches out. "Give me that thing. Let me snuggle with him." And Bolt winces as the snake is passed over into Elmer's arms, and drapes it around his hairy neck like a scarf. Bolt tries not to act nervous, just leans away a little, and the snake seems to pay him no mind.

But now the girls are looking at him, and Alberic, too, and maybe their attention is more discomfiting than that of a snake, so full are they of inexplicable and secret knowledge.

"So—" Alberic says. "Banjo," he says, and Bolt guesses that his name is now Banjo. "You're watching after the Rosalie, right?"

Bolt shrugs. There's a part of him that feels protective of her, a part of him that knows he shouldn't speak of it. "Yeah?" he says.

"She's gaffed, isn't she?" Alberic says. "That thing on her head ain't real, is it?"

"Well," Bolt says. "I don't know for sure. But it seems real to me."

Shyla slaps Alberic's forehead with her long-fingered hand. "Don't be rude," she says. And she shrugs apologetically. "It would be stupid," she says. "If she's gaffed, then why wouldn't they display her? Why would they keep her so secluded?"

"Um," Bolt says.

"But does she talk to you? Does she tell you things?" Shyla says.

"Well," Bolt says, sheepishly. "Sometimes. But it doesn't usually make much sense. Just—like—babbles. She ain't completely right in the head."

Alberic thinks this is funny and snorts, but Shyla nods seriously.

"Then it's good that they don't display her to the public," she says. "To be exhibited without consent, without awareness, that is so sad. These sideshows that offer up gimp babies in jars! Corpses! It's so disrespectful!"

"Aw, phooey," Elmer says. "They're dead, what do they care?" He sits up, cross-legged, holding his pink-soled feet in his hands. "Besides," he says, "what's the big deal about being looked at? I don't know. Some of these crooked people think it's insulting, but I relish it! I like it when they stare! I like to give them a show, tickle their imaginations a little."

Elmer strokes the python's head with his finger. "I'm telling you," he says. "That hootchy-cootchy I'm doing with Miss Alcott is bringing in lots of gapers. I think it's better than a bally act! It's good enough as people would pay tickets for it!"

"Ladies," he says, and gives Gladness and Shyla a saucy wink, "you should hear those bug-eater gals suck in breath when I take off my shirt. They're like to drop into a faint!"

Shyla laughs. "I can hardly keep from swooning myself," she says. She reaches over and puts her seven-fingered hand across Alberic's eyes. "Don't look! You will be overcome!"

"That's right," says Elmer and runs his index finger along the python's head as it tastes his neck with its tongue. "I mean to have a act with a banner, a big pitcher of me! ELMER JENGLING, HAIRIEST MAN ALIVE! PLEASING TO THE EYE, SOOTHING TO THE SMELL!"

"Oh yes, you Airedale!" says Shyla. "We'll collect the soothing odors of Elmer and sell it like ambergris!"

Bolt doesn't know what amber grease is, but he laughs anyhow. He wishes he could be as comfortable in his skin as Elmer is in his fur. He wishes that their minds would open fully to him, and he could be certain that they really do accept him.

One of us, he thinks, and he remembers all of them drinking from the goblet, the Loving Cup, and how they'd banged their spoons and forks on the table and chanted. *One of us! ONE OF US!*

Is he?

Well, he's more like part of the family than Eleanor is. She still says she's Eleanor Lambkin, but he's ready to be Bolt Jengling, if only she'd let him. She thinks that just because they are twins they have to follow a matching path, she thinks she will always be master and commander, the one who was born first, the smarter one, the stronger one—

"—the only one who can ever really know you for who you truly are," she'd told him. This was after they'd poisoned old Humberstone, after the burial service, and they were sitting in the backyard behind the boardinghouse in their black funeral clothes while the adults inside ate potluck food that had been laid out on a long table. Humberstone had not been very sociable, so there were fewer than a dozen mourners.

Eleanor squatted down and turned over a stone that sat under the lilac tree, alarming a salamander and a centipede and some roly-poly bugs. "It will always only be us, you know," she said. She poked the centipede with a twig, and it began racing around angrily on its many flowing legs. "Because we're murderers," she said. "No one else could ever love us if they knew how wicked we were."

Bolt was silent, watching as the centipede did battle with Eleanor's stick. Then he said, "Would they put us in jail, do you think?"

"Actually, I think they might hang us," Eleanor said. She didn't turn to look at him. "Or put us in a home for delinquent children. That'd be worst than death."

"But I ain't never going to tell nobody," Bolt said. "Even if I got married and had a wife, I wouldn't even tell her."

"Pff," said Eleanor, and gave the centipede a dismissive stab. "Yourn't ever going to get married! You don't even like girls in that way."

"Well," Bolt said. "I might someday. When I'm older."

She turned and gave Bolt a sharp poke with her twig, right in the thigh: ***No. You. Won't.*** And stabbed with each syllable for emphasis.

He feels the ghost of that poke even now as he sits with Elmer and Gladness and Shyla and Alberic, and he wonders what they would think of him if they knew he was a murderer. He leans back, trying not to blush, sucking his teeth.

"I don't care if they look at me, either," Alberic is saying, sitting cross-legged on Shyla's silk-draped bed. He crooks his knee and takes the corncob pipe from Gladness with his foot, clutching it between his toes and drawing it up to his lips. "But I'm not doing a show for them for free. I'm not twisting a pinkie for less than ten dollars a day!"

Gladness leans back and cocks one eyebrow at Alberic, bemused. As large as she is, there is nothing ungainly about her, nothing heavy nor awkward. Her movements are always precise and feathery smooth, as if she's planned out each gesture long before she executes it. People may come to gawp at her because she's fat, because once in another circus she was known as the Savage Half-Ton Head-Huntress of the Darkest African Jungles—but now that she is the Princess of Zanzibar, they stay to watch her dance with giant fans and feather boas and snakes because they are transfixed. They stay because she possesses a bearing that is as queenly as any of the gapers have ever witnessed, an unselfconscious majesty, not haughty but serene.

"Did I ever tell you," she says, and even her voice has a sloe-eyed elegance, an accent unplaceable but definitely not American. "I once heard of a gimp who worked for Monson and Monson. He said he was a no-arm, but he was only pretending, and in truth he kept his arms bound up at his sides with a girdle brace. But he was very gifted—he could shoot arrows from a bow with his feet and throw knives and even played the guitar with his toes. And then, sadly, it was discovered that he was a phony, that he had arms like an ordinary man. And I heard that the crooked ones in the circus 'took care of him,' as they say."

"Ha!" says Elmer. "What'd they do? Chop off his arms for him?"

"Oh, no, my sweet," says Gladness. "They cut off his toes. That was the source of his livelihood. His arms were of less than no use to him!"

They all burst out laughing, and Bolt joins them in their merriment though actually he's not quite sure what's funny about the story.

Maybe it's a joke about him?

Is he like the phony gimp—only pretending to belong?

Bolt tries to scope their minds and he can't sense any malice, but that doesn't necessarily mean anything. He's never been good at reading the minds of people that he wants to be friends with. The only telepathies that ever come through to him with perfect clarity are from people he doesn't care about, random strangers. He can always most distinctly hear the thoughts that he wishes not to know.

He can also hear Eleanor, of course. He has a sense of where she is, he can feel a compass point for her and a basic idea of her mood, sometimes fragments of her thoughts or what she's reading will flutter through him.

But even if she were gone, even if she were dead, she would still exist whole as a voice in his brain. He supposes that this is true for most everyone—if you have a lost loved one, they continue to speak to you in the back of your mind, their voice is so clear and distinct and surprisingly independent. Though he's spent years as a member of the Spiritualist Church, holding séances and asking for help from the astral plane, this is the most supernatural experience he can think of: that a portion of yourself somehow exists, separate from you, inside another person.

Eleanor occupies a full suite of rooms in his head, he reckons, there's almost a full-blown homunculus of her up there. She's noisiest when she's criticizing him, but she has kind words for him, too, she'll comfort him when he's scared or puzzled, or tell him a joke that makes him laugh aloud.

Meanwhile, the smoke in Shyla and Gladness's train car is hanging low and thick as marsh fog, and he doesn't need to be psychic to see that they are all dreamy and relaxed. Cozy.

Alberic leans back on his elbows. "I have some magical mushrooms, if anyone is interested," he says. "'Teonanacatl,' it's called—from down in Oaxaca, in Mexico. I got them from this hunchback dwarf I met in Omaha, who works for Buffalo Bill Cody's circus. He's got cousins down there. I'm telling you, you never felt nothing like it! It's like being awake and dreaming at the same time!"

Magical mushrooms!

Bolt is enchanted by this idea.

Though they don't look very nice. He thought they'd be more colorful, with sparkles or polka dots, or even see-through, like glass. Instead, they are brown as wood bark, wrinkled and ugly as the toe of a mummified monkey.

You'll get sick from it, says Eleanor, from her roost in his head. *It'll pr'y make you go insane. You'll make a fool of yourself. You'll pr'y strip off all your clothes and run around naked and all the girls will see your ding-dong and laugh!*

He pops it in his mouth and swallows it.

But nothing happens.

He doesn't feel any different, and everybody just keeps on chatting.

They wonder how Mr. Jengling became rich, and there is some discussion of whether there are precious gems amongst his collection, or pirate's doubloons, and Shyla says that she heard he owns a garment factory in Massachusetts.

"Aw," Elmer says. "He don't own no garment factory!"

Alberic does his imitation of Mr. Jengling, lowering his voice and gritting his teeth into a falsely earnest smile. "*Allow me to support your talents*," he says, and it is a pretty good mimicry, but then Gladness takes a turn.

"*My dear, I want you to see yourself as you truly are*," she says, and her Jengling voice is so exact that everyone goggles, astonished, and then bursts out laughing.

And Bolt also laughs but he's actually finding himself more interested in the brass box that sits on Shyla's dressing table.

A *Paar Daan*, Shyla calls it—an heirloom, she says, from her grandmother. It has an ornate hoop-and-staple lock, but it is propped open now, revealing six little compartments with seeds and spices in them. It makes him think of a music box.

Is music coming from it?

The box is decorated with engraved shapes—vines with three-leafed buds, and pointy quarter moons on their side like a smile or a frown, zigzags like waves of water.

The waves seem to be moving—a gentle, almost imperceptible flowing like thread unwinding from a spindle, and he can almost certainly hear a kind of tinkling music, but too small and distant to make out a tune. He watches attentively and the engraved vines seem to breathe and rustle.

"I think I'm a-feelin it," Bolt murmurs, and he lifts his head to look at the others, his eyes widening with wonder. "I'm a-feeling them magical mushrooms!" he exclaims, and they all laugh.

And their laughter isn't cruel, it isn't making fun of him or scornful, but warm and affectionate. *Oh, Bolt!* it seems to say. *Our Bolt! We accept you, sweet boy!*

And there is a shimmering tingle across his skin that feels real nice, and emanating from his friends is only welcome such as he's never before felt, from anyone—had Eleanor ever felt as joyful to have him present and alive as Alberic and Gladness, Shyla and Elmer do now?

Ah! He leans back and the figures of the *Paar Daan* animate and swim like sea creatures behind his closed eyelids. Ahh! Ahh!

"Balooey!" Elmer says, and Bolt glances over surreptitiously as Elmer leans back on his elbows and tilts his head back. "This stuff tingles real nice, don't it?" He laughs sleepily, and Bolt observes as he runs his fingers down the front of his bare chest, slowly combing through the thick mane of hair, and it seems like Elmer's fingertips move slower than is possible, and the hair seems to make a rustling sound like wind through the reeds, and there's that music again, like a soft glissando on the far east end of a piano keyboard—

"Hey, Bloke," says Elmer, and Bolt looks up startled and Elmer's teeth are so white and glinting and smiling. "Hey, Chum, do you wanna pet me?" he says, gently. "It's okay if you do. I don't mind."

Elmer opens his arms wide, puffing out his chest, and Bolt hesitantly reaches out and lets his fingers graze along the soft, tickling tips of the hair. He sees a pale pink nipple, erect in the center of a reddish-brown aureole and his breath hitches as he brushes it with his pinkie, as he lets his hand run down toward Elmer's belly button, which is a tight and perfect swirly shape, a spiral you could follow down and down.

And then Gladness is sitting next to him, and she puts her soft, lotioned hand across the back of his, her palm on his knuckles, and their hands seem to move together unbidden, the way a planchette moves across a Ouija board, circling around and around the circumference of Elmer's belly. Yes, it is a nice tingling. He can feel Gladness's soft breath on his neck.

Alberic is sitting on the other side now, and his alabaster-white, red-freckled hand runs along parallel to Bolt's and Gladness's, and then Shyla's seven-fingered hand joins his, and all of them are skating their fingers up and down Elmer's torso, you can feel his belly softly pulsing with breath, his ribs expanding, his eyes blissfully closed and his lips parted, his fur as silky as sable—

Bolt thinks this must be what love feels like.

Seven Cosmic Planes, Seven Principles and Bodies

•••••••••

Shyla brushes the hand of the boy, Bolt, and abruptly she feels the Eye of Rosalie fall upon her. It's like swoon, a faint, a deathly nausea that winds up her torso, it reaches her chest and neck and she can't breathe.

She knows suddenly that Alberic will die aged sixty-nine. He will be on his back on a floor and looming into his vision is the face of a blue-eyed orange tabby cat leaning over with an expression of thoughtful but unsympathetic curiosity, the vibration of a purr.

She knows that Elmer will be killed in the year 1973 and all his hair will have fallen out and she can see clearly his naked body, pale, wrinkled, crepey, floating in a river And she knows that as for she herself—her life is three-quarters over.

What does that mean? If she is seventeen, then . . . what?

Six more years?

Shyla flinches away before more can be foretold and transmitted to her, and she gasps when Bolt widens his eyes at her, startled, shy, dopey—

"Get away from me!" she cries, recoiling, and she feels the weight of her own death on her: *Oh! She will die, she will die before she is twenty-four!*

And they all turn toward her with sleepy surprise and slow concern, their faces growing transparent and splitting into two, wavering like they are reflected in a droplet of water and Alberic puts his arm around her. "Here, girl," he says. "Here, don't fear! You're safe!" and Elmer sits up on his elbows, smiling gently, and oh God! These two stupid boys will outlive her! How is it possible that they will exist long after she is gone?

It's the unfairness of it that wounds her most. Why should *they* get more? They won't even do anything with it!

Shhhh! says Alberic. "No no no, sweet one, no no no, it's just the magical mushroom playing a trick on you, it's nothing, it's nothing, close your eyes, take a big breath—"

From early on, Shyla had heard whispers about Rosalie's ability to foretell your death, but it was Billy Bigelow who first spelled it out for her.

He was following along behind her, barefoot and naked except for his boxer's trunks and not particularly welcomed, though she was too polite to ask him to leave her alone, and then they went past the pink-and-blue-striped tent outside of which Tickley-Feather stood guard.

"Hey! Girlie!" said Billy, and touched her arm, most unwelcome, but she turned. "Hey, you see that tent?"

She nodded. "Yes. I see it." And he tilted his head, showing his sharkened teeth.

"That where they keep the Rosalie," he whispered, confidentially. "She's a geek with a second head growing out the back of her skull—but if you look into her eyes, she'll tell you when and how you'll die. No kidding. It's not a gaff."

"Tsk," Shyla said, coolly. "How unpleasant."

Billy let out a soft chuckle, as if *she* was flirting with *him*. "Yeah," he said. He put his hands on his hips and slipped his fingers below the waistband of his boxer's trunks, unselfconsciously massaging his buttocks. "Yeah. If you knew—if you truly knew—it would ruin everything, wouldn't it?"

He cocks his hips in a vulgar way, and later she will speak to Mme.

Clothilde about Billy Bigelow, and Mme. Clothilde will tell her that she will have Tickley-Feather talk to him, and afterward Billy never spoke to her again, he averted his eyes whenever they crossed paths.

Billy had first heard stories about Rosalie from Minnie Wilks, the three-legged woman whom he had been sleeping with for a time, and one night they were in bed under the sweet patchwork quilt she had made for him, sewed her own self, and she was leaning her head against him, dreamy the way girls get afterward, wanting to canoodle.

She told him that Mme. Clothilde had asked her to come in and possibly tutor Rosalie—reading aloud from appropriate novels, offering lessons in basic conversational English.

Good morning! How are you?

I am well! And you?

And it all seemed to be going along fine until Rosalie suddenly jerked her head up and stared into Minnie's eyes.

"You want to have a baby," Rosalie said softly, singsong. "But you will die in childbirth. July of the eleventh, 1919. The little one will also die. It will never take a breath."

And then Rosalie gave her a shy smile, bashful, as if she were a grade school child offering her teacher a crude, handmade gift.

"**A**w, boosh!" murmured Billy. "It's just baby-babble. It doesn't mean anything." He stroked a finger along the edge of her hairline, tracing around the circumference of her ear, and Minnie shrugged away.

"Billy," she said. "She barely had a vocabulary of a hundred words, and then suddenly she spoke to me as if she were an adult."

"Pff," said Billy. "My birdie can parrot a lot of words. That doesn't mean she understands most of them."

He snuffled his face against her neck, sleepily, houndishly. "Maybe she was just trying to do you a favor, eh? Now you know not to get pregnant, and you'll live longer, right?"

"Oh my stars!" said Viola the Half-Woman, when Minnie recounted the conversation. "He said that to you? What a cad!"

Minnie only looked down at the quilt they were making together—a patchwork in a log house pattern, and she was cutting rectangles of cloth from an old periwinkle blouse.

"Well," she said, her eyes on her work. "If I wanted good manners, I wouldn't have Billy as a beau, would I?" Her scissors snipped, her hands precise in their concentration. "And I think he's right. I've been rescued, in a way, because now I can avoid one death, at least. No doubt the old shroud will catch me eventually."

Minnie laughed softly in that practical, ironic, introspective way she had. She ran her hand along Viola's forearm—as if *Viola* were the one who needed comforting.

People always said that they seemed like sisters, Minnie and Viola, and that could have come across as a cruel joke—one sister with three legs, one sister with none—

—which was not precisely true, anyway. Viola, born with hypoplasia of the sacrum, had tiny appendages like featherless bird wings where her legs and feet might have been.

Nevertheless, they did feel like sisters. They were both young women in their early twenties who had been born into relatively middle-class homes—Minnie's father was a grocer from St. Louis, while Viola's was a tailor in Quincy, Massachusetts—and as children, they had both dreamed of having unextraordinary lives: to be schoolteachers, or librarians, or marrying and having a husband and children. Even now, as circus performers, they find themselves attracted to homely, mundane hobbies—quilting and keeping little window gardens of herbs, reading novels and discussing them as if the characters in them were real.

Viola walked along on her hands and her tread was delicate, it was an almost panther-ish, stalking gait. She wore sturdy leather driving gauntlets and a frill-vested gray shirtwaist blouse with a black string bow and a high-necked collar. A skirt would be unnecessary, obviously, though sometimes she wondered if she would seem more human if she were dragging along a bottom half, a limp dress and a pair of shoes.

Sometimes she felt ethereal with rage at the world, this out-of-the-body tingling fury would build inside her for a while but then it always dissipated before she exploded, settling into a leaden load she was pulling along behind her.

There was something particularly cruel, she thought, about predicting that Minnie would die in childbirth. Of course, both she and Minnie were well aware that the chances were slim that girls in "their condition" could bear offspring.

Was it grotesque to hope that their bodies had functioning wombs?

Was it so very hideous to imagine them as loving mothers, raising families, living a life like anyone else might?

She walked into an empty tent where there was some gymnastic equipment set up for them—a balance beam and a pommel horse—and she crouched and launched herself, sprang up and grasped the gymnast's rings in her strong, heavy hands.

She had to practice.

She gave her torso a spin. Her arms were so strong, her shoulders were so broad and unladylike.

If only she had dreamed of being a ballerina, she might've enjoyed this.

When Herculea the Muscle Lady came in, Viola continued to practice but watched surreptitiously as Herculea flexed and squatted and stretched, grunting like a bear. She was an aloof sort of person, at least toward Viola—she seemed to prefer the friendship of men—and Herculea kept her eyes low, staring at her bare feet, pawing the sawdust. It wasn't clear if she was unaware of Viola's presence, or if she was simply ignoring her.

"Ahem," said Viola at last, dangling from the gymnastic rings, and Herculea lifted her head and shook her hair out of her eyes, droplets of sweat scattering.

"Huh?" Herculea said. "You need some help getting down?"

Viola felt like a piece of meat hanging on a hook, but she smiled politely and let herself drop onto the mat beneath her, falling onto the palms of her hands and steadying herself quickly.

"No thank you," she said. "I was just . . . wondering if I could ask you a question."

The Muscle Lady tensed, straightened, and squared herself, her arms loose at her sides and at the ready, like a gunfighter. "Yeah?" she grunted, but kept her eyes lowered. She was wearing a black-and-white-striped sleeveless singlet, and the glistening skin on her thickly muscled biceps twitched, the way a horse's hide does when a fly bites it.

"Do you know anything about that girl Rosalie? The one in the séance tent? I was wondering why she never eats with the rest of us, or . . . mingles. You've been here longer than I, so I thought . . ."

"Umm," Herculea said. Her eyes still downcast, she scratched her armpit thoughtfully. "I dunno? It can't talk." Herculea tapped her eyes. "It can't see," she said, and tugged her earlobes. "It can't hear." She zipped her thumb along her mouth. "There's prolly not much there. It's like . . . a animal."

Herculea was bashful around girls, and even half of a girl made her blush. For her whole adult life, something about women had eluded her—something they knew, something they expected that she'd know as well. What could it be? She wasn't sure. A type of understanding or a feeling of connection, of shared experience—a female "we" that she had difficulty fathoming.

She had spoken once to Dr. Chui about it. He'd had a similar transformation—"a metamorphosis," he called it. "Some of us are born with our conditions, and some develop them, you see, and it is a very different experience. As children, we had a taste of what it's like to be one of them, but our knowledge is incomplete."

In any case, somehow, during the process of her "metamorphosis," she'd missed out on some essential bit of femininity that other women seemed to carry with them naturally. A shape. A scent. A world invisible to her. She walked gloomily toward the mess hall after her conversation with Viola. *Couldn't you have at least looked her in the eye,* she chastised herself. *She must think you are very rude and stupid.*

She should have told the girl that what Rosalie tells you doesn't matter. You're going to die over and over for the rest of your life, that's what she wanted to explain. Little Mona Finkel and her crazy Totty both disappeared from this earth a long time ago; so, too, did the teenager Momo the Toad; and Lotta Mussels, the name she was given for her first vaudeville gig.

But this was hard to put into words that would make sense: the body that will eventually cease to function at some time in the future isn't your body. It will belong to someone else, some future you, an unknowable person who doesn't even care about you.

Still, it was true that the Rosalie might be dangerous—if what Mr. Lacis told her was to be believed.

She recalled a night when she and Mr. Lacis and Thistle-Britches were playing three-handed pinochle and Mr. Lacis abruptly reached over and patted Herculea's cheek, affectionately. "Ah, you're so young!" he said. "I worry about you. You're like me: always surprised by the inhumanity of mankind, though it shows itself over and over again." His eyes were red and watery with liquor. He drank all day long, she guessed, and by this time of night he could get squint-eyed and sentimental—not sloppy, but noticeably intoxicated. She watched as he swallowed another draught of brandy, as he ashed his cigar into a tea saucer and his expression grew contemplative.

"I have been here, with Jengling, almost ten years now," he said. "Ten years! And mostly I am happy, though I don't always like everything I see." He examined his wide, blunt hand, rubbed the pitted scar in the center of his palm, where he could insert a nail or an ice pick or a pocketknife all the way through without much apparent discomfort. "Hmph," he said, circling the spot softly with his index finger. "Do you know of the girl Rosalie that they keep in the séance tent?"

Herculea shrugged. "I know who she is," she said. "I've seen her a few times, but it seemed like she was witless."

"Maybe so," Mr. Lacis said. "Maybe so. But people come for private . . . viewings . . . of her, so she must have some use, I imagine. But it's strange, isn't it, how they keep her hidden?"

He drew on his cigar thoughtfully. "Do you know, I was here when she was brought in," he says. "She was, I would think, perhaps seven years old."

She came to the Emporium maybe six years ago, Lacis said. The one who brought her in was a dirty scarecrow of a man, long thin arms and legs, hollow-eyed, mustachioed, his hair swept back and oiled down. He wore a threadbare checked coat and a bow tie, as if he was trying to look respectable, but to Mr. Lacis he looked sickly—*diseased*—though it was difficult to say what, exactly, gave that impression.

This man came in carrying the girl in the crook of his arm as if she were a ventriloquist's dummy. He sat at a table in the mess tent across from Jengling, with the child limp in his lap. Mr. Lacis brought him a glass of water, and Mr. Jengling a glass of vodka.

"I've been her handler for quite a number of years," the man was saying. "But I'm ready to part with her for the right price. Let me show you how she works, and I'm sure we can come to a mutually—an understanding. I've heard that you have a keen interest in this sort of . . ." The man let out a ragged, involuntary cough, and spit into a napkin.

Later, when Mr. Lacis was clearing the table, he saw that the napkin contained what looked like a glob of vomit, coal black and flecked with blood.

"**S**o this seedy man in the checked coat, he went into the tent with Master Jengling and Mme. Clothilde, carrying his little girl, and I never saw him come out." Mr. Lacis gave Herculea a wily smile, his head wobbling with controlled drunkenness.

"And then!" Mr. Lacis raised his index finger like an exclamation point. "Then, two week, three week later, there is suddenly appears the one they call the Piltdown Man, the crazy one raging in a cage, and Mr. Jengling tells us that he is a newly adopted, that he was the last of his kind, captured on some island off the coast of Alaska, naked and not fully human, *more a part of the Animal menagerie,* Master Jengling says—

"But I recognize him, yes? I swear he is the same man in the checked coat who brought in Rosalie, only now he has long hair and beard and babbling and eating raw meat. And when I question this to Master Jengling he says no, I am mistaken."

He reached across the table and gave the back of Herculea's hand three short, sharp slaps. "But! I am not mistaken! It is same man!"

Herculea withdrew uncertainly. "What do you mean? You think—Father Jengling did something to him?"

"No, no," Mr. Lacis said. "I think it was the Rosalie. Her handler wants to get rid of her, but it was too late. She got rid of him! She made his mind go mad, that is what I believe."

The man had the improbable name of McGullian Heap, and Mme. Clothilde found him intensely distasteful the moment that Harland brought him into her tent.

She did not like the way Heap smirked at her, showing small, dirty teeth, appraising her as if she were a piece of merchandise, another oddity he might put on display, wondering what profit a tiny lady midget might bring in, with the right banner line and bally platform.

She did not like the way he held the child under his care, slung in his arms like a gunnysack, one pale limp hand dangling. She did not like his complexion, which was like a plucked chicken, dotted with small acne sores, nor his unevenly shaved face, nor his deep-set, sickly eyes, which showed only the basest of the seven principles: *kama rupa*—animal appetite, greed, low cunning—but no sign of the spiritual, no access to *ātma* or the sublime beyond ego. "*Bon soir*, madame," he said, inclining his head, smirking as if it amused him to address a person of her small stature politely.

"*S'il vous plaît, asseyez-vous*," she said coolly, and gestured toward the child-size stool across from her. His impertinence wavered, and he glanced toward Harland, as if this might be a joke, but Harland merely gestured at the seat, and Heap lowered himself into it, slinging the child against his shoulder, her head flopping at an angle like a discarded doll.

Harland bent down and stared avidly at the unconscious child's head. "Come, darling," he said. "I want you to take a close look at this. I think it's quite remarkable."

At first, when Clothilde approached, it looked as if there was a wound at the top of the girl's skull, a tumor with an eerie sheen like a raw oyster. And then, drawing closer, she saw that the protrusion was a sort of face, an infant-size head, fused, half-submerged in the larger head of its host. Its bulbous, almost amphibious eyes were closed but they scoped slowly under the thin, pink-veined eyelids; its nostrils flared as if it tried to take in breath; its lips moved as if it dreamed of suckling. She reached out and lightly stroked its cheek, which was as uncannily soft and tractable as a newborn's. "*Pauvrette*," she whispered.

This growth was not quite a human person, she didn't think, surely there was no soul in it, and yet perhaps a soul remnant lingered in the astral plane nearby, the unformed spirit of a person not born but not dead. She felt a pang of pity for the creature, and for this lost, insensate child it was melded to. She felt the sorrow of a childhood spent as a sideshow attraction, unloved, barely tended to. She smelt the fetor of old urine; the child's frock hadn't been washed properly in months.

But Harland was right: this was an extraordinary find.

"She's got sideshow potential," said the horrible Heap. "You know they'd pay money just to get a glimpse of that . . . growth." He looked down at his charge, considering, brushing his fingertips along her hair. "But I've never thought of her as a geek attraction, I don't like to have to display her to the public, you know."

He squinted an eye at Clothilde. "Her real value," he said. "From the perspective of a medium or spiritualist, she is an utterly exquisite Guiding Star. She can channel from any of the seven planes; she can draw spirits from eons past. I believe this is because she has two brains, one male, one female, and only one body."

He had the cloying voice of a concessionaire, and she didn't really listen as he parroted vague Theosophist dogma—a simpleton's version of the writings of Blavatsky, Colonel Olcott, Leadbeater. It was clear enough that this child was a powerful conduit.

Heap shifted on his stool and turned the poor child around so that she was facing forward, her head lolling as if her neck were broken. "Allow me to do a demonstration," he said.

It was shocking to Clothilde, how quickly he was able to achieve a trance—he slipped into a state of clairaudience so swiftly that for a moment she felt certain that he was a fraud, doing a lackluster, slapdash performance.

And then the child's head lifted with a jerk, she straightened in McGullian Heap's lap, and even as his posture grew limp, her eyes popped open. She had the plain, unremarkable face of a farmer's daughter, simple hazel eyes, a sleepy, pleasant smile. "Wither shall I wander?" she mused softly, as if reciting to herself. "Upstairs, downstairs, in my lady's chambers?" Meanwhile, McGullian Heap, his head thrown back, his mouth slack and leaking a trail of bubbling white spittle, mouthed along with her. They spoke as one: Heap's voice and the girl's voice, perfectly in unison as if they were singing together rather than mumbling words.

"I am the Princess Arsinoë," they said, their words twining together in a strange harmony of baritone and soprano, man and child, "daughter of the House of Ptolemy. What would you ask of me?"

Clothilde saw now why he could reach a trance state so quickly, and she saw, too, why he looked as if he were suffering from some wasting disease, some malaise that was corroding not just his body but also his mind and spirit. He *did* have a gift as a medium, after all, but he was wildly reckless—he had been casually opening a conduit and blindly offering himself as channel—perhaps not understanding the dangers, perhaps not truly believing in the powers he was conjuring, convincing himself that they were merely a ruse he'd invented.

She saw how he had, day after day, week after week, allowed himself to become the hapless tool of a variety of spirits such as this so-called Princess Arsinoë, spirits of whom he knew nothing but what they permitted him to know. How long, she wondered, had he been using these powers to perform amusing magic tricks, knowing nothing of the seven cosmic planes and their perils, benumbing his own astral spirit and allowing himself to become the passive instrument of any among numberless hosts—men that were, and those who will be men, but also unknown forces of Nature that lurk in the astral light, elementaries and elementals—what might be called "demons" or "fiends."

Perhaps McGullian Heap had finally begun to realize how heedless and foolhardy he had been and thought that he could rescue himself by selling off his poor little familiar. But it was too late. He was riddled with malevolent spirits, he was nearing the stage where he would become little more than a ragged, empty container that any host could enter and possess at will. She saw him stiffen, contort, cough up a dollop of blackish luminescent mucus as another passenger abruptly took his reins and rode astride him. The being that had saddled him rasped low in its throat.

"*Il y a quelqu'un ici qui aimerait te rencontrer, ma petite Adepte*," It—Heap—spat out in French, and at the same time the girl piped out in English, "I have someone here who would like to meet you, my little Adept."

Mme. Clothilde recoiled in alarm. "Harland," she said, but the two voices spoke quickly now, in English, in French, possibly in Thracian or Macedonian: *A spirit from before human consciousness*, they said, their voices wavering like a warped record on a phonograph, *a man before he knew himself to be man, without ancestor, first of his kind—Would you like to meet him*, mon petit morceau?"

"Harland!" Mme. Clothilde cried, for now Heap's eyes had rolled up in their sockets, and he gurgled and snarled out a string of gibberish, his mouth slavered with strings of drool like a rabid hound. She was on her feet and backing away swiftly, her hands protectively in front of her. "Harland! Put the cloche cloth over him!"

Heap sprang up with a raw, guttural bellow, tossing the child in his lap to the floor, knocking aside the table between them, and sending Clothilde's crystal meditation ball flying across the room where it smashed, and he leaped at her with his fingers contorted like hooks, his teeth gnashing and snapping before Harland struck him a blow to the head and felled him.

Heap would never recover. Not even a trace of his spirit lingered in the astral plane, as far as Clothilde could perceive, and whatever had taken possession of him during his final performance remained in permanent residence. Harland believed it to be the soul of a primitive hominid such as *Eoanthropus dawsoni* or *Pithecanthropus erectus*—an idea Clothilde privately found fanciful at best. It might be any number of entities, humanoid or not, and she hoped that Harland could eventually be convinced to trade the creature with another circus.

As for Rosalie herself, there was no way to know how or where or when Heap had acquired her, or whose offspring she had been originally. Harland and Clothilde would be her father and mother now, and she would be well and tenderly cared for.

Though it had proved more difficult than expected to find carers or minders or sitters for her. The first one had been Mrs. Euphemia Pettigrew, also known as The Lizard Lady due to her severe ichthyosis, and she had watched over Rosalie for two years until she developed brain cancer and died quite rapidly. Then it had been the fire-eater, Galina, but she had run off with a farmer's son and gotten married, and then it had been Ernesto, the elastic-skin boy, and they noticed that she seemed to do better with a male watcher but then he developed tuberculosis and had to be admitted to a sanatorium. By this time, it was becoming increasingly hard to find someone in the Jengling family who was willing to attend to her. There was a rumor, Tickley-Feather reported, that if you sat with her long enough she would eventually tell you when and how you would die.

Meanwhile Rosalie dreamed and dreamed, and most of the time she was barely aware of her caretakers, rarely awake in the material world for more than a few minutes a day—not unlike most of humankind. She drifted through lakes of soft wind in the astral plane, she felt the new mother wipe her face with a warm, silky cloth; she caught a glimpse of the manifestation of her half-born twin moving through dappled shade in what seemed to be a transparent garden, and then she saw, very clearly, the spoon that delivered rice pudding into her mouth but not the holder of the spoon.

Spirits came and inhabited her, and she became a different person for a time, and then another and another, and all the while her body was growing, muscle and bone and tissue raveling out cleverly in concert, steadily, without regret or uncertainty, and though time opened empty and vast on all sides it was not moving, and it had no central point, no compass. *Where is home?* one of her tenants asked, plaintively, and another wondered, *Is it too late?*

Ah. They asked such sad and pointless things: *Does no one remember me as I really was?* and *When will I be my true self?* and *What will become of me?* which was not the same question as *What will I become?*

The answer to that was always the same. *Dust*, she said, like a smart student raising her hand for the teacher.

She opens her eyes and a boy is sitting across from her.

Oh, she thinks, *this is a new one.*

It's so nice that he's giving her food! He's holding a spoon and putting delicious rice pudding into her mouth and she feels so grateful.

"The junction in the limbs is," she says. "Wrath of the clouds, I believe. Or not."

He gives her a sweet, puzzled look. "That's right," he says. "Uh-huh."

Bolt is his name. She remembers it—from somewhere. Something a spirit had told her once? Had they met in another life? A portent had been impressed upon her about him and she thought, *Oh, he's the one who doesn't die at the end, he never dies*, and tears of happiness come to the gutters of her eyes and she feels her mouth groggily move into a kind of smile.

"Say!" she whispers. "Don't I know you?"

And she wakes again and he's still with her! She isn't alone! He's across from her, kindhearted, homely-handsome, with uncombed, unruly auburn hair, and he's reading aloud from a book, his voice slow and awkward as he works his way through sentences, but not unpleasant. He reads to her of Tarzan, a boy raised by apes, and of how young Tarzan discovers a picture book in an abandoned cabin, and how the book is full of "odd little figures which appeared beneath and between the colored pictures," Bolt reads, "some strange kind of bug he thought they might be, for many of them had legs though nowhere could he find one with eyes and a mouth. Of course he had never before seen print, or ever had spoken with any living thing which had the remotest idea that such a thing as a written language existed."

Yes, she thinks. *Yes, that is exactly what it is like*, and she smiles and a sound comes from her throat.

"Ha ha," says Bolt, good-natured and friendly from across the table. She likes his big blunt-fingered hands, holding the book. "That's ziggety, ain't it?" He smiles. "I'm glad you like it! This is my favorite story!"

She moves her tongue and soundless drool comes out instead of words, and the boy reaches across and gently swabs her lip with a napkin. His fingers smell nice. She likes him so much.

It's so hard to stay in this world, she finds. The tug of the current of other planes is too strong, though she wishes she could catch hold of this boy and pull him down into the spinning astral air with her. Oh! To have a companion. A brother.

Eugenics & Phrenology, Chimaeras & Monsters

•••••••••

Eleanor uses a crowbar to open the crate, and the nails holding the lid closed crank in protest, but at last the wood gives way and she bends down and finds six jars packed tightly in straw. She is on one of the train cars that hold Mr. Jengling's treasures, a dark and windowless rectangular box lit only by the light of a kerosene lamp, and it must be about eight o'clock in the evening of Sunday, July 18, and they are traveling from Vermillion to Yankton, South Dakota—but in this space she can't tell if it's day or night outside, and even the sense of day, month, year seems somehow vaguer. The shadows of shelves and stacked trunks and suitcases and cabinets and boxes are on all sides, from floor to ceiling, all softly juddering as the train trundles along the track.

She lifts the first of the jars: here is another severed head, floating in brine.

There are so, so many of these heads that Jengling has accumulated. This one appears to be a toddler with a mouth as wide as a frog's, cleft all the way to the ears, and its expression is one of screaming, insane laughter, though its eyes are clouded with agony. The label on the jar says, AMNIOTIC BAND SYNDROME, and she writes this down in her notebook: "Head #73, Amniotic Band."

Then there is a kind of fetus, a malformed, ovoid lump of flesh that is mostly a head, she guesses, with fingers sprouting from the side of its face and toes growing out below its chin like a beard. She writes: "Finger-beard. Chimaera." Chimaera is what Mr. Jengling calls these unfortunates. "#105."

And in the next jar is a small doglike creature, but the hind legs have been fused together like a mermaid's tail, and the forepaws are tiny, gnarled hands tipped with black claws.

"Elmer," she writes, though she will probably erase it later.

Father Jengling does not like the term "collection." He feels that it implies a kind of frivolous hoarding—"which is *not*," he says, "why I am gathering these items." He sits at his desk cracking walnuts, and she sits in a plush wingback chair across from him. The floor vibrates as the train rushes along the tracks.

"I am preserving them," he says. "Protecting them from those in power who seek to extinguish all that is unique, all that is variant. Homogeneity is their religion, and they invent absurd scientific principles to support their views." He pinches the jaws of his nutcracker with a force that makes the shell splinter.

"Have you heard of these *supposed* sciences, Eleanor? Phrenology? Psychiatry? Have you heard of the Eugenics Records Office in Cold Spring Harbor?"

And when she shakes her head, he nods approvingly. "Good for you! You are wise to ignore them."

He picks up the notebook that has her catalog of his—what?—assemblage?—and frowns, flipping slowly through the pages. He makes a soft, thoughtful grunt.

"Eugenics," he says, "is actually a kind of Gnosticism. It is a belief, above all else, that some are more deserving of life than others. If you are rich, it is because you are a superior specimen of humanity—your very blood, your very heredity has elevated you above those who have less. If you see a beggar on the street, you know it is because he has weak genes, he is a pauper because he does not have your intelligence and acuity and serene sense of self-importance! How much harder you work, you think. How much more complexly you think than *them*. They, the lower orders."

He flips another page, scanning it with his iceberg-colored eyes, then looks up. "Is the Spirit of a man contained within a sperm and an egg? I think not! Can the Spirit be divined by scalp-kneading Phrenologists? Is it merely a slosh of chemicals stirred up in the brain? Once when I was in Portugal I saw the head of the fiend Diogo Alves, the Aqueduct Murderer, preserved in a jar of formaldehyde. He robbed and murdered more than seventy people and tossed their bodies over the edge of a bridge. And they think somehow an examination of the brain of this person will reveal the nature of evil? Nonsense! You and I know that the Spirit is much more than that, do we not, Eleanor?"

She nods in demure agreement, as Pollyanna would. In his eyes she senses some of her mother's bottomless sadness—but not the same despair. He is more focused, more attentive to the world outside his head. He's crazy, she guesses, but more interested in being alive than their mama ever was.

He lifts a fat, unlit cigar from a brass ashtray.

"I'm in favor of the opposite of eugenics," he says. "Take away the advantages of wealth and connection, the expensive educations, and give that to those whom they call freaks and undesirables. Then let us see how their good genes fare, eh?"

He starts to give her his Master of Ceremonies smile, then softens it, then lets it fade altogether. "Ah," he says, gives a little shrug—as if they are old friends, and she knows his foibles, and he knows hers. As if they like and trust each other.

"Must our forebears be our future?" he asks her, as if he is avidly interested in her opinion, and she looks thoughtfully down at her lap.

She feels him reach across the desk and touch her face. "Or—" he murmurs. "Can we be our own creations?"

Which is a lot to puzzle over.

But. But—

But she needs to keep her mind on her own goals, to stay focused and attuned.

1. To find out what Jengling wants with them, really, what his plan is.
2. To find out who her father was, what he wanted to tell her.
3. To escape.
4. To find the life that she was meant to live, her one and only true life. To know her forebearers *and* her future—it should not be so hard as this, it should not be so complicated.
5. Also, what to do about Bolt.

She hears a click and rattle behind her, and she turns just in time to see the handle of the boxcar door shift back and forth. The shadows flicker and stretch in the lantern light.

"Hello?" she says. She is bent over an open box of specimens—*miscellany*—and she is certain the door handle turns. *Click. Click.*

"Hello?" she says.

Silence.

Here is a specimen jar with a fetus that has no eyes or nose, only a mouth with a full set of little teeth. It doesn't have hands or forearms, nor calves, nor feet.

What of these things does Jengling want to preserve and protect? *Are we not all Spirits?* he asks, but these jarred remains ain't spirits, she knows that much.

The door handle moves again. There's a rattle and she sharply glances over and then the motion immediately grows still.

"*Is someone there?*" she says.

No reply.

And so Eleanor turns back to what looks like a withered, decaying hand floating in a jar. X-RAY TECHNICIAN, CATHODE EXPOSURE, it says, and she notes that the back of the hand is pocked with lesions and open sores, and the fingernails are sunken and ragged. She sets the jar down on the sideboard and the hand bobs slightly, translucent particles, maybe tiny pieces of skin, swirl around like a gust of snow.

She was never a scaredy person. When they were children, she was the one who took pleasure in telling horror stories, and she found that if she was able to get Bolt so affrighted that he couldn't sleep, a kind of peaceful feeling would settle over her. Ah! She rarely felt such a sense of warm comfort as when she'd truly terrorized Bolt.

Click. The door handle turns back and forth slowly, like a creature curiously tilting its head.

"*Who's there?*" she says sternly. "Bolt? Don't try to fool me! I know it's you."

She marches to the door, making her footsteps loud and cross enough that he will know she's thinking of clouting him upside the head.

But when she flings it open there's nothing there. It's twilight, after nine o'clock, she guesses, and the setting sun casts an eerie, golden glow across the stark badlands. Below the doorstep the wooden sleeper ties of the railroad track flicker past, blurred by the train's velocity. She hesitates.

Papá? she whispers.

The nice thing about Billy Bigelow is that he doesn't laugh at her when she comes to his train car and tells him about it—the slow twisting handle, the empty doorway, the train moving at highest speed down the tracks, *tickity-tackity*.

"Ay-yi," say Billy. "Gives me a shiver to think about. If it was me, I wouldn't open it, Garota. You're too brave for your own good."

He gestures for her to sit on his crumpled, unmade bed, and she does, primly. "Rest yourself," he says. "I'll get you a cup of cream to calm you."

He is not, of course, a very good housekeeper. There are two empty rum bottles on the nightstand, and some crumpled dollar bills and a scattering of nickels. The mynah bird has settled on a stack of dirty plates on his small dining table, and it releases a tiny, nonchalant droplet of shit before shaking its feathers and fluttering up to the curtain rod.

Billy sits down beside her on the edge of the bed—close, but respectful, and hands her a flowered porcelain teacup, and she takes it. She sips the cream, and it *is* soothing.

"It ain't bad to be wary in this place, girlie," he says. He brings his knees up to his chest, and his toes grip the edge of his bed frame. "I don't believe in *mate-klamar—fantasmas*—but I don't always know what these crooked ones are up to, eh? Madame Clothilde and that Rosalie? I don't know what kind of conjuring they are doing."

He lets his eyes rest on her as she takes another drink of cream, and he seems to be thinking of something sad from long ago. "You're one of those girls that think they have armor," he says. "You think you can't get hurt more than you already have." He reaches over and gently touches the tip of her nose. "That's the kind they like to eat up."

He hesitates, as if he could say more—as if he knows a secret she should hear—but then the mynah bird flaps down and lands on top of his head, and his face tightens. He gives her a sorrowful, inscrutable look.

"I'll walk you back to your sleeping car," he says. "And if you ever hear a tap on your door in the night again, don't you answer it, yeh? Just pull your pillow over your ear and roll over and face the wall."

Once she's in her own bed, she can't sleep. Her bed is tucked into a corner of one of Jengling's treasure cars, and it's not that she's surrounded by boxes full of skeletons and ancient talismans and who-knows-what body parts suspended in jars. That's not what keeps her awake.

She keeps thinking of the story she told Bolt that scared him so badly—

In Cleveland, she said, *there is a little old man who owns a candy store and likes to murder children. He'll tempt you into trying a special new treat in the back room, and he'll bid you sit in a high chair, and then he'll mesmerize you with a gold watch upon a chain, swinging slow and pendulously.*

"Relax," he murmurs in his kindly voice. "You must relax."

And you find that you cannot move a muscle. You cannot speak or make a sound. Your eyes are open and seeing, but you cannot blink.

And you watch as he prepares his special lollipop for you, as he coats it in arsenic dust.

"Here we are," the old gentleman says with a grandfatherly twinkle, and you feel him reach out and softly push your lower jaw down,

opening your mouth . . . just a little. You feel him slide the poisoned lollipop between your lips.

"It will take quite a long time for you to die," he murmurs gently, and strokes the hair above your ear. "And it will be very painful."

Your finger twitches. Your foot. A tear slips out of your eye. But you cannot even struggle. Now you see that on the shelves there are rows and rows of mummified children, taxidermied and stuffed with sawdust. Your tongue works helplessly, struggling, twisting, as the lollipop begins to melt in your mouth—

The story comes back to her vividly now as she stares at the door to her compartment, huddles back against her pillow, flips another page of her father's diary. She has made little more progress in deciphering it, but it gives her a kind of comfort—as if it can protect her. They were only two when he left home, but Eleanor thinks that maybe she can remember him, how he would come into their room and soothe them when they were crying, how he would lean over their crib and softly hush them to sleep, how he could pull a penny from his ear and balance it, spinning, on the tip of his pointer finger. Was this real? Or just her imagination?

She takes out the photograph, which she keeps tucked in the diary's pages, the only picture they ever saw of him. Except for his little mustache he looks more like an apple-headed boy, a gap between his teeth and a bit lazy-eyed—not strong, not a protector. But she feels as if he would be trustworthy and always loyal, *unlike some*. She believes that he would understand her, that he would know what was wrong with her spirit and how to fix it. *Must our forebears be our future?* Jengling had said, and how would she know? She has little insight into either one. If she could talk to her father, just once; even if she could read his words, maybe she would feel less unmoored, less like a floating particle, a fleck of dead skin in a jar of formaldehyde.

A-Roamin in the Gloamin

•••••••••

Yes, many's the time he hopped a moving train in his younger days when he was but a humble hobo, an itinerant laboring man, riding the rails from one job to the next. But you have to practice grabbing hold of a boxcar in motion and some perish before they perfect the technique, and even he—expert though he once was—is older now and has not the tigerish grace he'd had in the pink flush of youth. His catches the rung in his fists all right as it passes, but his pacing is a bit off so that his wrists are yanked almost out of their sockets and his feet are pulled from underneath him and he emits from his throat a sound like a cat whose tail has been stepped on.

But he makes it, by damn! He clings fast, and now he has hitched himself aboard the Jengling train, bound west, and his precious kidnapped children are near.

Some hobos who ride the rails will clamber onto the support truss rods beneath the train, to lie flat beneath the floor of a boxcar and close their eyes, but Charlie prefers to go up to the deck on top of the car. It takes a certain nerve and unbroken attentiveness, with the wind and the velocity tugging at a body constantly, and the clothes always aflutter and rippling, but to Charlie it's better than being stuck below, sealed like a corpse in a coffin. Up top, he can move about, crawling slowly along the rooftop, thence down to the blinds between cars, thence back up again, making his way like a caterpillar over the lid of the boxcars, peering down cautiously through skylights to see what might be seen.

Alas, he and Stardust have parted ways. He'd trailed the carnival train on horseback from Elk Point, where he'd first caught up with them, to the town of Vermillion, and he'd been increasingly conflustered by his inability to find a way to get his babies back, surrounded as they were by a small army of monsters and mesmerists and other sinister beings, and never let out to wander to a place where they could be decapacitated and captured.

Why he'd decided that Stardust was to blame for the predicament, he couldn't recall, only that he'd given her a sound beating due to her stupidity and stubbornness, and then, later at the campfire, had felt remorse and offered her a lump of sugar in recompense, but she had given him a hard bite on the finger for his trouble. Drunk on corn whiskey and enraged, he had retrieved his pistol and shot her through the forehead, which he now somewhat regretted. In retrospect, she had been a true companion to Charlie these past years, and he had not been as kind as he could've been.

Alas, for Stardust and all of horsekind, their time is mostly done. In these days of automobiles and telephones, zeppelins and aero-planes, radios and moving pictures, can the species continue to be valued as an important servant to man? No! No, sad to say, and when the time comes next he needs transport, he'll choose something with a piston motor rather than a heart.

Now, upon his belly with the hot wind flurrying his shirt and exposing his bare back, he hears the voice of the Ringmaster. A plummy and self-satisfied tone has he, one that carries despite the hiss and clank and rattle of the train, and Charlie inches closer to the skylight from which the voice is emitting. Dusk, and the shadows falling across the Missouri River and the hurtling northern plains, and he peers down and bespies them. Eleanor, his sweet Nellie, sitting across from the villain Jengling.

Due to the incessant chugging of the train, he can make out little of what they are saying, though he listens intently.

Can the Spirit be divined by scalp-kneading Phrenologists? Jengling asks.

No, Charlie thinks. *It cannot.*

He strains curiously to hear more as Fancy-Boots holds forth. **Must our forebears be our future? Or can we be our own creations?** Jengling says. Charlie considers. He has always been drawn to the speechifying of philosophical men: it gives him something to chew on when he's passing a lonely hour, and even though Jengling is his enemy the words he speaks are intriguing.

It puts him in mind of his dear Jasper.

"Ah, Charlie," Jasper once said—drugged to a stupor, unsteadily holding the haunch of a jackrabbit on a stick over their campfire. "Ah—" Jasper sighed. "If you were only you. If I were only me."

What did it mean? He was at first afraid that Jasper had divined that his true name wasn't "Charlie Prine," that Jasper had seen through his ruse as a Fraud and Confidence Man!

But, of course, Jasper would have known that already. Even from the beginning, when they first met, Jasper must've been aware of his true nature, he must've ascertained from beyond the veil that Charlie was naught but a common hobo, known by birth as Shadrick Crone, a runaway boy and crook, thief, murderer—

If I were only me . . . he thinks, and he can feel a tingle of meaning in the center of his forehead. *If you were only you, if I were only me . . .*

Ah, Charlie Lambkin! Ah, Chuck Lumpkin! What does it matter what name he bears? Now that he's set his cap on reclaiming his stolen darlings, he has a true purpose, and all the Charlies present past and future can bear down upon it, whate'er their names!

His personal belongings and treasures are secreted in hidden places he knows, and he has safe houses and shacks and caves ripped out in thirteen states, of which South Dakota is one that he knows best of all. Oh, once he has his childern he'll be sure they are snug and hidden and they won't never get away again.

He follers his Nellie as she leaves Jengling's car, crabwalks along above and behind her as she crosses from car to car until at last they've come to the lonesome boxcar she's been Rapunzeled into. Gazing down at her from above, o'er the lip of the boxcar behind her, he thinks he might be able to spring upon her and subdue her as she opens the door, but there is also the likelihood of around 30 percent that he would misjudge the jump and hit the side of the boxcar and be thrown from the moving train with significant force.

So he lets her go through the door and closes and locks it behind her, and then he drops down, presses himself close, crouches to put his eye to the keyhole beneath the handle, sees only a yeller light; he puts out the tip of his tongue and pokes it around the keyhole's edge. He feels through his pants pockets for the lady's hairpin and the nutpick, which he always carries somewhere on his person.

Usually, just a pick and a pin is all it takes, but this tumbler is unusually stiff, or heavy, and doesn't want to turn. He bears down and there's a listless click and he grabs the handle eagerly, but it doesn't give.

"Hello?" says his girl from inside, and maybe, he thinks, what if he called to her? What if he said, "Beloved child, it is your dear old Uncle Charlie, a-come to rescue you!" And maybe a 15 percent chance she'd realize that being his daughter was a better option than throwing in with a circus full of abhorable freaks. So he is silent. "*HELLO?*" she says, irritably, and she stomps a few steps toward the door, and he climbs up onto the deck and crouches for a time.

When it seems her agitation has ceased, he inches slowly to the skylight and peers down. It seems that they've assigned her to take inventory of their goods, and he observes as she unpacks a crate full of—severed heads? No doubt their plan is to expose her to the most awful of unholy deformity until she is accustomed to it, and then they'll have her in their sway! They'll have her believing that there's something wrong with *her* because she doesn't have toes growing out of her forehead.

She sets a jar down upon the sideboard and commences to write about it in her notebook, but even from this distance the head-shaped, fleshy ball in the brine makes Charlie like to yurp. And he shrinks back to the edge of the deck and then climbs down to the door to take another shot at that lock.

Nutpick. Lady's hairpin. Nutpick. Lady's hairpin. Nutpick. Lady's hairpin.

"Is someone there?" says his Nellie, and he stops. Waits.

They listen, together, to each other's silence, and then he guesses she turns back toward her hideous jars, and he—more stealthy now than ever!—turns back to the tumblers of the damnable lock. *Click. Click. Click*

"Who's there!?" she calls out angrily, with a startling abruptness that nearly makes him drop his nutpick.

"Bolt?!!!" she calls. "Don't try to fool me! I know it's you!"

Ah! So Jengling's not only separated them, but turned them agin each other, has he? Very clever, to separate and conquer, and Charlie might have done the same if the twins had not been snatched from his loving grasp.

He has just enough time to climb back up on the boxcar deck before she throws open the door in her fit of pique. "You can't scare me!" she cries into the dusk, into the rushing wind that runs in a ribbon along the side of the train, and he gazes down from above upon her be-pigtailed head. She looks left, right, sees nothing.

And now she's on the move again, stomping along down three cars as he scuttles along above her. A part of her knows he's here. A part of her can feel it, the way a jackrabbit can sense the eye of the coyote, but in Charlie's experience the poor innocents never grant credence to that third eye in the back of their head. You can blow your breath on the back of their neck and still they won't turn, assuring themselves it's only their imaginings.

She's almost his again. Not long now.

But he's managed to get her stirred up, she's restless and suspicious, so he has to be patient. Give her some time to catch her breath and believe herself to be safe.

He follows her silently to the cabin of the shark-tooth Gollywog, where she knocks and is admitted, and it is very troubling, very troubling indeed—shocking that they would allow a white girl-child, near to womanhood, to fraternize alone with one of such foreign and grotesque nature, covered from head to toe in godless markings! The indecency of this circus is boggling.

He watches down through the skylight and from above he sees the tattooed savage bringing his Nellie a teacup full of milky liquid. Charlie watches in horror as she trustingly takes the cup from the brute's hand, though no doubt it has been drugged. Then they sit side by side on the bed, heedless of propriety, talking too quietly for him to hear.

She seems not to know the danger she's in. Once they take the bone from their nose, these cannibals, once they learn to mimic civilized speech, they can trick an innocent like Nellie into thinking they're harmless. Any minute, Charlie expects her to pass out and have her clothes ripped off her, but all that happens is that the savage holds forth and gives her a lecture, raising his finger for emphasis, and Nellie nods grudgingly, and they both stand up.

Then the door opens and she's on the move again, and her tattooed friend walks along beside her, babbling as they go, and Charlie drags his belly along the top of the boxcar behind them as they emerge from one car and transition into another, taking the easy way while Charlie inchworms along behind and above, catching glimpses of them through the skylights.

Now they stand in front of Eleanor's car and he watches as the savage playfully taps Eleanor's nose with a tattooed index finger. "I'm not a-jokin, girlie," says he. "Don't pay no attention to knockings or rustles at the door. Nobody who wishes you well will be standing outside."

Eleanor gives him that smile of hers—as if she'd studied how to smile by looking at illustrations and hadn't quite figgered it out.

"Okay, then," she says. "Thank you. I'm sure it was nothing. Good night!"

And she steps inside her car and closes the door and then just as the tattooed one turns Charlie feels a sharp prick on his ear.

A bird swoops down at him and pecks his face and flutters at him as he swats it away, plucking at his nose with its sharp clawed yellow feet. "Billy-boy!" it screeches, in a hoarse singsong. "Billy-boy, charming Billy!"

And when it dives at him again he snatches it out of the air and tightens his fist as hard as he can and he feels its thin bones break between his fingers. Some juice comes out of it.

But it has done its job—it has called attention to him, and the young cannibal gazes up his eyes meet Charlie's.

"Hey!" he says as Charlie leaps down upon him.

Knocks the air out of him. Flattens him. The cannibal wants to cry out but when he opens his mouth Charlie crams the dead bird between his teeth to muffle him, and with his other hand he sticks the blade of the stiletto deep into the buttery-soft stomach and presses his palm hard over the boy's lips and pinches the nose closed and the cannibal lad's eyes widen—always, in the moment of death, you see the sweet, fat baby they once were—and then he pulls the blade out and then slides it in again, aiming for the liver.

"Off you go now, good journey," Charlie whispers, and the body falls backward off the moving train, and bounces when it hits the ground and the neck snaps and the corpse tumbles and flops away from the gravel-strewn tracks and down a slope and lands at last in a marshy bit of cattails and nettles and the tattoos on his skin no longer seem to move and shift. By the time his skin grows gray, the tattoos are also drab and faded, two-dimensional.

By the time the circus train arrives in Yankton, South Dakota, crows have discovered Billy's body. They settle and strut around the cadaver, examining it curiously. Yellowjackets buzz around it, and carrion beetles nudge beneath, and the largest male crow croaks and flaps his wings to chase the blowflies off of the face, then tastes of the eye socket, and pokes at the dead mynah bird which is curiously, incongruously, stuffed into the man-corpse's mouth.

And Meanwhile

•••••••••

It is the morning of July 20, a Tuesday, and the Jengling Emporium train has arrived in the town of Yankton, South Dakota. When Eleanor wakes up there is already a bustle of activity. The tent canvas is being unfolded and the poles erected, crates are being unloaded. Surely, Billy Bigelow is already overseeing the construction of the carousel. She misses it a little, even though she only worked that shift for a few weeks.

Oh, well. The canteen is set up, so Eleanor goes to get some breakfast. "Miss Bolt! Good morddnink!" calls Mr. Lacis, and spoons a clod of oatmeal into her bowl, to which she adds three spoons of strawberry preserves and some heavy cream, until it's palatable. When she pours herself a cup of coffee Mr. Lacis tsks. "Uch! Miss Bolt! You are too young to drink that, it will make hairs grow on your chin!"

"Well, then I'll be the bearded lady!" she says, as Pollyanna might. "And I'll earn a good living from it!" And Mr. Lacis's face crinkles with kindly laughter, despite the nails in his head.

She is sitting in the corner, reading peacefully, when Bolt and his friends come in, and she can hear them talking loudly over one another, competing to see who can be most noticeable, the vain things. How they love to be looked at! But she will not glance their way.

Her latest book is a volume of poetry called *Tender Buttons*, but she finds she can make no more sense of it than she can of her father's diary. She reads: "The change has come. There is no search. But there is, there is that hope and that interpretation and sometime, surely any is unwelcome, sometime there is breath and there will be a sinecure and charming very charming is that clean and cleansing."

She can feel Bolt looking at her as she falters through these lines. He is crawling along inside her head like one of those maddening houseflies that refuses to be brushed away, and she flicks at her forehead, irritably.

No, she thinks, hard, and she lifts her head and stares over at them and Elmer's coffee cup tips over and spills out onto his lap, and the dog-faced boy yelps and knocks his chair over as he jumps to his feet, and while they are in a ruckus she gets up and leaves.

And meanwhile, the clown named Thistle-Britches discovers that his costume trunk has been opened and rifled through. All his outfits have been strewn about by some careless person, and when he begins to pick up and fold the various articles of clothing he is puzzled to find that his "little old lady" costume is missing—the black dress and gray bun wig he would wear when he was playing an elderly widow in some of the clowns' skits. Scattered about are bits of coarse black hair. He finds a little braid with a bone and a ribbon and a matchstick woven into it.

Eleanor finds a spot in the shade next to Miss Alcott's cage and settles down on the hard-packed fairground dirt to puzzle over *Tender Buttons*. To think about her options. "Out of kindness comes redness," the book says, "and out of rudeness comes rapid same question, out of an eye comes research, out of selection comes painful cattle."

Painful cattle, she thinks, and glances over and sees a parade of red soldier ants carrying a conquered grasshopper toward their mound. The poor prisoner is still trying to struggle, still trying to kick his powerful legs, but he's held fast in the mandibles of his captors.

Eleanor regards the tableau attentively—it seems to be telling her something, she thinks, in the same way the poem seems to be telling her something—

But then she hears Jengling's voice from behind her, and the epiphany evaporates.

"Oh, no!" he says. "Not Gertrude Stein!" He is in his full regalia—his tight jodhpur pants and red tailcoat and top hat, his thin black whip holstered at his waist. "Dear me," he says. "What a terrible book! Are you enjoying it?"

She gets up and brushes the dry sod grass and dust off of her smock, and he stands there, arms akimbo, smiling secretively, and as always there is the awkward sense that he wants something specific and will be disappointed in you if you can't guess what it is.

Eleanor clasps the book in her hands like a ladies' handbag, and shrugs. "What makes it terrible?" she asks.

"Oh, I admit that the words feel good in the mouth, but it only flirts with sense," Jengling declares. "A pretense of depth and profundity that does not bear fruit under scrutiny! Reading it, I feel that it's the work of a *fraud*—an empress without clothes! Besides which, she is an unpleasant lady, in my experience!"

"Well then," says Eleanor. She looks down at the line of ants marching toward their city, and she guesses that the grasshopper has already been borne into the maze of tunnels below, where it will be dismembered, and its most tender, delicate parts given to the queen.

"Perchance," says Jengling, "have you seen Billy Bigelow this morning?"

She shakes her head. She thinks for a moment to say that she spoke with Billy last night, but then again, what business is that of Jengling's? He might want to know why she would go to Billy's berth in the night, and what they talked about, and so forth. Better to say nothing.

"In any case," says Jengling, "I will need to discuss with you my collection of skeletons and bones, which require particular care in handling and sorting. And—" he says, "I need to find you a better book. You should cast that one into the fire at your earliest opportunity!"

Eleanor nods, shifting *Tender Buttons* in her hands. Now she is certain that it must hold some secret, and she will have to find someplace to hide it.

"I'll meet you in half an hour," Jengling pronounces. "First, I must commune with Miss Alcott. I rely deeply on her friendship and wise presence."

And meanwhile, Charlie is feeling particularly thwarted. He's disguised himself as an old woman so that he can move undetected amongst the fairgoers and sneak close to his kidnapped little ones, and he'd felt a thrill of hope when he'd seen Eleanor headed off toward the edge of the carnival with a book in her hand. Oh, she always liked to find a quiet, private corner to read in.

But then she settles down next to the cage of a watchful gorilla! She leans against it with her back to the bars, the beast right behind her, so that it could easily reach through the bars and snatch her by the pigtails and give her head a deadly shake. Yet heedless she reclines!—even with the ape appearing to read over her shoulder—and soon enough along comes the villain Jengling, and Charlie's chance is lost.

His face burns. He'd hated to do it, but he knew that the disguise wouldn't be effective unless he shaved his face bare, so he'd taken up his stiletto and sawed off his beloved beard in chunks, and then used the edge of the blade to shave his cheeks as smooth as he could, painfully scraping the stubble and nicking himself a few times. He couldn't help thinking of the poor young savage he bestabbed with that self-same blade.

"Sorry I had to kill ye," Charlie murmured. "But now we're even."

He lathered on foundation makeup and rouged his cheeks and put on powder after that. Then just a touch of lipstick.

Thirty minutes is enough time to go back to the sleeping car and find a place to tuck away *Tender Buttons.* Eleanor doesn't think that Jengling would actually take the book from her, but now that he's mocked Gertrude Stein she feels both shame and a hard protectiveness toward the poetess. Perhaps Eleanor will never be seen with the book in public again, but in private she will read it fiercely.

She stashes it in a place of honor—underneath the mattress at the foot of the bed, wrapped in a pillowcase. Her father's diary is at the head, and inside the diary is his photograph and some money that Billy shared with her. She has some coins and pieces of stolen jewelry in the toe of a rolled-up stocking in the steamer trunk where she keeps her clothes.

She has always been a hider of things—and a thief—for as long as she can remember. Back in the boardinghouse, she used to like to sneak into the boarders' rooms and snoop through their belongings, perhaps taking something small—a charm off a bracelet, a single, tiny blue gem from an earring inset with nine gems in a circle, a jar of MUM deodorant crème from Miss Belieu's box of fancy toiletries, a marble and a pair of ivory dice from Mr. Duckett, a teething ring made of India rubber from Missus Berthe's homely baby, while it was sleeping. She kept her treasure in a hatbox—itself stolen from Old Mrs. Rocheleau—under her bed, but just as often she would decide after a while to take a stolen item out back and throw it into the pond. Flinging it, hearing it hit the water gave her a solemn, tingling delight in the lower belly, an inexplicable satisfaction.

Was there anything she'd ever owned that she missed? Certain books, she supposed, but those could be replaced, eventually. She didn't ever have a favorite toy or anything of that sort. It was Bolt who doted over the dolls she'd been given, and she'd never been particularly attached to clothing or adornments. The only thing she really missed from that boardinghouse was a cushioned armchair by the window in the downstairs parlor that caught the late afternoon light. The chair was just slightly too small to be comfortable for most adults, and it faced at an angle so that no one noticed you if you sat in it. She would like to have that chair back—or maybe just that particular light from that particular window.

As for the rest of it—their possessions, such as they were, she wishes she would have had the foresight to burn the house down before the bank took it from them. The only thing she's lost that she really regrets is a spring-fired stiletto switchblade knife that they found among Old Mr. Humberstone's things after he died. It had an amber bone handle and a thin, exquisitely sharp blade with a point as thin as a knitting needle, and it made a delicate but firm click when it popped open. She would still have it in her pocket now if Uncle Charlie hadn't taken it from her. "What's this?" he exclaimed. "A Irishman's toothpick? That's no toy for a girl!"

"That—that was my father's!" she protested. "He meant for me to have it!"

"Ha!" Uncle Charlie said. "Your dear departed pappy would've had nothing to do with such a foul instrument! This is something you'd find on the corpse of a common street hooligan." He clenched the stiletto in his fist and crammed it into the pocket of his dirty coat. "If Nellie wants to play with knives, there's a paring knife in the kitchen that she can peel some taters with!"

She's still thinking of that switchblade when she comes into Mr. Jengling's compartment and sits down across from him as he shuffles through the cavernous bottom drawer of his desk.

"One moment, Eleanor," he says. "I want to show you something."

He produces a wooden box and lowers it ceremoniously onto the desk between them. "Voilà!" he says and sifts gently through the wood shave packing, pulling out on the tips of his fingers what appears to be an elongated human skull. The bottom part seems normal—hollow eyes, hole for nose, grinning teeth—but the cranium is narrow and rises up bulbously like a narrow mushroom, a pope's hat, or a half-folded parasol.

"I love this skull," Jengling says. "I think it's my favorite."

"Surely," Eleanor says, politely. "It's a nice'un."

"It's the skull of an Amazonian girl, about your age," he says. "Recovered from a ruin in Ecuador. This particular tribe of natives practiced ritual skull-binding, you see. They would choose a female infant—perhaps some augur indicated that she would be . . . a sage, or priestess . . . and they would take the newborn and wrap its head very very tightly in swaddling cloths while the cranium was still malleable, the bones unyet fused, and thus they were able to shape the infant's actual head into remarkable contours. The brain itself matures into a container of a different size, a different form. Is it possible that the thoughts and perceptions are also altered—that this sculpted brain sees and experiences the world in ways that are unimaginable to the likes of us?"

"Well!" Eleanor says, in a soft Pollyanna-inspired voice. "I couldn't say!" She looks down at her folded hands, then can't help but glance up darkly at the grotesque object that Jengling is balancing on the tips of his fingers. She can't help but feel that he's suggesting she herself is like to this deformed priestess girl. Maybe if she'd had her head swathed and squeezed since she was a newborn, that would explain what was wrong with her, why she couldn't ever have the kind of mind that other people did.

"Then!" Jengling continues. "Then—perhaps as this otherly being approached womanhood—they would perform a trepanning upon her. Do you see this hole at the top of the skull?" He carefully tilts the cranium as if it is the most delicate, antique vase, and Eleanor sees a little tunnel has been dug into it, a few times larger than the entrance to an anthill.

"Trepanning is an ancient surgical practice," he tells her, "in which an opening is made by scraping, or boring, or cutting through the cranial roof, exposing a small portion of the dura matter of the brain. It was often a medical procedure, to treat head injuries—swelling and blood buildup and the like. But it was also performed for spiritual reasons. Some believed that it opened the Third Eye, the sight of the clairvoyant. That, by allowing the brain to freely pulsate, it would open a gateway to a higher state of consciousness, deeper access to the spirit world and visions—perhaps allowing us to commune not only with our own species, but with the others—"

"Mm," Eleanor says, politely. "I reckon you'd surely get visions if somebody drilled a hole into your skull."

"Exactly!" Jengling says. "And I've considered having the procedure done myself, but I've yet to find the right surgeon."

She watches as he lowers the elongated skull gently back down into the box. She notes the strange, unnatural peach-fuzz hair on the backs of his fingers, thick and downy and so pale it is almost invisible, except when it catches the light.

"In any case," he says, "there are about two or three hundred skulls or partial skulls in train car number thirty-three that need to be cataloged, along with a descriptive sentence or two. Let me open that compartment for you."

Herculea is unloading her barbells when she sees an old lady near the boxcars. This is not that unusual. Even more than children, the elderly are prone to wandering onto the carnival grounds to snoop around before it opens.

"Ahem," Herculea says. "Mad—? Madam? This is not a," she says, "not a safe area for—uhh—visitors . . ."

The doddering *alte kacker* looks at her and hunches, head lowered, and takes a step back. "Oh! Sorry!" she says, in a high, cracking voice.

Sometimes people are frightened by Herculea, because of her size and muscular physique, so she tries to soften her voice and gesture in a friendly way. "Carnival won't be set up until dusk, ma'am," Herculea says. "And they'll be unloading the elephant and the tiger soon, so—"

She folds her arms over her chest, and the old one hobbles off at a pace much quicker than expected, and Herculea turns her attention back to unloading her equipment.

At the commissary, Mr. Lacis had told her to keep an eye out for Billy Bigelow. "He's gone off again," Mr. Lacis told her, sadly. "He worry me, he should not drink that rum he likes."

She nods. A few weeks ago, in Omaha, Billy had been on the rum and he'd bet a hundred dollars that she could beat the Buffalo Bill Circus's strongman in an arm-wrestling match. "Don't fail me, girlie," he'd whispered, his liquored breath against her ear. "Cuz I don't have no money to pay if you lose." And he'd kissed her fist to give her good luck, and showed his sharpened teeth in a wide smile.

"I have faith in you!" he said fiercely, and maybe he was just inebriated but she had been moved—honored—by his trust, and her resolve had tightened so firmly that she'd accidentally broken Bill Cody's strongman's pinkie finger.

Eleanor spends the day withdrawing skulls from boxes full of wood shavings, and writing a short description of each, and putting a tag on it, and she tries to put together the pieces of all the things he's told her: eugenics and phrenology, monsters and chimaera, heredity and species, trepanning and spirit worlds and visions, and "can we be our own creations." For a while it all circles in a miasma in her mind, and then she wonders if the reason she can't make sense of it is because it doesn't actually make sense. Maybe it's just the blather of a man who likes to think of himself as a genius. He says that Gertrude Stein is an empress with no clothes but maybe he should look in the mirror.

Elmer is on his way to fetch another box of prizes for the ball toss, he wants to get a lot of those yarn-haired cloth dollies that the gillies are so excited about these days. But maybe, he thinks, he won't have to worry about dollies much longer. Word is that Billy Bigelow has gone off on a bender, and he's thinking this might be his chance. The carousel is a lot better moneymaker than the ball toss, and if he could get in on that, plus the bit with Miss Alcott combing him, he might soon be a serious attraction.

He likes Billy well enough. But if he never came back? Or got fired? He wouldn't die from it.

Up ahead, by the boxcar where Ringmaster Jengling keeps his collections, Elmer sees an old woman nosing around as if she's trying to figure out a way to get in. Probably senile, he reckons, and befuddled.

"Hey, lady," he says. "Are you lost? Do you want me to excort you back to the midway?"

She turns to stare at him, and for a brief moment he has the eerie sensation that she's about to pounce and attack him. His neck prickles. She's a very thick, broad-shouldered old bird, and she keeps her head low, her arms at her sides like she's used to fighting. Something wrong about her, something unnatural, and Elmer takes a step back.

And then the person hurries off into the darkness, toward the trees that line the river.

When Eleanor emerges from train car #33, she is still in a daze of thinking. It's the kind of trance you get into when you fall under the spell of a book, when you spend your afternoon reading and you lift your head to find that the sun has gone down and you've somehow missed suppertime.

It's already night when she opens the door, and the carnival is up and running, the calliope from the carousel is playing "In My Merry Oldsmobile," and barkers are calling, and townsfolk are wandering through the rows of booths and rides and exhibits. It's eerie that she's lost track of time so completely, somehow ten or more hours vanished while she sorted through the variegated skulls of the variant and unique.

Passing now through the milling crowd of fairgoers, she keeps her head down. Her plan is to grab some slop from the commissary and take it back to her room so she can read the diary while she eats—or, not *read it*, exactly, but examine the hieroglyphs and turn its pages.

But as she walks by the line for the Ferris wheel, she spies a horrible old woman standing off to the side, partially hidden in shadow at the edge of a tent. A staring hag in a bonnet and a high-necked dress, with rouged cheeks and dark lipstick and bushy black eyebrows, and large misshapen breasts.

They only lock eyes for a moment. Just a glimpse. Then the woman turns her eyes away and hurries on into the general flow of the crowd, a tall and grotesquely burly lady—

—reminding of?—

Up ahead, she sees Dr. Chui strolling serenely through the stream of gillies, his head a foot above anyone else's, his eyes focused on the distant horizon, but when she hurries toward him, he bends down to look at her with gentle concern.

"You look affrighted, my dear," he says. "Are you quite all right?"

He blinks. His distant kindliness. His polite skepticism. His hands clasped and held lightly just below his breastbone.

It seems foolish to try to tell him about Uncle Charlie. To say that she imagined she saw Uncle Charlie dressed as an old woman, with his beard shaved off and his face painted. It would only make her seem like one of those trepanned loonies, pie-eyed and full of visions.

"Oh yes, I'm fine, thank you," she says, as Pollyanna would. "I only . . . I only need to go back to my bunk and lie down."

"You shouldn't worry about Billy," Dr. Chui says. "He occasionally goes off on a bender, but he always comes home. I expect that Tickley-Feather will locate him before the end of the night! Still, we may need your help with the carousel tomorrow, if he's not back."

"Oh," she says. She's not really sure what he's talking about, but she nods vaguely, still thinking of the glimpse she had of that glaring, bushy-eyebrowed old woman. "Yes, of course."

The moon above. The moon above Yankton. The wide Missouri River, dotted with little wooded islands. The dazzle and glister of carnival lights, the smell of caramel and popcorn and candy apples and fairy floss, babbling chatter and laughter of the fairgoers, Eleanor plowing onward through them, a billowing dread passing across her like the waves of tiny river gnats and night insects that are drawn to the circus's glow.

Looking back, this may have been the worst moment of her life: walking into her train car and realizing immediately that she had been robbed. She saw that the flap of her bedspread had been pulled back and—

The diary! Where is it—?

She tilts the thin mattress off its frame and gets down on her hands and knees with a kerosene lantern crawling along the floor tracing her hand along the wall behind the bed, but even as she gropes around she knows that it's fruitless. It's gone.

Of course Bolt took it! She's immediately certain of that. No one else knew of it but him.

He had betrayed her as she always expected he would, and she hates him. HATES HIM! She can't even remember what it felt like to love him, she can only feel the treachery, the stupidity and disloyalty and brainless gullibility—

And so she storms back out and through the crowd again, pushing her way through a cluster of har-harring bumpkin boys. "Hey!" one calls, and when she glares at him his bag of peanuts breaks open and scatters in a burst. *"Hey!"* he cries.

Why would Bolt even want it?!? He couldn't translate a code if his life depended upon it! It would be meaningless to him. He just took it out of pure greed, maybe he's showing it to Elmer and Gladness and Shyla and Alberic and they're all fingering it and laughing. *Ha ha ha! Ha ha ha! What are these scribblings? Ha ha ha!*

She is so angry that her vision is blurry with tears, the faces and the lights dapple together as she stomps along the midway, she will never forgive him, no matter how hard he begs, never, never ever—

False! *Perfidious!* ***Unfaithful!***

Oh, she will hurt him. She will wound him in ways that he will never forget.

But when Eleanor comes to the entrance to the Séance Tent, she hesitates. She knows he's in there, but so, too, is that creature. The Rosalie and the Otherin. She doesn't need Billy Bigelow to tell her that it's dangerous—she can feel it in the back of her mind, a kind of low, gurgling singing—harmonic voices but guttural and out of tune. Whatever it is, she can feel its malevolence on her tongue, like the metallic taste of lightning weather.

She pulls back the flap and peeks in. It's a vast, dark space—somehow it seems larger on the inside than it does from out, and only the center is illuminated. At a table with a crystal ball in the center, Mme. Clothilde and a well-dressed older gentleman and Rosalie are all holding hands, and behind Rosalie, Bolt is standing in a black choir robe, slowly brushing her hair. His jaw is slack and his eyes are glazed—blind?—and he's panting shallowly as if he can barely breathe. His hand moves in a steady, mesmerized combing movement.

Off to the side is Mr. Jengling, standing stiffly with his hands clasped like a soldier at attention, seemingly intent on the proceedings.

But then he turns and looks directly at her and gives her *that smile.* That grimace: teeth bared, upper and lower. He slowly raises his index finger and puts it to his lips: *Shhhh.* And motions for her to back up.

One moment. I'll meet you outside.

Ringmaster Jengling emerges from the Séance Tent and takes care to ensure that the entrance is fully closed before he turns to Eleanor. He composes his face: an expression that she supposes he believes to be kind and helpful, but she can see a sort of self-satisfaction in his eyes as well, the subtle gloating of a card sharp who's been dealt a fine hand.

"Eleanor," he says. "Are you looking for something?"

"I . . ." she says, and she is trying her hardest to keep any sharpness or anger from her voice. "I need to talk to Bolt," she says, but her tone isn't as gentle or melodious as she'd hoped. Jengling regards her for a moment.

"Oh, Bolt can't help you," he says, his face chiaroscuro, his arms folded, the noise of the carnival in the distance. "But I can. I know what you're searching for, my dear. Follow me."

Ringmaster Jengling leads Eleanor back once again to his train car, he sits behind his desk and once again she takes the chair across from him, and he moves his lips as if he's not sure what shape he wants to make with them. "Ahem," he says.

She observes as he drums his fingers, once, against the green velvet blotter. He picks up his paperweight—a clear piece of reddish amber, with a bug sealed inside it—and considers it. At least he's not trying to look her in the eye. At least he's not giving her that Master of Ceremony smile.

"I assume," he says, "that you're concerned about your father's diary. Don't worry. I have it here. It's safe."

Her stomach sinks, as if she had ridden to the top of the Ferris wheel and is now lurching downward, the feeling of the heart in the throat, a brief sense of bodiless unreality as the new facts arrange themselves. *Why does he want the diary? What does he want it for?*

But she can do nothing but sit there, her hands in her lap, as he produces the diary from the top drawer of his desk and mildly turns the pages, pausing to run his fingers over the runes her father inscribed.

"You mustn't blame Bolt," Jengling says. "Bolt is a very talented Receptor but he's quite simple and entirely without guile. He adores you with all his heart and he would never steal from you. It wasn't Bolt who told us about the diary."

"Give it back, please," Eleanor says, her voice high, and, despite herself, fluting with emotion. "It—it doesn't belong to you!"

Jengling holds out his hand, as if he means to reach out and touch her, to pat her in sympathy. "You see," he says, "*Bolt* didn't tell us about the diary—your father did."

He may as well have slapped her. She opens her mouth and a tear spills out of her eye and drops into her mouth and she can taste the mild salt water even as her vision fishbowls.

"My father is dead," she says, and Jengling nods solemnly.

"Yes," he says. "Of course he is. But that doesn't mean he's not present. He came to Mme. Clothilde in a séance, channeled through Rosalie. He told us how special you both were, and that you would need our help. He was the one that led me to that grotesque child auction, so that I could rescue you."

She shakes her head. She remembers the way Jengling came striding forward in his Ringmaster uniform, his trombone of a voice, and she understands that of course: it was the diary he'd wanted all along, the diary and its secrets. That was why he adopted them!

"I know," says Jengling, in a voice he probably thinks is soothing and sweetly fatherly. "I know you don't believe me. You don't believe you're special. *But you will know what you are when it is necessary to know.*"

She doesn't believe any of it, that's true. And most of all she doesn't believe that her father's spirit would have sought out Jengling and Mme. Clothilde to be his proxies. More likely, she thinks, Jengling had met her father when he was alive, and that somehow Jengling had known about the diary—perhaps it led to treasure? A gold claim her father had made, or some other valuable collector's item—and Jengling had stalked them and hunted them down and bought them at auction just as he might buy a deformed baby in a jar or a dinosaur bone. Her father would've never wanted Jengling to have them.

"That's—" she whispers. "Sir, what you're saying is a lie. You're making it up."

"No," says Jengling, and he tries on a soft voice that is meant to convey sincerity. "No, Eleanor. I may not have been as forthright with you as I should've been, but I've never told you an untruth."

He puts his hand to his throat, puffs out his chest.

"He came to us today, again," Jengling says. "And he was concerned about his diary—he was worried that it might fall into *the wrong hands*. He was afraid that you would never be able to decipher the messages that he was trying to inscribe. The code is based upon ancient Cretan hieroglyphics, but I could help you translate it. We could unscramble it together—?"

He holds out his palms, earnestly, as if she'll clasp them and cry, "Oh, Father! Yes! Let's decipher it together!"

Ha! How stupid he must believe her to be—what a patsy, what a gullie, what a mark!

He is a cruel person, she thinks. Not just a collector, but a puppeteer—an arranger of dioramas, a producer of small, diabolical plays, and he thinks he can maneuver her into being an unwilling actress.

She glances past his outstretched palms to the ashtray on his desk, to the unfinished cigar, and the ash end of it begins to glow red. She stares more intently and the brass of the ashtray begins to vibrate and hum and Mr. Jengling looks down, puzzled, as it rattles and then springs toward him like a snake. He flinches back, surprised.

And Eleanor springs up and snatches the diary from his hands and runs out as fast as her legs will carry her, she hurtles forward and down the stairs and she hears the door slam shut behind her, and she feels the deadlock winch and twist as her mind hardens on it.

She clutches the diary hard against her chest. It's too late to save Bolt, she reckons, but she will get herself away, she will never, ever go back, she thinks, as she pounds away from the winking lights of the carnival and runs down a ravine filled with scrub trees and tumbles down a slope to the bank of the wide Missouri River. She lands flat on her back, the wind knocked out of her, but her father's journal is still cradled in her arms.

She opens her eyes and a shadow, a silhouette of a face leans over her.

"*There you are*," says the voice from above. It's that horrible old woman, leaning down, a hunched figure, black hollows for eyes, red painted lips, holding a dirty wig in her hands like a pelt.

"Gotcha!" Uncle Charlie whispers, triumphant at last.

Somewhere a Voice Is Calling

•••••••••

It's after ten o'clock at night when Bolt finally comes out of Rosalie's tent and his head is woozy. Everything looks like it's made of fog—the canvas of the tents and silhouettes of people walking by and the strings of electric lights and the line of river trees in the distance are all nearly transparent, seeming to drift apart in fingerlings like smoke, pulling a long blur behind them, and when he looks up at the Ferris wheel it seems to be carrying people up into a swirl of fiery embers.

Whoa, he thinks.

I like how you comb my hair, Rosalie whispers to him, and his legs wobble, he lurches against the edge of the tent like a drunk. His temples tingle, and he squints his eyes and massages his forehead with his fingertips.

I wish you could pet me the way you petted Elmer.

A sharp cramp clenches in his stomach, runs all the way down through his bowels to his colon, and he bends over, clasping his gut, and chokes up a bit of goop, which slides out of his mouth into the dust beside the stake of the tent. He stares. It's an opaque jelly-blob about the size of a chicken egg, but in a shape almost like a baby, like one of those creatures he's seen in the jars of Jengling's collection—fetus, they're called. Tiny veins seem to run across the surface of it.

He clears his throat wetly and wipes his mouth with the back of his hand and kicks some dirt over it and turns away. His mouth tastes cold, like peppermint.

It's pr'y nothing, he thinks. But . . . maybe he should ask Mme.

Clothilde about it? Or else ask Alberic? It might be due to them magical mushrooms he ate.

Anyways, it had been an uncomfortable session this evening. Not only had the tent been like a bake oven in the July afternoon heat, but the gentleman who came to see Rosalie had unnerved him. "Leftenant," Mme. Clothilde called him, and he wore a fine high-necked military jacket with golden braided epaulets and two rows of brass buttons down the front and a medal pinned over his left breast. But he didn't act like a soldier. He fidgeted his fingers like a squirrel, and his yellow brush mustache twitched and quivered. The hair of his bangs stood up in wispy tufts. "Mama," he rasped, and fat tears ran down his red face.

Bolt wasn't supposed to pay attention to what they were talking about, he was to keep his eyes lowered and concentrate on brushing Rosalie's hair—but he couldn't help but glance up when the Leftenant let out a ragged squall, just like a baby! "Waa-aa-aa!" he wailed. "O Mother! Will you sing to your little boy one more time?" And the plaintive, horribly childlike voice made Bolt shudder. The Otherin's swollen eyes rolled and caught Bolt's gaze with a look that seemed almost bemused. It spread its lips into a sort of sly smirk, and some pus oozed out of the slit. Then Rosalie's mouth fell open and the distant sound of an old woman singing a lullaby emerged from her mouth.

Next thing he knew, Bolt was outside the tent half-blinded and urping up a goober in the shape of an embryo.

Slowly, the normal sounds and smells come back to him. Here is the scent of elephant manure and buttered popcorn and he hears the calls of the hawkers and the sound of gullies laughing and he gives his head another shake and falters but steadies himself. He'd like to smoke some of that marihuana, maybe have a drink of whiskey and a cigaret. He scans the midway up ahead for Elmer's booth, lifting his head to listen for his busking—

But dang it if the voice of Rosalie doesn't abruptly cut through his thoughts again, and he freezes with his foot lifted to take a step.

NO NO NO! **RUN! RUN!**

It gives him a jolt, and he puts his hand to his forehead, flinching the way you would if you'd glanced at the sun on an August afternoon and her voice grows louder inside him, like a drill between his eyes.

NO NO HE'S BEHIND YOU
HE'S RIGHT BEHIND YOU

And before he can even turn, he feels the thick hand close over his mouth and nose, and the flick of a stiletto blade opened and pressed to his throat.

The hot rotten-fish breath of Uncle Charlie presses close to his ear; he feels the lips of Uncle Charlie against his earlobe.

"I got yer sissy tied up down to the river," Uncle Charlie whispers. "Come with me."

Charlie ties Bolt's wrists behind his back with a silk scarf and makes him put a rubber ball in his mouth, and his big hand can nearly fit around the whole circumference of Bolt's neck like a collar. They march slowly through the muddy stubble behind Rosalie's tent, past some empty crates and rolls of burlap, toward a darkened copse of scrub cottonwoods.

"That's right," Charlie croons in a whisper as the lights of the carnival grow distant behind them. "I always knew you were a good boy, and you won't be harmed, even though you've wounded my heart almost to bleeding, I forgive you, Bolt, you didn't know any better, did you? You just follered what Nellie told you to, didn't you? On your own, you nary would have left me, would you? Cuz we was good friends, weren't we? We was going to do good business together and make lots of money, weren't we?"

Rosalie is gone—if she was ever there. For a while it seemed like they were almost conjoined in their minds, but now it's just him alone.

Bolt glances backward and sees the neon circle of the Ferris wheel and the strings of electric lights glittering and the shadows of the tents great and small. He hopes to see the silhouette of Dr. Chui hurrying after him, Tickley-Feather, striding to rescue—if they only looked, they would see him and his captor walking through the bare edge of the fairground, they could see the silhouettes—Uncle Charlie is dressed in a granny's smock, his lips painted red and rouged cheeks, beard shaved off, holding an old wig in his right hand, swinging it loosely—but the hard left hand around Bolt's neck is not grandmotherly.

"You know," Charlie says, sorrowfully, "I expected just more gratitude. Exspecially from you, my sweet lad! I'm not atall surprised by your sister, but *you*?—well . . ." He tightens his grip, his fingertips pressing into the cords of Bolt's neck. "I thought you was groomable."

Maybe once that was so. Maybe once he would've accepted a position as flunky to Uncle Charlie and thought it was as much as he could expect, as good as he deserved. But now he's got Elmer, and Gladness and Shyla and Alberic, he has Tickley-Feather and Mme. Clothilde and Mr. Lacis, and Jengling himself, calling him "son"! They would've given him the carnival surname, if he'd asked, and maybe someday *he'd* have been Ringmaster—

The noise of the carnival is fainter now. He can hear the sound of the mud sucking on Uncle Charlie's boots, he can hear a great horned owl flutter off heavily, startled from its perch on a rotten branch.

But they'll come looking for him, won't they? They won't just think that he and Eleanor ran off, and move along without them to the next town and the next and forget he ever existed? Didn't he drink from the Loving Cup?

And then as he hesitates Uncle Charlie gives him a firm shove, and they head down a slope into the brush, toward the river.

When he sees Eleanor, hog-tied in some bushes in the mud, he begins to cry. She's been beaten pretty badly. Her eyes are black and blue and swollen shut, and there's a lump on her head and dried blood down the side of her face.

"Wa-a-a-a," Bolt weeps, and his mouth contorts around the rubber ball that's been crammed in his mouth, and fat tears roll out of his eyes. Does he look like a bawling baby, like that Leftenant calling for his mama to sing for him? He falls to his knees next to her body, squirming against the scarven binds that fasten his wrists behind his back. "El-eleanor!" he garbles through his gag.

"Oh, now, now," Uncle Charlie growls when Bolt starts snuffling. "She ain't hurt that much. I bought one of them candy apples and put it in a sock and used it as a truncheon. Knocked her out cold, but didn't do no permanent damage, I reckon. When she awakes, she'll be the same little treacherous ginger cookie as she always was."

Charlie gives Bolt a slap on the back of his head, and it knocks the sob right out of him. "Guh!" Bolt grunts, and Charlie bends down and lifts Eleanor's limp body in his arms, and then considers.

"Stand up," Charlie commands, and though it's not that easy to rise from a kneeling position with your hands tied behind your back by scarves, Bolt does it, and sniffs in the tears that are clogging his nose.

Could someone tell him what to do? Where is Rosalie? Where is Mme. Clothilde, where is Tickley-Feather? He tries to touch Eleanor's mind, but it's empty. *Wake up, wake up*, he thinks, and he remembers something she once told him.

"It's not *really* real," she'd said. "People can't actually read each other's thoughts. It only works if you're both pretending."

They are standing on the bank of the river near a thatch of cattails and brush, and the stars burble above them. In the distance, there is only silence and the whirr and chirp of bugs. He guesses the calliope has been shut down. How long will it be before they know he is missing?

Charlie hitches Eleanor's limp body in his arms, and grunts irritably, shifting from one foot to the other.

"You know what?" Charlie says. "Let me undo your hands. Then *you* can carry her."

They walk through the blackest of night down a rutted dirt road, the river with its dark audience of scrub trees and brush to their left, the empty rolling badlands to their right. Impossible to say where the lid of sky touches the land.

Bolt takes one of the tire tracks, struggling to walk with Eleanor limp in his arms, and Charlie takes the other, strolling along in his old lady smock, whistling almost imperceptibly. A mohawk strip of stiff grass and weeds runs between the ruts, and that makes walking even harder, trying to stay in his narrow path taking little scissoring steps and she's so heavy. So heavy that he thinks he might drop her at any moment, he keeps pausing to hitch her up in his arms.

"She's more of a burden than she looks, ain't she?" Charlie says. He's walking a little behind, slow and thoughtful, looking up at the starry sky. "I'll bet by the time we've gone a few miles you'll grow to hate the weight of her."

If he put her down and took off, he could probably outrun Uncle Charlie. If he put Eleanor down and dashed off toward the dark thatch along the river, he could make his way back to the carnival and alert them of the kidnapping, and they could gather a posse and come back to rescue her—

But he knows they would never find them. Uncle Charlie would vanish with Eleanor, and Bolt would be left with the rest of his life to know that he'd abandoned her. Uncle Charlie's thoughts are mostly impenetrable, a nest of thorned and tangled vines, impossible to traverse, but he has seen one image that Charlie keeps polishing in his mind—a picture of Eleanor sitting hunched on a milk stool, her head bent, her wrists and ankles broken. *Hobbled* is the word Uncle Charlie thinks of, fondly.

He's not sure what to do, he just needs somebody's advice, and then when he stumbles and hitches up Eleanor in his arms again he sees headlights in the distance coming toward them.

"Well, well," Charlie says. "Just what I was hoping for."

Bolt watches as Charlie fits the ragged gray wig over his head like a cap and waves his arms as the lights of a Model T come chugging along around the bend, and who knows what the driver thinks as the pedestrians come into view—a big, barrel-chested man in a dress, lips painted, flagging them down. A boy with a lifeless girl in his arms.

Bolt watches as they come to a stop, and he wants to call out a warning, but he can't think of what to say. It's confusing because this situation requires too much explanation.

So he watches mutely as a man leans out of the driver's-side window, a deeply wrinkled old codger in a cowboy hat, who bears a look of alarmed surprise. "Trouble?!" he chirps, goggling at them.

"We need a ride into town," says Charlie, and Bolt feels his lips move uncertainly but he just stands there holding Eleanor's limp body in his arms and he observes as if from above as Charlie plants his stiletto in the elderly gentleman's throat, and he watches as Charlie drags the man out, still struggling, making a terrible gargling sound like a crow and scrabbling at the blade in his neck, and Bolt almost loses his grip on Eleanor as Charlie pulls the knife out of the old man's neck and a stream of blood spouts up and the man scrabbles, enraged, clawing at Charlie's face as Charlie thrusts the stiletto repeatedly into the man's heart, *snik snik snik snik snik snik snik snik snik snik*, Bolt counts ten stabs before the man goes limp and Charlie kicks the body down the embankment toward the river.

"Oh!" Bolt keeps whispering to himself. "Oh! Oh!" Gobsmacked and silently watching.

Later he thought that he might have tried to escape, then. He could have carried Eleanor while Charlie was focused on his bloodthirsty work, he could have hurried them off to a hiding place—

But instead he just stood there, and Charlie climbed into the front seat of the Model T and put his hands on the steering wheel, and leaned out.

"Put your sissy in the rumble seat and get in," Charlie says, his face spattered with the blood of the old cowboy. "Come on, ye slacklips! I know a place for us."

Bolt sits in the back and holds Eleanor's head in his lap, trying to wipe the dried blood off her face with the cuff of his shirt.

Up front, Uncle Charlie throws back his head and begins to sing. "Somewhere a voice is calling—calling for me!" And he moves the steering wheel to the rhythm, so the car jogs and swerves along the road.

Morgue

Dr. Chui is examining the cadaver of Billy Bigelow in the "infirmary," as it's called—which is really just another boxcar with a couple of cots and a cabinet with some bottles of pills and cannisters of unguents and gauze and so forth, some drawers full of a miscellany of medical instruments, which he finds himself sorting through for no reason as Billy's body lies there—a reflex hammer and tuning fork, atomizers and nebulizers, injecting syringes and urethral catheters, uterine dilators and forceps, rubber gloves and a chloroform inhaler, catgut sutures and needles, scalpels and amputating knives, tourniquets, bone drills, a stethoscope. What is he even looking for?

He is not a doctor, despite the title he has given himself—the framed certificate from the Imperial College of Peking is just a forgery, only a bit of showmanship, a vanity diploma. And yet he has read many medical textbooks, both Western and Chinese, and his mother was an herbalist of some skill who taught him a little of what she knew.

In short, he's close enough to act as a physician for Jengling's Emporium. And as a coroner.

He fills a metal pan with water and begins to clean the nude corpse with a sponge, gently wiping off the mud and gore and dried blood. He uses forceps to dislodge the crumpled wreckage of Billy's bird from between his teeth and uses tweezers to remove the remaining bits of feathers from the mouth. There is still an expression of surprise and alarm on the young man's face, a last remnant, souvenir of the person that once animated this lifeless flesh. He'd been a cheeky, rascally fellow, playing the part of the flip and cocky pirate, but he'd always been polite and respectful when he spoke to Dr. Chui.

How old was this boy? Dr. Chui wonders. Certainly not yet thirty.

When Jengling and Mme. Clothilde come into the infirmary, Billy Bigelow is covered with a sheet up to his waist. His broken neck has been straightened, and his mouth has been closed and sewn shut with catgut thread. His eyes, which were predated upon by scavenger birds, have been tidied up and closed and covered over with gauze. But it's still gruesome, and Jengling reflexively turns his head and squeezes his eyes shut. "Uch," he whispers, covering his mouth, and Mme. Clothilde, in the crook of her husband's arm, gazes stoically at the remains.

"He was murdered," she says. "Rosalie was able to tell us this much, at least. He was wounded with a knife and thrown from the train, but she does not know who is the coupable. It would not be one of us, it is a stranger."

"Yes," Dr. Chui says. He does not hold the prophesies of Rosalie in such high regard, but this is unquestionable. "There are several deep wounds in his belly, delivered by a narrow blade and aimed rather precisely toward the liver, kidneys, and spleen—so it would seem that the assailant had some experience in stabbing, in that he knew which vital organs to seek out." He watches as his fingers straighten the edge of the sheet that covers Billy, his fingers trembling slightly, and he hears Jengling let out a groan.

"God! Gods!" cries Jengling, lifting his face heavenward and slapping his right palm over his eyes while Mme. Clothilde is leaned back against his shoulder as if reclining in a fauteuil chair, thoughtfully stroking her chin. "My sweet boy!" Jengling says. "My goodhearted young rogue!" His theatricality is an iron mask, Dr. Chui sometimes thinks, through which you sometimes glimpse human eyes. He seems to wipe at genuine tears. "He had so many talents—the ventriloquism, especially, was remarkable—and he was truly a part of our family, and he will be avenged. We will find the assassin and bring him to justice!" And he hardens his mouth to hold back a sob as he looks down at Billy's gray, immobile face, the once-bright tattoos now strangely muted.

Dr. Chui, too, feels his throat constrict—but not as much with sorrow as with rage. He cannot help but think of those Rock Springs men as they massacred the Chinese camp all those decades ago, he can picture the terrible joy that alit in their faces, the chortling ecstasy of taking a life with their own hands and believing that the life they were taking didn't matter, was not human as they were human, and that their victim's suffering was delightfully comical. Does Jengling understand that this country is full of such men, who could slaughter every person in his Emporium and not feel a twinge of remorse?

"I saw a man one night when we were in Elk Point," Dr. Chui says at last. "A suspicious man, lurking about after the carnival had shut down. A wicked-looking black-bearded devil, I thought, but when I approached him, he ran off. I didn't make much of it at the time, but now I wonder—"

"Yes," Jengling says. "This is information we should add to our store of knowledge." But what good is it now? Dr. Chui thinks. Can they scour all of South Dakota for a black-bearded white man he'd once glimpsed crouching behind some barrels and crates, and had a bad intuition about?

"But," Jengling says, and he and Mme. Clothilde exchange glances. "But—there is another problem as well, Dr. Chui. The twins are missing. They seem to have run off. We cannot be certain that the two . . . events . . . are related, but—" He clears his throat, and hesitates as Mme. Clothilde gives a long look. "But—we were warned by a familiar of Rosalie's of a danger to them, so—we must assume that . . ."

"I see," says Dr. Chui. Despite his skepticism, despite his doubts about the Otherin and theosophy in general, he must admit that, for whatever reason, Rosalie is occasionally accurate in her prognostications.

"So then," he says to Mme. Clothilde, "could we not ask Rosalie to reveal the location of our missing orphans? Could we compel her to speak with the ghost of Billy and have him tell us the identity of his killer?"

"*Οὐαί!*" she murmurs and gives him a softly imperious stare. "The spirits of the recently murdered are not reliable. They are—*embrouillés*—befogged. And besides, what would he know? He may be able to describe the attacker, he may not."

"I see," says Dr. Chui, and looks silently down at his folded hands.

Though Jengling has always assured him that he is third in the line of succession, Mme. Clothilde has never treated him as such. It is not that she dislikes him—only that she senses his dubiety, she knows he is not a True Believer and when she speaks to him of her séances and so forth, there is always the tang of regretful condescension, a Christian politely indulging an unenlightened agnostic.

"In any case," says Mme. Clothilde, dabbing her nose with a lace handkerchief, regarding the stained gauze covering Billy's pecked-out eyes. "In any case, it would be unlikely that Rosalie could be persuaded to contact him. She was developing a good rapport with the boy Bolt, but now it is very difficult to get her attention. We were fortunate that she was willing to tell us where Billy's body could be found. But beyond that? She has nothing to say."

Dr. Chui nods. "Then we must proceed with the knowledge that there is a killer loose who has slain one of our people, and who may murder more. Perhaps we should break down the carnival and pack up. Leave Yankton. Perhaps take a recess for a week or so."

The two of them look at him, blinking silently, and it is clear—as it should have been clear long ago—that he is *not* third in command but only a well-regarded head butler, a beloved young cousin, though he is older than either of them by some years.

"No, no," Jengling says. "We must see out the week here, as planned. Mr. Lacis can operate the carousel for now, until a replacement can be found. Perhaps Elmer—?"

"And Rosalie must not be moved," Mme. Clothilde says. "She can be a beacon that may help us find the missing children."

Dr. Chui purses his lips, nonplussed. "I see," he says, as politely as he can muster. "I understood you to say that Rosalie could not be persuaded to help. Perhaps I misunderstood."

"We believe," says Jengling, "that she could be motivated to help us find the twins."

"But," says Mme. Clothilde, "she would need a strong—conduit. Which is not so easy to find, you see."

"Although," Jengling says, "we could use—what was his name? Our Piltdown Man?"

"Heap," Mme. Clothilde says.

Of the One Previously Known as McGullian Heap

••••••••

He is no longer what would be considered a "person," at least not in the ordinary sense. His soul is like a helix strip of yellow flypaper in a butcher shop, upon which dozens of black, squirming horseflies are trapped, their legs grasping and stuck wings flexing.

The Swedenborgians believed these spirits were multiform, of countless kinds and species—creatures with faces like torches, beings made entirely of hair, or bone, sirens whose only pleasure was manipulation—and most of the ones who had attached themselves were not particularly intelligent or focused but they were stubbornly persistent. What little remained of Heap might grasp upward for a moment, like a drowning man emerging, gasping, from the water, only to be pushed down again into the murk as yet another eager, brute spirit clambered over him. Over and over, the marshy water fills his mouth and lungs; over and over he chokes and drowns and then rises again, scrabbling toward air.

He was born scrambling. That's the joke of it. He spent his whole life trying to get ahead of the bad luck that had been dealt to him, that's what he wants Rosalie to understand when he's brought before her, wheeled into the tent strapped to a bag barrow, atwitch with growling, giggling spirit voices. If he could only gain control for long enough he would tell her he did his best, such as he was capable of.

Back when he was a youth, children were not merely pets, as they are now—they were commerce, they were an important part of the economy, and the question when acquiring an orphan was not merely whether it was adorable and well-behaved and fawning with gratitude, but whether it might have some use.

Yes, he had used her to earn a meager living, he displayed her to gapers and channeled spirits through her, but he never did her injury as he himself was beaten and kicked and burned with a hot fork. He never ravished her, as he himself was, he made sure she had food before he himself ate, when she was barely more than an infant he fed her sips of milk from an eyedropper. He nursed her and kept her alive when most would have suffocated her and covered her up in an unmarked grave.

Ah, but no one bears a parent a grudge like an adopted child. You can never, ever give them enough love to fill them up, for they always will be burdened by a dream of a True Mother, a True Father—no matter that the man who planted the seed that became Rosalie most likely never knew she existed, and the woman who whelped her left her in a stye in a farmer's barn, to suckle at the teat of a sow amongst a farrow of piglets.

No matter. Even her forgiveness could not help him now.

He sees her in the center of the tent as he's wheeled in through the flap. She's at a little table with a lantern on it, wearing a large white bow in her hair, and a white sash over a pearl-colored dress. Seated beside her is the French midget, Clothilde, and the procurer of freaks, Jengling, and beyond them is an expanse of darkness, much larger that the space of a tent. As he's brought closer to them, Heap tries to twist his head and squeeze his eyes shut but the tall one they call Tickley-Feather grasps him by the ears and holds his head steady and uses his forefingers to peel McGullian's eyelids open, and his index fingers to pull the lower lids down.

"Nnng," Heap gasps as his eyes lock with Rosalie's, as she *hooks*—enters—

O Pioneers!

Eleanor is laid out on a makeshift cot in the dirt-walled root cellar and tornado shelter of an abandoned homestead just north of Scotland, South Dakota, and Uncle Charlie tenderly pours a few drops of strong liquor into her open mouth. She makes a soft gagging sound, but doesn't cough nor sputter, she doesn't rouse, and so he lifts her limp hand and slaps her cheek lightly with it.

"Why are you hitting yerself?" he asks playfully as the palm smacks against the flesh of the face. She's as unresponsive as bread dough. "Why are you hitting yerself? Why are you hitting yerself?"

"Stop it!" pipes Bolt from behind him, his voice high and whiny like a scolding old laying hen. "She's hurt! I'm scairt she's dyin!"

"Pshaw!" says Charlie, frowning, itching at the stubble on his face—he hates having to regrow a beard from scratch. "I'd say thirty to fifty percent of it is playing possum!" he says. "Preparing to play Ophelia upon the vaudeville stage." He peels back the eyelids. The right is dilated so large that it almost encompasses the iris, while the left is but a pinprick. He blows a puff of breath across the damp eyeball surface, but she barely flinches.

"Huh," says Charlie, and forces another drink of corn whiskey down her gullet. She has a lump the size of a meatball at the crown of her head, but the swelling seems to be going down. She's breathing just fine, and he can feel a steady pulse of blood when he presses his finger against her wrist.

"Nothing to be worried about," Charlie says to Bolt, who is holding the kerosene lantern above his sister with trembling hand. "She'll snap out of it here tirectly and she'll be as saucy as ever."

He fixes a stern and disgusted eye upon the lad, and when he reaches for the lamp Bolt flinches and cowers.

"Oh, for Pete's sake!" Charlie snarls, snatching the lantern by the handle. "Cease your blubbering! Go lay down!"

And Bolt backs away from him, toward a dark corner where terrible jars full of rotten jams and long-forgotten canned vegetables are lined up on cobwebbed shelves. The chain on the boy's ankles clinks irritatingly.

"You ought to be ashamed," Charlie says. "I once thought you might be worth something as a helper, but you're nothing but a blubbering bawl-baby. What would your daddy think if he could see you now?"

"Please," Bolt mewls. "*Uncle.* We got to take her to a doctor!"

Fie! He should probably give the sniveller a good hard licking, but he only turns away and carries the lantern up the ladder out of the cellar—let the mealy weakling weep and tremble in darkness. Charlie slams the cellar door behind him.

It has been a flabbergasting few days. Though he'd performed a daring rescue of which a minstrel might one day write a song, nothing has gone to plan ever since. The hijacked Model T is nearly out of gasoline, and they find themselves now stranded in the midst of the badland prairie, in an abandoned sod house with its roof of mud and thatch and grass collapsing, the water-pump windmill only spurting out muddy liquid that tastes of moss. He'd told Bolt to boil it hard in a pan before drinking it.

They say that 50 percent of the homesteaders who take the government up on its offer of 160 acres of free land will abandon the property within the year. Drought, blizzards, swarms of grasshoppers. Despair, madness. *Hum.*

He takes out his makins and rolls himself a marihuana cigarillo. Thinks back to that long-ago day when he and Jasper were talking and he'd joked about the fool farmers and their houses made of mud and cow pies: *I'd sooner swaller poison than live in a house made of dried shit*, Charlie had said, laughing. *Put a noose upon my neck and tie my feet to a fast horse!*

He didn't like to think that he'd planted evil ideas in his friend's head.

Hum.

He slowly releases a long breath of smoke, watches as it hangs and dissipates in the still summer air.

Ah, would that Jasper knew what lengths Charlie had gone to, for his memory's sake. Would that Jasper could appear vaporously as specter or vision, to thank Charlie for saving his little'uns from the clutches of the carnival!

He gazes off at the badland desert beyond the edge of the dead farm, the way the sunlight makes shimmering phantoms that glint and ripple like water puddles. Thinks to that time Jasper rubbed mentholated liniment onto his sore back, so gentle but also matter-of-fact, and Charlie had wondered if that's what a mother's touch felt like.

Hum.

Jasper may not feel like Charlie did a very good job. Jasper may not be pleased about the condition of the girl.

He hadn't intended to hit her so hard—and in any case, it was only a candy apple in a sock, how much damage could it do?

Though it's possible she hit her head on a rock when she fell and broke her skull or bruised her brain.

But if so, he couldn't be held to blame. That was an accident!

"Goddam it, Jasper!" he calls out, forlornly. "I was only trying to make you happy!"

But there is only the soft *creak-creak* of the metal blades of the windmill, rotating without conviction in the dry heat.

All in the Golden Afternoon

•••••••••

Eleanor wakes up.

She is in the downstairs parlor of the boardinghouse, in her favorite cushioned armchair by the window, with the golden afternoon light falling over her face. *What a curious dream I've just had!* she thinks, and a twinge touches the back of her neck.

She glances down at the book spread open in her lap and sees the first lines of a poem:

All in the golden afternoon
Full leisurely we glide;

But that is all she can read. She finds that she cannot tilt her head to follow the text down farther, nor can her fingers turn the page.

She cannot part her lips, she can't feel herself breathing.

It doesn't feel like she's frozen like a statue, but rather like she's two-dimensional, like a photograph, and only her eyes seem able to move.

Outside, through the window, she can see two small children playing near the chokecherry, pretending to search for something, their hands stroking at the air. They must be about five or six, and it makes her think of the game she and Bolt used to play—Eleanor dressed in Bolt's clothes and Bolt dressed in Eleanor's. Sometimes she thought they would have been happier if they'd never switched back.

But when these children turn with their outstretched arms, she sees they are not her and her brother, but different twins entirely. They are both blindfolded with a strip of cloth around their eyes, and they run off in different directions, swinging their arms as if trying to grab an invisible prize.

What are they doing in her yard? she wonders—if, in fact, it *is* the yard behind the boardinghouse. The trees and flowers and bushes and clothesline are all in the right place, but they have the look of props on a stage—cut-paper silhouettes that tremble slightly as if balanced from hidden wires. She notices her own transparent reflection in the window glass, the outline of her own silhouette—a girl in a high-backed armchair with a book in her lap.

Behind her, in the parlor, she can hear adult voices, but she can't make out the words. Is it her mother? Her mother's soft, aggrieved voice? Her eyes widen, and dread ripples across her paper self, across the shadow of her that's pinned to the chair facing the window—

—and then the craggy voice of an old smoker man

Where's my stiletto?

Old Man Humberstone, she thinks, and a shadow passes over her like a cloud pulling along the sky and she can sense him somewhere nearby, behind her. She hears the tread of his high-laced boots, which give off a faint, shimmering sleigh-bell echo. His smell of pipe tobacco and whiskey and male bedclothes. His phlegmy, gloomy chuckle, on the verge of a cough.

"Well, well," he says, like an old shopkeeper, pleasantly surprised by an unexpected customer. "Look who's here."

She squeezes her eyes shut, and maybe it's just a nightmare she's having, she thinks, but it doesn't feel like one. It feels like—what?—like the place you were before you were born. She and Bolt used to be able to peek into it when they were little, and Bolt said that Mme. Clothilde had told him that it was called the astral plane, that it was the borderlands between the living and the dead. Rosalie, he said, mostly lived in the astral, and only the smallest piece of her remained in the Mortal Realm.

"Stuff and nonsense!" Eleanor had said at the time—but now that she is here, she wishes she had asked Bolt more questions. For example, how do you get out?

You've arrived sooner than expected," Humberstone says. He's right behind her now, she can feel the weight of his shape leaning over her, though she can't turn to look. Sweet-musky scent of rotten fur.

She keeps her eyes squeezed shut. "I'm not dead," she whispers to herself. *"I'm not dead!"*

"Well, you're close enough, I reckon," Old Humberstone murmurs, wryly. From the corner of her eye, she sees his gnarled, tobacco-stained fingers rest on the edge of the high-backed chair, right near her arm.

"It's funny," he says. "I thought you kids liked me. Your brother always laughed when I recited a limerick. It made me feel good, the way he smiled when I talked to him. And then you went and poisoned me!"

Bolt said that the spirits of the dead clustered around Rosalie because she could offer them a portal, a passageway—she would allow them to put their hand inside her as if she were a sock puppet. They were most of them unhappy, Bolt said. They bore grudges or festering wounds or were insane. The murdered and brokenhearted were commonly represented amongst the clustering spirits, as were those who generally wished ill upon the living. Very few remained in the borderlands to pass on their love and blessings.

But Humberstone doesn't seem especially angry. She observes as he brushes his fingertips along the velvet of her chair's upholstery. She feels the flutter of his breath.

"Sixty years old!" he murmurs. "Sixty years alive and not a shred of wisdom did I gain, and then put down like a dog—and for what? A few bars of gold and a watch? A wallet with fifty dollars in it? Just money. Didn't do you a lick of good, did it?"

"I'm . . . sorry," Eleanor says. What else does one say to the man you killed as he hovers behind you? She would run if she could. She would scream herself awake, but she is only a shadow flattened on a chair in a memory of a house that they lost long ago.

"Aw, pshaw," Humberstone says, and gives off another exhalation of whiskey and pipe smoke and moldering bedclothes. "I know your mother put you up to it. You were just children; you didn't know any better."

Well, Eleanor thinks.

And despite herself she can't help but be a little offended by his beneficence. *Just because I was a child doesn't mean I was stupid*, she thinks, though she knows she should be apologizing with all her might.

"It doesn't matter," Old Humberstone says. "Life was all a big nothing anyway. And the sad thing is, you and your brother might be the only people left on earth who ever think about me. Ha! You're not a very nice little girl, but I forgive you. Tell Bolt I forgive both of you."

Well, Eleanor thinks. For some reason, *you're not a very nice little girl* weighs more heavily on her than *I forgive you*. But she should say something. She should acknowledge that she appreciates being absolved, she should thank him for his lack of resentment.

What would Pollyanna say, she wonders. She glances down at her lap and the page is different now—

Oh, I'm so glad! I'm glad for everything. Why, I'm glad now
I lost my legs for a while, for you never, never know
how perfectly lovely legs are till you haven't got
them—

"Are you still reading that dumb book?" says Billy, and she lifts her head and she's sitting on the edge of the carousel and Billy is beside her. "I thought you were done with it." Beyond them is a thick fog through which she can see the carnival lights, dappled and glistening like candles reflected in a pane of glass, a beaded veil of lights rustling in unison. She feels the wooden platform circling around the center pole and the bobbing of the fantastical mounts—but though she senses the steady turning, the view doesn't change.

"Where are we?" she says, and Billy reaches down and thoughtfully scratches his big toe, upon which a flowered little vine is tattooed.

"Hard to say." He shrugs. "No place, I guess."

He turns to look at her, and his face is wrong. His eyes are two hollows, full of wet, attentive shadow. His mouth is open and she can see a little face inside it—his bird peeping out from between his parted teeth like a hoot owl in a hollow tree. The bird's beak moves and speaks with Billy's voice. "*Merda!* I feel so woozy!" He wipes the back of his hand across his nose, and Eleanor glances away quickly. She doesn't want to think about what happened to him, why he's here in this place with her.

"I don't want you to be dead," she says. The rows of electric lights with their golden filaments blink peaceably in the fog.

"Nor I," Billy says. "It sure didn't turn out the way I planned it!"

And they are both silent, considering. A curious benumbment seems to have settled over them. She supposes this is how it feels to try to accept something you cannot believe. She lets the toes of her shoes drag along through the gravelly dirt as the carousel turns, turns.

Billy gets to his feet. "C'mon," he says. "Let's ride."

He climbs on the back of a bare-chested, long-bearded man with a fish for a tail, and she takes the mount beside him—the plump body of a sheep with the head of a wolf. The calliope plays "Daisy Bell," and for some reason she is presented with the useless foreknowledge that "Daisy Bell" will someday be the first song sung synthetically by a machine—an invention called "IBM 7094"—in 1961. What a grim place the future seems!

They ride along quietly for a while astride their wooden chimaeras, two silhouettes jouncing gently through the fog, which she guesses is the astral plane, or something. Not so different from the flatlands of Nebraska and South Dakota.

Billy humphs. "I wish I would have never saved one penny! I should have spent it all!"

"Well," Eleanor says. "But then if you *hadn't* died, you'd be sorry."

"*Ai de mim!*" Billy says. "I should have had a baby with Minnie."

"Minnie!" exclaims Eleanor. "The Three-Leg Girl?!"

"She sew me a blanket!" Billy says. "And she made pretty good food for a white lady."

"Well," Eleanor says. "She would've died in childbirth."

"*Damn!* That's what the Rosalie said, too! Are you going to turn into one of those?"

"I don't know. I'm never sure what I'm going to be one minute to the next."

"Yeah," Billy says, sympathetically. They sit silently again, bobbing slowly along on their carousel mounts, and then he surprises her by leaning over and giving her a dry, gentle kiss on the side of her head. "Yeah . . . I saw that about you. You the lostest and loneliest person I ever met, Garota—other than me," he says. "But I liked your grit. We would've made good pals, if we had more time together."

Yes, she thinks. *Maybe we would've.*

But she doesn't say it, she doesn't know why she hesitates and yet her tongue stays dormant, and she looks off to where his bird is gliding along beside the circling merry-go-round, dappled by the blinking gold electric lights. *Say something, at least*, she thinks, and stares down at her lap, where her book is open to another page.

But now it's not letters, it's the squiggles and hieroglyphs of her father's journal.

And when she lifts her head, Billy and the carousel have vanished, and she's in a dark, closed space. There is a smell of damp dirt and mildew and cobwebs that makes her think she must be in a cellar, or a cave, or a tomb.

Then the scritch of a match being lit. A tiny flame illuminates the face of a man who is lighting the pipe in his mouth. She hears him draw in smoke, and the embers in the pipe grow bright and then dim.

"That book is not really meant for you," a man's voice says. "I'm sorry that you became fixated upon it. It won't tell you anything that will help you."

The outline of a figure apparates out of the dimness, walking slowly toward her: a thin man in a dapper tweed coat, his face alit from below.

It is her father. She recognizes him from his photograph, and she might have cried out *Papá!* She might've actually run to him with her arms open, but she finds that once again she can neither move nor speak.

"It's just a field notebook," her father tells her, and he looms above her. Is she supine? It seems so as he peers down at her. "A record of my observations concerning my experiences with lucid dreaming and out-of-body travel, but it's useless. I was entirely wrong about the cosmic planes and the realms beyond death."

His face is simple: round and boyish, a densely freckled snub nose and big, sheepish eyes. In a moving picture you would think he was a comic character, but as he stares down at her she feels only a shudder of dread. *Was* this her father? She had imagined that some great feeling would burst open in her chest—in both their chests!—when they met; that the connection between them would be instantaneous and complete, that he would fit into her like the teeth of a key into the pins of a tumbler lock. She thought his eyes would be more tender, but his expression is matter-of-fact.

"I owe you an apology," he says. "I never intended to bring you into this wretched world, and you obviously had no opportunity to give your consent."

He gives her a small, wistful shrug, but he might just as well have slapped her. Anything she might have said to him is smacked out of her head, and all she can do is open and close her mouth, as if all the air has gone from her lungs. Oh, how she'd longed her whole life to believe that he wanted her—

"In any case," he says, "you don't have to return. You can stay here, and it will be almost as if you'd never been born! It will be so much easier for you to shed the chains of the physical plane."

He casts his hand dismissively toward the dark cave that contains them. "Once you're fully dead, you'll eventually be able to move about. You can linger here and read your books for as long as you like, any story you've ever wanted. If you need to, you can mingle with those who cluster here at the edge, peering into the world of the living like Little Matchgirls—or you might even be able to catch the attention of a vessel like your brother's friend Rosalie, and speak to the loved ones who remain behind. If you need to. For some, it takes quite a long time to lose interest in the material realm."

He itches his little mustache, thoughtfully.

"But for you—it doesn't seem like there's much to miss, is there? Even if you were to live a full life, you'll never be satisfied with what is on offer, given your means. Without wealth, a person's only value is as livestock—as a servant to someone else's story. It's not really worth becoming what there's left for you to become."

Well.

What would Pollyanna say?

What would anyone say, who looked at her? Had she ever had even one premonition of the future that suggested she'd find happiness?

"You could still go back if you wanted," her father says. He reaches down and brushes her hair back from her eyes, as if he's clearing away a cobweb, but even this brief stroke of phantom fingers makes her ache.

"Of course," he says, "you'll have to sacrifice the thing you love the most."

The thing that she loves most?

Whatever could that be?

He doesn't say, and she's afraid she doesn't know. What is it? What must be sacrificed?

But also: *Yes. Yes. Yes, I will. I want to go back—*

Hansel and Gretel

Bolt listens hard for voices.
For Eleanor.

For anybody.

Hello?

He's sitting in the dark on the dirt floor of the root cellar where he's been confined and it's not clear if it's day or night. He leans his back against the cot where Eleanor is laid out, holding her chilly hand, and he checks again that she has a pulse. He finds the vein in her wrist and presses the pad of his palm onto it and counts its beats.

Hello? Nell? he thinks. He tries to find that place in his brain where other people's thoughts appear—a ticklish spot in the center of his forehead that beams out an invisible light in front of him like a miner's headlamp. In the field of this light, people's voices will come to him as sparks, or shocks, or stings. He will feel them before he hears them in his mind.

He closes his eyes and puts his full attention on the tiny pinprick in his forehead, but all he hears is the sound of Eleanor's radial vein—a soft, steady thupping sound, not unlike the noise his mother's Victrola made when the needle came to the end of a record.

It's too dark to see, but after a while his eyes get used to the murk, he can sense a shadow when he waves a hand in front of his face, and he gropes around in the opaque soup of it. His ankles are fettered but otherwise he's free to explore the circumference of their prison.

They are confined in a dug-out hole six feet under the ground, a square space of about twelve feet by twelve feet, with walls made of stacked rocks that were mortared together with sticky red clay, a roof of boards and slabs of sod bricks. Some shelves along one wall have canning jars full of unknown ingredients—possibly jellies or jams or pickled vegetables—and there is a gunnysack of rotten potatoes sprouting pale tendrils, and a bag of moldy flour. It's not clear how long ago the former residence abandoned this homestead, but it's probably more than a year.

What else? Mice, probably, spiders and daddy longlegs, earthworms and sow bugs, centipedes, a few mosquitoes, which insistently land on his sweaty neck and face.

This is like the story of Hansel and Gretel, he thinks. But he can't quite recollect the way that the story goes. He remembers that the witch lures them into her Candy House, and holds them prisoner, but how exactly do they escape? There's a part about how they hold out a bone or a chicken foot so the blind hag doesn't realize they are getting fat. And then somehow they get the witch to crawl into the oven and they burn her up alive. But he can't recall which steps they took to trick her.

Well. Somehow, they excaped, that's all that matters. And he and Eleanor will, too! If only he could get her to wake up.

He kneads her hand in both of his, he kisses her palm, gives her thumb a pinch. *Eleanor*, he thinks. *Nor-Nor*, he whispers, the babyish name he'd called her when they were very small.

Smelly Nelly, he thinks, hesitantly—the nickname that would make her chase him down with a stick. She could never brook being teased, had no tolerance for it, and if there's one thing that surely would get her to snap out of her trance it's an insult.

Nothing. In the dark, he traces his fingers along the contour of her face, which feels more like clay than skin. He puts his finger between her lips, inside her mouth, which is unnaturally dry and sticky rather than wet like it should be, and he pours a tiny bit of water in and pinches and un-pinches her cheeks to slosh it around. He can't tell whether she swallows any or not.

Back when things were perfect, they used to be able to play checkers together just in their head. They would sit cross-legged on their bed, facing each other, hands clasped, and they would close their eyes and picture a checkerboard between them in their minds' eyes, and Eleanor had the black team and Bolt had the red, and they could sit there for hours moving their imaginary checkers across an imaginary plane, and they could both see it, they were there in that shared space together.

He gently pours a little more water between her lips. *ELEANOR!* he thinks, as hard and as loud as he can. *ELEANOR! ELEANOR!*

Does she want him to beg? To grovel? He will. *Sister, I know you're mad at me. I know you've given up on me but please just give me one more chance. I will never disappoint you again, I swear it on a stack of Bibles. Please come back to me. Please come back to me. Please come back to me. Please come back to me. Please come back to me. Please come back to me. Please come back to me. Please come back to me. Please come back to me. Please come back to me. Please come back to me. Please come back to me. Please come back to me. Please come back to me—*

And then the outer door opens and a brick of sunlight is thrown upon him. Uncle Charlie stands at the top of the stairs, arms akimbo.

"I'm home!" Charlie exclaims. "Where's my supper?"

"Wh-what?" says Bolt.

"I'm a-kidding with you, idjit," says Uncle Charlie—just a dark silhouette in the doorway above, backlit by dazzling sun. "I'm not eating nothing that's been moldering down there in that godfersaken pit. So I walked to the nearest town and got us some provisions. Come on up and I'll feed you some beans and applesauce."

Bolt is very hungry. It's been a day—two days?—since he's had anything to eat, and he feels the animal part of himself wake up at the mention of food.

"But what about my sister?" he says. "I'm real worried about her, she's terrible sick."

"Pah!" Uncle Charlie says. "I got her a tonic, said to be expecially helpful for those suffering from concussings." He raises his voice, directing toward Eleanor. "And I'm told," he says dramatically, "that it's got the BITTEREST taste, and if it's given to a girl who is ONLY PLAYING POSSUM then that girl will REGRET it."

Despite the threat, Eleanor doesn't stir.

"So!" cries Uncle Charlie. "That's the way it's to be, is it? You think you can play the rag doll game with me? Well, then! My Bolt and I will go up and sit by a nice fire and eat some vittles, and then when we're done I'll come back down here and give you a teaspoon full of the worst medicine you've ever tasted! And then if you don't choke on that, I'll give you yet another teaspoon! This nonsense has to stop, Young Lady!"

And Bolt squeezes her hand as Charlie blusters at her. *Come back to me*, he thinks, *o come back to me—*

Then he follows Uncle Charlie up the stairs, hobbling one step at a time, his ankle chains rattling as he goes.

He has always thought that they would die at the exact same time. Even if they were separated by mountains, even if they had been apart for decades, it wouldn't matter: when one soul left the world, the other would be pulled along behind.

He is sitting in the sod house and Uncle Charlie watches with interest as he spoons applesauce into his mouth.

"Ha!" Uncle Charlie says. "Look at him go to town! But he doesn't even know what being hungry really means. That's the problem with the young these days! None of you have ever been truly starved!"

"Mm," says Bolt, and makes a soft, shrugging apology for his feckless generation.

come back to me please

Uncle Charlie takes the jar from his hand and carefully runs his finger around the rim, collecting applesauce remnants on his index finger, which he then puts in his mouth and sucks on thoughtfully.

"We're having a hard time finding gasoline, goddam it," he says. "I pr'y should've never shot that horse."

Bolt lifts his head. "You . . ." he says. "You killed Stardust?"

"I was overcome by a fit of pique," Uncle Charlie says. "I regret it. You don't need to rub it in."

The Searchers

Imagine seeing this by moonlight: let's say in silhouette—

First comes the one known as Piltdown Man, with his wild, matted hair and his filthy porcupine-quill beard, slouched and scampering, wearing a rope around his neck for a leash, and behind him is lanky Tickley-Feather in a wide-brimmed ten-gallon hat, riding a bareback mule, *tan galan,* with a rifle slung over his shoulder—and beside him on a mule of her own is Herculea the Muscle Lady, in chaps and big boots and a sombrero, holding the mule's reins in one hand and Piltdown Man's rope in the other.

What would people think, Herculea wonders, if they were to spot the three of them parading down the empty, rutted road alongside the railroad tracks?

She had been surprised when they asked her to accompany Tickley-Feather. "A person such as yourself may be helpful," Ringmaster Jengling had told her. But what did that mean? She is surely one of the strongest amongst them, and she has some experience with torch swallowing and knife throwing, so she assumes that they chose her for her brawn and prowess. She'd like to think that they see her as a kind of knight, sent off to rescue and avenge. In another life, perhaps that's what she would've been.

At the same time, in the two years she has been with Jengling's Emporium, she has rarely been off the carnival grounds. In many ways she is still a city girl from Philadelphia, with little knowledge of this part of the country, with its rattlesnakes and mountain lions, its lawless cowboys and Indians such as Herculea had seen in magazines, with their loincloths and face paint and feathered headdresses. She is dumbstruck by the great expanse of sky, unobstructed by trees or human habitation, so vast and foreboding as to sometimes seem that she's on a different planet. What little she knows of Dakota comes mostly from *The Life and Adventures of Calamity Jane*, which she had read so avidly as a girl, and from dime novels about Deadwood Dick that she doubts can be trusted for their veracity.

They come to a crossroads and the Piltdown Man lifts his head and tenses and peers around, tilting his gaze left and right, up and down, panting. Herculea and Tickley-Feather sit there on their mules, waiting for him to come to a decision.

"Is he like a dog?" Herculea had asked him when they first set out on their journey. "Is he following a scent? Or . . . ?"

Tickley-Feather shrugs. "I don't know how it works. They say he'll lead us to them kids if we're patient, and that's all I care to understand about it."

She nodded and kept her thoughts about Piltdown Man to herself after that.

Still, it's hard not to feel a bit guilty as the unfortunate soul cringes there at the crossroad, snuffling the air and slobbering, eating a bug or a piece of dirt from the ground. It's hard to feel like a noble knight when she's got a scrawny, slavering lunatic with a rope around his neck, and she herself holding the end of the leash.

They'd put him in a pair of farmer's overalls but that's it. He's barefoot, no shirt, running hunched over, sometimes using his knuckles like a chimp. It's pretty easy to believe that he's not a human being, but then sometimes he'll glance over at her and she thinks that she gets a glimpse of the person that is submerged down inside him, a frightened flicker of eyes, as if seen through a mask. She imagines a spark of terrible sadness, pleading—*help me*, he seems to say, *I'm trapped*—and then the brief spark of consciousness fades back into something animal, or empty.

They walk northward along the rutted dirt road track for a while in silence. In fact, most of the trip so far has been wordless, just the clop of the mules' hooves and the strange yips and snorts and muttered gibberish of Piltdown Man. For as long as she's been with the Jengling Emporium, Tickley-Feather had always been aloof, actively friendless and unsociable, and she admired that about him. She wished she herself had his ability to be comfortable with loneliness.

So now she's surprised that Tickley-Feather has begun to whistle. It's almost imperceptibly soft at first, but then he seems to lose himself in the strange, forlorn music, and it turns out that he's a beautiful whistler, his notes full and clear with a slow, softly burbling vibrato beneath them. The tune is one she doesn't recognize, but even without words she knows it tells a sad story—love lost forever, home yearned for but far away and unreachable. For a moment, it seems that they are all enveloped in it, she and Tickley-Feather and Piltdown Man and even the plodding mules, all of them held in a snow globe of this song which must surely be ancient, a keening of quiet grief that humans learned even before they had language.

"I'm not sure I've ever heard that song before," Herculea says at last, shyly, after he's finished, after they've ridden along for another few quiet minutes. "What's it called?"

He glances over at her, and for a moment she's not sure if he's going to answer. "Mm," he says. Considers.

"I reckon it's just a song I made up," he says. "When I was a kid."

She nods. The Piltdown Man scrabbles onward down the road, and on either side, dark empty tracts spread out toward ink-black silhouettes of rocky hills. "Did you—" she says, hesitantly. "Did you grow up near here? Or—?"

He thinks about this for a while as well.

"Born in Canada. Manitoba," he replies, finally. "Lived a lot of places since."

"Yes," she says. "So have I."

She looks down at her hands—the mule's reins in her right, the rope attached to Piltdown Man looped around her left. "Have you—? You've been with the Jengling Carnival for a while, I imagine?"

"Yep," he says. He gives her a hooded look, appraising. "I reckon I've been with Harland longer than any of them," he says, in his rumbling, mumbly voice. "Purty much since the beginning. Worked together as partners but then we decided that he'd be a better Ringmaster and I'd be a better clown."

There are so many things that Herculea would like to ask him. But she is aware that this may be a rare moment of openness, and that her questions must be oblique and casual—not prying, not demanding an answer. Just passing-the-time conversation, take it or leave it.

"So," she says, at last. "Do you like being a clown? Is it fun?"

"Fun," he says.

Considers.

Considers.

"Well," he says. "I like being invisible. It's good when nobody knows your real name."

"Yes," says the former Mona Finkel, says the former Lotta Muscles. "I agree."

And then Tickley-Feather tenses.

"Cht," he hisses. He points with his chin, and in the distance she sees the headlights of an automobile coming toward them, and they get over to the side of the road and she pulls Piltdown Man close so that he stands next to her as the Model T's headlights flare over them and then Herculea sees a girl child in a loose bonnet staring out at her from the passenger-seat window, a pale dappled face like a reflection on a pond.

"Let's keep going," Tickley-Feather says, after the automobile has passed.

But at last they must stop, because the Piltdown Man can go no farther. It must be after one in the morning, and the poor creature is exhausted, and Tickley-Feather pours water from his canteen into a bowl and Piltdown Man laps it up like a dog.

"We'll get some shut-eye for a couple hours and let him rest," says Tickley-Feather, and she nods, and quietly helps to make camp. She makes a little fire and tries not to look reproachful as Tickley-Feather fastens fetters around the Piltdown Man's ankles. It seems inhumane to chain this mad wreckage of a man, but she supposes it must be necessary. Tickley-Feather is firm but not overly rough, and once the man is shackled, he settles peaceably down on a bedroll and huddled into a ball to sleep.

Tickley-Feather crouches down on his haunches near her by the fire and begins to fastidiously open a can with his pocketknife. He pries back the jagged lid and puts a spoon in it, then offers it toward her.

"Beans?" he says. He doesn't meet her eye as she takes the can from him, and she scoops a spoonful and passes it back, looking off into the distance. The sky was never so vast back in Philadelphia; she could have never imagined such an expanse of emptiness—the horizon only distinguished by the dark lines of cragged buttes along the horizon. They sit there silently for what seems like a long time, passing the can back and forth, looking at the silver and purple stripe of the Milky Way. She spies a shooting star; it's that time in August, when they come out.

"So," she says finally, when the beans are gone and they've been wordless for a while. "This man we're looking for. The one that took the twins?" She hesitates. "The one they think stabbed Billy—" She clears her throat. Ever since they left the circus, she's been trying not to think about this question.

"We're going to kill him, aren't we?" she says.

Tickley-Feather gives it some thought.

"Yes," he says. His voice flat as a stone.

She nods. She had been aware even before they set out, but she kept trying to talk herself out of the idea. She pokes at the embers of the fire with a stick. In the distance there is a yipping of coyotes, a high, mystical babbling, as if they're experiencing a religious ecstasy, and then the sound fades, and she guesses they're off on their hunt.

"I've never murdered anybody before," she says, softly, and he looks her in the eye and holds her gaze for a long time.

"Well," he says. "I hope you never have to again."

He reaches his big hand out and touches the back of her wrist, and she startles at the press of his fingertips.

"We're not assassins at heart," he says. "But neither can we call on a U.S. marshall to bring this man to justice, nor ask a judge to bring him to account for his crimes. What proof do we have that he's guilty? What help would a lawman be to the likes of us? What satisfaction could be expected in a court of law?"

He shrugs heavily and turns away, and Herculea keeps staring into the fire.

Oh Herculea, oh Lotta Muscles, oh Mona Finkel—how far she has come from the person she once was, and how many new people will she be in the future, a new person and another and again and again for the rest of her life—

The Piltdown Man sits up from his bedroll as they stare into the fire, and he speaks in the voice of a little girl.

"The sister—!" Piltdown Man exclaims.

The sister

is with us

Who Is Us?

•••••••••

At first, when she dies, Eleanor sails up free of her body. The part of herself that she thinks of as her "self" dislodges, lifts out. She can feel the lights shutting off behind her as she leaves—the heart growing slack, the breath ceasing, the electric impulses of the brain blinking out one by one. Suddenly she is fluttering near the wood-and-mud root cellar ceiling above her—not like a butterfly but more like a bit of ash or ember, carried off on the night breeze, pulled upward like a spark in the narrow trail that leads from a campfire to the dark sky.

She moves easily, but it's hard to hold herself together. She's aware of herself as particles that are beginning to dissipate, she's aware that it might take more willpower than she has to stay together, and so she settles into the first cohesive thing she touches.

A mosquito. That's a shock—entering a living thing! It's like lying down on a nest of pins, and then inside is the bright, quivering moiré pattern of the mosquito's mind and vision, a pulsing of hunger and movement, too difficult to bear—

And so from the mosquito she slips into a bit of thistle seed fluff, which is the mind of a sleeping infant being pushed along in a pram, and she floats along inside that for a while on the late summer air.

So this is death, she thinks. *What am I now? A ghost?*

But no, she is not a ghost, for soon the drowsy spirit of the thistle seed is pressing down upon her, bland and sleepy and unconcerned, and she sees that what she rides upon also rides her, and when she gets the chance she leaps into a pendulous bit of cobweb before the thistle seed could envelop her in its endlessly drifting patience, and the cobweb is nothing, it's the way a paper bag tastes when you chew on it, and she's safe for the moment. She hangs there with the husk of a dead gnat caught in her fibers and she rests for a good long while.

How long? She doesn't know. The problem with inhabiting a nonliving thing is that there is no heartbeat, no sense of time, and she can see how it would be so easy to get stuck, to waft for years and years in a kind of half-awareness, until someone came along with a broom and swept you away.

She sees how very hard it is to remain alive, what a constant and heavy effort—inhabiting a sod brick is like sitting in a darkened and empty train car that has stopped along the track for some reason; and the eyes of potatoes have a fervid, competitive anxiety, constantly worried that someone else was going to get more light. Crickets are fine for short periods though their single-minded lechery is exhausting after a while, the shuddery, insistent pleasure of rubbing one wing against another, the excruciating, piercing intensity of it. Earthworms are easier to handle, though harder to navigate. They're nuzzling creatures, humming and dozy, their sweetly muzzy philosophy of life actually very seductive—

Traveling this way, you have to be alert. You can readily become occupied by the thing you are occupying, and the longer you stay the more it seems that you and your host are synchronizing into one mind. She wonders how many a poor soul had made the mistake of trying to ride an ant and found themselves so overwhelmed by the urgent weight of chores and duties that they never got out again.

It would be easy to lose yourself. She could settle into something from which she could not escape, and it would subsume her, and the bit of Eleanor that remained would grow smaller and smaller until it forgot itself entirely, and this is why, she thinks, she's so jumpy and ill at ease. Whatever this is—whatever *she* is—it's extraordinarily fragile, and she wants to preserve it for as long as she can.

I am me, she thinks, as she leaps from a sullen tiger salamander to a molding, discarded child's shoe into a jar of succotash swarming with botulism bacteria. *I am Eleanor! I am myself! I am here!*

Where now is the astral plane? Where is her father, where is Billy Bigelow, where is Old Humberstone? Can they hear her? Can they help her? She tries to flatten her thoughts, reaching around hesitantly in the long vast plains of her mind, scoping for a doorway, a window through which she could make contact with the spirits—

—but the material world pulls her in the opposite direction, her attention drawn by the succotash she's bound up with, the fizzing, celebratory exultation of bacteria as they multiply, and she recalls back when they were first with Uncle Charlie, how impossible it was to try and read when one of his drunken card games was ongoing. There's no way to concentrate. It's hard enough to hold on to her own thoughts with the carousing festival of decay all around her, urging her to join it.

I am me! I am Eleanor! she thinks, and tumbles into a daddy longlegs that is clambering thoughtfully along the surface of the jar of putrid succotash.

She has made a mistake, she guesses. She should have gone toward the light; she should have dissipated instead of grabbing that mosquito and holding on. What was it her father had told her? *You could still go back*, he'd said, *of course, you'll have to sacrifice the thing you love the most*. But he hadn't told her what it was: herself. Her *Self*—her thoughts, her feelings, her *Eleanor-ness*—would fade and fade, decline into a random disorder of glints and glimpses of consciousness, and then, finally, would be dissolved into the pulse of rot and rebirth that was the universe.

The daddy longlegs cannot hear, but can feel vibrations. Its two eyes are on short stalks, but the vision is poor. He is cautiously indecisive and easily distracted, and that, Eleanor thinks, is manageable. She gently steers him along the shelf and down to the floor. He was supposed to be watching over the eggs that a female had laid on the underside of a rotting plank, but his hunger and thirst had overcome him, and he was hoping he could find a quick drink and maybe a bit of mold to eat and then hurry back to his guard post.

But he is not particularly strong-willed, and she is able to steer him along the floor toward the cot where her corpse rests. She thinks maybe if she could get back inside it—it would be safe there for a while.

She can feel Bolt before she sees the giant, blurry presence of him. She can sense his heat, and his voice tingles against the forelegs she has lifted like antennae. Whatever anger she'd once felt toward him is forgotten now, and she runs toward him—*Bolt!* she calls out in her mind, and the daddy longlegs is no match for the force of her resolve, the poor arachnid has never experienced the wave of love and sorrow that fills them to bursting, and it does as she bids it to, running as fast as its spindle legs can carry it. When it touches the tip of his bare toe she doesn't hesitate—

She leaps.

He sucks in a gasp of breath when she enters him. She feels his spine arch, and his hands spasm, and she hears the glottal strangled sound the throat makes as she alights and settles. *No!* she hears him think . . . *Wait . . .*

And then they open their eyes.

They stare down at the dead face of Eleanor. They put out a finger and touch her cold lips, from which no breath will ever come again.

Them

They is weeping over the corpse of the dead girl when Uncle Charlie comes down the stairs. Stomp! Stomp!

"What in the Sam Hill are you caterwauling about?" he says, sloe-eyed and bed-headed, arms akimbo. "I'm trying to sleep!"

They turns to stare at him, and though their eyes is red and wet from crying, their face is expressionless.

"She's dead," they says.

"Aw, for the love of Pete!" he exclaims, and strides forward assuredly. "If you'd just quit picking and poking at her, she'd be fine."

He pushes them aside and they observes silently as he examines her. He pushes the eyelid up with his thumb and sucks in a surprised breath. "Oh!" he whispers. He puts his paw on her and gives her a shake. "Oh, oh, oh," he says, and slaps her lightly on the cheek, and then harder. "No," he says. He clutches his scalp with both hands. "Noooo! It can't be!"

They watches as he lifts her corpse off the cot and cradles it in his arms. "My child!" he cries. He throws back his head and howls at the ceiling, and fat tears roll down his face. "Lord! What have they done to my girl!" he cries out, and the head of the corpse flops loosely on its neck stalk as he rocks it and kisses it and sobs.

Bolt peers out from the left eye, and Eleanor peers out from the right, and together they waits silently as Uncle Charlie thumps his chest and calls out protests to the Heavenly Father.

A spirit possession hurts quite a lot at first, but Bolt already knew that from acting as a vessel during Rosalie's séances. Eleanor, however, found it a shock. She was entirely unprepared for the intensity—a slow, steady stabbing sensation, surrounding the skull but outside of it, pain in the very air around one's head, like a throbbing crown of knives. It was so abrupt and agonizing that Eleanor almost leapt back out with a shriek, but Bolt had learned how to acquiesce to an inhabiting spirit, how to step aside and make room.

The pain slowly subsided to a low, throbbing ache, circling around the cap of their skull like a halo, and Eleanor felt herself ease in and settle a bit. There was plenty of room in Bolt's mind for her to spread out.

They were still two individuals, still Bolt and Eleanor—and yet they were also aware of a muddy area of comingling. It wasn't always clear who was thinking, who was the inner voice and who was the outer voice, who was feeling an itch and who was scratching it. Memories stacked upon memories in multiple versions, and whatever their separate moods might have been mixed together like two colors of paint on a palette. Thoughts entangled and contradicting.

The soul is eternal, of course, but ever changing; bound, like all things, by the law of entropy. The thing we call a *self* is more ephemeral—a series of costumes the soul tries on, a loose collection of stories and yearnings and wounds, barely stable from one moment to the next.

So who is to say where Eleanor's mind ends and Bolt's begins? Even from the beginning, they have not always been sure themselves.

Uncle Charlie finishes bargaining with God and sets about planning a funeral. He has decided, for some reason, that Eleanor was afflicted by some unknown wasting sickness, "Pr'y terbercolosis," he tells them. "She was more fragile than we knew, but she hid it from us to spare us from worry." He takes a wadded handkerchief from his pocket and reverently drapes it over her face.

"We'll bury her right next to her daddy," he says. "In Murdo! We'll dress her in silks and laces, with ribbons and flowers in her hair, and get her a nice, varnished box, fit for a lady!"

He hums to himself, rubbing his stubble beard and they imagine how they will murder him. *Not poison this time*, they think. Bolt feels strongly that it should be a bullet through the forehead, while Eleanor likes the idea of an axe or a sharp shovel.

A person might have imagined he'd be able to feel their hatred rippling over him, that he'd feel the spike of their glare right into the back of his skull, but he busies himself over Eleanor's body, arranging her arms neatly at her sides, combing the tangles in her hair with his thick, ungentle fingers.

"Problem is," he says, "Murdo is maybe two hundred miles away to the west. So we have to get the automobile problem situated, and then it'll be a couple of days at least before we can get there, buy the plot next to your dear daddy, have her embalmed, buy the funerary clothes, and so forth. And horrible as it is to imagine, she will begin to ripen over that time. No, not good to leave a corpse to its own devices."

They has not considered this—the inevitable decomposition—and it gives them pause. Uncle Charlie reaches out and puts his big palm against their cheek. "You'll need to warsh her down with vinegar and water," he says. "T'would be better if we had a woman to do it, but you'll have to suffice, since you're her brother and won't be as much of a offense to the Lord if you see her nude. Then we'll beshroud her in linen cloth that's been soaked in river mud. It's complicated, but I've done it before, and you'd be surprised at how well it slows down the rot and festering and so forth."

Uncle Charlie hesitates and then he abruptly encloses them in a hug, pressing their face deep into the metallic stink of his armpit. "It was God's will," he says, crooning. "Valiantly though she fought, she has been elevated to the Pearly Gates, where she kneels at the boots of our Maker."

Upstairs, they boil water in a pail over a fireplace built of sod slabs, with dried cow dung for fuel. The roof is so dry and crumbly that bits of dirt and grass fall from the sod ceiling like autumn leaves.

We could just throw boiling water on him while his back is turned, Eleanor thinks, and they shifts their shackled feet, watching as Charlie paces back and forth near the windmill, muttering to himself.

Would that for sure kill him? Bolt wonders. *'Cause if he was just wounded, he'd shoot us dead.*

They take up the jar of vinegar and pour some into the water. The vinegar had been left behind by the previous occupants—"Must've been Bohunks or Russians, those are the ones that love vinegar," Uncle Charlie said—and they stir with an old wooden spoon.

What if, Bolt wonders, *you got back into your own body? And then you could raise up and point your finger at him, and that would like to give him a heart attack. At least he would go running away, screaming, wouldn't he?*

Eleanor pictures what might await her in the corpse—a carousing festival of decay that will be eager for her to join in. *I don't think that's a good idea.*

Uncle Charlie comes in to check on their work, and there is a moment when he holds his face over the steam above the boiling pail and they could possibly move swiftly and push his head down into the scalding water. Or shove him into the fireplace, though the blaze isn't large enough to engulf him. *How big was that stove in Hansel and Gretel*, they wonder.

Maybe they could pour kerosene on him while he was in bed and drop an oil lamp onto his covers. Wrap a piece of barbed wire around his neck and strangle him until his head pops off. Slice his neck artery with the stiletto and watch him clutch his neck, gurgling, trying to stanch the geysering blood with his hands.

Problem is, they are almost a foot shorter than he, and a hundred or so pounds lighter. They is aware of his strength as he clamps his hands onto Bolt's shoulders (*their shoulders*), as he kneads the trapezius muscles.

"Ah, Bolt," says Uncle Charlie. "I can see how deep you're grieving, and I can tell you from my own experience it's a pain as won't never go away. But I can show you ways to make it lessen—and over time, you and I will forge on, even if we can hardly bear it, because everything we do will be in honor of her memory, and that of your dearly departed daddy. And our Journey, henceforth, is in their name, until such time as we are reunited with them in the land of Heaven!"

As he speaks his massaging becomes tighter and his grip grows harder. "You and me are going to be swell pals, aren't we?" he murmurs. "And

I'm going to take good care of you from now on. I'm going to squeeze you in my arms and always keep you safe. You know that, don't you?"

They wince as his fingers dig in. "Yes," they say.

"I do recall the one time that you tried to poison me," Uncle Charlie says, softly. "But you won't try that ever again, will you?"

Though they share the same mind they still disagree on some things. Did Eleanor make dirt clods fall out of the sky and drop a dead tree branch on a Pinkerton man? She still denies it—still insists she didn't intend to do anything.

They is washing the hair of the dead body, they coils it and twists it, wringing out the excess water. They combs it out smooth, in a fan around her face. They scrubs her eyelids and along the curling hollows of her ear and inside of her nostrils and they wipes her lips.

But didn't she telepathically knock Elmer's coffee cup out of his hand, didn't she make Mr. Jengling's cigar explode in his face?

No.

Or *maybe*, but it wasn't as if she'd sent out a mental ray beam. It just happened. It wasn't as if she had the power to make Uncle Charlie's head explode, or make him catch afire.

They washes the back of the dead girl's hands, and they buffs her fingernails with an emery board.

But what if they concentrates, if they puts both their minds together, if they really joined?

They gently cleans the soles of the dead girl's feet and rubs away the calluses with the emery board.

Try and bend that teaspoon there. Just a little bit.

Nothing.

Try to make the dead girl lift one finger.

Does it quiver? Or is they just imagining things?

They is winding the dead girl up in the mud-soaked linens, wrapping them around her arms and legs and torso, making a mummy of her, when Uncle Charlie comes down the stairs into the cellar.

"I've got some good news!" he exclaims, stomping down in his big boots, his mood hideously jolly. They turns silently from their work to stare at him.

"I got us two big cans of fuel!" he exclaims. "Pr'y enough to carry us all the way to Murdo with our poor dead angel!"

He holds up his lantern, grinning, the whites of his eyes wide and glimmering. His face and the front of his shirt are spattered with blood.

"Found some friendly neighbors who had some kerosene to share!"

Would You Like to Know How You Will Die?

Rosalie rides the body of McGullian Heap through the wild badlands of South Dakota, she has him saddled and bridled, so to speak, and she spurs him and he gallops along the wagon ruts and over the sod-grass hills and red clay. He is more or less an empty vessel now, mostly occupied by a primitive, simpleminded spirit, some kind of early prehuman soul who doesn't give her too much trouble and willingly follows directions.

She can feel Bolt out there in the distance, and she urges her steed forward. *We must find Bolt, we must rescue him*, she sings like a lullaby to her McGullian and it wants water but she whispers *just a little while farther, we can't lose time*—and he gibbers and slavers but obeys.

Meanwhile, a hundred miles or more to the east her body lies, recumbent on a feather bed in a tent, attended by Mme. Clothilde, who holds her hand, and wipes her brow; and by trembling, terrified Shyla, who brushes her hair; and stern Gladness, who squeezes droplets of honey water and lemonade from a silk handkerchief into Rosalie's softly parted lips. She can't believe how far she can travel from herself without losing her grip, though it *is* a strain. Her brother, small as he is, makes their single heart weak, she has to pump so much extra blood just to keep his little head alive, and she can sense how very hard the heart is working now, how fast it thumps in her chest.

But she must have her Bolt back—her special one, her soul's delight, her boy-bride—never has she had a more perfect conduit. For years she has suffered inferior vessels to act as a channel—dull, literal-minded Miss Pettigrew who sat still as a sawhorse and only moved her lips and whispered when Rosalie mounted her; and then stupid Galina, who thrashed around and exuded ectoplasm melodramatically, gagging like she had a braid of hair in her throat the entire time; and then poor timid Ernesto, who allowed himself willingly to be ridden, but he could barely breathe when she was astride him, and he only got weaker as time went on. Mme. Clothilde herself was too dense and vain to allow Rosalie to truly drive her—she was, in truth, a medium of quite limited psychic ability that she augmented with clever jugglery—but sometimes when Madame was enjoying a cigaret, she could be made to hear a few words after much screaming.

Well. *Bon . . .*

Before all that had been the long time she'd been attached to Heap—the only true conduit she had known before Bolt—though also most foul, most hateful, for to ride him meant sitting on his lap and feeling his erection, it meant being enclosed in his stink of old beer and cigars and whiskey and unwashed balls and the slime of his interior thoughts.

And then Bolt had come along, and he had been as easy to mount as Heap had been, but so much nicer and cleaner, so open and good-natured—and after only a few months with him she had felt herself growing stronger and more truly present in the world, and she knew she could with only a little coaxing make this Bolt tame and obedient and teach him lots of tricks—

When the twins first came, Rosalie thought she might be able to make use of the girl as well, but Eleanor was sealed up tight. Eleanor was one of those frustrating people who had no entryway, not even a crack, not even a stray, glancing thought could be heard. Rosalie was a bit afraid of her.

The body of McGullian Heap gets a prickly pear cactus stuck in its paw, and tries to pull it out with its teeth and yelps with surprise as the fishhook spines catch in its lips—

And this gives what little is left of the old McGullian a chance to grow hysterical like a moth in a jar beating its wings—

Let me out!
Let me out!

But his voice is only a gurgling from underwater and she makes him grow even smaller. "No! No!" peeps Heap, and then he tucks his scrawny, hairy body into a ball on the ground, with his torn feet curling like a baby's, and his bloody hands cupping his genitals for comfort and she doesn't make him stop. It's pleasant enough.

Heap's body does not have long left—he's burning hot, his kidneys, his liver, his boiling innards. Oh, his poor, poor heart! But he'll do as he's told and like it till the end.

YOU'LL DO AS YOU'RE TOLD AND LIKE IT, BY GOD!

Wasn't that how he'd always explained things?

Still, she can't help but feel a little tenderly toward this wretched, gizzardy rodent of a man, she can manifest herself as the spirit of a sweet and innocently kind girl in a clean frock, who can gently pet the filthy creature's matted fur as it gulps up its piteously endless sobs, pissing itself a little. *Shhhh*, she can say, soothingly. *Shhhhhhhhhhhhhhhhhhh.*

Now, get up!

And he does. He must. He gets up and takes some sustenance from the hand of Tickley-Feather, some mix of herbs and mushrooms and meat that he reverently lips from Tickley-Feather's extended palm. There is experience of rapid cicada-like vibrations from several planes, communicating back and forth.

Otherwise, the man who goes by Tickley-Feather remains, like Eleanor, irritatingly shut off from her—she's not even certain if he *is* an actual person, though he must be the semblance of one, since the Muscle Lady called Mona seems to recognize him as one of *her kind*.

Whatever that is.

Over the years, Rosalie has touched most of them and taken stock. She knows their beginnings and endings, she knows when they'll die, most likely, but she has never been one of them, she has never been a passenger of Jengling's Ark, his fantasy commune with one of every kind. She will never sit at a table and drink from a Loving Cup with them, she will never be part of their social dramas, though she occasionally observes them from afar with mild interest. But with most of them, the first thing she always learns is how they will die—and once she knows that, it's hard to take much interest in the day-to-day worries and minutiae that they are wasting their remaining life with.

For better or worse, she has always been the daughter of Heap. She can recall nothing of the past before Heap acquired her, before she became his property, his child, his puppet—and then the reverse—this—this thing—whatever his remnant is—

He drinks from an algae pond full of late-brood tadpoles, and sucks them up in big slurping swallows. He bites lightly but furiously on the wounded knucklebone of his forefinger, like a squirrel trying to open a nut. He pauses from running to grab his ankle and lick a sticker from the sole of his own bare foot.

But also he is singularly obedient. Singularly her own.

At least until they can find Bolt.

You Will Never Love Again

Actually, Charlie didn't really want the girl anyway. Having the boy is good enough, he decides, and probably better! Together, the pair of them would have conspired against him, and Charlie would've always had to be constantly on watch for runaway or murder attempts or other such betrayals; alone, the lad will behave himself and mind what he's told. Look at him! Not even crying no more, just sitting quiet and solemn, with his hands in his lap, next to the cadaver of his sissy.

Still, he keeps an eye on them, just in case, he glances back occasionally as he drives. He has the girl beshawled with a blanket because nobody wants to see the mummy-wrapped corpse of a thirteen-year-old girl propped up in a rumble seat of a Model T as it passes.

They're making good time. Mostly, the roads are smooth and flat here in the badlands of the Dakotas, and he can reach speeds of thirty or forty miles per hour—though he has to take care, since sometimes the roads can be rutted and wagon-worn and if he broke an axle he'd be bum-swiggled.

But if they keep going at this pace, and the kerosene holds out, they'll be in Murdo in no time, and he'll have the damned little Albertine in the ground next to her daddy.

Murdo, says Rosalie's mount.

Tickley-Feather lifts his head from the stick he's whittling. Stiffens.

Murrrrrdo, says the *wîhtikow*, and Tickley-Feather gets up and walks over to where it's hunched on the ground with its ankles chained. He toes it with his boot.

Acch! Acch! it gurgles, coughing up black-flecked phlegm. It gazes up at him with hostile misery, and he places his hand over its mouth and nose until he can feel the dewy condensation of its breath on his palm.

"Speak," he commands.

A human body can be infected with any number of spirits, but never has he seen a person so riddled with them. The one they call Piltdown Man is like a lump of meat squirming with maggots. Pustules in the shape of tiny faces have broken out on his forehead, along the edge of his hairline. He lent himself out as a conduit for too long, Tickley-Feather reckons, and now his soul is as thin as lace, and as full of holes.

His slobbering mouth licks and lips Tickley-Feather's palm and Rosalie's voice comes up out of his throat.

"Ruined!" she mutters. "She's taken him and ***RUINED*** him! I'll never love again!"

I'*ll never love again!* Bolt hears himself gasp—he doesn't even know why—very often the spiritual air is full of little voices and snatches of phrases, and from time to time they catch hold of you.

That's right you won't, Eleanor thinks. *You don't need to.*

And anyway, they have other concerns at the moment. They have arrived now in the little town of Murdo, and it is bleaker than they could have ever imagined—a cluster of houses on the edge of the railroad, maybe home to three or four hundred people, no trees, no hills, just an endless stretch of flat, sepia-colored dirt, a main street made up of a few weathered stores with high false fronts, an old cowboy wandering along the dusty road with a starving, wire-haired mutt hobbling along behind him, its spine hunched and all of its ribs visible.

Oh, God, is this where Eleanor is to be buried? Uncle Charlie seems to have forgotten that her remains are riding in the rumble seat behind him, and he's cheerfully holding forth on the history of Murdo, as if he's the president of the Chamber of Commerce. "Named for Murdo MacKenzie, the famed cattle baron, manager of the Matador Land and

Cattle Company and most well regarded! He was given a honorarium by Teddy Roosevelt hisself, and put on Murdo's neck a medal with a silk ribbon! Now, I never met him, but I was present when his son Dode was shot in LeBeau, and there was a big to-do about it because he was a MacKenzie, and also worked for Matador."

Soon, Eleanor thinks, they'll put her corpse in the ground here, and that's where it will remain forever, until it's nothing but bones and dust. What a strange thought, that she and her own body will soon be parted, that she'll never again see the flesh that once contained her. Bolt strokes her mud-caked, mummy-wrapped hand with his fingers. They gaze upon her pale, cold face, her eyes closed and her mouth a flat, inexpressive line. In death, she is not so homely as she thought she was. It's not a dainty face, but—not horrible to look upon, after all. Why had she thought that? What part of her had felt such a strong need to be ugly?

Now that the body is lost to her, she misses it. Being in Bolt's body is not the same—it's not hers. She's only a resident—a boarder—and it would be very difficult for she herself to take the steering wheel of it. She could make Bolt's feet take steps forward and maintain her balance, she supposes, but it would be quite another thing to maneuver the fingers to turn the pages of a book, or to pick up a knife.

"I'd like to check us in to the Crosbie Hotel," Uncle Charlie is saying. "That's where your father passed, and it'd be nice to say a little prayer and let him know that his dear daughter has gone to her greater reward. Despite all that loving and caring hands could do!"

Charlie steers Bolt through the front door of the hotel with his hand locked on the back of the lad's collar in a firm but fatherly grip, and guess who he sees? Why, it's that sweet little Norwegian lass whose neck he suckled upon when he was aghast with grief at poor Jasper's funeral and had on accident given her a love-bruise most black upon her creamy skin. She looks terrified to see him again.

He gives her a warm and kindly nod and approaches the front desk with a gentlemanly reserve. Best, he decides, to pretend that he's never met her before.

"Afternoon, miss!" says he, polite as you please, but still she keeps her head down and won't look up. He has a charming twinkle in his eye that is going completely to waste. "I'd like a room for myself and my nephew," he says.

"Two room?" she says and pinches her mouth just as tiny as it will go. She pushes the open guest-register book toward him, as if it will provide a barrier.

"No, just one!" Charlie beams. "Me and my nephew, we're as close as peas in a pod!" He takes up the fountain pen and writes in his prettiest handwriting: *C. W. Lambkin and Nephew.*

"I'd like to have the second room on the left at the top of the stairs, if it's available," Charlie says—that's the room where Jasper hung hisself—and the Norwegianess glances up despite herself, startled. Her thin and delicate fingers tremble.

"That will be seventy-five cents for the night," she mumbles, and with a flourish Charlie puts a quarter and a fifty-cent piece on the counter. *Click. Click!*

And she gives him the key and up he goes, with Bolt be-collared by his palm, whistling a Norwegian song called "*Eg ser deg ut for gluggjin*," which he'd learned from a tiresomely talkative gambler name of Knausgaard, back in the days of his youth.

The room is not much to speak of, but it's clean and tidy: a nice-size bed, big enough for two, and a little writing table with a chair by the window, and of course the big closet where Jasper had hung himself with his belt.

He reckons that Bolt doesn't need to hear about that.

"Do you need to make water before I tie you up?" he says. "I'm going to leave you here for a while. I got to get your sissy out that rumble seat before somebody tries to steal her and get her over to the undertaker. Then I got to go to the courthouse before they close and buy a grave next to your daddy if it's still available. But don't worry, I'm sure it is, I doubt if they've had a run on cemetery plots since last I was here."

He turns his back and faces the wall as Bolt tinkles into a bedpan. The wallpaper is a winding floral pattern, white on Regency pink, pretty fancy for a Podunk town hotel.

Charlie bids Bolt to lie on the bed and hog-ties him with rope, and the lad doesn't put up any kind of resistance. If anything, he's a bit limp and almost like he's half-asleep, and Charlie hopes that the boy isn't prone to the woofits as his father was.

"I imagine you're pr'y tired and sore from our ardorous journey, eh?" Charlie says, and Bolt doesn't look at him—a bit pouty, Charlie thinks. "Now, I'll give you a little something to help you sleep. And when I get back, I'll give you a nice foot rub!"

Charlie takes a bottle of laudanum from his inner coat pocket and sucks up a tot of it with an eyedropper. "Open up for the medicine!" he croons, and catches hold of Bolt's jaw and drips the drug between the boy's parted lips.

Hum.

Hum.

"Now, listen here," he says. "I'm thinking I should best put a gag in your mouth so you won't decide to yell and holler while I'm gone."

"I won't," says the boy, with sullen dreariness. "I'm not going to make a peep," he mutters.

"Hum," Charlie says. "That's what someone who's planning to cry out for help would say." And to be on the safe side he digs through his rucksack until he finds a soft, chewy piece of leather and balls it up and stuffs it into the lad's mouth cavity—not rough at all, but tenderly.

"This is only tempererry," Charlie murmurs, and gives the boy's hair a gentle stroke. "We're going to be pals, you and me," he says, and watches as the laudanum begins to work, as the eyes grow dim and unfocused. "You're going to learn to trust me, and we're going to be forever friends."

Tickley-Feather instructs Herculea in the art of sharpshooting. She carries a Smith & Wesson Model 10 revolver, not a bad weapon, and they stand in the dusk with the sun in her eyes and she takes aim at empty cans of beans that he's lined up on the fence posts.

He's a good teacher—patient, encouraging, articulate—albeit a little cold. Still, in a few hours' practice, she will learn enough to keep herself alive.

He himself is an expert marksman and quick-draw—he could hold his own among the cowboys in Buffalo Bill's Wild West Circus crew, and he sometimes regrets that he is too young to have had the opportunity to have been a gunfighter, to face a villain in a duel on the street of some cowboy town, to shoot a white man dead in the presence of other white men, and walk away. That would have been something.

He stands behind the girl and adjusts her posture. She'd told Jengling that she'd had experience with a gun, but he can't see it. He takes her hand and shows her how to hold her fingers.

He is an excellent chess player—better than Jengling. He is a decent tracker and scout. He is an electrical hobbyist with a good grasp of the principles of magnetism. He can recognize birds of the region by their song, and mammals by their scat.

He is a middling clown—his mime is more sinister than humorous, and he's never known how to make people laugh—but he *does* know how to be propelled out of a cannon, how to hold his body still, arms at his sides like a diver, arcing through the air toward the waiting net.

As for the spiritualist realm, it's harder to gauge. He has some skill as an exorcist, and as a reader of auras. He can project his thoughts when necessary.

But he has no idea how to handle a creature like this Piltdown Man, nor the one they call Rosalie, for that matter. Both of them seem to have gone into a funk, but he does believe that the last thing she told him is right: they'll find the twins and their captor in Murdo, and they should go to the graveyard where the twins' father is buried. Beyond that, there has only been sullen muttering: *She can't stay in there, it's not allowed,* burbles the Piltdown Man in the voice of a fourteen-year-old girl. *The right of the stream, a glowstone, I suppose—*

And so: target practice. He just wants to get the muscle girl to the point where she's not a complete liability, because who knows what they're walking into.

In the opium dream, Bolt is in the Big Top with the audience applauding him on all sides. He's wearing Mister Jengling's top hat and bright red coat, his black jodhpur pants and high black leather boots, and they clap, thousands of faces in the bleachers gazing down at him raptly as he stretches out his hand. "Ladies and gentlemen," he booms, and gestures broadly with his whip, "I present to you my beloved family!"

And they all come parading in—here is Gladness, holding a thurible censer that trails pink smoke, and behind her is Miss Alcott, carrying a naked Elmer in her arms like a baby, and Jengling with Mme. Clothilde perched on his shoulder, and Shyla and Alberic prancing and tossing candies, and Mr. Lacis, his body stuck through with railroad spikes like a pincushion; and the man with the tiny head, his face skeletal like a starving person, playing his accordion, with his dog dancing on its hind legs, and all the rest of them striding along behind, and as they pass each one gives Bolt a look of admiration and love. The marching band is playing that song they sang to him and Eleanor once: *One of us, one of us, we accept you—*

And meanwhile Eleanor, not drugged, observes her brother's dream with stoic impatience. There seems to be no way to wake him, and no matter how hard she flexes she can't make him hear her or stir. She can't even change the tenor of the dream to something they might both enjoy.

If only she could make this body move. Even hog-tied as they are, they could struggle off the bed, they could caterpillar along the floor and pound against the door until the girl downstairs came up to see what was the matter.

But try as she might, she can only wiggle the fingers a bit. She can only open the eyes and blink at the window where she can see a hawk drifting in the clear sky at some distance away. Maybe if she tried, she could leap into the bird?

You should, says a little voice. *You'd be better off there, I think.* It comes to her as if from a distance, as if from a memory of a long-ago conversation. Not her own voice, but—familiar, somehow.

You'll never love again, says the tiny voice. *You'll shrink him and belittle him and take over everything, like you do, but why do you deserve to be the boss? You don't even like to be alive.*

Yes, I do! Eleanor thinks. *I do!*

She contorts as hard as she can muster, and Bolt moves a few inches toward the edge of the bed.

Charlie and the undertaker are in the charnel room at the back of the Tillman Funeral Home, and Eleanor is laid out on a slab, slathered in red river clay and wrapped in linen cloth. On a table next to her are the embalming tools—the tubes and pumps and hoses, the brass syringes and array of surgical instruments. There's a stack of pine coffins in one corner, and a shelf full of jars of formaldehyde on another, which perfume the entire room with their pungence.

"My God," says Tillman the undertaker. "What happened to this poor child?"

"She passed of a wasting disease over near a little town called Scotland," Charlie says solemnly, and clears his throat. "But I brung her here so she could be interred next to her beloved father. It was her last wish, and I felt that it would be heartless not to honor it."

"Why is she coated in mud?" The undertaker frowns, touching the cracking layer that covers her forearm, and Charlie feels judged by the bald, pinch-faced old feller.

"Well," Charlie says, sheepishly. "I read it somewhere that a bath of clay could postpone the discompensation of the recently deceased."

"That's nonsense," says the bespectacled corpse diddler rebukefully. "If anything, you've quickened the process. I'm afraid getting all of this mess off her is going to take some time and effort. It'll cost you extra."

"Of course," Charlie says softly, and looks down at the card he'd been given. D. H. TILLMAN, GENERAL UNDERTAKER, it says. KEEPS ON-HAND AND FURNISHES TO-ORDER COFFINS, CASKETS, BURIAL CASES, ROBES AND SHROUDS, PRICES VERY REASONABLE!

"I can give you a diamond ring if you can make her look purty. I'd like to put some ribbons and flowers in her hair and paint her face so it looks rosy and dress her in a funerary robe of white satin material or equivalent. And a white casket with pink flowers painted on it."

"I can't promise anything until I've got the mud and rags off of her," says Tillman curtly. "Depending on the level of decay we may prefer putting her in a shroud. And the only casket I've got on hand is oak with a red velvet cloth interior."

"I see," says Charlie. He knows he definitely read about this clay and linen-wrap treatment in a book, but he doesn't think arguing about it will get him anywhere. Still, he feels that the man could at least compliment him on his initiative.

"And I'll need to see this diamond ring of yours," says the balding scoldy-lips. "I don't usually take trade. Or bank cheques."

Charlie nods, and stares covetously at the assortment of sharp instruments laid out on the table—gougers and peelers, round-tipped scalpels and nail trimmers and long-toothed sawing blades, hollow pokers and hooked scrapers and long needle-y things. What fun it would be to try them out on somebody living.

"Hum," Charlie says, and hands over the ring, which he knows for a fact to be a pretty valuable piece of jewelry. He has come to be a fairly good appraiser over the years of acquiring such stuff.

Mme. Clothilde holds her cool, soft palm on Rosalie's wrist. One hundred and twenty beats per minute, much, much too fast, particularly for a child with a weak heart. She looks at Dr. Chui, on the other side of the bed, and Harland behind him. "Can anything be done about this *tachycardie*? She seems quite frail."

Chui frowns, passing his enormous hand softly across the girl's red, sweating face. "There is a tea that can be made," he says. "Containing epimedium, ginseng, hazel leaf, wild ginger, sage, and a powder of dried leeches. Whether such ingredients are available, though . . ."

"I will see what I can find," says Jengling. "We have an extensive assortment of herbs." And he strides out.

You'll never love again, Rosalie whispers feverishly, barely audible, as Chui wipes her brow with a cool cloth.

Elmer the dog-faced boy, in his baseball-toss booth, in the midst of his patter, abruptly feels his arm muscles twitch. "You'll never love again," he hears himself blurt out, involuntarily, startled, and at the edge of the fairgrounds a young mother hands her five-year-old daughter a stick wrapped with fairy floss and the child looks up at her sweetly. "You'll never love again," the tot says, and back in their house in Yankton the little girl's grandmother wakes from dozing and coughs and spits delicately into a handkerchief. "You'll never love again," she chokes, and a white-breasted nuthatch near her window flutters with sudden alarm and flies off. *You'll never*, it cries, *love again-gain-gain*—

This reaches the ears of a mule pulling a hay cart toward the little town of Tabor, where a small group of Czech immigrants have settled, and the horse's driver feels a kind of electrical shock. *Už nikdy nebudete milovat*, he thinks, and he drops the reins for a moment—

And from there the message passes through mosquitoes and minnows, through Charles Mix County and across Goose Lake, up the Missouri River to Oacoma, where it finds a ten-year-old boy on a dock and he jerks his fishing pole and it feels like he's caught something. "You'll never love again!" the boy cheers and gives his line a yank and pulls up a monster of a catfish, and his mother jolts from hanging sheets on a clothesline behind their house as if the clothespin had bit her and she hears herself let out a sharp little cry, *you'll never love again*, and a locust picks it up and lifts off out of the weeds toward the roiling prairie, beating its wings faster even than Rosalie's heart.

Eleanor hears it in the back of their mind as they looks down upon the corpse of her own face. They are in the funeral parlor for the viewing, and the undertaker stands off to the side with his hands clasped respectfully in front him, surreptitiously watching as Bolt and Uncle Charlie stand before the casket.

Eleanor's face has been powdered and her cheeks have been brightly rouged; her lips have been painted bright red, and a blond wig with ringlets has been fitted over her scalp and decorated with ribbons and pale pink paper flowers. Her hands have been crossed over her chest, and she wears a thin white gown, like a nightdress.

It is slowly beginning to dawn on her that this clownish mannequin will be her final version. Her body cannot be revived or recovered—and though she never once loved it, she now sees that it was more than just a suit of flesh that she was wearing. It was an idea—a sense of a true, unquestioned *home*—and now that she's only a spark of consciousness, she'll never be able to get that back. She intuits now that if she still had a body, she would have grown and changed with it—in two years, in ten years, in fifty years, her spirit would have been completely different. The Eleanor she is now would've still been present, but along with layers of other selves, other lives.

Alas! Now she will be a confused and unhappy thirteen-and-a-half-year-old girl forever, or at least for as long as this glimmer of herself can stay awake. For as long as it clutches hold of the material world, for as long as it wants to remain.

They are still groggy with laudanum, and they lurch at the edge of the casket, unsteadily. Bolt reaches down as if to stroke the corpse's folded hands. *Don't*, Eleanor says. *Don't touch it.*

And they rest their fingers on the lip of the varnished wood casket where it meets the red velvet interior.

"It sure is a purty casket, ain't it?" Uncle Charlie says. "I think they did her up real nice. She looks so life-like."

They can feel Uncle Charlie's hand stroking the back of their head.

"Go on," Charlie says, and tightens his grip, pressing their face downward. "Plant a tender kiss of farewell upon her porcelain cheek."

They pucker their lips and close their eyes.

Once they've finished with the viewing, they carry the casket out to the hearse, Charlie and Bolt pallbearing on one side, Tillman the undertaker and his assistant on the other. The helper is a grimbly-muscled young Bohunk buck, square of head, with eyes that seem like they are two different sizes, and it's not clear if he has all his wits. The Bohunk isn't ugly enough to sell to a circus, but he definitely must turn heads when people see him coming toward them.

Anyway, he's sturdy enough to dig a hole in the ground and strong enough to haul a barrel of human guts out to whatever ditch they dump the offal into, and he's steady enough getting the casket loaded into the horse-drawn coffin-carriage.

They all climb in and ride about three blocks to the cemetery.

It's a sunny day, clear-skied, as they solemnly pace down the main street, and Charlie waves at a drunkard who has just hobbled out of the saloon and who takes his hat off as they pass. It feels like they're in a parade, and he waves also at two grubby barefoot urchins in knee-high breeches who are chasing after a wounded chicken, and salutes a prim, churchy-looking lass with a tiny lacy bonnet atop her braided bun.

It's not much of a town, he has to admit—just a cluster of junk alongside the railroad tracks, a few brick and clapboard shops, a shoddy church, a smattering of shacks hardly bigger than a shithouse, and stacks of cement bags and pine two-by-fours and clinkers. South Dakota is going to the dogs, he thinks. Time to look toward brighter horizons!

He's been thinking about ambling down to Ruby, Arizona, or possibly Abilene, Texas. He had some good times in Fort Griffin, back in the day.

He's done here now, he's finished what he's had to do, and you know what? It's a good feeling of accomplishment! He may not have Jasper anymore, but he kept his promise, and now he's got Jasper's son, which might be even better. Hopefully, Bolt'll have his daddy's gifts without the woofits and suicidal urges.

Things are looking up, that's what Charlie is thinking. He has been blessed with so many lives, so many transmogrifications, from humble and hateful beginnings, through more adventures than you can count, and he just keeps striving to improve and improve—he's not just murdering random families anymore, but now he's MAKING a family of his own! And he feels certain that he and Bolt will come to share the most secret of their secrets together.

The horse-drawn hearse, draped with black crepe, comes to a stop in the little cemetery, and Charlie recognizes the site from Jasper's funeral—a tombstone at the edge of the treeless, unfenced patch of graveyard, with the barren stretch of badlands behind it. The hole next to Jasper's gravestone has already been dug, and they hop out and unload the casket and place it on a pallet that can be lowered into the grave with a rope and pulley.

Goddam, he realizes that he has forgotten to hire a preacher!

Now what? It's sad that he and Bolt and the undertaker and his idiot will be the only ones in attendance, but admit it—little Nelly had never been the kind of girl who would've ever drawn a crowd of mourners.

Let's get this over with, he thinks. He clears his throat and steps forward, hands clasped. He looks down at the casket, and can't think what to say, and so he decides he'll sing a little.

Rock of Ages,
Gold to be!
Let me hiiiide
My face in
thee!

And he can't remember any more of it, so he just hums a bit and glances over at the Bohunk, hoping the simpleton will get the hint that it's time to lower the goddam coffin.

You will never
Love again!
You will neeever
Love
again.

He sings, and he thinks: that's not right.

No! He will! He WILL love again! Why would he even think such a thing?

And then, as if in a hallucination, they appear as he's singing—as his baritone strains toward tenor, he sees them.

There is the tall, lanky half-breed on a mule with a rifle cradled in his arms; and to his left is his young friend, feminine of face but quite muscular in physique; and to her left, a wild man with a thatch of long hair and a shock of beard who looks like a stick of dynamite blew up in his face.

The circus folk have found him, somehow, and Charlie feels the old rage gurgle in his stomach. "What is the meaning of this infusion?" Charlie bellows.

But they just keep approaching. No expressions, just a kind of cold intentness. He feels a tingle of unease. They were wise not to bring any obvious deformitaries with them but still they are *freaks*, who should've been put in a sack and dropped in a river at birth! Any normal, natural man will stand with him against them.

He looks to Undertaker Tillman and his half-wit, who are both observing the approaching strangers with mild puzzlement, and he takes a step behind Bolt, placing one firm hand on the boy's waist, and with the other hand withdraws the stiletto which he gently pricks into the small of the lad's back. "We may have a problem here," he murmurs, and pulls Bolt a little closer. "Don't make it worse, nephew. I won't kill you right away if you cause trouble but I *will* cripple you for life."

This has been on the agenda in the back of his mind anyway—making sure that the boy could never leave him—whether that meant breaking one of his shinbones so he'd be unable to run fast, or cutting off the tip of his tongue so he could only talk like a moron, Charlie hadn't decided. But once this showdown is over he'll get to work on debilitating his young ward in some way as soon as possible.

Meanwhile, D. H. Tillman doesn't like the looks of this. Most people don't realize how often violent conflicts erupt during graveside services, but as a funeral director he's seen it over and over, and he has no intention of getting involved in family squabbles. "*Tsssst,*" he hisses at his sister's brother-in-law, Ivar, and when Ivar catches his eye he points with his thumb. They both begin to back away, stepping slowly toward the hearse.

Herculea has her revolver unholstered and holds it at her side. She is going to kill this man, she thinks, and she is aware of how sad her Totty would be, to see his daughter become a *Tvtshlag'r,* a murderer! But what can be done? He is an evil man who must be stopped, yes? She has no choice.

The unshaved, black-haired man maneuvers himself slightly behind the child, and it outrages her to see him using the boy as a shield. Coward!

"You don't belong here!" the brute calls. "This is a *Christian* cemetery. They got ones for you circus folk up to Wisconsin, I think. You should head out, lest ill befall you!"

And then Tickley-Feather speaks from atop his mule. "We've come to bring a killer to justice," he says, and his voice is clear and solemn and almost princely, she thinks, and her eyes burn.

Yes. She also would like Justice.

As the tall one speaks, Piltdown Man inches forward, crouches like a cat, so low to the ground that the scrub grass brushes his belly. He grips the dirt with his fingers and toes, creeping along the edge of the thicket of wooden crosses and headstones, just out of the prey's line of sight. If he can remain unnoticed, he might circle around behind the man his mistress hates and the boy she covets. He feels a shiver run in a tickling shimmer all along his skin. He can hear the men's voices gnarling but he long ago lost interest in human language. All he wants, all he's ever wanted, is to bite and rend and tear with tooth and claw.

There is no greater pleasure in life, no greater hope.

"**L**et loose the child!" calls Tickley-Feather. He is trying to calculate. How stupid he'd been, not to foresee that the villain would hunker down behind the boy instead of facing them. Again and again, he miscalculates the willingness of these people to commit acts that would make he himself die of shame.

"Oh, you want the boy, too, do you?" calls out the Murder Man in a mocking singsong voice, and he clutches Bolt close and swings him back and forth in a hideous, swaying waltz, three-stepping in front of the casket, which hangs suspended over the open grave. "C'mon! Shoot me in the eye and win a prize!"

And Bolt's head swims as he's rocked and weaved roughly back and forth. He's still loopy on laudanum, but he can definitely feel the needle stabs of the stiletto, piercing the skin on his lower back with little sharp pricks as they swivel. He gazes down into the hole where they were going to put Eleanor and his eyes smart with tears.

"Go! Leave!" he cries toward Tickley-Feather. "I—I want to be with my uncle Charlie! Get out of here!"

It's the only thing he can think to say that will make Uncle Charlie quit dancing and poking, and he hopes that somehow Tickley-Feather will know that he's just faking. He hears his voice, high as that of a turkey calling for water.

"That's right," Uncle Charlie says, sounding pleased and pleasantly surprised. "Yer my special baby," he whispers, and gives Bolt's ear a nuzzle. "Don't worry. I'll save you."

And Eleanor apprehends the voice of her father, a half-heard whisper carried on the filth-breath of Uncle Charlie murmuring against the side of their head. She can feel him nearby, his corpse in the grave next to the one that has been dug for her.

Isn't this what you wanted? says Jasper Lambkin, his voice dreamy and disinterested. *You wanted to stay alive. Now you must fight for it.*

She can't see her father. She looks out through their eyes and only sees Tickley-Feather with his rifle, astride a mule, and that muscle girl, and she doubts that they are going to save them.

Father, help us, she thinks, but there is only silence.

Bolt? she thinks, but he doesn't seem to hear her.

All right, she thinks. *All right.* And she buckles down as hard as she can.

A clod of earth falls abruptly from the sky and strikes Charlie on the top of the head. "Why, you!" Charlie cries, and looks up, gape-mouthed toward the sky, and a sudden rain of pebbles comes pouring down, and he gasps, gags as they fall into his face. "Gaaa!" he sputters.

Piltdown springs from behind onto the prey's back, and he latches his teeth as hard as he can onto the fat neck and clutches the hair between his fingers and bites and gnashes, bites and gnashes—

And Herculea thinks she has the perfect shot and fires just as Charlie twists around and the bullet meant for Charlie's brain finds Piltdown Man instead—

And Charlie stumbles, burying the stiletto deep into the small of Bolt's back—

And Bolt falls forward, onto the casket, and the pallet collapses under his weight and he falls into the pit and he thinks, *Okay, it's*—

And Rosalie lets out a gasp as her mount is downed and she sits up back in her bed in the tent. She sucks in air like a person who has been drownding.

"They're killed! They're killed!" she shrieks, and Dr. Chui and Mme. Clothilde try to hold her down as her body goes into convulsions and her hardworking heart strains to stay pumping.

"**H**a ha! You can't catch me!" screams Charlie, and his legs perform a crazy jig, he feels the clown's bullet graze him and feints and dodges and starts running toward the wide-open prairie, toward the darkness, tumbling and panting, scrambling and ducking and evading—and they'll never get him, THEY'LL NEVER GET HIM—

But from the corpse of the Piltdown Man are so many souls released—dozens fly out bodiless, desperate, and they pursue after him like hornets and his body writhes and twitches, his arms thrash and his legs pump as all of them riddle into him like buckshot.

AIEEEE! Charlie utters: a rageful bellow—a terrible, yodeling laugh—an anguished cry—all at once piercing—

And then he is running and dancing, giggling and nimble, and above him he feels the jolly moon and the strip of purple Milky Way that pirouettes with uncountable stars. He's going to be alive FOREVER! He feels the vastness of time, he feels the clustering merriment and swirling agita of the many souls inside him, he cackles because he can apprehend the eleven billion years between the birth of the Earth and the death of the Sun, and he has at least that much time before—

Even as the bullet of Tickley-Feather the clown approaches the back of his skull. Milliseconds. Eternity.

It Wasn't a Dream, It Was a Place

••••••••••

Bolt will recover with time and rest, Dr. Chui says. He is very, very lucky. The blade did not pierce any vital organs, nor did it nick the bowels or he would surely be dead. Still, by the time Bolt is returned to the arms of the Jengling Emporium, his wound is seriously infected, and he's lost a considerable amount of blood. He will be severely ill and bedridden for several weeks, but Dr. Chui feels certain that he will survive.

Bolt wants to live so badly. Eleanor cannot experience the pain he feels, the fever and chills and nausea, the dull terrible throbbing at the site of the puncture—but she can perceive him fighting against death, and even though his mind is blurry with the struggle, it is clear to her: Oh, how frantically he wants to be alive!

Well, so be it. She'd thought it was over when the knife slid into their back, when they fell into the grave on top of the coffin that contained her body, she thought, *All right, this is the perfect end*, but then Tickley-Feather was in the hole and lifting them out, passing them up to Herculea, who cradled them in her powerful arms. Tickley-Feather looked into their face and though Bolt was unconscious Eleanor was awake, and the tall man's voice spoke in Eleanor's mind.

You're going to come back home with us, he told her. *And you're going to behave yourself. You owe us a debt. You are beholden to the Jengling Carnival, and to Billy Bigelow, who died for you, and to your brother, who let you in and gave you shelter. You are liable and honor-bound. Do you understand?*

She did not appreciate his haughty and condescending tone, but she assented. *Yes*, she said, and Bolt yelped as Herculea tried to stanch his wound.

They are in the same body, but not in the same place. The physical suffering makes him distant to her, it takes so much of his attention. Dr. Chui rubs the lesion on his back with a tincture of honey and garlic, and they winces and tears fall down their face. *Eleanor!* he calls, and she says, *I'm here, I'm with you—*

You made stones fall out of the sky, Bolt whispers. *You saved us.*

Yes, she says.

And Bolt falls back to sleep, smiling vaguely, comforted.

After a week, he's well enough to receive visitors. They line up outside the tent where he is convalescing, all of them—*all of them!*—one by one, they come to tell him they hope he gets better soon, and they are so sorry that he lost his sister, and they are praying for him to get better soon, and they care for him.

It's hard for Eleanor to believe that they are in earnest, but what other reason is there? Maybe there was a code of love that she'd never learnt, that she'd never known existed. Would they have lined up for her, if she were alive and Bolt were dead? She doubts it.

First comes Miss Alcott, accompanied by Jengling.

"She's been positively *desperate* to see him," Jengling tells Dr. Chui, and Miss Alcott hovers behind him. "She would like to hold him in her arms."

Dr. Chui nods, and Miss Alcott steps forward and lifts Bolt's body so gently, so gently, and rocks him and croons a song in gorilla-ese, and strokes his brow, and her eyes stare down at him with a deep and sorrowful concern.

"She is gifted with an empathy beyond human comprehension," Jengling tells Dr. Chui.

And Mr. Lacis gets on his knees and kisses Bolt's hand. "Oh, boy!" he says. "I hope you will be better soon!" He strikes his breast with his fist. "I am so sorry of your sister!" He weeps, and bows his head, and cries into the blankets on their bed.

The price he pays for his open, fatherly affection is despair. Most people expect cruelty as the normal order of things, but for poor Lacis, it is a constant shock, he has always believed in the essential goodness of people.

When he touches their skin, Eleanor has her first clear presentiment. She knows that he will remain with Jengling for the rest of his life, and that he will use his big toe on the trigger of a rifle to shoot himself in the mouth on or about July 7, 1919.

When Mme. Clothilde comes in accompanied by Shyla, Eleanor gets the same glimmer. It seems that Shyla has been reluctantly elected as Mme. Clothilde's handmaiden, and she hovers in the background uncomfortably as the little woman seats herself regally at Bolt's bedside and takes his hand.

"How are you feeling, *mon cher*," Mme. Clothilde says, and they open their eyes hazily.

"Not that bad," says Bolt, and smiles wanly, but Eleanor finds herself looking at Shyla, and she can sense the girl's eminent and horrific death at the age of twenty-three, on or about February 10, 1921, and she recoils at the brief flash of images before pushing them away.

And Mme. Clothilde looks at them sharply. "Ah!" she says, and turns her head to glance sternly at Shyla, and then back to Bolt.

"Ah! I see that you are not alone, are you, my darling?" Mme. Clothilde murmurs. "Ohhh—she is there with you, isn't she? Your sister? *Je l'ai sous-estimée.*"

"Whu—?" Bolt says, and Mme. Clothilde wipes their face with her handkerchief. "*Plus tard*," she says. "Now we must only think about getting well."

And Shyla's enormous brown eyes widen and quickly shift away. Doomed. Poor girl.

Things flow into them so easily, now—where once, Bolt could only catch brief snippets of thoughts, together they can scan through the pages of a person's mind like flipping through a book.

Eleanor finds herself surprised that people are, for the most part, not nearly as full of vicious intentions and cruel urges as she'd thought them to be. When Gladness and Alberic come in for a visit, Eleanor is aware that they feel genuine compassion for this boy, who was kidnapped by a madman and had his sister murdered.

Alberic squats down lithely by the bedside. "Hey there, Banjo-Eyes," he says, teasing playfully, like an older brother. "Gladness was going to bring her snake to see you, but I talked her out of it."

Bolt laughs, then winces when it hurts the wound in their back, and Gladness gives their hair a soft stroke with her palm. "My snake," she says, "is sending you all its best wishes for a speedy recovery. And I'm so sorry about your sister. I can't imagine how such a loss must grieve you. I wish I might've known her better."

And Eleanor apprehends that Gladness believes she didn't like her and Shyla because they were colored. And that Gladness had been hurt by her refusal to sit with them in the commissary. And she sees that Gladness and Alberic will have a mostly blessed life. They will marry, and they will not want for money, and they will have four children, none of them with any special skill but all of them—two boys, two girls—will grow up to be handsome and beautiful, and they will each have success in their chosen fields—in law, in business, in singing and performing, and in sculpting. And Alberic and Gladness will die within a year of each other, both of them in their sixties, but generally content with what they'd accomplished in their lives.

When Minnie the three-legged tightrope walker and Viola the Half-Woman drop by to sit by Bolt's bedside while he sleeps feverishly, Eleanor discovers that they have a book discussion every week, and that they'd recently read *Ethan Frome*, which Eleanor had been meaning to get to. In another life, she might have joined them, and they would have found much to talk about, and they could have all been great companions.

Oh, she thinks. *I died without friends.*

And the man with the small head, and Strong Baby, and the noseless clown called Thistle-Britches all come in one afternoon to pay their respects and Thistle-Britches produces a magician's bouquet of paper roses and makes a little bow. He blows Bolt a kiss, and Strong Baby opens his mouth in a wide, drooling grin, and makes one of his high, cooing noises; and the man with the small head takes off his top hat and holds it over his heart, his thin lips pulled back from his rictus teeth.

She'd thought that they were all simply imbeciles—feebleminded unfortunates on display for their deformities—but it seems that they actually have complex thoughts and feelings, and she can feel them looking deeply into her, solemnly. Staring at her, not Bolt.

You have found the place where you belong, thinks the small-headed man, whose real name, she knows now, is Berk Ozdemir. *You will learn to be happy as you are, in time.*

You are one of us now, thinks Thistle-Britches.

And the enormous, hairless man known as Strong Baby—who was given the name Andrew Albright when he was born—gazes down on her with tender pity.

Don't despair. You are still you. And you are not alone. We will remember you.

And so, she had misjudged almost everyone—except for Elmer, who is, in fact, as glibly oblivious and self-regarding as she first took him to be. He comes in with a swagger and cocky head tilt, visiting because others have visited, and he doesn't want to be left out. "Hey—Butch!" he says, and he still genuinely can't remember Bolt's actual name, and he has no sense whatsoever of the intensity of Bolt's feelings for him. He sits down and crosses his legs at the ankle, itching the back of his head absently.

"They got me running the carousel now that Billy's gone," he says, cheerfully. "I like it! I think it could be a real good thing." He considers, casts a quick eye back. "Oh, and I'm sorry about your sis. She was a peach."

Very soon, his hair will begin to fall out, Eleanor thinks. In six months, his career as a circus freak will be over, and he'll head out whistling with a knapsack.

"Well, folks!" he'll say, with his upturned half-smirk and his winsome squint. "I'm off to join the normals! But I won't forget you!"

In fact, he'll be drafted into the army, and he'll fight in the no-man's-lands of Flanders Fields; and when he comes back he'll get married and have two sons, but he'll become quickly the kind of shiftless drunkard Uncle Charlie once cheated at cards, the kind who hunches over a shot of whiskey at the end of the bar, slurring mumbled grudges into his glass, the kind who might try to tell people he used to be with the circus, the kind who cringes and slinks away when he is jeered at, who goes home and beats his resentment into his kids, who has screaming arguments with his wife, who is ultimately abandoned by her and estranged from his children, the kind whose hands tremble so badly he can't light a cigaret until he's had a few drinks, and who, in his middle seventies, is robbed on his way out of a liquor store and shoved off a bridge into the Chicago River, where he will perish, unloved and forgotten—forgotten except, perhaps, by Bolt.

And then there is Herculea. She is the last of them to come in, and she stands in the doorway, gathering her courage for a long moment before she walks toward them. Her muscles are tensed and trembling, and her hands are balled into fists at her sides, and her face is tight with the struggle to hold back tears. She gets down on one knee as if she's a knight of old, and clasps her hands in front of her, and bows her head.

"I wish—" she says and pauses. She takes a few long breaths, as if preparing to lift a great barbell.

"I wish," she says. "I wish you strength to overcome your grief at the tragic loss of your"—and another shivering pause—"your sister."

She fills her lungs again. "Uff," she says. "We can. Never. Lose the cherished memory. Memories," and grunts softly with the effort. "All that we love deeply becomes part of us."

Despite her struggle, a tear manages to expel itself and hangs pendulously for a second from the tip of her nose before falling onto the carpet. A small droplet splash, though given the energy it took to produce, it should well have burned through the floor.

It is not only that she failed to save Eleanor, that she was unable to keep Uncle Charlie from stabbing Bolt—it is, most of all, that she killed an innocent. Poor Piltdown Man! She will never in her life be able to forget that pitiful yelp he let out as her bullet struck him in the back, the way his hands thrashed and scrabbled as if trying to catch the air. She took a human life: she can't get over it! It seems that it will haunt her every step from now on, until the end of her days.

Bolt woozily reaches over and pats her clasped, white-knuckled, shivering hands. "Thank you," he says, hoarsely. "Nobody ever tried to rescue me before."

And to Eleanor he thinks: *We could be her friend. Maybe.*

Maybe, Eleanor thinks.

But she doesn't choose to look into the future to see if it will be true.

When Jengling appears in their chamber, Bolt is asleep—exhausted by the parade of visitors, and the effort of fighting the infection, and benumbed by the bitter tea that Dr. Chui had urged him to drink—to ease pain, and encourage healing, the doctor said.

Still, their eyes are open, and Jengling settles himself into the little upholstered chair beside their bed.

"I knew from the moment I saw the two of you that you were very special creatures," he murmurs, and pauses. Strikes a match to his cigar. Puffs, and produces a perfect smoke ring. "Two souls bonded in the astral plane—and now one body and yet two people—astonishing! You are an important discovery!"

Eleanor cannot move Bolt's lips or operate his voice box, and so she only blinks, slowly.

"You are adopted of our family, and I would like to offer you a position of importance here. Percentage of profits. Partnership. Let's say—a degree of autonomy, based upon your interests?"

He peers down at her face. "We think the name Evelyn Jengling would suit you," he says. "Because there isn't really a 'Bolt' or 'Eleanor' anymore, is there? It's better, I think, to start afresh. Would you like to call this day your birthday?"

Meanwhile, in his dream, Bolt is walking through a foggy ruined garden, overhung with weeping willows and hanging moss, with delicate fern fronds underfoot and statues draped with clinging vines. And then he sees Rosalie standing in a clearing at the edge of a pond on a misty shore thick with cattails and reeds.

"Oh!" she says, as if startled, and turns. "Bolt! I was hoping I would see you again!" She is wearing a fashionable blue serge dress with a red kerchief and a striped sailor collar. Her hair is tied back and coifed prettily, and he can't help but notice that the Otherin is not protruding from the back of her head.

"Hullo," says Bolt, shyly, and when she offers her hand he touches it awkwardly and then drops his arm back down to his side. "Is this—a real place? Or a dream?"

She gives him a small, kindly laugh. "Why, it's neither, really," she says. "It's the place you go when you die—or one of them, at least. But don't worry, you're not dead. You're just visiting."

He glances around. There are fireflies slowly glowing and bobbing along around their ankles in the dewy grass. There is a wood of silvery trees circled around them.

"Uh-huh," he says. "I think Eleanor was here once."

"I doubt it," says Rosalie. "If she had come this far, she would have never been able to go back. But then again, I don't know how she did what she did." She takes his hand in both her own and holds it tightly, with a wistful smile. "But let's not talk about her. Let's just have a nice time together. I don't imagine there will be another opportunity."

She takes Bolt's index finger and leads him along a stone path that runs along the circumference of the pond, and the fog around their ankles dissipates as they walk. "Let's go sit on those rocks by the water," she says. "And you can comb my hair and tell me a story about Tarzan, or Barsoom, or—whatever you like."

It *is* more like a dream, he thinks, because when they sit down on the edge of the pond he has the pretty, ivory *brosse à cheveux* that Mme. Clothilde gave him in his hand, and she lets her hair down and he sets about to running the teeth of the brush gently through it, and he tells her about how John Carter met the Red Martian Princess Dejah Thoris. They can hear the soft chirping of frogs and insects, and the air smells like sweetgrass and lilacs.

And then he comes to the end of the story and he isn't sure what else to say. She touches his wrist, to signal that he should stop brushing.

"I probably won't be alive much longer," she says, after a silence. "I suppose I put too much strain on my heart, and I've gotten very weak."

"But," Bolt says, "Dr. Chui can probably help you. He's a real good doctor."

"Being alive is such a *strain*," she says mildly. "I don't think I was ever meant for it. And it does grow very tiring, to be made use of. You'll see." In the center of the pond, a silver fish jumps up and catches a dragonfly and then disappears again beneath the surface of the water, leaving only slow ripples spreading outward.

"But you like it, don't you?" she says. "You like being alive?"

"Yeah," Bolt says.

"The problem with being dead," says Rosalie, "is you never get to eat again, nor touch someone's skin. You never get to feel tears coming out of your eyes, nor your legs pumping when you run. Nor music," says Rosalie. "You can *hear* it, in a way, but you don't have a body to *feel* it. That's a great loss."

"Well," Bolt says. He hesitates. "You could always—I don't know—could you be inside me like Eleanor is? I reckon there's room. I could be like a boardinghouse for spirits."

"*No*," she says, and her voice surprises him with its sharpness. "You can't do that, you'll end up like Heap—Piltdown Man, isn't that what they called him?"

"Old Chicken Guts?" says Bolt.

"Yes," she says. "And in the end, I'm glad I didn't have you as my conduit, I probably would have destroyed you, like I did him." She bends down and sets to undoing the laces from the silver eyes of her calf-high shoes. "Though—so, probably, will your sister . . ."

He watches as she pulls off her shoes and stockings and sets them down by the shore. She splashes her bare feet in the water.

"I didn't think it was allowed," Rosalie says. "She shouldn't be able to stay inside you. Not—permanently, at least. In the end, it will be one of you or the other."

She stands up and lifts her skirt a few inches and wades into the shallow water. The pond is so glassy clear that he can see tiny minnows flitting around her ankles.

"But what about your own brother?" Bolt says. "The . . . Otherin? Ain't he inside you?"

"Ah," she says. She takes a step deeper into the pond, far enough that the water wets the edges of her dress. "No. *He* doesn't have a soul to speak of. He was my twin, but I absorbed him in the womb. I manifested him when I was learning to travel the planes, I pushed him out of the back of my head like a woman pushes a baby out from between her legs. It's called a thought-form. A *tulpa*. Not like your sister at all. ***She*** was a fully formed spirit, who took up occupancy inside you. I wonder why she would dare settle into you, unless she intended, ultimately, to take control of the material body?"

He watches as she reaches around and unbuttons her dress from the back, and peels it off over her head, and stands there in her one-piece underclothes. And then she steps back deeper into the water, and she is just a head and a pair of drifting, swimmy arms.

"I suppose," she says, "that your sister is possibly *a kind of* manifestation. A kind of thought-form."

She submerges herself, and then rises up and shakes her wet hair. "But are you manifesting her? Or is she manifesting you? I guess you'll find out, sooner or later."

And then she lets herself sink under the water. Her hair floats like algae on the scrim of the pond, and some bubbles rise.

And then she is gone altogether.

MAY 2015

•••••••••

The limousine stops in front of the gate that leads to the Jengling Institute—about twenty miles outside the tiny, unincorporated town of Animas, New Mexico, in the midst of a sagebrush savannah. The wall around the compound is twelve or so feet tall, made of thick, corrugated steel, and then above that are rows of electrified fencing, and then, at the very top, a glinting fluff of razor wire. Riordan can see the brutalist-style Institute building rising up behind the wall, a textural concrete facade with long, narrow windows, fifteen stories high, built directly into the side of a butte. He guesses it must extend into some kind of underground bunker.

The driver gets out and opens the back door for him, and he notices for the first time that there is no handle on the inside. "You may step out of the car, sir," the lanky chauffeur says.

Riordan stands, spread-eagle, as the tall man with the long dark ponytail pats him down. He is divested of his sunglasses—billfold—cell phone—earbuds—vape pen: solemnly stripped of his items of identity.

"These will be returned to you upon departure," the driver says sternly. "May I have permission to touch your hair?"

"I beg your pardon?" Riordan says, but the man has already reached up and is gently combing his fingers along Riordan's scalp and down to his neck.

"This is just a precaution," the man explains, and Riordan can't help but feel he is about to be murdered.

Given what he knows about the Jengling Institute, assassination does not seem outside of the realm of possibility. But people know he's here. His editor, for example, and his agent. If he doesn't come back to New York, there will be inquiries into his disappearance.

He is led through the doors of the Institute by a small man in a black suit, with the distinctive head and body shape of a person with achondroplasia. "Right this way, Mr. Riordan," the man says. He is about three feet tall, with very striking pale blue eyes and white-blond hair, and he ushers Riordan into an enormous, open first-floor lobby, reminiscent of a metropolitan hospital. Riordan thinks it's about three o'clock in the afternoon. Usually, he would check his phone and make a voice note on his recording app, but. Well.

"Excuse me," he says to his escort. "I'm wondering—is it possible to get a pen and some paper? Usually, I record my interviews and then transcribe them, but they confiscated my device at the gate so—"

The man stops and glances back at Riordan, and his mouth turns up in a brief commiserating smile.

"Sorry," the little man says.

Riordan has been working on his book about the Jengling Institute off and on since he was in his twenties, and it's possible that—aside from the cultists themselves—he knows more about the organization than anyone. Very few are aware of its origins as a traveling "Freak Show" in the early twentieth century, nor how, sometime in the 1920s, it came to be called the Temple of True Science, a sort of offshoot of the Theosophist movement. Mostly, they were known for their vocal opposition to eugenics and sterilization laws, and for the strident advertisement they purchased in multiple newspapers, a caricature of a top-hatted rich man perusing a line of cringing, ragged children. DON'T LET MILLIONAIRES DECIDE WHO HAS THE RIGHT TO BE ALIVE.

There was also a poster, now prized by collectors, attributed to J. Allen St. John—noted for his illustrations of the novels of Edgar Rice Burroughs—showing a group of humanoid figures of all shapes, sizes, and hues of skin, some of them quite grotesque, and including a gorilla, dancing together in a ring in a forest glade, and below them the words: *Temple of True Science: Unusquisque enim verum sui.*

Conspiracy theorists claimed that the Temple of True Science was implicated in the death of Harry Houdini—a debunker of spiritualism and mediums—and this had received a little minor press when, in 2007, one of Houdini's grand-nephews had put in a request to allow the exhumation of the body to investigate the possibility that he had been murdered by a cabal of Spiritualists.

The Temple was also mentioned briefly in an addendum to the U.S. Senate's Pecora Commission Report on the causes of the 1929 Stock Market Crash, noting that they were one of the few large investors who had substantially *benefited* from the collapse.

For a while in the 1950s and 1960s, the Temple of True Science, now known as the Jengling Institute, was in the news because of their research into cryonics. It was a punch line for edgy young comedians that all of the cultists had their severed heads frozen and preserved when they died. But they were also at the forefront of research into cryopreservation of embryos, and it has since been speculated that they may have successfully implanted a previously frozen fetus as early as 1965, nearly twenty years before Zoe Leyland, the first official "test-tube baby," was born in 1984.

Otherwise, they remained remarkably unnoticed by trusted sources and recorded history. Between 1925 and 2015, the *New York Times* had only fifteen records that mentioned the organization. Today they were known, if they were known at all, primarily for their support of orphanages and foster home programs.

They were not evangelical. They did not seek out the spotlight. Membership was said to be by invitation only.

Riordan is ushered at last into a room that looks like a curio shop. Yellow recessed ceiling lights glow softly down on shelves lined with jars full of what appear to be various kinds of organic specimens—octopi and deformed monkeys and severed hands and bobbing eyeballs and so forth—as well as display cases with skulls and bones, masks and puppets and totems. He tries to take in as many details as he can as he steps toward the far end of the room, where a very old person is sitting in a wheelchair behind a Dalbergia wood desk, taking oxygen by a tube through the nose, absorbed in a book.

"Hello! Hi!" says Riordan, as softly as if he's in a library. "Mr. . . . Jengling?" One thing he knows is that they are all called "Mr." or "Ms." Jengling—they take on the surname when they join (are "adopted") by the cult. He stops a few paces from the desk and folds his hands in front of him. "I'm Wessler Riordan." And he waits, holding himself very still, as the ancient being traces a finger down to the bottom of the page, and then, with a wobbly hand inserts a bookmark, closes the cover, sets the little book down upon a green velvet blotter. Riordan gets a glimpse of some sort of boil or wen on the back of the bald head before the old man turns his face up to regard him.

Riordan doesn't think he's ever seen a face with so many deep creases and wrinkles—like cracked mud in a dry riverbed, he thinks, and hopes he can recall the turn of phrase. He read somewhere that the noses and ears of the elderly seem to be larger because the cartilage tissue wears down with age and the skin sags, but here is an extreme example of the phenomenon.

Jengling's lips shift vaguely, and a dry, whispery voice comes out. "Please," he says. "Have a seat, Wessler."

Riordan does. He feels adrift without a recorder or a pen and paper, and his fingers fidget in his lap. "First of all, sir, I want to thank you so much for agreeing to speak with me. I know it's extremely rare for a member of the Institute to speak to a journalist—though I actually think of myself more as a writer of literary nonfiction than a, ha, reporter." He pauses. He'd had pages of organized notes and questions on his phone, he'd spent a lot of time arranging the questions into categories, and figuring out the order of his approach. But now it's all jumbled up in his brain. "In any case," he says at last. "As you may know, I have been trying for quite some time to get a chance to speak to a . . . representative of your organization. So, I'm deeply thrilled to have a chance to—"

The way that Jengling's eyes fix on him is terribly unnerving. They are so cloudy that Riordan isn't certain if there's much actual eyesight at all, but still Jengling's gaze gives him a ticklish feeling on the back of his neck—the kind of sensation you'd have if someone was creeping up on you from behind. Riordan glances at the thick closed wooden door. "Thrilled," he says.

Jengling shrugs mildly. "Your letter was very persuasive," he says, and thoughtfully touches an unlit cigar that is resting in an old-fashioned glass ashtray. "You know a great deal about our history. But I must admit I was very surprised indeed at your mention of the names Bolt and Eleanor Lambkin. I wouldn't have thought there'd be anyone alive who knew those names."

"Right," says Riordan. There is a stack of old books on the desk—*The Book of Mediums* by Allan Kardec; *Lo!* by Charles Fort; *Thought-Forms* by Annie Besant and C. W. Leadbeater, and on top of the books is a deformed skull that looks a bit like a space alien.

Begin with a gesture of generous honesty, Riordan thinks. He's pretty sure that was the original plan when he'd written it down. *Be disarmingly open and sincere. Create an atmosphere in which intimacy is possible.*

"So," Riordan says. "I suppose the best thing to start with is a little personal background: I actually first became aware of this story because I inherited some papers from my great-aunt, Helen Peattie. She was a newspaperwoman for many, many years, probably best known as the film critic for the *Des Moines Register* for almost four decades. But before that, her first job, actually, was as a reporter for a newspaper in a little Iowa town called Shenandoah. And she became fascinated with a—confluence of events—that occurred the summer of 1915."

He hesitates, watching uncomfortably as the man strokes along the length of the cigar in the ashtray, the gnarled old finger slowly curling and uncurling, as if beckoning. "There was a week when first, the Jengling Carnival came into town; and then an orphan train—I'm sure you've heard of those—also arrived; and then there was an axe murder of an entire family of five in a nearby village. My aunt had an intuition that all these strange events happening at once could not simply be a coincidence—but she couldn't quite put the pieces together in any logical way, nothing quite came together. Still, she couldn't let it go, either. She kept investigating, probably over the course of her entire life—it's reductive to call it a hobby, of course, but she was never able to publish any of her research."

He clears his throat yet again. It feels like he has the husk of a popcorn seed lodged at the back of his tongue, and that crept-up-on feeling doesn't dissipate. "In any—in any case," he says, "when she died, she willed me these boxes and boxes of papers, and I was confused at first but then I started to go through them and—" He gives Jengling a modest shrug. "You know, I was the author of a couple of fairly well-received books in the true crime genre, and when I started to dig into what she'd—she'd—she'd *bequeathed* to me, I thought, 'Wow, there's the core of a book in this!' "

"I see," Jengling says. The droop of his ancient eyes is astonishing—he has wrinkles on his eyelids—but at the same time, they seem alert. "And how was she able to glean the names of the twins, I wonder."

"She was there in the audience, when the twins were selected—adopted—" Riordan says, and he's aware that he's being a bit more open about his sources than he would usually feel comfortable with, but he keeps on talking. "And she took down their names because she was writing an article about the adoption proceedings, or whatever you want to call it. And then later she was able to trace them back to a boardinghouse in Oberlin, Ohio, where there had been some suspicious deaths, including the sudden death of their mother, and for a while, my aunt had the idea that these twins might be murderers, and I have to omit—I have to add mint—I have to *admit* that this really piqued my interest, and I submitted a preliminary proposal to my editor at Scribner: *America's First Teen Serial Killers*, or something silly like that, and they did give me some money, but—"

He's babbling. He would never, ever speak to an interview subject about book proposals and the business side of his work, it made him seem like a hack, he thought, like a grubber, and yet he hears himself talking and he feels like he's stoned and chatty and unable to shut up. Jengling, meanwhile, is taking snail-like, methodical notes in a Moleskine journal.

"But eventually my aunt had decided that they weren't," says Riordan. "Killers," he says. "And ultimately I couldn't find enough evidence to build a book around it either. Yet there were so many paths that opened up—it just kept unfolding and unfolding like a root system or a maze, and I thought it could be like a sort of . . . you know, like a historical collage, focusing on the mystery of these twins, but from that vantage point incorporating a sweeping examination of that particular moment in the United States, with its dizzying technological advances and political upheaval, not unlike our own—there are so many rich subjects to explore here: the carnival and freak show and the Theosophist religious beliefs, and then how this little traveling circus began to develop into a sort of utopic community for the disenfranchised and, ah, people with disabilities. And how that dovetails with the topics of eugenics and the development of the infant adoption industry—big-picture American history things. But there's also murder, which adds a touch of thriller spice to things. So yes, it—it—was a rabid—rapid—*rabbit* hole for me just as it was for Great-Aunt Helen."

Jengling picks up a paperweight in his hands—a reddish piece of amber with an insect embedded in it, and strokes it with his thumb.

"My aunt," Riordan hears himself say, but it has begun to seem as if he isn't really talking anymore. It's as if he's thinking and the thoughts are somehow being broadcast out loud. "My aunt spoke to a man named Elmer Googins, who once worked for the—for the Jengling Carnival—and he told her that Eleanor had died, and that Bolt took on the name of Evelyn Jengling."

"Ahh," the old man says. "Elmer." Riordan watches, unmoving in his chair, as the old man loses himself in thoughts for a moment. "But Elmer was far from reliable," Jengling says at last. "I am myself Evelyn Jengling. And Bolt is . . . not really with us anymore."

Riordan feels his lips move, but no sound comes out. *Evelyn Jengling would be, like*, he thinks, *a hundred and thirteen years old.*

"I do like your aunt," says the ancient creature, still fondling the paperweight. "She was a pistol, wasn't she? I've always felt a kinship with pioneering women."

Riordan nods. Or rather, his head is nodded, and his body settles more deeply into the plush armchair across from the person who calls themself Evelyn Jengling.

"So I will tell Miss Helen Peattie a story," says this elder being. "And I will hope to answer all her nagging questions."

After Wessler Riordan has been escorted out, Evelyn sits for a while with her elbows on the desk and her face in her hands. It was necessary to speak to the writer to find out the sources of his information, but there was no reason for her to tell him the story of that summer back in 1915—not that he'll remember most of what she said, and in any case, when he returns to New York his boxes of Miss Peattie's papers will be gone.

She supposes that she felt compelled to recount her long and rambling tale because of the spirit presence of Miss Peattie herself—so close by in the astral plane, so eager to have her questions answered. And so Evelyn had done her a kindness. People are curious, even in death. Or some people are.

At last she lifts her head and adjusts the flow on her oxygen regulator, just a touch higher. Considers.

No—she had not done it for Miss Peattie's benefit. She'd done it for herself, succumbing to some sentimental need to relive and explain, as if telling someone else might make the past clearer and cleaner.

Or else she'd done it *to* herself. To give herself a little punishment of memory. To touch the place where Bolt once was, to feel the stiletto stab of it. *Remember at your peril.*

At times, as she'd recounted their story, she'd almost felt as if Bolt awakened for a moment. She felt a spark of objection, disapproval, disappointment in the back of her mind. She had not told the reporter how much she'd hated the Jengling Carnival at first, how she'd wanted to run away, how deeply isolated and friendless she was those first months; she didn't mention their estrangement that summer, how the covenant between them had been broken and how she might have left him behind if Uncle Charlie hadn't knocked her over the head; how willing Bolt might have been to let her go. Bolt seemed to stir softly at these omissions, these lies, this version of herself that she mostly believed, day to day.

It must be almost sundown. It feels as if she talked and talked for hours, as if she actually traveled back in time for the space of an afternoon and now it seems she hardly has a foot in the material plane. She touches the mouse ball on the arm of her wheelchair and backs away from the desk.

In the beginning, she had truly believed it could be managed. It wasn't that different from being twins—growing up together, as close as they had been, body and mind. They didn't think it would be so hard for the consciousness to be shared. But then, when Eleanor found that she was able to begin to operate the voice and speak for herself and even move their limbs a bit—if awkwardly—a resentment began to fester. As if she were expected to always be a guest, just a passenger riding along?

It's my body, Bolt told her once, which, yes, technically was true, but also, under what law did he own it? Now that she was there, she was also a citizen of the body, and was it forever to be his property?

And so they agreed to split time, and she made space for him to socialize. He went off to his parties with Alberic and Gladness and Shyla and Elmer, and she found a corner with her own private thoughts.

Her wheelchair glides along the marble floor through a tunnel of shelves until she gets to the watercooler. It is such an effort to move Bolt's hands, these days. She paws the air until she manages to get a grip on a paper cup from the dispenser. Then she has to keep the hand steady and accurate enough to be under the spout, and she has to push the button that makes water come out, and then, somehow, she has to somehow bring the hand holding the cup toward her face without spilling all the water, and finally she has to somehow cause the hand to tilt into her mouth. She would like to manage it, but she'll probably eventually have to call a nurse.

After a while, it became harder for them to split time equally. The truth was, she was needed more than he was. By the time they were twenty, she had become a part of the management, trusted and consulted by Jengling and Mme. Clothilde; whereas Bolt was focused on trained monkeys and motorcycle daredevil arenas. He seemed to think that they would continue to be a carnival, whereas it had already been determined that they would begin to move away from that source of income. They would begin to move toward a charitable model, with religious tax exemptions, and their focus would be on preserving human diversity and acceptance of difference. Even as the population of the world began to exponentially multiply, the heterogeneity decreased. A mass extinction was underway, the government was literally sterilizing anyone it deemed abnormal or unworthy of producing offspring, and they needed to rescue and preserve as many as they could.

But what if we just want to be a carnival? Bolt said. *What if we all want to perform and do a show? It's fun!*

She had channeled a dismissive disapproval toward him. *Why would someone set themselves up as laughingstock, to be a clown for people who hate them?*

She maneuvers the wheelchair away from the watercooler and along a wall lined with items she remembers cataloging, a hundred or so years ago. Bolt's eyes are almost completely useless now, but the eyes that she has manifested are pretty good, and she tilts the head downward and looks out through the back of the skull.

As they grew closer to thirty years old, she felt it was necessary to rein him in a little more. He had become a regular smoker of marihuana, he would have puffed away all day long if she'd permitted it, until finally she had to put a stop to it. It was her body as well, and she had no intention of becoming a dope fiend. And she tried to encourage him to make friends with a better class of people. Once Elmer left the carnival, she noticed that he was consistently drawn to the bad element that any carnival will have among their number—drug users and gamblers and drunkards and flimflam men and dirty-joke tellers, and she wanted him to spend more time with those who could be a positive influence.

She didn't understand his desires. It's possible she had been too quick to thwart his longing to touch and kiss and—all the sexual nonsense that occupied him.

It's possible that she did him a great unkindness. That she had withdrawn from him the experience of physical intimacy with another person. That she had perpetrated Rosalie's final curse: *You will never love again.*

Evelyn stops the wheelchair and listens. There is the low hum of air conditioner and dehumidifier, the constant white noise that runs through the building like wind-rustled grass, which after a while you cease to consciously hear. For years, she'd imagined that she heard Bolt speaking her name: *Eleanor—Eleanor*—buried just below the steady static hiss of the building. But then she supposes she became inured to that as well, so that the ghostly whisper, too, became part of the background.

Do you remember the story you once told me about a boy who lets a ghost inside him and then becomes the ghost's prisoner in his own body? Bolt asked her once.

I never told such a story, says Eleanor. *And you're not a prisoner. The two of us are doing important work.*

I don't want to do important work, Bolt says. *I want to have a say in how I spend my days.*

They was in their thirties by this time, and they had become an important part of the organization. They had valuable abilities, and it seemed that more and more Harland listened to their opinions as much as he did to Mme. Clothilde, or Dr. Chui, or even Tickley-Feather.

Meanwhile, Bolt's main job was to ruin any pleasure she took in her accomplishments with his sullen boredom.

He *is* here, she thinks now. She's almost certain of it and nudges the mouse on her wheelchair so it turns slowly in a circle, 360 degrees at the speed of the second hand of a clock. She can sense his presence—though whether he is in her mind or in the other plane she can't quite tell. Or is it just a wishful hallucination?

In the end, the thing that they'd most disagreed about was a project that the Jengling Institute began working on in the mid-1950s. They had been very interested in cryonics, and in finding ways of preserving the most important and unique specimens as frozen sperm or egg or embryo. And they were having some success when Eleanor had a great realization. All these embryos could be vessels, she thought. When members of the Jengling family died on the material plane, they could take habitance in one of the fetuses, and thus they could continue on, indefinitely, altogether changed and yet the same.

Sounds nice, said Bolt. *But what of the souls of the babies? I reckon they're just pushed aside, are they?*

And Eleanor was made haughty and irritated by his judgmental tone. *It will be a hybrid*, she said, stonily. *The infant souls will adapt.*

Oh, right, Bolt says. *As I have.*

What would you have done without me? Eleanor said. *You would have wasted your life.*

He stopped talking to her then for a long time. He was still present, still a part of their body, but mostly as weight, a resentful stone she was carrying on her back, a finger that pinched her when she was sleeping.

You're a parasite, he whispered. *I should have never let you in. I could've been happy.*

As it turned out, that was the last thing he really said to her. She occasionally heard muttering, or he'd hum an old song from their childhood over and over, or she'd occasionally have a certain kind of dream that she was *quite* sure was not of her own imagination.

But by the 1970s he seemed to have disappeared altogether, and she had become increasingly anxious. She had always thought that he would cool down with time, and she promised that things would be better if he came back, she would share the body freely—even though now it was growing old—she would give him the driver's seat as often as he wanted. She knew she had been bossy, she knew she had overstepped, but couldn't he just say one word? *Bolt? Just tell me you're here.*

But as hard as she tried, she could not reach him, and though she held many séances and called for him, though she even set foot into the astral plane for a few paces, she saw no sign. Was he alive or dead? Had he somehow ceased to exist? Or was he just eluding her?

Bolt? she called. *Bolt! I know you're there!*

Her little face, her thought-form, her *tulpa*, grows out of the back of Bolt's skull, and at this point it's the only way she can keep things running. She tilts Bolt's head and begins to maneuver back toward the desk.

She has lost the ability to sleep.

She is afraid that maybe she cannot die.

"Bolt?" she whispers, rolling on imperceptibly humming treads through the rows and rows of Jengling's specimens. "Bolt?" she says as she has so many times over so many years. "Please come back. Please don't leave me alone like this."

But nothing answers. Only the steady current of cool air blowing out endlessly from the vent.

Author's Note

Writing a novel about the circus means being in conversation with many deeply influential works of fiction on that subject. These include the 1932 film *Freaks*, directed by Tod Browning; Ray Bradbury's *Dark Carnival* and *Something Wicked This Way Comes*; Angela Carter's *Nights at the Circus*; *The Circus in Winter* by Cathy Day; *Geek Love* by Katherine Dunn; *Nightmare Alley* by William Lindsay Gresham; *Curious Toys* by Elizabeth Hand; *The Night Circus* by Erin Morgenstern; *The Unholy Three* by Tod Robbins; and many others.

Sherwood Anderson's stories helped me with period detail and provided me with some of the slang of that era. Thomas Tryon's novel *The Other* was also a big influence—as it has been since I first read it when I was thirteen.

For some reason, the children's picture book *The Little Engine That Could* by Watty Piper was a big part of my visual mood board when I was picturing this book. So, too, were the Disney films *Dumbo* and *Pinocchio*. I'd like it if you imagined this book as a lost Disney animation from the early 1940s, or possibly the film that Charles Laughton directed after *The Night of the Hunter*. Or picture it in the gaudy Metrocolor of *7 Faces of Dr. Lao*, the last film directed by the great George Pal.

I quote from a number of works from that period that are now in public domain. Eleanor H. Porter's *Pollyanna* is a book that haunted me when I was a child, and I'm happy to haunt it back in this book. The works of

Edgar Rice Burroughs are frequently referred to and excerpted, as are a few poems by Gertrude Stein.

Joseph Payne Brennan's story "Levitation" is alluded to in the chapter "Blair, Nebraska."

The story "The New Mother" by Lucy Clifford is referenced in several chapters.

The story Gladness tells in the chapter "Seven Cosmic Planes, Seven Principles and Bodies" is inspired by Tod Browning's silent-era classic film *The Unknown* (1927). Uncle Charlie's killing spree is partially based on the crimes described in *The Man from the Train: Discovering America's Most Elusive Serial Killer* by Bill James and Rachel McCarthy James, and the book was also a useful reference for period detail.

Dr. Chui's chapter draws heavily on *The Chinese Massacre at Rock Springs, Wyoming Territory, September 2, 1885* by Isaac H. Bromley.

Two important resources about the orphan trains were *The Orphan Trains: Placing Out in America* by Marilyn Irvin Holt, and *We Rode the Orphan Trains* by Andrea Warren.

I consulted many books about carnivals and sideshows during the early twentieth century, but two that were especially important to me were *Secrets of the Sideshows* by Joe Nickell and *Very Special People* by Frederick Drimmer.

Theosophist and Spiritism concepts are drawn from a number of sources, including Allan Kardec's *The Book on Mediums: Guide for Mediums and Invocators*; *The Spirit World Unmasked* by Henry Ridgley Evans; *Thought-Forms: A Record of Clairvoyant Investigation* by Annie Besant and C. W. Leadbeater; *Isis Unveiled: A Master-Key to the Mysteries of Ancient and Modern Science and Theology* by Helena Petrovna Blavatsky; and *Madame Blavatsky's Baboon: A History of the Mystics, Mediums, and Misfits Who Brought Spiritualism to America* by Peter Washington.

I am deeply grateful and indebted to all of these writers and artists.

Acknowledgments

I was fortunate to have the support and advice of friends and family while I was working on this book. My agent, Renée Zuckerbrot, has been a guardian angel since we first began working together, and I'm so grateful for her wise counsel and enthusiastic advocacy of my work, her patience and kindness and practicality.

Thanks to all my early readers for their thoughts and advice: Simona Mkrtschjan, who read along as I was writing and whose penetrating insights into character and psychology helped me enormously; Dan Riordan, who pushed for plot and action when I was floating; Dr. Lynda Montgomery, not only a great reader but also an imperturbable source of medical advice whenever I needed to murder or injure a character; my son Philip Chaon, whose uncanny instincts always gave me clues that led me forward along the way; my dear pal Imad Rahman, unfailingly astute and perceptive; my sister, Sheri, for practical advice and emotional support; my old friends Tom Barbash and John Martin, who always have smart things to say; the wise-beyond-her-years Charlotte Tate; Billy Hallal; Mike Rocheleau; Sylvia Watanabe; and my younger son, Paul, who has taught me so much these past few years.

Thanks to the entire team at Holt, including Leela Gebo, who was always on top of things. Thanks to Tim Duggan for stepping in at the final hour. Thanks to Andrew Miller. And, finally, thanks to my wonderful editor, Caroline Zancan, who was unflappable as the book got weirder and weirder, and who gave me a free rein while pushing me to do better.

About the Author

Dan Chaon is the author of several books, including *Ill Will*, a national bestseller that was named one of the ten best books of the year by *Publishers Weekly*. Other works include the short story collection *Stay Awake*, a finalist for the Story Prize; the national bestseller *Await Your Reply*; and *Among the Missing*, a finalist for the National Book Award. Chaon's fiction has appeared in the *Best American Short Stories*, the Pushcart Prize Anthologies, and the O. Henry Collection. He has been a finalist for the National Magazine Award in Fiction and the Shirley Jackson Award, and he was the recipient of an Academy Award in Literature from the American Academy of Arts and Letters. Chaon lives in Cleveland.